IF YOU WERE MINE

TEACHER CHRONICLES BOOK 3

IDA BRADY

To all the Enemies-to-Lovers fans,
The slow-burn is going to hurt, but it'll be worth it in the end. I
promise.
To Team Brida,
For all the love, family cuddles and chocolate.

AUTHOR NOTE on TRIGGER WARNINGS: This book contains the following references (please skip this description if you don't want potential spoilers): mental health, swearing, child abuse, physical and verbal abuse, domestic violence, death of loved ones, body image abuse, eating disorder, substance abuse.

On the plus, it contains spicy sex.

CHAPTER ONE

*H*aving a dream-gasm should have made Maddie happy. Having a dream-gasm should have left her feeling limber. Instead, having a dream-gasm at approximately 7.34AM that Monday morning in the second week of term two made Maddie Fitzgerald angry enough to commit murder.

As far as orgasms went, Maddie's was leg-tremblingly good. So much so that she had to wait a few minutes for the blood to stop pounding in her ears before she could think straight.

The problem wasn't the dream-gasm as such, or the power of it, but more so the person who had got her off . . . figuratively speaking.

Gabriel. Fucking. Steele.

Vice principal of Woodbury High and all-around pain in her ass, Gabriel Steele.

He had no right causing her to lose her mind on a Monday, of all days, when he *knew* well and good that she would have to see him at the after-school leadership team meeting.

The effrontery.

The sheer freaking nerve of that man.

Maddie sat up in bed, shoving aside the covers with a muttered curse. "Who the hell does he think he is, invading my dreams like that?" Maddie spoke to the empty room of her two-bedroom apartment. She really had no time for this.

Like it wasn't hell enough to have to deal with his arrogance day in and day out. Like she really wanted to have sexy dream thoughts about those cold gray eyes that only ever looked at her to criticize.

Nuh-uh. No way.

And yet, the evidence of her orgasm dampened the auburn curls between her legs, mocking her.

Maddie stomped to the bathroom, wishing like hell she could wash off the dream and be rid of the jittery feeling that wreaked havoc with her nervous system.

No such luck. It followed her as she dressed, sat beside her on the way to work, and stared back at her in the reflection of the sliding glass doors of her office at Woodbury High School.

Dumping her bag on her desk, Maddie mentally slapped herself. She hated Gabriel. That fact remained true. And the dream? It didn't mean anything. It *couldn't* mean anything. It went against every rivalry code since the dawn of time to lust after your archnemesis. There was a definite line between her and Steele and it would remain that way forever.

She was juiced up from the big O, that was all. And to prove it, she would trawl through a dating app until she found someone decidedly *not* like Gabriel Steele to distract her. A short, blond, bearded Viking should do the trick. And she would take him home and screw his brains out until she forgot about the stoic vice principal and his stormy eyes. She would do it until he was a distant memory.

Satisfied, Maddie smiled for the first time that morning.

It had nothing to do with the dream, or even the pleasant humming in her body at all.

Not. One. Little. Bit.

"Stalking me already, Steele? It's not even 9AM."

Gabriel shut the sliding door behind him. He took his time walking through the rectangular office space until he reached Maddie's desk at the far end by the window. He thanked heaven that the rest of the staff weren't in yet.

Affecting his best bored expression, Gabriel looked at the hellion in question. "I have nothing in my life but you."

Maddie's head jerked up. "What?"

He raised one eyebrow. It took a split second for her to register his sarcasm, but the shock had been well worth it.

Maddie's mouth compressed in a thin line of disdain. A shame, really. It had been that pouty bottom lip that had gripped his attention in the first place. Her flaming red hair had come in a close second. And those eyes . . . Mismatched and full of mischief, they completed the trifecta.

Gabriel gritted his teeth.

All the years he'd spent learning how to control his wicked ways would not be undone by the redhead sitting before him. He was no longer that man; he would no longer give in to temptation. He'd learned self-control a long time ago. It was what had helped him thrive.

But Maddie . . . . Maddie was a constant waterfall of emotions. He saw it in their every interaction: the flicker of resignation in her eyes, the disgruntled downturn of her mouth. Her whole body screamed of her dislike of his presence. Not that she ever had a problem telling him the truth to his face. Mind and body, Maddie Fitzgerald despised him.

Which suited him perfectly.

Everything about her pissed him off.

Everything about her reeled him in.

Stop. Focus on something else.

Gabriel noticed the collection of felt pens and markers on

her desk. Scented, no doubt. Her stationery was an extension of herself. Loud. Colorful. Well put together.

As his blood pumped through him, Gabriel examined the collage of pictures she had Blu-Tacked on her wall—images of Maddie with her best friends, Sera and Ally, in various poses, looking carefree and happy. The news he was about to deliver was going to shock her on many levels. He stifled a sigh. No better man for the job.

"Now that I have your attention, did you see my Post-it Note?"

"Ahh, the infamous Post-it Notes." Maddie's bright purple fingernails danced across her desk until she plucked the note out from a pile. "'Please see me. Important,'" Maddie mimicked in what he assumed was her best 'Gabriel' impression. It would have annoyed him if he hadn't found it so amusing. Not that he would be caught dead admitting that to her. "Naturally, I ignored it."

"I have news."

"Uh-oh. That sounds ominous."

Gabriel bit back a retort. "I needed to speak to you about this in person."

"Goody for me."

"Penelope won't be back this term, and most likely for the remainder of the year."

"What happened?"

Gabriel grimaced, trying his best to be as considerate as possible. He sat down on the chair opposite. "She suffered a stroke on Saturday."

Maddie gasped, crunching the Post-it Note in her hand. "Is she . . . ?"

"It was severe enough that they think she won't be able to return for a while yet. One of her daughters left a message with Jacinta over the weekend."

"I saw her on Thursday. She seemed fighting fit."

He understood her shock. Even though Penelope was not far off retirement, she was a powerhouse, filled with a wealth of knowledge that Gabriel could only hope to have at her age.

"We'll be making an announcement at break today."

Maddie's eyes became vacant, her lips parting. "Her students! What's going to happen to them? They're seniors. They'll be devastated." She stood, pacing. "They're all so close with Penelope. This is the last thing they need right now."

"I'll be breaking the news to them today. And we've briefed the student welfare team. The kids will be upset, but we're handling it."

"Fuck."

"I know you were close."

"Everything I know about teaching literature I learned from Penelope. Hell, everything about teaching, we learned from her."

"I know this must be difficult, but we—"

"Are handling it. Yeah, I get it. Always down to business."

"I'm simply telling you the logistics."

"Logistics this, then. Who's taking her lit kids? I can't take them because half her classes clash with my senior drama ones. By the time we advertise and hire someone, we'll probably be at the end of the term."

"I know."

"And?"

"Take a seat."

Maddie scowled. "Why?"

Gabriel shifted slightly to look up at her. "Because we're filling the role in-house."

"Internally? Who in the English department is even remotely qualified to teach literature? We've been actively trying to recruit grads for the past few years, but none of them are ready or, hell, willing. Who is dumb enough to agree to take on a senior literature class at the beginning of term two, while we're implementing a new study design no less?"

Gabriel's stare was direct. "Me."

He had the satisfaction of watching Maddie deflate into her chair.

"*You?*"

"Don't look so shocked."

"I mean, I know you're English trained but—"

"Master's in education, double bachelor's in literature and gender studies. Taught seniors for a few years before moving into leadership roles in my last school."

"How did I not know this?"

"Maybe you didn't want to know."

"So wait a minute, why didn't you take seniors before?"

"We were consumed by the new department initiatives at the time. Jacinta felt I should work on that and connect with staff given I was new to the school back then. And when we had you and Penelope, we didn't need anyone else. Until now. Is the interrogation over?"

Maddie's eyes opened wide in horror. "So you and I—"

"Will be working closely together for the next eight months."

"Jesus Christ."

"I'm sure he's turning in his grave."

"What did Jacinta say?"

"Our esteemed principal was the one who suggested it."

"Fuck me," she muttered.

"I'll pass."

Her eyes narrowed. "It wasn't an offer."

"For that, I'm grateful. Look, I'll need to get up to scratch on the outcomes you've completed and what texts you're studying at the moment. I looked through the list this morning and I'm familiar with most of the books, not so much with the poetry."

"It's a new study design so we've been winging it a bit, as

are other schools in the network. They haven't really given us much to go on in terms of sample pieces for outcomes, but we've another briefing soon so that'll help us out a bit. Penelope and I have been meeting pretty regularly so we're both on the same page. You're lucky I suppose, as all the other schools are also figuring it out."

"Evens the playing field."

"Something like that."

"So when are you free?" Gabriel stood, motioning to her chronicle.

Maddie flicked it open.

Gabriel leaned in, bracing one arm on the desk, the other on the back of her chair. His mouth twitched as he glanced at the timetable in her planner. Color-coded. Of course. He found a few free periods where they were available to meet, pointing to the classes he'd be able to attend so they could team teach.

Gabriel glanced down at Maddie, who hadn't moved an inch. She was unusually quiet.

"Maddie?" he muttered. When those witchy eyes looked up at him, Gabriel gripped the back of her chair. There was something swirling in the blue and brown depths of her eyes that drew him in. Something that he had no right claiming. "Your timetable," he prompted after a moment.

She blinked, and it was as if her spirit landed back in her body. If she hadn't been sitting down, he was sure she would've fallen flat on her ass.

"My timetable," she repeated slowly, looking down at her chronicle.

"You have a free period later in the week. Maybe given the circumstances, I could cover your junior drama so we can have the double period to get things started? I know you have a lot going on with after-school drama and your seniors, and the last thing we need is to be staying back late."

"Right. No all-nighters."

Gabriel swiveled her chair to face him. "Are you alright? Your pupils are dilated." Before he could stop to caution himself, Gabriel gripped her chin, tilting it to examine her face. "I think you might be in shock."

Suddenly, his fingers were itching to have their own way, to trail down the smooth column of skin to the whisper of cleavage peeking out of her dress.

As if burned, Maddie jerked back. "I'm fine, too much coffee."

Gabriel straightened. "I thought it might shock you given how close you were."

"Huh?"

"Penelope's stroke?"

"Right, Penny." Maddie stood, looking everywhere but at him. "Okay, so thanks. I mean, no thanks, that was bad news, but thanks for the bad news?"

Gabriel crossed his arms and watched as she picked up her phone and planner, movements wooden and stiff. She usually moved with such grace that it took him by surprise. Clearly, he'd underestimated how the news would affect her.

When she turned to face him, he reached out, holding her arm. A blush, red and bright, flourished on her pale cheeks.

"I've gotta go. I'll, we'll . . . Later. Talk later."

Before he could utter another word, Maddie all but ran out of the office. In all the years he'd known her, Maddie had never retreated.

He was wise enough to know not to follow her.

CHAPTER TWO

*M*addie congratulated herself as she walked back to her office at the end of the day. She hadn't even thought about that *thing* at all. Well, not much anyway. Not when the news of Penny's stroke hung over her like a storm cloud.

How the hell would she manage to work with Gabriel of all people? Having to navigate the new literature study design together meant being in contact. Close contact.

The thought alone had her stomach performing cartwheels.

And if that wasn't enough, she now had to suffer through a leadership team meeting with the man. As days went, this Monday was shaping up to be a big ol' bitch.

"Madds! Big M, wait up!" Sera called after her as Maddie marched across the courtyard back to her office. She wanted to catch up with Hugh to discuss his section of the drama proposal before their meeting in ten minutes.

"Hey, have you seen Hugh by any chance?"

"Hugh Gandy? No, not since first break."

"Hmm."

"Oh no."

"Oh yes." Maddie wrenched the door open and stomped through, her best friend trailing after. "I've got a bloody leadership team meeting where Hugh is supposed to be presenting information about the new drama course, and do you think he sent his half to me? I asked him for it this morning, and he said he would send it by lunchtime. God, the guy is such a fucking flake."

"Shit."

"And I know Gabriel-why-did-you-leave-this-to-the-last-minute-Steele is going to have *my* ass."

Sera raised her eyebrows.

"Metaphorically of course."

"Uh-huh."

"Speaking of ass . . ." Maddie stopped outside of her office, making sure nobody else was in the corridor to hear before drawing Sera closer. It was times like these that she loved working with her best friends. She had met Sera and Ally in college and had remained close ever since. The fact that they'd all landed jobs at Woodbury High at the same time was a delicious bonus.

"Ooooh, spill!" Sera's brown eyes lit up.

"Ok, so this is *not* a big deal, but it's been driving me crazy all day and I have to get it off my chest."

"Bigger than Penelope's stroke?"

"Not as serious." Maddie paused, gathering her courage. "I had a sex dream last night."

Sera's eyes lit up. "Love it!"

"It was one of those amazing ones where you wake up coming."

"The best."

"Right?"

"So why do you look like it was a Dementor who gave you the big O?"

Maddie pulled a face. "It wasn't far off."

"Huh?"

Maddie lowered her voice even further. She was going to be late for this meeting, but right now, in gossip mode with her bestie, she didn't care. "The thing is . . ."

"Yeah."

"It was kinda with . . ."

"For the love of all that is holy and sacred, Maddie, spit it out!"

"It was with—surely it's a sin to say this aloud—*Gabriel*."

Sera frowned. "Gabriel . . ." Then her eyes popped. "Wait, Gabriel, as in vice principal of Woodbury High, Gabriel? Like, you had a sex dream about *Gabriel Steele, Gabriel*?"

"Would you stop broadcasting his name!" She covered her face with her chronicle. "And yes, *that* Gabriel."

Sera looked up at her, brown eyes wide with shock. Maddie didn't know whether to laugh or die of mortification.

"What's going on?" Ally, their bestie and the third in their tight-knit friendship group, rushed over, cradling her impressive baby bump. "Sera looks like she ate a big, fat, juicy piece of gossip."

"Hey!" Sera protested. "How could you tell?"

"We love you, darling, but you have the worst poker face known to man. You're a horrible liar to boot."

"That's true, but what you're about to hear is a whopper of a gossip burger."

"This mama-to-be is hungry for a double whopper. The juicier, the better. Spill, I can only last so long on my feet these days."

Sera's eyes lit up. "Madds had a sex dream last night."

"Oooh, *très* juicy."

"Uh-huh, and you'll never guess who it was with."

Ally leaned in, her straight black hair falling over her shoulder. "I'll bite. Who did Maddie have a sex dream about last night that's left her looking so mortified?"

"I'm certain that information can wait until after school hours." The deep rumbling reply behind her set Maddie's teeth on edge.

She wanted to die. To bury herself in a hole and possibly never ever come back out. Ignoring the adrenaline pumping through her, Maddie turned, shooting daggers at none other than sex dream star himself, Gabriel.

She ignored the little shiver that ran through her, schooling her features as best as she could. His deep voice surrounded her, triggering a sudden remembrance of all the *things* that dream-Gabriel had said and done. Dirty things. Things that had no right infiltrating her brain at this very moment.

"This is a private conversation."

"During school hours."

"The bell has rung." Maddie refused to break eye contact.

"And you have a meeting to attend."

"So do you."

She wanted to wipe that smug smile off his face, but all she could think about was the image of his mouth on her . . .

Was it any wonder she was frustrated at having had the best imaginary sex of her adult life with *him* of all people. He was insufferable and arrogant and so bloody sanctimonious! She'd rather have monster sex. She'd always had a thing for *Beauty and the Beast* . . . Now, if she could just have a library and a big castle, she'd be set.

"I have some news."

"Well, I'm having a private conversation."

"And one entirely inappropriate for school hours."

"Castigating me again? How original."

"I thought you'd be used to being brought to heel."

Equal parts shock and pleasure flooded through her. One point to Gabriel. "I didn't realize you could see us peasants from your lofty tower. Must be tough issuing orders all day long."

She watched in satisfaction as his mouth compressed in a straight line. Pointing out his position as vice principal never failed at getting a rise out of him. Not that she ever really saw him lose his temper. He was the epitome of self-control . . . all the bloody time.

What would he be like if he let loose a little? Went a bit wild?

Images of his cock doing X-rated things punched through her. Perhaps a little too wild.

"In case it hasn't dawned on you, schools are social places as much as they are learning institutions."

What bugged her about Gabriel was the way in which he put up walls. Maddie thrived on developing relationships with her colleagues; Gabriel constantly rebuffed them.

Workplace banter? Zilch. Office gossip? *Nada.* Personal life oversharing? Nope. For all Maddie knew, the man could be living as a monk in some monastery on the weekends.

"The later you are to the meeting, the longer we stay back, Maddie."

"Did you come here to call me tardy?"

"As much as pointing out your flaws fills me with glee, no. I'd rather not spend a millennium trying."

Maddie glared at him. "Low blow, but I'd expect nothing more from you."

"Giving as good as I get. We have a change of agenda for this afternoon's meeting."

"Speaking of." Ally tugged at Sera's arm. "We better go. C'mon, Sera."

Maddie envied their freedom. All she wanted to do was follow them and talk about the weird feeling she had every time she thought about the sex dream. She couldn't quite look at Gabriel the same way.

Which made everything worse, as the man only ever opened his mouth to find fault with her.

"So why am I finding this out two minutes before our meeting?"

"Hugh's gone home sick—"

"Again," they both said in unison.

Maddie huffed. "Aren't you just full of great news for me today?"

"I thought it best to tell you that I'll fill the slot with a few items the welfare team wanted to talk about, in light of Penelope's stroke."

"So I'm not presenting?"

"No."

Maddie narrowed her eyes. "Why are you doing this?" It wasn't like Gabriel to save the day. Usually, he was prodding her into oncoming traffic, not rescuing her like Superman. *Not the time to think of the man in spandex, Madds. Seriously.*

"I thought you'd be happy."

"Happy? Far from it. Not only do I still have to present this with Hugh at some future meeting, but given I'm the acting head of arts, I have to reprimand him. Again. And hope he doesn't pass out like the last time."

Gabriel's mouth curved. Was that a smile? Maddie was so stunned by the show of emotion that she almost missed his comment.

"I'll handle him."

Maddie opened her mouth, but no sound came out. She could only stare as he continued.

"I think you've had enough shocks for one day. In case you've forgotten, I'm in charge of staffing issues, and I think the situation with Hugh has become unmanageable, don't you think?"

"Are you saying I can't handle him?"

Gabriel's sigh was so deep, she almost felt sorry for the man.

"Maddie, you can handle just about anything and you know

it. But we need to escalate things if we want Hugh to . . . step into another direction, if you understand my meaning."

Maddie understood perfectly and was glad that they were finally taking action. The man was a lost cause, coming in hours late to work without letting anyone know, never going to meetings, and, if the recent allegations were true, offering weed to seniors at a weekend party. The guy needed help.

"I believe I do."

"We're in agreement then. I'll handle Hugh."

Agree? With Gabriel-I'm-always-right-Steele? Never.

"That way you'll have more time to think about that sex dream of yours." Gabriel smirked before walking away.

Well, *fuck.*

CHAPTER THREE

Gabriel paced his study that evening, unable to quiet his mind.

Walking along the rows of books, admiring the shelves he had built himself, would usually offer him comfort. How many nights as a child had he dreamed of having a home like this, filled with peace and stability?

But he'd learned at the tender age of five that happy families were reserved for fiction. Or other people. The Steele family was not one of the blessed, lucky few.

Knowing it had haunted him as a child. As a rebellious teenager, it had made him rage. As a man in his mid-thirties, it only made him ache for something he would simply never have.

Gabriel's hand hovered over the wrinkled and concertinaed spine of a well-loved book. He retracted it as if burned. Not tonight. Not when his mind was already full.

Anger wanted to rear its ugly head, to rail and shove at his control, at the measured life he had built for himself. One of peace. Of calm.

But even if he was itching for a fight, tonight he lacked the spirit. Try as he might, he couldn't get the image of Maddie out of his head. She had no right being there. And he had no right thinking about her. But the tantalizing piece of gossip that he'd heard before this afternoon's meeting heated his blood.

Maddie had had a sex dream.

So what? Millions of people around the world were probably having one right now.

Big enough news to gossip about it at school.

Not his business.

Who was the guy? Or girl?

It didn't matter.

Gabriel stood by the window and made every effort to slow his breathing. When that didn't work, he focused on the cobblestones. Then on his car p—

"For fuck's sake."

He refused to indulge in any fantasies. His control was all he had. He wouldn't risk his position and reputation—as boring as it seemed to the outside world—for . . . what?

Lust?

Frustration?

A maddening combination of both?

The Gabriel of old would have had no qualms in seducing the stunning redhead. But he wasn't that man anymore. If people thought him boring, uninteresting, and not worth the gossip, then that suited him well enough.

The past didn't matter; he was a vice principal at a school he loved. He'd studied his butt off to finish top of the class at university, to work on his English literature degree, to persist with his master's of education. He wouldn't even recognize his old self anymore.

His life was above board, and nobody would know any differently.

Frustrated with himself, with the world at large, Gabriel

stormed upstairs, changing out of his suit. He needed to move, to sweat.

Instead of hitting the weights, he headed out to the far end of his backyard. Against the tall trees sat a pile of logs ready for cutting. What had once been a random hobby, had turned into a form of therapy.

More often than not, chopping wood was one of the many physical things he could do that calmed him. One of the many ways he'd coped when life had felt out of control.

After the first few swings, the knot in his belly began to unravel. By the time he was halfway through the pile, his shirt was damp from sweat and his muscles were shaking. Yet still, his mind churned.

The vibration of his phone on the stump of wood beside him made him curse. It was uncanny that his best friend knew exactly when to call, when he needed a chat. Leaning over the axe, he picked up his phone.

"Harps."

"What is going on, Gabe? I swear you're like a fucking buzzy bee in my head right now."

Gabriel wasn't a religious man by any stretch, but over time he'd begun to accept that there were some people who lived life connected to the spiritual world. His best friend, Harper, was one of them. Even though he'd known her since he was a kid, he still found himself shocked at her ability to see things, to sense things that nobody would know. It was like she operated on a different frequency. "I appreciate the concern, but I'm caught up in a few things."

"Who is she?"

Gabriel sat down on the nearby stump, wondering how best to answer.

"I don't know what you mean."

"You can't bullshit your way out of this, Gabriel. I've known you for forever, so shut up and tell me."

"If I shut up, then how can I speak?"

His chest warmed at her chuckle. She had a rich, raspy laugh thanks to the cigarette habit she hadn't seemed to kick since she was ten years old. Harper was bold and brassy and had been through more trauma than most. When she wasn't traveling the world and experiencing life, she was working or bothering him. She was his first real friend and he loved her more than he had loved anything else in the world, except his mother.

"You haven't pulled that line since you were eight."

"Keeping it real, Harps."

"You, my friend, are stubborn."

"Yeah, but you love me."

She chuckled. "I do. And it's not just 'coz of your pretty face."

"Yeah, yeah."

"Who's the woman? The vibes I'm getting are strong, so it isn't some fleeting fling. Two bright, powerful auras are there, but I can see you'll clash."

"Harps." His sigh was one of resignation.

He didn't want to hear this. Not when it came to any woman or relationship. But more so, it was unsettling that the woman whose face came to mind was the one woman he would never touch.

No way. Not happening.

"Tell me this, were you thinking about a woman when I called? Yes or no."

Gabriel winced, knowing that his best friend was as ruthless as a hound on the scent.

"Yes."

"This woman has you by the balls, Gabriel."

"She does not." He stood, more than a little pissed off by the suggestion.

"If it wasn't true, you wouldn't get so snooty."

"You know, you're starting to—"

Harper was relentless. "Who is she?"

He could imagine Harper in her small flat, surrounded by her crystals and tarot cards. She was such a bright spark in his life and always would be, but she had a way of picking at him when he least expected it. Or wanted it.

She'd gone through hell and back, and he had to remind himself sometimes that the positive, open spirit that she was had nearly been broken. But through all the shit, Harper had proven that she was stronger than anything. She could have chosen to remain scared and jaded after her breakup with her abusive ex, but she was resilient and strong. Still a pain in his ass though.

"Nobody, like I said. I'm dealing with stuff at work, Harps."

"I want you to be open to what's coming. Not everything is going to be cut and dry. Not everything is easily controlled, Gabe. When you open your eyes, you'll see her. You'll know."

"And what if I don't want to know? I'm very happy with my life."

"What, living like a monk? No, Gabriel. That's not happiness. And it's not your fate either. Your future isn't one where you're alone."

"If I want a reading, I'll let you know. But for now, you can butt out."

"Ooh, she really must be pulling a number on you."

"I'm hanging up the phone now."

Harper made smoochy, kissing noises. He cut off her laughter with a modicum of satisfaction.

This was why he was single. He'd found peace in his life, away from the carousel of models and week-long benders, from constantly searching for the next thrill. He was happy with this new life. His *boring* life.

A portentous feeling stole over him. A presentiment of a

future that he had no right believing in. A future he had no right to claim.

There was a real fear inside him that if he gave into temptation, to the hungry, gnawing ache inside, that he would fall back into his old habits, his old life. He wasn't that man anymore. He'd grown up, found his purpose.

He was happy enough. And happy enough was good enough, despite Harper's predictions.

Sometimes, even psychics got it wrong.

CHAPTER FOUR

Maddie decided that she would rather get a root canal while resetting a broken collarbone than actually visit her mother. Sharon Fitzgerald wasn't the type who evoked any warm and fuzzy feelings in anybody, let alone her daughter. She was a hard, bitter woman who loved nothing more than pointing out Maddie's flaws. According to Sharon, she had many.

Too fat.

Too loud.

Too opinionated.

Why couldn't you be kind like that soft-spoken friend of yours?

Why couldn't you be skinnier like that fit friend of yours?

Why? Why? Why?

For many years, Maddie had become an expert in maintaining low and sometimes no contact with her mother, which, to be honest, suited Maddie perfectly. But then the world had gone to hell in a handbasket; the global pandemic—and living in lockdown—had left Maddie questioning everything she knew, including her relationship with her mother.

The occasional phone call had turned into the occasional video call. And before she'd known it, the pandemic had been over and she'd gone back to visiting her mother and questioning her own sanity in the process.

Her mother was not a soft woman.

Her mother was not an understanding woman.

In fact, if it weren't for the birth certificate that Maddie had found when she was ten years old, she wouldn't believe that she was related to Sharon Calway Fitzgerald.

Maddie knew from years of therapy that she was still yearning for something more than her mother could ever give. But in her usual belligerent, mean way, Sharon used the short visits to berate Maddie on her weight, her lack of a boyfriend, and her inability to change her fiery red hair.

If Maddie had been worried about her mother's health, the scathing commentary upon her arrival would assuage any concern. But the pandemic and her stupid nostalgic weakness had unfortunately opened the line of communication, one which Maddie wished she could take back. Which she could, of course, at any time, her therapist reminded her.

But lately, there was a yawning chasm inside of her that couldn't be filled. She knew it was because of her dad. And for some reason, her gut instinct told her that her mother would be able to help her.

That Wednesday was her millionth attempt to make some kind of headway with the woman who birthed her. She didn't hold out much hope that anything would change.

"Why are you here?" Sharon barked as she entered the kitchen of the small cottage-style home. It had been one of the many homes she had known throughout her childhood. It hadn't been until Maddie was completing her final year of high school that her mother had decided to finally stay put. As always, too little too late.

For as long as she could remember, they had been on the

move. She'd never had a stable childhood ever since her dad had left. They'd never stayed in any place longer than a few years, which had made trying to fit in at another new school akin to torture.

By high school, she'd had the 'new kid' routine down to a fine art. Maddie had learned to be open and engaging, bold and brassy. Naturally, that meant she'd gravitated towards the drama club. They had been the same everywhere she'd gone. A melting pot of weird, whacky, and confident individuals, happy to take in another stray.

And that had been how she'd felt for a long time, bouncing from rental to rental, wishing her life had been something different. Wishing that her mother hadn't always been so angry and bitter. God forbid Maddie should come home happy, or with a friend, or—horror—a boyfriend. Her mother found every reason to be dissatisfied.

"I said, why are you here, child?" Sharon's eyes narrowed, and Maddie could feel her disapproval through her clothes.

"Fucked if I know, Mother," Maddie muttered, shutting the back door.

"You should be at the gym."

"Well, I'm here, so deal with it."

Her mother grunted. "That stomach of yours is only getting bigger. You don't watch yourself, you'll end up like me."

Maddie bit her tongue, taking a couple of dirty mugs to the sink. "Is this some kind of an attempt at concern?"

"No man will want you looking like that."

Maddie tried to absorb the stinging words and found an object in the room to ground herself. A trick her therapist had taught her. Maddie focused on the picture of herself as a child, taken outside their first home, a small unit on the outskirts of the city. If she studied the roundness of her face or the lopsided pigtails, then maybe she wouldn't be so conscious of the hate spewing out of her mother's mouth.

Maddie noticed her toothy grin in the picture. She was holding a floppy doll she had loved and adored for years, Punky. Why her mother had that picture up in a frame confused her. Was it just to dig the knife in an old wound? Punky and that little gap-toothed kid were long gone.

Drawing in a deep breath, Maddie braced herself against the memories. That home had been both comfort and curse. A safe haven and a nightmare. As if it were yesterday, the sound of her father's laugh, that deep, belly rumble echoed in her memory. It reminded her of roaring hearths and cigar smoke. She could almost hear his deep Irish lilt, the drawn-out vowels and round consonants.

But then she would recall the nights when her parents had thought her asleep, when the fighting began. Her doll, Punky, and her odd assortment of stuffed animals hadn't been enough to block out the bickering and hollering that had seemed to rattle the windows. And her tiny heart.

Maddie had learned that making them laugh would often diffuse their anger. That had been all she'd ever wanted. To make the fighting stop. To keep them happy.

She shifted a pile of newspapers and sat down in the uncomfortable kitchen chair.

"Maybe we can start again. Hi, Mom."

Sharon sniffed, looking at her, *assessing* her in her usual habit. "What do you want?"

Maddie felt the lick of temper, the hot spitfire sensation creep up her chest, hovering around her mouth, ready and eager to burn. Her tolerance for her mother was decreasing with every passing month.

"I was stopping by to check up on you."

"Why? The pandemic is over. Everything is back to normal. You don't have to pretend to fucking care anymore."

Maddie opened her mouth to shout back, to defend herself against the twisted truth her mother always seemed to spew at her, but she clamped her lips shut. She'd worked through this already. Her therapist had warned her that she would be pulled back into their old routine, the only familiar routine Sharon knew: Maddie as punching bag for all the hate she seemed to bottle up inside.

She refused to be tricked into arguing with her, into reminding her of all the times she'd visited against rules and regulations to see if she'd been alright. Because her mother had a myriad of health problems, that had meant she'd already been high risk. But as usual, Sharon Fitzgerald had prevailed in spite of, or perhaps because of her circumstances.

Her mother was a Rottweiler, ugly, tenacious, and feared by many. With good reason.

"I thought you would appreciate the sentiment."

"Ha! Sentiment never paid any bills around here. I don't see you contributing to the household or offering to get my medication."

Maddie ground her teeth together.

Bait. She would not take the bait.

Because she knew that her mother was goading her to pick a fight, to release whatever it was that plagued her. But they were her mother's demons, not her own. She was a grown ass woman and didn't need any more shit in her life.

"So you're still on those blood pressure meds?"

"Fat lot of good they do. I'll have a stroke and then you'll be happy. Just like your father. Not that he ever cared."

"You need to let that go. It's been decades. Honestly, Mom, you're sitting here, eating yourself up over something that happened nearly thirty years ago. Give it a rest already."

"Give it a rest?" Her mother shook her head, eyes blazing. "I'll rest when I'm dead. Until then, every day is a reminder of what your father did. I'm like this because of him." She gestured to the wheelchair she was in, and Maddie couldn't help but notice that her mother was even heavier than the last

time she'd seen her. Doctors had warned with all the medication she was on, that being obese wasn't going to help. But
everything was someone else's fault. Someone else's problem.

She knew Sharon could walk but refused to. Out of spite.
The doctors had tried every incentive to get her back to the
gym, but she refused. Maddie was afraid that her mother's
diabetes and high blood pressure would take its toll sooner
rather than later.

"You can very well do as you please, Mother. You're single
and able."

"Able? *Able*? You call being stuck in a wheelchair able? Like
you can talk. I don't see you bringing any fellas around here."

And she never would.

"I'm very happy being single, thank you."

And yet the sentiment sounded foreign even to her own
ears, like listening to a recording of herself from decades ago,
recognizable but altered. Because while she had no intention of
settling down with anyone, Maddie had a feeling that her old
life, the one filled with endless first dates and casual flings,
wasn't appealing anymore.

But neither was being in a relationship.

The thought put her in a bad mood. Like everything else
that she couldn't explain or understand, she cast it aside. The
answer would come eventually or not at all. Whichever way, it
would be.

"Not so happy as you make out to be."

Maddie glanced at her mother's lined face. A pair of shrewd
brown eyes stared at her, knowing and a little smug with it. Her
mother was never gracious in victory.

"I'm not sitting at home moping about my life at least."

"Good to know. Men will only hurt you if you let them get
close."

It was a sentiment echoed in her childhood often enough
that Maddie didn't blink twice upon hearing it again.

"Not only men, Mother."

Try as she might, she didn't want to think about her sixth birthday. The wonderful excitement, the thrill of a present, the promise of a chocolate cake with icing fading away in a flash. Maddie rolled her shoulders as the memory played out. She could still picture herself, hair in braids, in her pink pajamas, racing into the living room to find her mother sitting by herself, eyes hard and wet, and her father nowhere in sight.

From then on, birthdays had been a somber occasion. And while Maddie had wanted to hate her father for leaving, as she'd grown older, she'd begun to wish he'd taken her with him.

"Have you heard from—"

"Your father's dead."

"Mother—"

"He's *dead*. And that's the end of it."

"You don't know that. Look, I think I might want to fi—"

"Stop it, Maddie! Don't come around here talking of that man. He left us years ago. As far as I'm concerned, he's dead."

Maddie gestured to the groceries she had brought with her, like she always did. "I'll put these away and go then."

"Don't bother, child. Just go."

She wanted to press her, to get some clarity, maybe even find some answers about whether her father was alive and well. But just like every other time she'd asked, her mother had shut down the conversation.

Maddie picked up her bag and glanced at the framed photograph one more time before leaving. How could Sharon harbor so much hatred still after decades of living alone?

"Why won't you tell me the truth?"

Her mother seemed to revert to silence as her answer. Always silence, but never any peace.

She was starting to think that perhaps there never would be.

"What's up?" Sera's gentle nudge broke Maddie out of her reverie. They were clothes shopping, a pastime that usually made her feel euphoric. That Saturday, it seemed to reinforce all her feelings of inadequacy.

"Everything at the moment." Maddie ran her hands along a soft, blue, stretch-cotton dress, glancing up at Sera only momentarily before studying the sexy outfit again. The slit up the side would show off her legs, but the cut of the bust wasn't right. As a woman with a full figure, Maddie sometimes found it challenging to find dresses that showed off her body in the way she liked. She placed the dress back on the rack.

"Your mom?"

It was a blessing and a curse to have friends who knew her so well. Friends who were only happy to engage in some much-needed retail therapy to celebrate the end of another busy working week. God knew her visit with Penelope yesterday after work had been hard enough. She'd always looked up to her over the years, both as a mentor and a friend. Seeing Penny in the hospital bed like that, her speech slurred from the stroke, had left her shaken.

After a sleepless night, Maddie had woken up this morning with clarity about her life and what she wanted from it.

"She doesn't get that I want to know what happened to Dad. I know she's hiding something. She gets that twitchy eye thing any time I bring up whether she's heard from him."

"What makes you think anything has changed?"

"I don't know if it has, but I get a gut feeling that she isn't being honest with me." Maddie shrugged, feeling stupid, but she trusted her instincts. Her mom was hiding something. She just wasn't certain what that something could be.

"So why keep it from you?" Ally stroked her ever-growing baby bump. Finally, after six months of awful morning, noon, and night sickness, Ally was beginning to hold food down without rushing to the restroom. Her dark hair was past her shoulders now, and there was a soft, glowy look about her that only seemed to intensify with every passing week.

For all of Maddie's reservations about having kids of her own—she had no desire to be a mother—she wholeheartedly loved that Ally was going to have a baby. And that she, an only child who had always longed for sisters, would be able to share in her joy.

This kid was going to get spoiled rotten.

"Your mom isn't the . . ." Sera struggled for words.

"Calmest of people," Ally finished.

"Girls, please. My mom is a raging bitch."

"So what are you going to do?"

Maddie picked up a sexy black pencil skirt. "First, I'm going to try this beauty on, and then I suppose I'll try to find my dad on my own."

Sera gripped her arm, soft brown eyes wide with surprise. "Oh my god, Madds."

She hugged the silk against her chest. "I know."

"This is big."

"Huge," Ally echoed.

"Why now?" Sera squeezed her arm.

"After those awful years—"

"It shall not be named." Ally raised her hand.

"Right, well, after the *pandemic*"—Maddie whispered the word as if some dirty secret—"it made me reassess a few things. Then, after seeing Penny in the hospital yesterday, everything kind of shifted into perspective.

"I don't want to keep living my life as if my dad doesn't exist. It works for my mom, well, aside from the raging anger and bitterness she still carries 'coz of it, but hey, I'm not touching that with a ten-foot pole. But for me? I'm sick of not knowing. I'm sick of doing a double take every time I see ginger hair or holding my breath whenever I hear an Irish accent. Shit, I don't even know if he *has* hair anymore."

Maddie swallowed, hearing the desperation in her voice. It had been building for years, this need to know the truth. But she hadn't been ready. Until now.

"That's hard, the not knowing," Ally soothed.

"It is. And if he's dead, well then, I want to know. Pretending like he died got me through school, but it's not cutting it anymore."

"So what will you do?"

"I don't know. I'm still trying to figure it all out. Not like my mother will be much help."

"Trust me, I get it." Ally nodded.

Maddie knew her friend understood. Ally's parents, while a lot better than they used to be, still had their issues.

"I know you do. And trust me, I'm not getting sucked back into her pity party if I can help it. She's so damn miserable and nothing I do seems to help. She doesn't give a shit and spends more time pointing out my flaws than actually trying to get over the fucking past and move on."

"It's like a tape recorder," Ally added.

"Yes! She's on rewind, and I can't stand to hear it anymore."

"It must be so painful," Sera, ever the soft heart, noted. "To have your husband walk out on you like that."

"I bet it was painful. It was nearly thirty fucking years ago. But like, if I can get over it, or at least keep living, surely she can?"

"She needs help," Sera muttered.

"She needs . . ." Maddie put up her hands, not wanting to get caught up in her mother's bullshit. She forced herself to take in a deep, cleansing breath. "Help, she definitely needs help. And to stop giving me advice about men or how I need to better myself."

"You're perfect."

"Damn right I am. I love my life, I love my body, and I'm sick of drifting because I'm afraid of what I'll find out."

Sera shoved back her mass of brown curls. "You should check the Births, Deaths, and Marriages offices. They'll be able to tell you if there's a record of his death."

"I will, thanks. That'll be a good place to start."

Ally followed Maddie to the changing rooms. "Speaking of new beginnings, how's it going working with your archnemesis?"

Maddie grinned, hanging up her clothes. "I've annoyed him to my satisfaction and it's only been a week."

"Oh boy," Sera muttered.

"I don't know why you two don't get along." Ally rested on the bench in the corner of the large changing room. "I think he's great."

"Then you work with him." Maddie picked up an emerald-green dress with spaghetti straps.

"There's worse people to be stuck working with," Sera threw over her shoulder as she tried on a cap-sleeved dress. She looked like a Mediterranean goddess, her golden skin glowing against the white. Or perhaps it was the fact that she was in happily wedded bliss with her Hollywood movie star husband.

Maddie studied herself in the mirror from every angle. The dress was a winner. Her working relationship, not so much. "Not in my book. The guy is seriously annoying. And you know those Post-it Notes he leaves? They've increased now that we have to work together. By the way, you've got to buy that dress, Sera. Jack would cream his pants seeing you in it."

Sera laughed. "You're so crass . . . and so right. But honestly, I don't think Gabriel means to piss you off."

"Oh really? Notes like: 'Wrong! Needs fixing.' Or 'This doesn't make sense.' He may as well just say, 'Give up now.'"

Maddie glanced in the mirror and caught the look that passed between her two friends.

"Don't be giving each other coded messages. I have eyes." She whipped around to face them. "And before you start with all the, 'oh, but Gabriel has the sun shining out of his ass' nonsense, I have a right to be pissed off at him. He has, since the get-go, treated me like I'm an inconvenience at the best of times. He was rude to me ever since his first day at Woodbury, and don't even get me started about what happened at his first Christmas party.

"To top it off, he's always judging or telling me how to do things better. He's arrogant and cold and . . . *boring*. So I think as my friends, you both need to be sympathetic to the fact that I have to work closely with him until the end of the year."

"So it's going well, you'd say." Ally pressed her lips together.

"Har, har. Honestly, he's lucky I haven't been applying for other positions. We have so much pressure with this new study design, but that's only going to work if we're on the same page. Not sure if the Lone Ranger even knows what teamwork is to be honest."

"I don't think Gabriel will cause any difficulties," Sera pointed out.

"Not intentionally. But he doesn't need to do much to piss me off."

"Look, think of it this way: you're both doing this for the kids. Get through the year, and I'm sure next year you'll be able to hire someone else to take on the role."

"One can live in hope."

"You might even want to try for the head of arts?" Ally nudged her arm.

"Like I'm not busy enough."

"Like you aren't doing it anyway. You're in the acting position. All applying for it would do is make it official," Sera replied, buttoning up her cardigan.

"Point taken."

"Try to have an open mind when it comes to him," Sera advised. "Jack and Gabriel have been hanging out a lot more since opening Bridgelake, and I've gotten to know him a bit better because of it. He really helped us figure out how we could make our arts and tech school a success. From the planning stage all the way through to the grand opening, Gabriel was there. Madds, he really is a nice guy."

"Gabriel? Nice? What the hell has happened to the two of you?" Maddie turned back to examine herself in the mirror again. The dress was definitely a keeper. "No, I'll eat my words before admitting that Gabriel Steele is anything but a pain in my ass."

"Well, said *ass* looks amazing in that dress," Ally pointed out. "I approve wholeheartedly."

"Agreed."

Now she had to find a man worthy enough to take her out in it.

CHAPTER FIVE

*O*nce upon a time, Gabriel had been wild.

He'd lived fast and loose, waking up from benders with anonymous women, and unable to remember his own name.

Once upon a time, Gabriel had been destructive.

He'd broken every single law imaginable just to feel something, *anything* but the white-hot anger that boiled his blood.

Once upon a time, Gabriel had been broken.

He'd looked in the mirror and seen the face of his father.

That had been the moment when everything had changed.

It hurt enough knowing he had his father's likeness, which he supposed had served him well in his old career. But that wasn't his life anymore. That wasn't him.

Gabriel only had to remember his upbringing and that churning, aching sadness would keep him on the straight and narrow. He'd promised himself that if he changed his destructive ways, he would make a difference. He reminded himself of that as he stared at yet another directive sent from the department. Sometimes it felt like nothing he did would be enough to change the lives of those who really needed it. It was difficult not to feel the creeping sense of frustration at the bureaucratic nature of the job. But if he wanted to make a difference, then he'd do it properly.

Working with the regional head of education on literacy initiatives was another step towards implementing better policies and change. If he could do that—make a difference in the lives of all those struggling students—then he would die a happy man.

But seeing his father last night had brought up this feeling of dissatisfaction and disappointment, as it always did. Seeing him struggling to remember anything, let alone his only son had been heartbreaking to say the least. It was only a matter of time before his dad's health deteriorated even further.

Gabriel straightened in his chair and tried—for the fourth time—to focus on the document in front of him. He didn't have time to wallow at work. Especially not now that he'd taken on a senior class.

He'd spoken to them last week, bracing himself for the fall-out. Many were, understandably, distraught that Penelope had fallen ill. But he'd spent all of last week's classes establishing a good rapport with the kids, not as the VP, but as their teacher. One who wouldn't be leaving them anytime soon. Gabriel glanced at his to-do list. Given the pile of work he had to get through, he might very well have a stroke too.

He'd spent the weekend cramming poetry, finding himself lost in possible interpretations, researching review papers, and forming his own ideas. He was looking forward to sharing them with his class, teasing out their interpretations in the process.

"Knock, knock."

Gabriel looked up and smiled, welcoming the distraction despite his workload. "Come in."

He waited patiently for Ally to sit down, knowing that if he offered her help, she would bat him away. She seemed steadier than she had been, less wan looking, a little livelier.

"Is this an okay time?"

"It is. I was off in my own world anyway."

"Tell me about it." Ally patted her stomach. "Sometimes I feel like a greenhouse, large and warm and . . ."

"Blooming?"

"Smelly."

Gabriel smiled. "How big is baby-no-name now?"

Ally tapped her phone. "According to the app, at twenty-five weeks, bub is the size of a cauliflower. Though Charlie insists that the website she found says it's a zucchini."

"So it's safe to say she's excited about becoming a big sister?"

"Obsessively so."

"Pregnancy looks good on you."

Ally beamed. "Thanks. Now that I can kind of keep things down, I'm eating at all times and all things."

"As it should be."

"Not when Charlie is baking up a storm every week. I tell you, between her and Mrs. De Lotto, I swear this bump is 90 percent food baby."

"It's hard to resist her baklava."

"Ooh, someone hit the jackpot." Ally winked.

"Sera's mom would come over with food while we were working out the plans for Bridgelake."

Ally's eyes narrowed. "And you were too afraid to say no."

"Petrified. Do you know when construction began, she was stopping by the site multiple times a week to make sure the builders were adequately fed?"

Ally nodded. "Sera told me they were all sad to finish up, knowing she wouldn't be there."

"The woman should've been in politics."

"I don't think she can help herself. She's been beaming ever since Jack came back into town. It's not every day that a Hollywood hunk returns home, falls in love with your daughter, and helps her build her dream school for disadvantaged kids."

"Good point."

"Speaking of points, there *was* a reason why I stopped by. Maternity leave. What's the plan?"

"Ah. That's a bit of a hot topic." Gabriel explained the staffing possibilities, discussing her current timetable and the responsibilities for the remainder of the school year. She'd need an acting junior school leader to cover her while she was away.

"Peter could do it. He's done it before. The question is, will he want to again? It's not like the job has incentives. Unless you count more work."

"If that's who you want in charge, I'll make it happen. Leave it with me."

"People can't say no to you, can they?"

Images of a fiery redhead telling him where to put his 'initiatives' came to mind. "That's not *entirely* true."

Ally grinned. "That settles that then. Oh, and before I go, I have something for you." She pulled out an envelope-sized invitation. "Open it."

Gabriel studied the pastel-printed paper, smiling. "Your baby shower."

"You're invited. I feel like since our wedding, Jack and Sera's wedding, and the opening of Bridgelake school, we've gotten to know you. We consider you a friend. You've helped me a lot over the past few years, and I feel like it would be remiss not to have you there. I know you have a no mixing outside of school policy—"

"It's more of a loose guideline when it comes to the McVeigh-Davies family."

Ally beamed, and Gabriel could understand why Owen had been smitten with her from the get-go. She was beautiful and lovely and the perfect stepmother Charlotte had needed when she had turned up at Woodbury, lonely and lost.

Despite all the grief with Charlotte's grandparents fighting for custody, Ally had stuck to her principles, doing what was right even if it had landed her in hot water. Perhaps she had bent the rules here and there, but nobody could fault the fact that Ally had the students' best interests at heart.

Her friendship with Maddie and Sera always struck him as interesting. Three very different women had come together in such a strong connection, he knew they were more like family than friends. He also knew that bond was very rare.

"Great! So I take it that's a yes?"

"Count me in."

"Awesome! And no presents. We have so many things already. Owen has reinforced a no gift policy."

"Jack?"

"Bingo. He's showered us with so much baby stuff. I think sometimes he rocks up with yet another must-have item just to spite his brother."

"He's in full uncle mode."

"Totally. Oh, and if you want to bring a date, feel free. Or a friend. Whatever you like."

"I'll think about it."

Ally stood gingerly. "By the way, how's it going with Maddie and the new study design?"

Gabriel leaned back in his chair. "Surely Maddie has told you how harrowing it is to work with me."

Ally wrinkled her nose. "Your relationship isn't exactly . . ." She circled her hands. "*Simpatico.*"

"That's putting it mildly. As usual, Maddie believes what she sees."

Ally's eyes sparked in interest. "And is what she sees what's actually true?"

"This is getting vague."

"Or deep."

Clever woman.

"Like I said, your friend is intent on finding fault with everything that I do. I don't mind arguing with Maddie when it's warranted, but if you're worried that we'll be donning the boxing gloves at your baby shower, don't. We'll be on our best behavior."

Ally's eyes narrowed, and Gabriel found himself struggling to not fidget. She had a spine of steel and a perspicacity that he hadn't initially appreciated. But he wasn't stupid. He knew that Ally and Maddie were best friends, so he would tread carefully.

"*You* might be. With Maddie, I'm not so sure. Look, sometimes she can get stuff in her head and . . . well, it can be hard to get it out. Give her the benefit of the doubt."

"I appreciate the concern, but I think if Maddie and I get through the remainder of this year without blood on our hands, it'll be a miracle."

"Yikes. Maybe this is a good first step in getting to know one another better?" Ally flashed him a hopeful smile.

"I won't hold my breath."

Gabriel waited until she left before picking up the invitation again. He couldn't say he'd ever been invited to a baby shower before. Did Maddie know Ally had included him on the guest list? Would she try to talk him out of attending?

Gabriel unlocked his phone and added the event to his calendar. He wouldn't miss it for the world.

"So . . ."

Gabriel looked up, eyes sparking with mild irritation. "What is it now, Maddie?"

"I didn't say anything."

"You did. You said 'so.'"

"So what?"

"*So*, it wasn't what you said, but how you said it. It wasn't just 'so.' There was tone. Spit it out so we can keep working."

Maddie tossed back her hair, only mildly annoyed. If she was going to be forced to work with the most insufferable man on the planet, she might as well take the opportunity to annoy him as much as humanly possible. That way, she would look forward to their meetings rather than dread them.

"It's this room." She gestured, bangles dancing. She'd chosen the multicolored beauties not just because they sparkled, but because of the tinkling sound they made any time she moved. What good was working with the devil if a girl couldn't have a little fun?

"It's the conference room," Gabriel replied slowly. "I booked this space so we wouldn't be interrupted."

"It's huge." Maddie gestured down the length of the table. "Were we expecting both our classes to join us as well?"

She noted how Gabriel gripped his pen. This was going to be too easy.

"I thought you'd appreciate the privacy."

Maddie wriggled her shoulders. "Yeah, but it's a little *too* private."

The glare she received made her want to smile. She sipped the glass of water he'd offered her at the beginning of the session instead. Needling Gabriel was thirsty work.

"Where would you suggest?"

"My office. Or yours. Or the staffroom. Or—"

"Do you realize how often I'll be interrupted?"

"Oooh, aren't we Mr. Popular."

"What are you, seventeen?"

"In youth and beauty. So you actually got this room to hide away, not because you thought I'd appreciate the privacy."

"Does it matter why?"

"I like to know people's motivations."

"I think you like being a pain in the ass."

Maddie grinned. "That too."

"Can we continue?"

"Sure. Did you find the file?" Maddie walked around the lengthy conference room table to where Gabriel sat on the other side.

His face was the very picture of concentration. She noted that his normally pale complexion had seen some sun over the summer. It suited him, adding an exotic depth to his angular features. His strong jaw, straight nose, and impossibly long lashes were annoying as much as they were arresting.

While he was always clean-shaven, she wondered what he might look like with a bit of scruff on his cheeks. What would facial hair do to his usually severe expression? Would he look a little wilder? Less severe?

Maddie wasn't an idiot. She wasn't going to pretend like Gabriel wasn't an attractive man. If you liked your men cold.

Like a dead fish.

His hot mouth on her breasts had been anything but frigid . .
. .

Get a fucking grip, girl. Are you honestly that horny that a sex dream with Gabriel is still on your mind?

Maddie sat down beside him, pressing her thighs together, making sure to avoid any contact. That had been a week ago. Why the hell was she still thinking about it? Ever since that demented dream, she had been noticing all sorts of things about him that she had no business noticing. She could appreciate someone's good looks without being attracted to them. Right?

It was that stupid dream giving her stupid ideas. That was all. And her man drought. She totally blamed her dry spell for being extra frisky.

Maddie froze when a pair of gray-blue eyes locked her in place. Try as she might, she couldn't quite seem to focus on anything else. How had she never noticed the small flecks of amber in his irises before?

It was as if all the oxygen in the room had been sucked down the vortex of some black hole.

Not that *hole, dirty bitch.*

Gabriel was the first to break the silence. "Did you hear anything I said?"

"You found the file?"

"We're never going to get anywhere if I have to keep repeating myself, Maddie."

"Well, if you brought some snacks, maybe I'd be able to concentrate."

She noticed the way his chest rose and fell under his suit. Deep breathing wasn't going to save him now.

"Does it look like I have snacks on me?" Gabriel motioned to the empty table.

"It's nearly half-past ten."

"So what?"

"So, Mr. Robot, normal people like to have morning tea around this time."

"We're working."

"Correction: planning. Planning requires brain food. Brain food requires snacks. Or is it only the executive leadership team that gets food at meetings?"

"You're some work, Fitzgerald."

Maddie grinned. "Thanks."

"That wasn't meant as a compliment."

"I refuse to cower to your sullen attitude."

She simply stared as Gabriel turned towards her fully. Had his shoulders always been that broad?

"I don't have an attitude. I'm simply trying to get this meeting back on track before I get called away to some emergency or other. I really don't want to waste any more of *our* time, and I'm sure you don't either. Given the importance of—"

There was a quick knock on the door and Elaine, one of the receptionists, popped her head in. "Sorry to interrupt."

"What? What is it?" Gabriel glowered at the lovely white-haired woman.

"I beg your pardon."

"I think he needs a snack," Maddie whispered to the eagle-eyed receptionist.

She glanced back at Gabriel and silently applauded Elaine's timing. The man was practically grinding those pearly whites.

"Is that how you speak to your colleagues?" Elaine shoved the door open. "I'll have you know that you may be in a senior position around here, but that does *not* mean you can take your temper out on me." Her glare alone was intimidating.

Gabriel still gripped his pen, but his voice softened. It was an odd and interesting combination. It must be exhausting being so restrained all the damn time. The man was cold. Or maybe simply devoid of emotion. Which was probably why she didn't get along with him. *Her* friends were down-to-earth. *They* shared their thoughts and feelings. It was as if he were trying to not be human sometimes. It was just plain weird.

"Apologies, Elaine. You're right. I shouldn't have spoken that way. What's happened?"

"Altercation in Lewis' senior prac class."

"Be right there."

Elaine merely sniffed and turned on her heel.

"You can wipe that smart-ass grin off your face now."

"Who, me?"

Gabriel hovered at the open doorway. "I'll be back in ten. Maybe you can point out what I need to add to my lesson plans for this poetry outcome?"

"Sure thing, boss."

"*Don't* call me boss."

"Sure thing, Vice Principal Steele."

Gabriel pinched the bridge of his nose. "God, that's somehow even worse."

Maddie only felt a slight pang of remorse at pushing his

buttons but quickly batted the feeling away. Drawing his laptop over, she focused on the document in question. She might enjoy getting on Gabriel's nerves, but she wasn't about to jeopardize the students' chances at success.

When he returned twenty minutes later, he threw down a packet of crisps on the table.

Maddie's eyes lit up.

"Oooh, must have been a good bust-up to get those."

"Yeah, I beat up a sixteen-year-old for them."

"Nice one, boss. You the real MVP."

"Now can we get started?"

"Finally." Maddie sighed, rolling her eyes. "I've been waiting for aaaages."

The look he spared her was well worth the wait.

CHAPTER SIX

The following week, Maddie closed the door of the new drama room at Bridgelake, the brand-new arts and tech school outside the inner city of Melbourne.

She loved everything about this school, and it wasn't just because Sera and Jack had built it. It was one of the best things to come out of the shitshow that was the pandemic, and it was every disadvantaged student's dream.

So when the school opened and began taking on pupils, without cost to struggling students or their parents, it meant that those kids who didn't have a chance, or even a bright future, could be supported. They could learn a trade, get experience in the hospitality sector, even work on their basic literacy and numeracy skills so they could get a job at the local store.

One thing Maddie enjoyed more than anything was running drama workshops with those kids who never had the luxury of enrolling in drama studies. For some, it was a chance to do something creative, and for others it was a crash course in something they wanted to pursue once they graduated.

To think that Jack Davies, Hollywood megastar and heartthrob, could be found running sessions at Bridgelake rather than flying back to LA still made her shake her head in disbe-lief. Hell, the fact that Sera had married the guy was like some-thing out of a Hollywood blockbuster film.

She didn't want to feel jealous of her best friends, but a part of her couldn't help it. Some days she longed for her own happily ever after. And it hurt to think that perhaps she would never get it.

Shaking off the green-eyed monster, Maddie packed away the props and costumes before heading out of the hall and down the maze of corridors to where she'd parked. Everything gleamed and shined, but even though the building was new, it wasn't intimidating. Sera had made sure of that.

Many of the kids who attended on scholarships had dropped out of school to work or because they'd gotten caught up in the wrong crowd, but thanks to the flexible learning environment, students were able to attend either morning or evening sessions to meet the requirements. And the guaran-teed apprenticeships and placements lined up for them once they finished made being in school an attractive option over crime.

But it was the satisfaction on their faces that never failed to delight her. It was a little bit of good that she could do to give back. Lord knew her childhood hadn't been the brightest, but she'd had a roof over her head and cooked meals to eat and that was a lot more than some of these kids had ever had.

Maddie was about to turn right down the corridor that led to reception when she heard it. The deep, authoritative rumble of a voice she had spent only this morning silently cursing at.

She backtracked a few steps, turning towards the half-open door. Sitting on the desk, with his suit jacket off and his sleeves rolled up was Gabriel.

Mercy, was his shirt collar unbuttoned, too?

Maddie had never seen him without a tie or a haughty atti-tude. Watching him casually propped on the desk half-dressed was almost akin to seeing him naked. Something about the whole image felt off. She couldn't quite figure it out.

He, blessedly, had his back turned to her, so Maddie hovered beside the door, listening to the students' discussion. They all appeared utterly engrossed in what he was saying.

And then it struck her. Gabriel Steele, all-around pain in her ass and bane of her existence, actually looked . . . approachable.

Somehow, he appeared relaxed and in his element as he sat in front of the class, a book in hand, his face almost . . . Wait, was that a smile? Maddie gaped at the transformation. She hadn't thought he knew how.

Gone was the severe, draconian vice principal, and in its place was someone that Maddie didn't recognize at all. If she was a generous woman, she would have said it made him look almost appealing.

But she wasn't.

Though, she would give him props for the cut of his suit. And hello, she was right about those shoulders. She watched him gesture and was bemused by the ripple of muscles beneath his blue shirt.

She took a moment—thirty seconds at most—to admire him before the realization hit her smack in the face.

What in the hell was Gabriel doing teaching at Bridgelake?

Maddie crossed her arms, contemplating the situation as if staring at swatches of paint at the hardware store. What color was Gabriel here? Almost a warm canary yellow. Inviting, calming, and hell, if she didn't dislike the man, she'd even go as far as to say somewhat arresting.

Odd given that he normally radiated waves of icy blue.

Maddie shook her head. She'd never understood why she saw people in colors. It was a weird quirk of hers. But then, she wasn't the most traditional of girls, which made working with him extra painful. Gabriel was strictly business, pure reason and logic and not at all someone whom she'd choose to work with closely this year.

"Snooping again?"

Maddie gasped, clutching her bag to her chest. She turned to face Jack and his shit-eating grin.

"You scared the hell out of me!" she furiously whispered.

"Mission accomplished."

"Real mature."

Jack motioned her away from the door. "How'd your class go?"

"Spying on me?"

"I know everything that goes on here. Good and bad." Jack winked, but his pride shone through.

"Are you telling me you're considering a career change?"

"Something like that."

"Is your agent still calling you?"

Jack rolled his eyes. "Only every six months now. He's certain he has the next big script that I won't be able to refuse."

"And what did you say?"

"I'd have to ask the boss."

Maddie grinned. "Sera wouldn't stop you."

"I don't want to change things, Madds."

"Not when you're swimming in success. I saw the write-up in the paper last week. There's talk of tech schools coming back in fashion because of Bridgelake."

"We're trendsetters alright. But I told them we're not just any arts and tech school. Some of these kids come in here for short courses, others for the extracurriculars, and then there's the rest that want to do trades. We can handle all the turning cogs in the wheel, but lots of other places view schools as businesses. Sera wants this to be as much about pastoral care as it is a bridging step towards other pathways."

"Hey, no need to sell it to me. I think this place is amazing."

"Fucking A, it is. And with the long list of community clubs wanting to use our courts and rooms outside of hours, it's starting to make some money. Not that that's our goal, but I've found I've a new passion for finance."

"Yet another career option . . . Do you miss it? The Hollywood life?"

Jack shrugged. "Hollywood, heck no. But sometimes I miss the challenge of taking on a character, of testing my limits as an artist. But all the other bullshit is still too fresh for me to go back. And with Bridgelake and all the food canteen work we're doing on weekends, I don't have time to think about anything else."

As the students began trickling out of the classroom without screaming or crying in fear, Maddie sidled closer to Jack.

"So, what's Steele doing here?" She jerked a thumb over her shoulder.

"He volunteers."

"I gathered that. Is this a regular thing?"

"He requested it."

Maddie heard the words but couldn't quite make sense of them.

"How did I not know about this?"

"Maybe you didn't *want* to know."

Huh.

"Sera said you two have been pretty buddy-buddy since opening the school."

"Gabriel has been a big help getting this place up and running. He has a lot of contacts in high places, and I had no idea where to begin. Naturally, we built a friendship over the years, but he told me from the get-go that he wanted to help out with the literacy classes and any additional English ones that needed to be filled. Given how busy he is with the leadership stuff at Woodbury, I didn't think he'd be able, but the guy makes it work."

"And *he* asked?"

"Insisted."

"You think you know a guy."

"Don't think, Maddie. You might hurt yourself." Gabriel's voice was soft, but she heard the smug satisfaction in his tone.

"As opposed to your sparkling humor and wit. Oh wait, you don't have any."

Gabriel stood beside Jack. "And here I was mildly surprised to hear that *you* of all people volunteer here. Don't you have a cauldron that needs stirring?"

Maddie gritted her teeth. "Do you ever get tired of being so, so . . ."

"There are minors here," Jack interrupted.

Maddie silently cursed. The man was—

Jack's phone broke the tension, startling her. "That's my cue. Try not to kill each other while I'm gone." Jack threw her a wink over his shoulder as he walked away.

"So you landed the lit role at school and now that means you're back into teacher mode?"

"I volunteer here, just like you, Maddie."

"Why?"

"None of your business."

"What's with the secrecy, Steele?"

"What's it to you, *Fitzgerald*?"

"I'm curious."

"You're nosey."

"Why can't you seem to answer any question that isn't work related?"

"Why do you only want to know things that aren't work related?"

Maddie huffed. "You're impossible."

"Has anyone ever told you that you should mind your own business?"

"Plenty of times, actually."

Gabriel leaned in, arms folded. "So now would be the time to listen to that advice," he whispered pointedly.

"Uh-huh. Don't you have anything better to do with your life than hang around school kids?"

"No, I don't. Clearly."

Maddie felt a stab of remorse, suddenly uncertain of what to say. "Oh. I didn't—I mean, lots of people take up volunteer work when they're lonely. I'm not saying that you're—"

Gabriel's small smile was the only evidence that she'd been played.

Bastard.

"Yes, I have a life, Maddie. Though, my friends might think otherwise. I volunteer because I want to. That should be enough to satisfy you."

"There it is."

"There *what* is?"

"That ol' reliable Steele, shutting down the conversation."

Gabriel rolled his shoulders back, the look on his face summing up exactly how she felt. Frustrated. "That's not true."

"Oh really?" Maddie flicked back her hair, revving up. "Any time anyone tries to have a remotely human conversation with you about life, *your* life, we get shut down. Like you're doing now."

"I disagree."

"You would." Maddie watched as the steam all but puffed out of his ears. "Nothing to say?"

"Never mind."

"See? Exactly my point! You can't seem to do the basic thing."

"What's that? What *is* the basic thing, Maddie? Please, in all your wisdom, enlighten me."

Was she imagining it, or did she catch a glimpse of human emotion beneath the ice? Could her words have actually hurt him?

Impossible. That would mean he had a heart to hurt.

"You're a closed book. I barely know anything about you, and most people would say the same. It's not only me who thinks it. What do you do for fun? Do you go to parties? Do you even know what a party is?"

"Funny, Fitzgerald."

"I should know something about you other than the fact that you're a rule-abiding know-it-all."

"Here's something you didn't know. This 'closed book' has already accepted Ally's invitation to her baby shower."

Maddie's mouth fell open. It took her a good few seconds to cram it shut again.

"I see your friends didn't keep you abreast of *that* bit of gossip." Gabriel gasped in such an exaggerated way that it would have been comical had it not pissed her off. "Are you the last to know?"

She hovered somewhere between annoyance and embarrassment. All she could think about was wiping that smug expression off his face.

"I'm sure the invite was out of pity."

Gabriel leaned in. "Is that the best you can do, *Red*?"

"Original."

"Fitting." He glanced at her hair.

Maddie jerked back when he reached out to tug at a loose strand, then froze, heart thudding frantically. For the life of her, she had nothing to say. She realized she was holding her breath but refused to move an inch. For some reason, she knew she had to keep very, *very* still.

He was close, so much so that she caught a whiff of his aftershave and felt the heat emanating from his chest.

While his voice was above a whisper, the tone was anything but sweet.

"Perhaps if you stopped running your mouth and listened to what other people are telling you, you might pick up on a lot more than you think. And maybe, just maybe, you'd see something that would challenge your assumptions. But if you must know, the life I used to live would have made the devil himself blush." Gabriel studied her face, and whatever was on it seemed to satisfy him.

He stepped back and slung his jacket over his shoulder. "But that's information you don't need to know. Isn't it?"

Maddie tilted her chin and watched him walk away.

"See you tomorrow, *Red*," he called out, slipping his free hand into his pocket.

Maddie brushed at the chill on her arms. She was hot and yet shivery. And as usual when it came to Gabriel, she was utterly frustrated.

What the hell had just happened? More to the point, what had Gabriel done in his past that had been so very wicked?

Was he playing with her, or was Gabriel hiding some deep dark secret?

Maddie walked down the corridor, her mind conjuring all sorts of scandalous scenarios. She was so engrossed in her thoughts that it didn't even occur to her that she thought of Gabriel all the way home.

CHAPTER SEVEN

Gabriel had never liked visiting his father. Even when the man had been in his prime and full of life, the exchange had often felt brittle. Not that he'd made the time or effort back then. He'd been too full of rage to taste any other emotion. And even though he'd grown out of feeling anything but blame for his father, having Leo sick and unable to have proper conversations, ones that actually mattered, was heart-wrenching.

Gabriel parked his car and walked through the entrance of Malton Mews, the nursing home his father had been living in for eight years now. In some twisted way, he supposed it was a blessing that Leo was plagued by dementia, not to mention a host of other health issues. He ground his teeth together against the jolt of sadness that rushed through him. They couldn't have their time again, and the ugly truth was, neither of them would have made better choices.

After registering his name at reception, Gabriel placed his visitor badge on his chest and walked down the hall to the communal area. Sitting down in an oversized chair, he glanced around the room, making a mental note of the familiar faces and one or two new ones, evidence that death waited for no man.

The pervading feeling of loss sat beside him. The man whom he once remembered as fun and dependable had disappeared when Gabriel had been a boy. He'd been five when the accident had happened, and after that fateful day, his father, the man he had once known and loved, had never returned. The man he'd hated as a teenager was long gone too. Instead, what was left was a shell of a human.

In a cruel twist of fate, Gabriel had lifted his no-contact rule with his dad not long after he'd begun teaching. But it had been short-lived. The connection he'd craved seemed to slip through his fingers as his dad's mental health deteriorated. At first, he'd thought it forgetfulness, but the disease had seemed to increase in severity and speed until Gabriel had had no choice but to find a home that would care for him.

And all through that time, Gabriel had fought against his frustrations; there'd been no outlet for his sadness and regret. He'd never had the chance to say the things that he'd wanted to after all those years apart. Gabriel could hardly rail against this fragile, lost shell of a person. To do so would be cruel.

The staff at Malton Mews had made everything easier. They were supportive, careful to contact Gabriel should his father be a little more lucid, a little less lost. They told him it would be foolish to hold out hope given his father's advanced state, but Gabriel still insisted that they call him at the slightest sign of improvement. But often by the time he reached the nursing home, his father had reverted to being a stranger. It had been chilling at first, to witness the vacant expression, the utter detachment, the anger.

Maybe it was better this way.

"Gabriel, can I speak to you for a minute?" Silas, one of the few male nurses whom his father liked and tolerated sat beside him. His dad had always been more of a ladies' man, and even dementia hadn't taken that away.

"I wanted to speak to you before your dad came out. Look, there's no easy way to say this, but the doctors have some concerns."

Gabriel's back straightened. "Concerns?"

"His heart is giving him trouble."

"Don't sugarcoat it for me, Silas."

"They don't think he'll make it to Christmas."

Gabriel crossed his arms. His own heart began to tremble.

"Gabriel?"

He didn't quite know how to feel. "Just processing it."

"We can make an appointment with the physician for you to speak to her and get some clarification on the matter, but I thought it best you know now."

"I appreciate it. Thanks, Silas. How is he today?"

"The usual."

So it was a bad one.

Gabriel looked around him. A few men and women were playing board games, most others in conversation with family or friends. The culmination of all of these people's lives, their contributions to society and whom they loved, was masked in nursing homes like this. What had they done in their youths? Who had they loved or hated before ill health had robbed them of independence? He felt helpless knowing that age ravaged some of them so harshly, while there were others who lived in good health until the end.

What would he give to have his father remember? His cynicism said his dad would have carried on being selfish and absent, consumed by his own grief even if he were sound of mind.

"Hey, Leo."

He never called him Dad. He had made that mistake—once —at the beginning, and his father had been so startled, so damn confused, he'd lashed out. It hadn't been the first time that he'd been struck by him. The anger and confusion usually came after an episode of remembering. When he forgot, he was usually as docile as a lamb.

His dad sat down gingerly in the chair in front of him. "Hah? You'll have to speak louder, young man."

He would never get used to it. Growing up neglected by his dad should have made this easier to handle, but it somehow only made it worse.

"I said, how are you feeling?"

"Ah, well enough. They played checkers with me today. That guy, Silas, is a dirty cheat though."

Even though his dad didn't remember him, it oddly pleased Gabriel that glimpses of Leo's personality would shine through. But these days, those brown eyes seemed to only skim the surface. There was no depth there, no recognition.

A wave of anguish washed over him, seizing him now as it did whenever he visited his father. "You say that every time."

"Every time, eh? You a regular?"

"Regular enough."

"What's your name, son?"

He knew the moniker was only his way, not because his father recognized him. It still stung all the same.

"Gabriel."

"An angel. Hero of God. If I had a son, I would name him Gabriel. But I was never blessed with children."

He noticed the blue of his father's sweater then focused on the sticky substance on his chin. When that didn't work, he listened to the sound of voices around them. He did everything to avoid feeling the ache in his heart. It wouldn't help. It didn't change things. There was nothing he could possibly do to take this disease away or to rail against his father for all the hurt he'd caused.

Because the little glimpse of his old personality—the one

who loved knowing the origin of people's names, the meaning behind words, even though he'd spent most of his life practically illiterate—was a painful reminder of whom he'd lost.

So Gabriel would carry on as normal, pretending like he was just any other person, that it was any other day. And all that he felt, all that sadness that wanted to swallow him whole would have to find another outlet.

Because the old Gabriel, the Gabriel who was reactive, the Gabriel who lived for conflict and emotion would have taken all that sadness and anger and gone on a week-long partying streak. Not necessarily boozing, but women. All types of women, in all different ways. The alcohol might loosen him up a little, but the women, their soft bodies, their sweet smells had drowned out any other feeling or fear.

And the more he'd partied, the more numb he'd felt to everything else. Which meant he'd needed a bigger thrill.

But that wasn't his life anymore.

It didn't fulfill him anymore.

He was happy now. Well, happier. Less wild, more contained.

He'd taken control of his life in a way his father had been incapable of doing. From a young age, he'd known that he couldn't rely on his dad. Over time, he'd grown accustomed to it. And if he hadn't met Harper, he was certain he would have died long ago.

It had only been when he'd grown up, when he'd been able to compare his father to the other ones in the school, the ones who had time to volunteer for committees or show up at concerts that Gabriel had realized he was different. He couldn't exactly bring in his father, the drunk. His father, the—

He squeezed his hands into fists. It didn't bear thinking about. Leo was a broken man who had in turn broken him.

"I did have a sweetheart." Leo was watching him now with a bit more awareness behind his eyes.

"I've heard about her."

"She was a beauty. Fair skin and the most glorious silver eyes, a bit darker than yours. Ahh, she was too good for me." Leo shook his head slowly.

"A nurse."

"That's right." He beamed. "But not like these dowdies here. She was beautiful. A classic beauty. And I loved her." His face creased as he tried with some difficulty to remember. "God, what was her name?"

"Annabelle."

"Hmm? No, I don't think so."

"Everything okay here?" Silas walked past.

"Fine, thanks," Leo replied, wiping at the spit that had gathered at his mouth. He frowned down at his pants and then his head whipped up. "Grace. Annabelle means grace. None of that for the old. We don't go gracefully. One day you're in your prime, pulling all the birds, and the next you're a face full of wrinkles." His dad sat back and sighed. Gabriel was used to the sudden changes in topic. "I don't know anymore. I'm not sure what happened to her, you see. The mind isn't as sharp. Still here though." He patted his chest, breathing shallowly.

Leo reached inside his trouser pocket.

"This is my sweetheart." He handed over the small picture of his wife, Annabelle. Gabriel braced himself against the pain as he gazed at the image of his mother, immortalized and forever young in the picture.

She was on her own, in a simple printed dress, standing on the cliff of a beach. One of their favorite spots, according to what his father had told him. And a place that his dad had been unable to visit for a very long time.

Gabriel had vague memories of her, but what he did remember comforted him decades later. The soft sound of her voice reading to him at night, the way she'd tucked him in bed, calling him her burrito baby. How she'd always read to him every evening, even when she'd had a late shift.

He recalled waking up one night to her sitting in his room, the summer light filtering through the blinds. It had been daylight savings, and he had protested to his dad about going to bed while the sun was still up. But he'd dozed off and eventually awoken hours later to the sound of his mother's voice.

She'd been reading beside him, still in her nurse's uniform, and he'd kept himself awake so he could feel her fingers brushing through his hair.

There had been something so soothing about the way she'd read to him, encouraging him when he would try to sound out the words and letters on his own. She'd said he would be the smartest kid in school. That he would shine bright and do great things.

A sick, lurching sensation tugged at him now. He was glad that she hadn't been around to witness his destruction. He didn't think he'd be able to bear it.

Gabriel handed back the picture.

"A looker, eh?" Leo winked.

"She was beautiful . . . . What else do you remember about her?"

"Who?"

Gabriel scratched his chin, trying his best to contain his anger.

"What are you doing here, talking to an old codger like me, eh? Handsome boy like you probably has all the girls chasing after him."

Gabriel stood. "I wanted to say hi, but I'm on my way out."

"I bet you are. Enjoy those beauties while you're still young. Before you know it, you're in a wheelchair eating cardboard and being fed like an infant."

"Take care of yourself, D—"

"Hah?" His dad clucked his tongue, waving him off. "I always do."

CHAPTER EIGHT

"What?" Gabriel spared a quick glance across his desk at Maddie.

He was trying to focus on the document on his laptop, given that they only had the period to get through their planning session—which had already been interrupted three times—but all he could feel were a pair of witchy eyes drilling holes into his brain.

"Nothing."

"Then get back to work."

It was week five, halfway through term two, and he was juggling a full schedule. It didn't help that he felt the pressure of the job. Not his role as vice principal, he was so used to dealing with student and staff welfare that even the larger than normal spate of student expulsions of late didn't make him break a sweat. It was the fact that he had a senior class for the first time in a long while coupled with the pressure of a new study design that had him sweating.

Students were looking to him for guidance. And while Penelope's sudden departure had been a shock to her senior students, he'd been able to reassure them that he was in fact an experienced teacher and they were safe having him as their substitute for the remainder of the year.

Penelope had recovered enough to hand in her notice, taking an early retirement much to the delight of her grandchildren. But it was a loss to the students and the school, as she was taking decades of knowledge and experience with her. It would have been good to have her for a handover period. Especially as he hadn't taught literature in a while.

It made everything worse when the woman in front of him seemed to delight in setting him on edge.

When the words on his screen turned into crawling black caterpillars, Gabriel sighed. "What is it?"

"What?"

"Why are you staring at me, Fitzgerald?"

"I'm not . . . Well, I *am*. I—"

"Are we ever going to be able to get through a working session together without you digressing into a thousand different segues?"

Maddie tapped the pen to her lips, which were pursed in a thoughtful expression. "Hmm, probably not."

Gabriel shoved his chair back from his desk and stretched out his legs, resting his hands on his stomach. He was expecting a call from the head of the region any minute now, so what was another interruption?

He glanced at his watch. "I'm waiting."

"I'm curious is all."

"About me?"

"Well, yes."

"Were you a cat in your past life? Actually"—Gabriel held out his hand—"don't answer that."

"I'm just trying to figure you out."

"What if I don't want to be figured out."

"Ha! See, anyone who says that has something to hide."

"I've nothing to hide. I'm an open book." He fought not to squirm when every part of him wanted to move.

Maddie snorted. "You're like a closed book buried in a tomb, buried in the sea, buried in the—"

"Enough. I get the point. I'm not an open book."

Maddie shook her head. "Not in the slightest. For instance, you have a tattoo on the inside of your ring finger."

Gabriel fingered it now, remembering the time when he'd had it done. The writing was small enough, running from the bottom of his ring finger and ending just at the base of his nail. "How very observant of you."

"I never really paid attention to it before."

"And why is this so important?"

"You know, I've always wanted a tattoo, but I keep talking myself out of it," she replied, ignoring his question. "Was it painful?"

"It wasn't. But then again, everyone's tolerance to pain is different."

"What's it say?"

"None of your—" Gabriel gritted his teeth at her 'told you so' expression. He could almost hear her singing 'closed book' in a taunting fashion.

"*Per sempre.*"

"What's that mean?"

"Forever." Gabriel sighed, fighting against the memories.

"And why on that finger?"

"Because the person who I make a commitment to, the one who I'll eventually marry, will be forever." He shoved aside the memories, the day he'd made himself that promise that he would never be like his father.

Gabriel shivered. His dad had never recovered from losing his wife. But unlike his father, Gabriel wouldn't . . . He shook his head, blocking out the memory. He would never be like his old man.

"Is that all, Maddie?"

"No. Why Italian?"

"My father's Italian."

"But Steele—"

"Drop it."

Maddie held up her hands. "Sore subject, got it. So answer this, why do you really volunteer with literacy classes at Bridgelake?"

"Will you get back to work if I answer this question?"

Maddie shook her head. "There might be more."

"You might find yourself with an extra yard duty, too."

He noticed how her lips—painted a pastel pink today—twitched slightly. "That's an abuse of power."

"No, that's a sign you've tested my patience."

"Grumpy."

"Time-bound."

"Boring."

"Focused."

Maddie rolled her eyes then leaned forward, bangles at her wrists dancing. "Yes, I promise to go back to work if you answer my question."

"Good."

"So why volunteer with the kids at Bridgelake?"

Gabriel sat up now, drawing his chair closer to his desk so that he mirrored her position. "Those kids are disadvantaged."

"Yes."

"So it's important to give back."

"That's it?"

"Does it have to be more than that?"

"In my world, nobody does something for nothing. Or without some other kind of motivation or reason behind it. Usually an emotional one. But given you're a robot incapable of feeling, I'm wondering what your reasoning might be."

"Consider it a flaw in my hardware. And news flash, Red, I'm fine and dandy not living in your world."

"Who says 'dandy' anymore?"

"I do." Gabriel leaned even closer, temper flaring. "The grumpy, boring, vengeful vice principal who is one phone call away from giving you a few more after school meetings for the next calendar month."

"Punishment?" Her eyes narrowed slightly, a sly expression stealing over her face. "Kinky."

Gabriel placed his palms flat on the desk, ignoring the knee-jerk reaction in his groin. *Not today, Satan.* He refused to be tempted by this woman. "This is an entirely inappropriate conversation to be having in a workplace."

"Depends on your aim in the workplace . . ."

"Fitzgerald." He resisted the urge to do something that would get them both fired, but with Maddie running her mouth, he might make an exception.

"Ooh, was that a growl? Very *not* boring."

"I signed up for literature teaching. I didn't sign up for gray hairs in the process."

"Oh, hey, if I don't give you gray hairs, my kids' close analysis skills will."

"Finally, back on topic."

"Hmm, not really. Why those kids?"

"Literacy is important to me, okay? Teaching kids who screwed up and don't have a proper chance means something to me, and yes, it's personal. And none of your business."

"Oh." Maddie closed her mouth, seeming to rethink her initial urge to speak. After a few seconds, she shrugged. "Okay, cool. Why didn't you say so in the first place? Now we can get back to work."

Gabriel was sure he'd developed dangerously high blood pressure since working with the harpy. Their principal, Jacinta, owed him big.

"Not so fast, Fitzgerald."

"What?" Maddie's gaze was direct. He liked that about her. She never flinched from him even if he was being a dick. And sometimes his job meant he had to be the disciplinarian. Gabriel tried not to let his imagination run away with him.

Not here.

Not with her.

But there was something so damn sexy about a woman who was confident. And Maddie Fitzgerald, as annoying as she was, had confidence down to an art.

"I'm listening."

"I have questions of my own. Why do *you* volunteer?"

"That's an easy one. I'm helping out a friend."

"Wrong answer."

"Well, that's the only one you'll get from me."

"And now who's being the boring one? The closed book?"

Maddie fake laughed, glancing at her well-manicured nails. "Nice try, but I'm the master of verbal manipulation. I wasn't born yesterday."

"Well, at least we can start a new boring teachers club together. Maybe take up knitting."

"Hey, knitting is cool. It's made a big come back in recent ye—"

Maddie's frown disappeared. She was quick, he'd give her that. Which was why besting her felt so damn good.

She cursed at him for goading her, and Gabriel had to hand it to her for cussing him out in Spanish. They didn't even offer it in the curriculum.

"I'm not a big, hairy ass, but I appreciate the sentiment."

She smiled sweetly. "I learned a lot in Spain ten years ago."

"I bet you did," Gabriel muttered.

"What's that supposed to mean?"

"Let it go."

"I will *not*."

"Fine, you wanna know?"

"Yes."

Gabriel stood, walking around the table to perch on the desk in front of her. "Then I'll tell you. All that fiery red hair and a mouth like yours would have certainly gotten you into trouble. Not to mention those curves. Spanish men, from my experience, wouldn't have seen you coming. So the fact that you know a few choice Spanish swear words doesn't surprise me in the least."

Maddie's mouth opened, but her voice had a breathlessness to it when she spoke. "This is an entirely inappropriate conversation to be having in the workplace."

"Is it?"

"Yes."

"Good. Then I've made my point. Now, can we get back to work?" He waited a beat, watching the way she challenged him, body taut, eyes direct. "I don't care whether you volunteer at the school for your own ego or out of the goodness of your heart. I don't care whether you spend your Saturday nights knitting or having torrid affairs with Spaniards. I don't care about any of that stuff, Maddie, because that's your private life and we are in my very public office." He gestured to the glass doors behind her. The blinds weren't drawn. Anybody walking along the corridor could see them.

"A—" She cleared her throat, tried again. "And what if we were in a private office?"

Gabriel glanced at her mouth, the one that drove him a little crazy but was off-limits. He was caught by whatever spell she seemed to conjure and, because of it, gave into temptation.

"Then the last thing we would do is talk."

Gabriel breathed in her response like a smoker dragging in his first hit of nicotine. It sent a thrill through him that had no damn place being there. None at all.

Reel it the fuck in, Gabe.

"Oh . . ."

Gabriel stood then forced himself to take a few steps back. But he still felt the charge of whatever simmered between them. "Let's get it straight, Red. What you do in your spare time is none of my business. What I do in mine is off-limits to you. We keep up that agreement and things between us will go a hell of a lot smoother. Is that understood?"

A basic part of him was pleased when it took a minute for her to snap out of it. If he wanted to, dear God, if he put even a little effort in, he could have her floating on a bed of pure hedonistic pleasure. What he could do . . . What he *would* do . . .

Maddie sat up taller, adjusting the laptop that threatened to slide down her long legs. She mock-saluted. "Yes, sir."

God, he could spank her for that.

"Good."

Gabriel sat behind his desk before his body had any other ideas. Typing in his password, he forced his brain to focus. He'd crossed a line.

Damn it and damn her for the mistake. And it was a mistake, one he wouldn't allow himself to make again.

Far better to keep things professional.

Far, far better for them both to pretend like that slip-up had never happened.

But something still hovered in the air between them, and if Gabriel wasn't careful, it would suffocate them both.

CHAPTER NINE

"So what is this thing I *have* to see?" Maddie shoved her sunglasses on top of her head. "I was in the middle of a steamy historical, girl."

"You can get back to your Heathcliff later." Sera ushered her into her parents' home. Why they were meeting at Maryam and Tony's house was apparently top secret over the phone.

"I finished re-reading *Wuthering Heights* last weekend, thank you very much. I'm on to a totally different book, a very slow-burn Regency romance that had me up until the wee hours."

"Which makes sense as to why you're so grumpy this morning." Sera smiled sweetly sitting on the sofa.

"It's still middle of the night according to my body clock."

"It's one in the afternoon, princess. And stop complaining, my mom is making falafels."

"Oh, God bless Maryam and her culinary hands." Maddie flopped on the couch beside her.

"I thought you were going out with your fellow thespians last night."

"I did. But the pub was a bust and the club wasn't any better."

"Man drought?"

"Bingo. I should've been having glorious morning sex followed by brunch at a café, but my vibrator and a fictional duke kept me company instead."

"Not a terrible end to your evening then."

"No . . ."

"Any news about your dad?"

She'd contacted the Births, Deaths, and Marriages office to find out whether her dad was dead or alive earlier that week. They'd put her in contact with a family history expert, so she was waiting for the results. Every time she thought about it or even checked her email, the sick, nauseated feeling would return.

"No. But it hasn't even been a week. I've sent through all the relevant information, so now it's just a waiting game."

"And you're ever so patient."

Maddie grinned. "Ally here?"

"She'll be around soon. Everything moves a little slower when you're pregnant."

"Do I have to wait for her, or can you tell me what this hot goss is now before I *really* test your patience?"

"I wouldn't inflict that pain on either of us."

"So?"

"I was clearing out some of my things in the attic, looking for baby blankets Mom was certain she'd stored up there, but then I got sidetracked."

"Attic. Nostalgia. Totally makes sense."

"Anyway, I found all my *Girlfriend* and *Seventeen* magazines as well as a slew of other teen mags and started looking through them."

"And?"

"And I found this." Sera picked out a magazine from the box on the coffee table. She flipped the cover over so Maddie could see.

"'Do you want more sex tips to rock your lover's world?'" Maddie read the headline then shrugged. "What am I supposed t—" Maddie gasped, sitting upright. "No!"

Sera placed her hands on either side of the young guy's long, dark hair. He had sunglasses on, which were tipped down slightly to reveal a pair of gray eyes, and suddenly the man on the cover was someone whom she recognized all too well.

"No," Maddie repeated, grabbing the magazine.

Now that she'd seen it, she couldn't unsee it.

His face was smooth, soft, still that of a teenager, not yet a man. But that dark hair and those gray-blue eyes were the same. So was the smirk.

His shirt was unbuttoned, revealing smooth, hard skin.

It was Gabriel. Gabriel fucking Steele.

"Oh my god." Her brain was furiously trying to fit the two images of him together, but it didn't compute.

"Right?"

"But . . . but . . . Gabriel *Rossi*." Maddie pointed to the name beneath his image.

"Maybe he used a pseudonym."

She recalled the conversation they'd had in his office. "He said his dad was Italian, so maybe that's his surname." Maddie read the caption beneath his picture. "'Gabriel talks of family, following in his father's footsteps, and his quick rise to fame.'"

"Read the article."

Maddie flicked to the double page spread where Gabriel was sprawled in a lounging position, his arms behind his head, a smile—she didn't even know he was capable of grinning with such wicked intent—plastered across his face. Gone was the stern, steely-eyed man who didn't seem capable of emotion. Was this the wicked past he'd hinted at when she'd seen him at Bridgelake? Or was this merely the tip of the iceberg?

Maddie gasped. "He lost his mom when he was a child." Despite her dislike of the man, her heart ached for the five-year-old boy who'd had to go through that. She understood the feeling all too well. It struck her as odd that she'd learned more about his life in a few minutes than she ever had in the . . . six years of their working relationship. Surely it hadn't been that long?

Sera leaned in, looking over her shoulder. "I know, he was only five."

"And his dad was a model."

"Doesn't say much more than that about his parents. Just stuff about modeling and what he'll do next."

"Did you find any other magazines with him in them?"

"A few from an awards show." Sera picked up a second magazine, flipping to the page. "His arm around a leggy blonde, him with a few celebrities, that kind of thing."

"Oh my god, Sera! That wasn't *some* leggy blonde. That was Casey Stevens!"

"Okaaay."

"She had big, *natural* boobs and no tummy fat. I used to obsess over her."

Sera nodded. "She is pretty dazzling to look at."

"Bitch."

"Total."

Maddie shook her head. "I can't believe Gabriel Steele was a model."

"Gabriel *Rossi*."

"Right."

"Uh-oh."

"What?"

"Madds, I know that look."

"What look?" Maddie tried to appear innocent, but she'd known Sera since college, and it was hard pretending with someone who knew you as well as a sibling.

"That devious 'I'm going to go digging until I find out more information' look."

"I don't know what you mean."

Sera's tone was dripping with disapproval. "Madds, if he wanted everyone to know he was a model, then we'd know already."

"I only want to do a bit of googling." She reached for her phone then sighed a few minutes later when there wasn't anything of consequence coming up. "That's odd, isn't it?"

"Maybe he didn't like social media."

"But surely there would be *something*."

"Let it go, Maddie."

"Weird to think we may have looked at this very magazine, never even imagining that we would one day work with the cover model."

"I wonder why he stopped modeling. With Gabriel's looks and from the sounds of the article, he was poised to be the next big thing."

Maddie chewed her lip, but her mind was trying to piece together the puzzle. "Can I keep this?"

"Maddie," Sera warned.

"I promise I'll give it back."

"You cannot throw this in his face." Sera's look was pointed and disapproving. Her friend had always had a kind heart.

"*Moi?*" Maddie's faux indignation was barely believable. "There's nothing to be ashamed of."

"But don't you think if Gabriel wanted us to know, he would tell us?"

"What, rock up the first day and be like, hi, my name is Gabriel, and I used to be a cover model? Doubtful."

"Okay, so maybe not that, but surely it would have come up over the years. Jack and Gabriel spend a lot of time together, especially with all the help Gabriel has given us with Bridge-lake. Surely, it would have . . ." Sera gasped. "I wonder if Jack knows."

"Oh boy."

"No." Sera frowned. "He would tell me if he knew."

"Bros before hoes."

Sera nudged her. "I'm his *wife*, hardly a *ho*."

"Lady on the street but a f—" Maddie sang then squealed as a pillow smacked her in the face.

"Watch it, Fitzgerald." But Sera's hazel eyes were warm.

"So, can I keep this?"

Sera sighed. "Wait until Ally sees it and then you can borrow it."

Maddie grinned, feeling brighter than she had all weekend. "Excellent."

Maddie slapped the magazine on Gabriel's desk and had the utter pleasure of seeing his jaw clench. It was a sure sign that he was pissed. She'd been waiting for the best time to do it, almost squirming with impatience all Sunday afternoon.

She'd waited all day Monday because Gabriel hadn't been there, and when Tuesday had rolled around, she'd been positively bursting with excitement.

"Where did you get this?" His eyes had narrowed, but she noticed he didn't pick up the magazine. In fact, he reared back as if afraid to even touch it.

"You know, when I thought about all the jobs you might've had prior to teaching, none of them included being a magazine pin-up boy. Is that where you perfected your Steely smolder?" Maddie did her best impression of a serious model pose before sitting down on the chair opposite.

"I said, where did you get this?"

Maddie continued as if she hadn't heard him, "I have to say, there would be plenty of single moms loitering around after school who would *love* the chance to be set up with a former model. I wonder if you could do a catwalk down the hall for our fashion design showcase. That is, if you still remember the moves?"

"Where. Did. You. Get. This?"

She shrugged her shoulders. "I have to protect my sources. I'm not a rat."

It was only then that Maddie noticed Gabriel's demeanor. He was stiff and withdrawn, his hands bunched in fists on the table.

She peered at him closely and caught a brief glimpse of what looked like pain flash across his stoic features.

"I can take it back." She reached for the magazine then flinched as Gabriel slammed his hand down on the cover. "What the hell!"

He was visibly fighting for control. She'd never seen him worked up like this before. Suddenly, the smug, satisfied feeling she'd championed when she'd walked into his office a few minutes ago was gone. A feeling very akin to regret stole over her now.

Maybe Sera had been right.

Gabriel shoved his chair back then paced the length of his office. He was already imposing at well over six feet, but his anger was palpable, making him appear larger, his office smaller.

"Hey, it was just a joke."

"Have you shown this to anyone?"

"Did you not see the whole school email?"

Gabriel stopped pacing, pinning her with a mutinous glare.

She raised her hands in surrender. "Kidding."

Gabriel was around the table in a flash. Maddie barely gasped when his hands gripped the arms of her chair, trapping her in place.

This should not be sexy. This should not make you aroused.

How many men had such vibrancy to them? Her traitorous

brain was thinking of all the ways he would use that energy, all the ways he *could* use it. On her.

Maddie's stomach pitched. The usual feeling of disgust that normally surfaced when she thought of him that way had disappeared. Panic seized her spine, stiffening it. Then annoyance took its place.

"Where did you get this, Maddie?"

"I—"

"Or do I need to—"

Maddie dragged in what little air there was between them. His face was so close, his expression hard and passionate. This was not the Gabriel she knew, the detached, cold vice principal. This was a man, a very pissed, very powerful man, who made her tingle in all the right places.

Fuck. That wasn't supposed to happen. Not with him. Not at all.

"Do what?"

She was goading him. He was fighting to control his emotions, and here she was, egging him on. Why?

It dawned on her that she wanted to see him crack. In a sick, perverse way, she wanted to figure out what it was that drove him wild, what it was about him that made her have that sex dream. Now that she'd had a glimpse of this passion, she was curious to discover more.

Get a better vibrator, Madds.

Gabriel's face hovered close. She felt him almost shaking with anger and . . . and what? Something more. Something elemental, raw, and downright sexy as fuck.

"You run that mouth of yours, Red, but there are consequences to your actions."

"Consequences. Good or bad?"

Gabriel shifted even closer. "Depends on what you're into."

Maddie's mouth parted. She watched in fascination as his eyes traveled over her lips. There was a storm brewing, and she wasn't sure if she wanted to run away in search of shelter or stand outside in the elements.

She was afraid to find out.

"I—"

"Play stupid games, win stupid prizes, Fitzgerald."

"What are we even talking about?"

"You tell me."

"As soon as you maintain the appropriate distance, we can have a conversation." She tilted her chin and froze as it closed the distance between them. Her heart was a racing rabbit, bounding in her chest. But she was trapped, caught by his gaze, imprisoned by his arms.

Dear God in heaven, she was turned on. She felt a heavy, pulsing ache between her thighs. Her body was a traitorous bitch, it seemed.

And just when she was about to do something wild, something unthinkable, Gabriel drew back. It was like someone had flipped a switch and the man who'd looked like he wanted to kiss her had disappeared and the person who emerged was the vice principal once again.

Who was this man? What the hell did she really know about him?

Gabriel sat beside her, frozen still.

She studied his profile. The straight nose, the dark sweep of lashes, the firm, compressed mouth.

In a voice that was deeper, a little darker, he spoke. "Where did you get the magazine from, Maddie?"

"A friend found it in a box of her old things stored away in her attic."

Gabriel's shoulders lowered a fraction. "Has anyone else seen it?"

"No."

"The truth?"

"Only my friend and I, who you don't even know."

"You're a terrible liar."

"I lie very well, thank you." She sat up, slightly miffed.

"No, you *think* you do. But your voice changes." He turned to look at her, and she knew that whatever was going on was deeper than she could have imagined.

"My voice?"

"Yes, it changes, gets a little higher in register, and you do this breathing thing."

Maddie swallowed, eager for him to keep talking but wanting to make it all stop. It was almost intimate, this knowledge he had of her.

She'd thought he was oblivious, distant, and unobservant. But she supposed the reason he was so good at his job, that he dealt so well with staff and students, was because he understood them.

"What . . . breathing thing?"

"Does it matter?"

"I—"

It didn't matter and yet it did. How was it that he knew that about her? Something she hadn't even known herself?

"Not very comfortable when someone pries, is it?"

"I didn't pry. S—my friend found this magazine, and I thought you might like to see it."

"You came here to crow about it. Well played. One point for Maddie. But you're wrong if you think I want to discuss this. I don't care for my past and don't want to be reminded of it. Ever."

"Clearly."

"Is there—"

"This is the only copy that I know of."

Gabriel sighed, his shoulders deflating. He spared her a glance before turning back to study his desk. "Good. You can take your copy and leave."

"Gabriel, it was a joke. I didn't realize you would be so—"

"Out, Maddie."

"Look, I didn't—"

"I said out."

It was the cold, measured finality of his voice that had her rising. There was no heat to it, no temper, just weary resignation. And it was that tone that had her standing unsteadily.

"And take the damn magazine with you."

Maddie snatched it from the table. Turning, she shoved it at his chest, jolting at the firm heat beneath his white shirt.

"You keep it. Something tells me you need it more than I do."

Shaking slightly, she stormed out. This wasn't what she'd expected at all. She felt hot and cold and not at all pleased.

Damn that Gabriel. Damn him to hell.

CHAPTER TEN

That Thursday afternoon, instead of going out to the pub with a few other teachers, Maddie had driven to see Sera's mom, Mrs. De Lotto. She needed a mother figure to talk to, and the thought of even asking her mom for advice made her cringe.

Not that her mother had paid her any attention when Maddie had visited her last night. Except to tell her that she had taken up a delivery service with the local supermarket and wouldn't be needing her to stop by anymore. Every attempt that she made at establishing a connection was met with rejection.

Maddie had been dismissed. Like a stranger. Or a servant.

"What is it, *habibte*?" Maryam passed her a tray of biscotti, her eyes filled with patience.

"Everything is awful." Maddie bit into one and the burst of orange and pistachio was so good it nearly made up for the shit feeling inside. Almost.

Maryam had been a surrogate mother figure ever since she'd met Sera in college. When she'd had a problem with subject selection, she'd called Maryam. When she'd broken up with her boyfriend, she'd cuddled Maryam. When she needed someone to give her strength, she looked to Maryam as the person who filled up all the holes inside her.

Maryam De Lotto was the only parental figure in the world with whom she could seek advice.

And she needed it, bad. Because she'd fucked up. Big.

Gabriel had ignored her all day yesterday. There hadn't been any Post-it Notes with terse orders on her desk. At their staff meeting, he'd been almost polite, speaking to her to simply agree or disagree with her ideas. Nothing new there, except he'd barely looked at her when he'd been doing it. Usually, he pinned her with that uncompromising expression.

And this morning? He'd acted like she didn't even exist. They'd meant to have a planning session after school today, but he'd canceled it with a very polite, neutral email at the start of the day. Normally, she would have shrugged her shoulders and gone out to the pub with the crew, but not this time.

This afternoon, Maddie was in agony.

It surprised her, feeling so very bad about someone she disliked. And everything she did to make herself feel better didn't seem to work.

"Warm milk?"

"Cold is fine."

Maryam settled opposite her at the kitchen table. "So tell me, what has you so upset?"

"I crossed the line with someone."

"Work problem?"

Maddie slumped in her chair. "Yeah." She explained what had happened with her unnamed co-worker on Tuesday, minus the sexy atmosphere in the air part.

"And you're feeling bad about yourself?"

Maddie straightened. "I hate that he made me feel that way. Maybe he's rubbing it in." But then she recalled the pained expression on his face and knew that wasn't the case. "I did it to grill him. I mean, he's so damn controlled all the time. I wanted to see him react to *something*. I thought he'd fire back, and then we'd do this bit where he gets all broody and I tease him and —" Maddie took a deep breath.

"But he didn't."

"No. He didn't. Ugh! I really can't stand the man."

She saw Maryam's mouth quirk, but wise woman that she was, she didn't interject. Such a difference from her own mother, who would only use this as another way of lecturing her. Of pointing out her flaws. Of course he wouldn't be able to work with you, Maddie. You're too fiery. You don't take advice. You, you, you, you . . .

God forbid her mother ever took accountability for her actions, let alone offered a kind word of advice.

"Anyway," Maddie continued, "when Sera found his picture in this magazine, I thought it would be fun to needle him about it. I mean, we know next to nothing about him. The guy is super serious and private, so, like, finding that he had this secret, past life as a *model* . . . Well, it was only natural that I brought it up. He would've totally done the same to me."

Maddie knew she was pouting, but she didn't care. She'd assumed he'd get all uppity and annoyed. They would banter. Throw a few sparring comments. She would emerge the victor, and they would carry on as usual.

What she hadn't expected was him to react like this.

"So you're feeling a bit sorry for yourself."

Maddie gestured with her biscotti. "I mean, he was all, you need to mind your own business and I don't care to remember that life, super serious . . ."

"And perhaps you liked that you had information over him, private information that you knew he wouldn't like."

Maddie shrugged. "I s'ppose."

"And that makes you feel not so good, as he isn't playing by these invisible rules you've both set up."

"Yes! He didn't play by the rules."

"But you uncovered a sore spot. A wound."

"I—" She chewed on her biscotti, mulling it over. She hadn't thought of it that way. Yes, she wanted to needle and dig at Gabriel at every opportunity, but did she want to cause him pain? A year ago, hell yes. But now? She wasn't quite so sure.

On reflection, bringing that magazine seemed to have triggered something in Gabriel that wasn't just annoyance about being a model. The article had said he'd lost his mom at a young age. Perhaps seeing the magazine brought up those memories. She understood all too well what it felt like to lose a parent so young. Could that have been it? Or was he ashamed of his past life as a pin-up boy? Or was it something else?

"He said he didn't care for his past, but I didn't think it was anything to be embarrassed about." She toyed with the crumbs on the table.

"And how did Gabriel act?"

Maddie's head whipped up. "So you guessed who it is."

"*Habibte*, I've sat back and watched you and Gabriel verbally tear each other apart for years now, so yes, I knew exactly who you were talking about. And if you want my advice, then I think there's a lot about him you don't know."

"It's because he refuses to talk about anything personal."

"And perhaps you're feeling regret for causing him pain."

"Did he actually think I would go around telling everybody?"

"I can't answer these questions, but it seems to me like you care about what he thinks."

Maddie straightened. "No."

"Would you be sitting in my kitchen and eating biscotti instead of out with friends if you didn't?"

Maddie fidgeted with the rim of her glass. "I don't like this line of questioning."

"It seems to me that this magazine and Gabriel's past are

private things that have brought up feelings you didn't expect to see. Otherwise, he wouldn't be so upset."

"You can't be a model and think that stuff won't ever come out."

"And it also seems to me that you have some repair work to do because this relationship is important to you."

"It's not—"

"You came here for the hard truth, and there it is, child."

"I don't have to like it."

"This is true. Well, let's have a look at it then."

"What?"

"The magazine."

"I let him keep it. Even though I told Sera I'd give it back."

"That was good of you."

"I wasn't feeling so magnanimous when I did it."

"Oh, I like that word. Hold on." Maryam took out a small notebook from the kitchen drawer and wrote it down. She had been doing it for years in an attempt to expand her vocabulary. Maddie's heart swelled. She loved this woman to bits. "What does it mean?"

"Generous . . . forgiving."

Maryam looked up at her before shutting the notebook. "And you were in a temper, no doubt. But *habibte*, there is always more to the story than what is told. And what I've learned about Gabriel is that he's only too happy to keep his life private, for whatever reason, but that's because he's been hurt before."

Maddie's shoulders slumped. "And I've gone in and dug up all this dirt."

"So he's probably feeling a bit defensive."

"A bit!"

"A lot . . . and it is only respectful that you let him have his privacy. It isn't nice to pry, Maddie. Even if the man annoys you. I'm sure whatever unkindness on his part was from a need to defend himself. He was clearly embarrassed by it, for reasons which you don't need to know."

"Now I feel even worse."

"Perhaps you need to speak to Gabriel and sort this out. Even if you didn't intend to hurt him, you did. And it makes you a decent person to apologize for your mistakes, even if you dislike him."

Maddie pushed aside her glass. "I know . . ." She was going to have to apologize. To Gabriel. Her archnemesis. She *never* apologized. Well, at least not to him, and she didn't think she much liked making it a habit now.

But she realized that Maryam was right. She *had* hurt Gabriel. Deep down inside, she was beginning to realize that perhaps she didn't want to wound him like that.

She recalled the look on his face and a fresh wave of regret made her reach for yet another biscotti.

Who knew that beneath that cold exterior, the man had feelings?

Even worse was the realization that she cared.

CHAPTER ELEVEN

That Friday evening, instead of heading home to have a long, hot soak in the bath, Maddie drove forty minutes up the mountain to apologize to Gabriel. She briefly wondered if she was overstepping by visiting him at his house, but she figured he'd just have to deal with it—she was going to apologize after all.

After her conversation with Maryam last night, she was determined to make things right. But as luck would have it, Gabriel had been out at a leadership seminar for the whole day. Given that Maddie didn't quite like spending the weekend sweating it over an apology, she'd made the decision to visit him at his home.

Maddie sighed. She hated being the one at fault. Knowing that she'd hurt his feelings, that she'd caused him pain didn't give her the perverse satisfaction she'd thought it would.

Girl, you've changed.

Too much of the De Lotto influence, it seemed.

Maddie bit her lip. Perhaps it was for the best?

She drove up the winding paths, enjoying the way the trees shifted and swayed, dancing along the darkening skies. Her stomach rumbled, and she thought she might go begging at Sera and Jack's place for a meal later. But first she had to eat some humble pie. Her favorite.

Maddie's stomach dipped and dived. She distracted herself by picturing what Gabriel's house might look like. When she finally arrived, grateful that the iron gates were open, she couldn't help but be impressed. Driving along the gravel path, flanked by an overhanging corridor of trees, she came upon a large, two-story home.

It was fairytale-like in its largess, slightly Tudor in its style, with pitched roofs and stone exteriors that gave the house a stately appearance. She wanted to walk around the property, to admire the different elements and angles, to watch the way the light filtered through the windows or perhaps lounge in what looked like a sunroom by the side of the house. It was warm and inviting, the total opposite of what she had expected.

Gabriel's car was parked in the driveway and there was plenty of space for more, she noted with a little envy. As much as she adored her apartment, she was impressed by the grandeur of his home.

Not ostentatious, but comfortable and warm, she noted, with smaller shrubs and flowers planted around the base of the porch in welcome. She'd never been a plant person, and she wouldn't know a petunia from a pansy, but she could admire the beauty of it all the same.

She was a water baby, through and through. There was something about the sea that called to her, and even though she could admire mountains and hills, if she ever had the chance and extra money to invest, she would put a down payment on some seaside shack. And maybe get a dog.

Maddie parked then climbed the stairs to ring the bell. She waited a few minutes before knocking. Then she rang the bell again. And again. And again.

After trying one last time, she stepped back from the house. Her apology would have to wait until next week.

Maddie trundled down the stairs and towards her car. If he wanted to ignore her, she supposed that was his prerogative. It was his home and she was encroaching on it, but it still annoyed her that he was freezing her out. It was also rude.

She didn't mean for the stupid magazine to cause such a damn uproar.

Sera's warning jangled through her brain, which made her scowl even more. Ally had also warned her against teasing him with it, but of course she hadn't listened. She bet the two of them would look at her in that knowing way—

"Hey."

Maddie paused with her hand on the car door. She turned, ready to give him a piece of her mind about the etiquette of greeting guests in a timely manner, when she froze.

And her mind went blessedly blank.

A buzzing sound replaced the soft trilling of the birds in the trees.

Oh.

Oh. My.

Oh. My. God.

Maddie swallowed the saliva that pooled in her mouth and her eyes traveled over him. He was naked. Well, semi-naked but for the faded jeans that sat low on his hips.

His torso was broad and firm and glistening with sweat. He looked warm despite the winter weather. His hair was slightly damp at the temples and a ruddy flush had spread across his cheeks.

Jesus, he was hot.

Muscles she didn't even know existed rippled on his arms and down his abdomen. His shirt was tucked into the back of his waistband and an axe—dear Lord—an actual lumberjack-in-the-woods axe sat over his shoulder.

He looked entirely in his element, and Maddie was at a loss for words.

Because the Gabriel standing before her was not the Gabriel she knew and loathed.

This Gabriel was all man.

This Gabriel was appealing as fuck.

This Gabriel was the lover straight out of her sex dream.

And the lust that pierced through her was swift and sharp and deadly. It rattled every bit of the armor she had in place against this man.

As if in a trance, Maddie took a few tentative steps, meeting him halfway.

"I didn't hear you at first. I was chopping wood out back."

"Wood."

What was wrong with her brain? Oh, that was right, it was glued to his bulging biceps. The man had no right looking like that without a shirt. He should be entirely unappealing and dowdy. Boring.

The way he'd been since she'd met him, right?

"Come with me. The side gate is open."

Oh lord in heaven, his back was just as sculpted.

Maddie swallowed, silently following behind.

Don't look at his ass. Don't you dare look at his—

Hello!

Maddie pressed her lips together, afraid that she was going to say something else she regretted.

Already dug that ditch for yourself this week, love.

She focused on the paved path that led to the sprawling backyard. Gabriel walked her over to the pile of wood that lay neatly in the corner at the far end of his property.

"Wood." He pointed, a smile threatening the corners of his mouth.

"Fun."

"It is for me." Gabriel wiped his face with his shirt and, instead of putting it back on, tucked it inside of his waistband.

She stared. Like a teenager ogling a cute boy on the bus, all she could do was stare.

"I take it you didn't drive all the way to my house to watch me chop wood."

Hello, new kink.

"Given that I had no idea you had lumberjack tendencies, I'll say no."

"You're puzzled by it?"

"Truthfully? Yes, I am. You don't strike me as the rugged, outdoorsy type. But then again, after this week, I'm not sure what you're like."

Gabriel crossed his arms, his eyes lighting with interest. "Tell me, what do I strike you as?"

"More meditation, soy-chai-latte-sipping philosopher than outdoorsy, down, and dirty."

"I can get down and dirty as well as any man."

"Hmm. Yes. Well. So."

"So."

"Can you—can I watch?"

Gabriel's eyes warmed a fraction. "Watch me chopping wood?"

She jerked her shoulders. "I'm intrigued."

And aroused.

"As you wish," he said with a bow, walking back to the small pile.

Maddie approached, not sure what to expect. Gabriel bent down to pick up a log, placing it carefully on the stump. He threw a look over his shoulder before swinging the axe up and letting it fly, splitting the log clean in two.

Maddie simply stared as his back and shoulders rippled with strength. He repeated the action, and a low stirring began in her belly.

Who knew that chopping wood was such a turn-on?

Gabriel paused then turned to face her. "Happy now?"

"Do a bigger one."

Gabriel smirked, finding one of the thicker logs. This time, he faced her, and the view was even better. He looked relaxed, his body loose, his expression calm. But the fact that he was in control and confident, doing something he clearly enjoyed, made the act even sexier. And when he cleaved the massive log in two in one go, Maddie knew she was in trouble.

She felt that familiar tingle of awareness *down there* and wanted to tell him to put his damn shirt back on, but she refused to give him the satisfaction of showing that she cared.

Gabriel walked back, leaving the axe on the ground beside the pile of chopped wood.

"Satisfied?"

Not nearly enough.

"Mm-hmm." She cleared her throat. "That was . . . impressive."

"Look at you, all but choking on your words while giving me a compliment."

He was watching her with those cool gray eyes, and he no longer seemed angry, so she supposed that was a plus. But he was making her sweat beneath her woolly cardigan. He must have figured out why she was here, but he wasn't going to let her get out of it so easily. Fair play. She begrudgingly admired and respected that.

"I came here to apologize," she blurted before she lost her nerve.

Gabriel patted down his pockets. "Can I get that in writing?"

"Funny."

"So not here to watch me chop wood after all. Pity."

Maddie tossed her hair back. Only this man would make her

feel pissed off when offering an apology. Figured. She continued, "I hurt you earlier this week, and I'm sorry for it."

"I accept your apology. Even if it looks like you want to use that axe on me instead."

Maddie huffed. "What? Just like that?"

Gabriel frowned. "I've wallowed enough for one week, I think."

"You've been a right ass is what you've been."

"I've had a lot going on."

"Oh yeah, like what?"

"Like my dad is unwell in a home and he had a heart attack on Monday which is why I was absent. Or how about this, it was the anniversary of my mom's death yesterday, which is why I cancelled our planning session."

Maddie gasped. *Fuck. Fuckity fuck, fuck, fuckeroo.* She rubbed at her forehead. How stupid, how self-centered was she to think he'd been holding a grudge?

"I thought . . ." She breathed out slowly. "So you're not angry with me still?"

"No. I said my piece that day in my office. Though I may have been a bit terse given the news about my dad, so for that I'm sorry."

"But you've been so, so . . ."

"Preoccupied? Busy? What did you expect? It's been a big week, Maddie. On top of all my personal shit, we have four weeks left until the end of term, so there's a lot going on. I haven't had the capacity to add much more on my plate. Yes, I was angry about the magazine, but I'm not going to hold a grudge over it."

"I didn't expect you to react the way you did."

"I don't like to talk about my past."

"Because of your mom?"

Gabriel sighed. "Because it's private. Just like my dad's health. It's none of your business and the last thing I want to be thinking about at work. Something which a Nosey Parker like you doesn't seem to understand or respect."

"I respect it. At least now I do. It bothered me that we were working together but you didn't want to share anything about yourself. This whole thing, the constant planning and team teaching and sharing ideas, will only work when we understand each other. And it irked me to think I didn't know anything about you. I thrive on connections."

"And I'm happy keeping to myself. But I take your point."

Maddie frowned. "You're agreeing with me?"

"I can see your point of view. Is that so strange?"

"Frankly, yes. But I see your point too." Maddie looked up to the evening sky. "I feel like lightning is going to strike us down now."

"I think the universe can handle a truce between us."

"Don't know about that." Maddie stepped towards him. "By the way, modeling isn't something to be ashamed of. Lots of men model."

"It's not the modeling that I don't wish to remember."

"I didn't realize it would be such an issue."

"I'm not saying you did. Like I said, I'm entitled to my privacy, as you are yours."

"I'm an open book."

"Really?"

"Yes, ask me anything."

"Anything?" He stepped closer.

"Yes."

Why did she sound so uncertain? Why was her heart galloping like a racehorse?

Gabriel stopped in front of her now. He was so close, she had to lift her head, just a fraction, to look into his eyes. "Why are you such a pain in the ass?"

Maddie gasped then laughed. "You'll have to ask my parents that one."

"And where are your parents?"

Maddie's back straightened. She was an open book, right? "My dad's no longer in the picture, and my mom isn't someone I want to associate with."

"You don't have to tell me. I'm trying to make a point. For some people, for *normal* people, talking about painful shit is . . . painful."

"Open book, remember?"

"Okay then, do you see your dad now?"

Maddie rolled her shoulders. She had every reason to tell him to mind his own business. She could simply walk away. But a part of her wanted to tell him, to share it with him for some reason. Maybe it was his calm manner or the fact that he didn't look so much like the stuffy, rule-abiding VP at that moment. But just a guy who liked chopping wood.

Now that she had learned a bit about him, it was only fair to share.

"No." She swallowed the pain. "I'm not sure what has happened to my dad. I'm waiting on news about whether he's even alive."

"And that bothers you?"

Maddie shrugged. "I'd like to think it doesn't, but it does. After all the crap over the past few years, after the pandemic and Penelope's stroke, it made me want to find out what happened to him. Your turn."

"Haven't you pried enough?"

"I thought we were being candid with one another."

Gabriel shook his head. "I shouldn't have snapped at you, but that magazine reminded me of a time I would rather forget."

"Hey, can I ask, why couldn't I find images of you online?"

"I paid good money to erase as much of the past as I could. I never had social media accounts, so it was easy to have some distance. But I dated a supermodel, so I couldn't avoid the spotlight altogether."

"Crafty."

"If you dig hard enough, I'm sure some stuff will come up. I was a different person back then. I'm not that person anymore."

"What person?"

"Reckless."

"You? Mr. Follow-the-Rules?" She almost snorted in disbelief.

"Yes, wild, reckless, but without depth of character. Appearances can often be misleading."

"So it would seem."

"Take you for instance."

Maddie raised her chin. "Me?"

"Yes, you . . ." He was close enough that she could smell the sweat of his skin, feel the heat of it in the cool dusk. And it was as if a bubble cocooned them both now, keeping her close to him.

"What about me?" She would not let this half-naked man intimidate her. She wasn't much shorter than he was, but he still felt bigger. Powerful.

Not many men could make her—a tall, curvy girl—feel, well, small.

"You look like you should be chanting in the forest, half-naked with all that fiery hair trailing loose down your back. Your witchy eyes and that lush body would glow in the moonlight, bewitching any man who dared to approach."

A thrill shot through her. "That's an entirely inappropriate thing to say," she whispered.

Tell me more.

"We aren't in the office right now."

"Good point. It's still inappropriate for . . . for . . ."

"Us? I wonder why that is." His voice dropped, his body almost brushing against hers.

"It—"

"Let me finish. Like I said, impressions can be misleading. Instead of being a witch in the woods, you're a schoolteacher. Sure, you're dramatic, but you're also bookish. Organized. And highly intelligent.

"You use drama as a form of self-expression, in your clothes and your career, but you know the new study design inside out. You volunteer to be on panels for the department and understand the changes in the curriculum before most people have even read the damn document. You have an interest in learning and education that would put most people to shame. In short, you're a nerd."

Maddie grinned. Damn it, she couldn't help herself, but it seemed that Gabriel had tickled a funny bone. Who knew?

"You seem to know a lot about me, Steele."

"I know a lot about a lot of people, Fitzgerald. It's my job."

Maddie didn't know why that put her back up. Why she felt a little wounded by it. No, he hadn't taken notice of *her* specifically. He was simply anal retentive and had a good head for observing people. *Part of his job, Madds.*

Not that you care.

She might be standing toe to toe with him, half-naked and verbally sparring, but that meant nothing. She recalled the gorgeous blonde he'd dated in the magazine and couldn't help but ask.

"One more question about the modeling days and then I won't bring it up ever, ever, ever again."

"I doubt that, but I'll bite. What?"

"Dating Casey Stevens, what was that like?"

"Boring."

Maddie blinked. "Excuse me?" When his facial expression remained the same, she sputtered, "I don't believe you. She was the 'it girl,' the one to watch. The, the—"

"Casey was a model too, if you recall."

"I do. I had pictures of her pinned up on my bedroom wall."

"As did half the population at the time." Gabriel paused as if deciding whether to proceed. Lucky for her gossip-hungry heart, he did. "Casey was as beautiful as the pictures and just as dazzling. But she was shallow and wildly unhealthy. We only dated for a short time."

"You're ruining my image of her." She shook her head.

"Her diet consisted of crackers and almonds. Sometimes lettuce or bits of tuna the size of my thumb. And drugs. Lots and lots of drugs."

"No!"

"She didn't feel like eating when coked up."

"Wow."

"Yeah. And for the record, for all my wild ways, I drew the line at drugs."

"Double wow. Okay." Maddie chewed on the information, processing it slowly. Gabriel had been a bad boy?

"Plus, I like a woman with an appetite." Gabriel flashed a rare grin, and Maddie had barely any time to react to it before it was gone again. But in its wake, she was left stunned.

What in good God's name was Gabriel Steele doing being so . . . so . . . *sexy.*

Nuh-uh, he had no right to do that. She had him all figured out, didn't she? She knew exactly what to expect when it came to Gabriel, right? *Right?*

Gabriel had been a bad boy. He had a wild past. Suddenly those thoughts didn't seem so far-fetched. Or so unappealing.

Maddie caught the way his eyes raked over her body. It was brief, but it was heated. And it did something to her insides that he had no right doing. Something she had no right feeling.

"Maddie?"

How was his voice so tempting? So soft and smooth and . . . The way he said her name made her want to melt into a puddle on the floor.

"Yeah?"

"I think it's time for you to leave. Don't you think?"

While a part of her was relieved, she was appalled to admit that an equal part was disappointed.

Gabriel stepped back, seeming to rein in whatever it was that hovered between them. Maddie nodded and followed him silently back to her car.

She refused to admit that she checked out his butt the whole way there.

CHAPTER TWELVE

he next day, Maddie studied her naked body in her bedroom mirror. She sucked in her stomach then looked at herself from a side profile. She pressed her hand against the curve of her belly, flattening it, then cursed. She was letting shit get to her.

"Gorgeous. Your body is gorgeous," she affirmed to her reflection.

Long gone were the days when she hated herself or, worse, compared her body to other women's. But any time she heard a vicious comment in her head, it was invariably in her mother's voice. She had spent way too much money and time in therapy trying to heal. To love herself.

She had curves, she had a real body, and she wasn't going to let anyone or anything make her feel less for being herself.

And then the image of Casey Stevens resurfaced in her brain. She'd been thinking about Gabriel and the woman he'd dated last night.

She glanced at the curve of her ass then slipped on her underwear and sweatpants. No chance she was ever going to look like the stick-thin model. Not that she wanted to. Perhaps when she was fourteen and filled with self-loathing, but not anymore.

Maddie rubbed her face, wishing she'd gone to bed earlier last night. She'd tossed and turned and woken up this morning knowing she'd needed to talk through everything that had happened.

She smiled, remembering what Gabriel had said.

I like a woman with an appetite.

Had he said it to tease her?

She was a full-figured woman, one who loved her body and her life. She ate well, mostly healthily, and worked out a few times a week. Walking, yoga, some light weights. She no longer starved herself because of her mother's harsh comments or because she wanted to impress a boy. She'd found exercise and yoga helped quiet her thoughts, and since she didn't have a man to do some horizontal cardio with, she'd have to settle for a more traditional routine.

She slipped on her workout bra, added another one for good measure, and picked out a black tank from her cupboard. God, she needed a man. A real one who knew how to make her see stars, who was assertive and generous and—

Gabriel's half-naked body flashed in her mind. She shut her eyes against the image. Jesus, she was a live wire these days. The slightest brush of her lace bra against her nipples or the whisper of silk against the curve of her hips and she was all but vibrating with arousal. Hell, even her bland cotton workout gear seemed to turn her on.

Maddie bit her lip. She hadn't been this lusty since college.

She craved the feeling of flesh against flesh, the hot, heavy weight of a man's body pressing into her. She wanted to be touched.

Dear God forgive her, but she wanted Gabriel to be the one to do the touching.

Maddie groaned. What the hell was wrong with her? Okay,

so she thought Gabriel was hot. And the fact that he had this hidden past made him a bit more appealing. So what? There were plenty of hot guys out there. It didn't have to mean anything.

Maddie cursed when her phone pinged. She was going to be late for her workout with Sera.

When she pulled up outside the large exercise park twenty minutes later, Sera was already waiting for her on the lawn.

"Look at you all pumped," Sera called out. "I've just done my pre-workout."

"You're a machine, you know that, right?"

"I live for the burn."

"Psychopath."

"This morning, you're all mine."

"Why am I suddenly regretting this decision immensely?"

"Coward."

"And proud."

"C'mon, let's start with some cardio. Is there anything you want to work on specifically?"

"My stomach could use some love." She felt embarrassed to even admit it. Saying so felt like she was self-conscious, which she wasn't normally. It felt odd to even say it aloud. To admit there were things about her body she wanted to improve on, especially after the decades it took for her to love herself.

She sighed. Her fucking mother was in her head again.

"Sounds like you need to talk more than a workout."

"Workout first. I never know how you can do both at the same time."

"My special talent."

They started with a light jog around the perimeter of the park, passing slow walkers and children on scooters. Then Sera upped the ante, and Maddie found herself huffing and puffing at the sprints.

By the time they returned to the machines littered along the exercise track, she was ready to call it a day.

"Nuh-uh." Sera waggled her finger. "You said you wanted upper body. Let's go, Madds. Time for some resistance training."

Maddie had only enough energy to whimper. They worked on her abs, but also her arms and shoulders, and eventually every part of her body was screaming. Sera explained that it was good to work more than one part of her body to start strengthening her core, which would help with her back in the long run.

Maddie would have complained but she hadn't the energy. She didn't think she'd ever have enough energy ever again.

Forty minutes later, they lay on the grass, sweaty and spent. But Maddie had to admit, she didn't have room to care about much else when she was fighting to stay alive.

"See? Almost as good as the big O."

"There really is something wrong with you."

Sera laughed. "I said *almost* because let's face it, my man knows how to please his woman."

"Ugh, you make me sick." Maddie made gagging noises but smiled at her friend. Happiness radiated off her golden skin. Gone was that little slice of sadness that Sera had carried around with her. She had her fairytale ending with her Hollywood hunk and all but floated on air these days. Jack had helped her heal, and in Maddie's mind, that made him pretty special. Not that she'd ever tell him that. Man had an ego the size of Texas.

"So why the workout?"

"What? Can't a girl wanna hang out with her bestie and get fit?"

"It's a Saturday morning. Workout Maddie doesn't normally appear until at least Monday evening, normally Tuesday afternoon." Sera rolled up off the grass, holding up her hands in defense. "Hey, don't get me wrong, I'm pumped that you're committed to your fitness. You're much stronger than a few years ago, that's for sure. But I know you, Madds. Up early on a Saturday for training isn't really you. Something's going on."

Maddie sat up, picking at the grass then quickly flattening it back down. "Two things. My dad's alive. And I spoke to my mom."

Sera spluttered. "What?!"

"Oh, and I apologized to Gabriel yesterday, so that makes three, but more on that later. When I got home, I saw I had an email from Births, Deaths, and Marriages. They'd sent the document confirming that no death certificate had been registered. So we can assume he's still alive. That's assuming he still lives here."

"Oh my god, Madds. How do you feel?"

"Scared, happy, in shock. I mean, it's the news I was hoping for, but now I'm wondering what I should do. Do I really want to find him? Or do I live happy enough with the knowledge that he's alive?"

"Oh, love, only you know the answer to that. But this is a great start, isn't it?"

"Yeah. It is. I was wildly happy last night. And then my mother called."

"Did you tell her?"

"I was tempted to, but no. She's never wanted to talk about him over the years, so I assume telling her won't make a difference. Plus, she was more concerned about telling me of some diet pill all these celebs are taking that will help me shed weight than talking about things that matter."

"That's awful."

Not for the first time, Maddie wished she'd had Sera's mother growing up. Her friend had been lucky to have the stability of her parents. But she still wanted and craved that for herself. It was stupid to do so at her age, and she knew she always had Maryam and Tony if she ever needed them, but what she really wanted was for her own parents to be there. For them to love her and care for her in a way that they never could.

Maddie gnawed at her lip. She didn't like sharing her mom's abuse. It almost made her feel oddly defensive if someone spoke out against her, like she needed to protect the woman who was a right cow towards her. It was twisted and fucked up, but over time, she understood that doing so was only hurting herself.

"She likes to comment on my weight."

Sera only nodded.

"She gets in my head, and I know I shouldn't let it bother me, but then I find myself getting back into old habits, ones I was sure I would never worry about again. I stood in the mirror this morning dissecting every part of my body, with my mother's voice in my head. And it felt like all the progress I've made has been for nothing."

"I know you don't like to talk about it, but I've known you since college, and I've picked up enough to know that she fat-shames you, Madds. And I'm sorry for it. I know you think I probably don't get it, and on some level, you're right. Here I am with a supportive mother, a fitness-loving sports fanatic, but I don't want you to feel like you can't talk to me about it."

"I feel embarrassed."

"Fair call. But you're more than just worrying about your weight. I don't want you working out or trying to change yourself because of that woman. She's not been a mother to you in a way that counts, and she's made you see yourself in a warped way. Look, I'm the first to encourage people to exercise, but that's because I love and feel great doing it."

"And are a size zero." At Sera's scathing look, Maddie rolled her eyes. "Okay, bitchy and unnecessary."

"Very unnecessary. I'm sorry if I've ever made you feel uncomfortable. I'll always want to include you and Ally on a run or a walk, but that's only because I love working out with you. If you wanna work out with me, say the word, and I'll be there. But you have a beautiful body, Madds. It's strong, it's yours, and she can't stand for you to be happy in it because she's not happy in hers. Hurt people—"

"Hurt people . . . I know."

"I know you know, but sometimes you need a reminder. You don't have to be strong around us. We've got your back, always."

Maddie pursed her lips, letting her friend's words heal her a little. "You know I envy what you have."

"You've told me this."

"And I would steal your identity if I could and make your mom and dad my parents."

"That's a little creepy, but sure."

Maddie chuckled, grateful for Sera's kindness.

And then it came to her: the reason why she'd felt so embarrassed earlier. Admitting the parts of her that she was less than happy with meant exposing her flaws. Admitting it aloud meant she was self-conscious about a part of her that she shouldn't be. And that left her vulnerable, open to ridicule and judgment, for others to comment on her like she was skin and fat and not a human being with feelings. Which was exactly how her mother treated her.

Because being vulnerable meant she could get hurt. And she had learned from a young age to hide those flaws, her weaknesses, and then she'd be less of a target.

Screw all that to hell.

She refused to let her mother get to her. To get in her head. She'd progressed too far for that, loved herself too much to let that bring her down.

"You know my parents love you. In their eyes, you and Ally are their daughters too."

Her friend had a big heart. It was a De Lotto thing. Again,

she wondered what traits she'd inherited from her parents. Fear. Jealousy—

"Feeling better?"

Maddie sat up straighter, not wanting to succumb to that kind of negative thinking. She wouldn't know who she really was without knowing her dad. Which meant she had to find him. "Yeah . . . the exercise has those endorphins rushing through me."

"See? Almost better than—"

"Not even close."

They both stood, walking slowly back to where they'd parked. "So what happened with Gabriel and the apology?"

"He accepted it."

Sera raised an eyebrow. "You're holding out on me."

"We can talk about it when we see Ally."

"Oh my god, something happened."

"I don't know what you're talking about." Maddie stopped at her car. "I apologized. That's it."

"Girl, you better get ready for the interrogation of your life."

Maddie laughed. "Can't wait."

An hour later, after she had washed and dressed, Maddie drove as slowly as humanly possible to Ally and Owen's house.

She felt a little brighter after talking to Sera. She was happy knowing her dad was alive. It was a good first step.

When she arrived, Sera and Ally were already in the living room, unpacking containers of takeout food.

"That smells so good."

"Hello to you, Big M." Ally leaned over to give her a kiss. "Sera told me you have gossip."

Maddie filled her in on the details, repeating what she'd told

Sera earlier and the fact that she was thinking about finding her father so she could move on.

"I think you'll feel relieved once you make contact with him."

"I hope so. It's like these past few years, I've been in limbo. Even lately, everything feels unsettled. Hell, I went out last weekend and didn't even pick up. I'm off my game."

"Speaking of men, you need to start talking about what happened with Gabriel on Friday night."

Ally settled back, plate loaded. "Something happened?"

"Nothing happened." Maddie piled her own plate then sat next to Sera on the sofa.

"Well?" Ally prompted after a few minutes of silence. The food really was that good.

"Maddie went to visit Gabriel to grovel about the magazine incident on Friday after school," Sera supplied.

"Oh?"

"At his *house,*" Sera emphasized.

"Ohhhh. And?"

"Hello?" Maddie waved a fork in front of her friends' faces. "I'm the one with the goss."

"Well, get talking, girl, because I've been waiting hours for more info," Sera whined.

"So, I felt bad for rubbing it in his face about the whole modeling thing."

"I bet."

"I know you guys told me not to do it in the first place."

"We did. Go on," Ally muttered around her mouthful of food.

"Soooo, I suppose this is where I should tell you that I kind of saw Gabriel half-naked. Chopping wood."

Maddie covered her ears at the twin squeals of shock and delight.

"Girl, you *have* been holding out on us!" Sera swatted at her arm while Ally had her hand over her mouth, chewing furiously, desperate to comment.

"Okay, for all the hate I have for Gabriel, I will say this"—Maddie looked at both friends, pausing for dramatic effect—"that man is ripped."

"Ohhhh, tellll ussss!" Ally was beaming. "I can barely tie my laces, so I need tales of wild, steamy romps, or almost romps. And is it just me, or is this mixed gyro like the best you've ever had?"

"That's your pregnancy taste buds doing a happy dance." Maddie sampled hers. "Or maybe it is the best. Anyway, there are no or will ever be romps when it comes to Gabriel Steele."

"Never say never," Sera warned. "Tell us every detail!"

"I asked him to chop some wood—don't give me *that* look. I was curious. And let me tell you, that man knows what he's doing. It's weird, but I felt like seeing him stripped back like that was the real Gabriel. He seemed . . . relaxed. And honestly, I don't know why I've never noticed how muscly he is."

"Maybe because you were too busy hoping he'd fall off a cliff."

"Good point. But seeing him shirtless with an axe slung over his shoulder makes me believe that he *was* a little wild . . . once upon a time."

"Hubba hubba."

Maddie laughed. "I mean, yeah, the whole thing was hot as hell. Though also weird. I'm used to boring, rule-abiding Gabriel, not the half-naked, ex-model, chopping wood Gabriel. There was also a . . . Well, we . . ."

"Oh my god, you kissed!"

"No, baby mama, we didn't. But, oh god." Maddie buried her face in her hands. "Maybe I'm reading too many romance novels, but I think"—she peeked out from behind her hands—"we almost might have."

"Holy shit." Sera stared at her. "You and Gabriel!"

"There is no 'me and Gabriel,' so before you and your runaway brain start concocting fairytales and happily ever afters, know that I have no intention of acting on anything at that level with that man. Yes, he may be eye candy, but that way lies disaster."

Her friends made kissing noises—which, she knew she was going to cop—but she also loved nothing more than sharing goss with her besties. And Gabriel looking fit and fine was pretty big goss.

"I think I'm still reeling from the fact that he has a wild past."

"Which makes him suddenly more appealing to you. Not interested in the guy you say? He's so your type. Tall, dark, handsome." Sera listed off her fingers.

"And big from the sounds of it," Ally added.

"Jesus, the two of you."

"Aaaand he's coming to my baby shower."

"So I heard. Hey, before you start designing my bridal dress, let me remind you that I actually can't stand the guy. And he will most likely be bringing a date."

Ally paused with the forkful of food hovering in front of her mouth. "Wait, what? Gabriel has a girlfriend?"

"How should I know?" Maddie shrugged. "But a guy like that probably does. He was a *model*, Al. He dated a supermodel. I don't think he's in any way single or in need of a girlfriend."

"I'm gonna get Jack to ask him." Sera's eyes glinted in determination.

"No. Please don't." Maddie shook her head. "I don't care either way."

"We do." Ally winked at Sera. "And I wanna know."

Maddie ate, listening to her friends concoct wild theories. She savored the herbs on her tongue, refusing to feel guilty for enjoying a healthy appetite. But it struck her that she would never be like those models he'd dated.

And that part of her knee-jerk reaction today hadn't just been about her parents.

Not that she was jealous. She'd never be a size zero. Not that she even really wanted to be . . . anymore.

Her days of purging were over. She loved her body and made sure she took care of herself. She wasn't going to obsess over how she looked because of a guy. Even a hot one. Gabriel was a pleasant distraction. Nothing more. Noticing Gabriel had a six pack and fucking amazing shoulders didn't mean she was going to jump him.

The image of him naked, axe slung over his shoulder flashed in her mind.

She would *not* be fantasizing about Gabriel chopping wood. At least, not for much longer. She'd start getting ideas in her head, and ideas like that were best kept to fiction novels.

"So now that we've all indulged in the juicy gossip, let's focus on the pregnant mama." Maddie lounged back on the sofa. "Time to start planning this baby shower."

"I've started jotting down some ideas." Ally picked up a notepad beside her then yawned.

"Naptime?" Maddie suggested.

"I had one before lunch."

"Second naptime then?" Maddie reached out and plucked the notepad out of Ally's hands.

"No, I'm supposed to have *more* energy, not less at this stage, aren't I?" Ally sighed then lay down on the sofa.

"As a woman who's never been pregnant before, I can't say I have the answers," Maddie supplied.

"Nap it is." Ally closed her eyes.

"So . . . food." Sera began.

"I'm listening." Ally waved a hand around in the air.

"Mom and I have a list of things we think might work—"

"I can bake some stuff—"

"Al, my mother would have my neck, and yours, if you

suggest that again. She's given permission for Charlie to bake a few things, but you're to do nothing but laze about. We're going to sort the whole thing."

"And don't even think about getting on chairs to decorate the place. Charlie and I have a theme and Jack's enlisting helpers, so the house will be a baby shower paradise," Maddie added.

The girls began writing out their list, discussing everything from color themes to games. An hour later, they had an outline for the party complete with duties for all the helpers.

"We still discussing baby shower business?" Owen, Ally's husband, walked in with a glass of sparkling water for his wife. He placed it on the table before sitting on the arm of the sofa. His hand automatically came to rest on Ally's foot.

Maddie's heart melted a little bit watching how tenderly Owen treated her best friend. After all the crap they'd gone through, to see them together, a family, made her want to cry a little. Owen had been the best thing to happen to Ally, and while Maddie knew she would never have a family of her own, she also knew she would be happy being the doting auntie.

"We are," she said, handing him her list. "Do you have anything you want changed?"

"Not a change, but an addition, I suppose. Instead of having my pregnant goddess pottering around here while we decorate, I've booked a mini getaway for her."

Ally's eyes popped open and she scrambled into a sitting position. "What?"

"Charlie and I found a place that does pampering for expectant moms. Twenty-four hours of total relaxation, room service, and great food. It'll give us time to set up the house and you'll get a chance to be treated like a queen. You'll spend all Saturday there and I'll swing by and collect you the next day for the party."

"That's so lovely." She looked up at him, holding his hand. "I think I might cry."

Owen gathered her close as she wept a little bit into his side. He rubbed her back and handed her a box of tissues.

"Feel better?" he murmured.

"Yeah."

Ally's stomach rumbled, making them all laugh.

"Baby's hungry." Owen stood, crossing the room. "Cheese and crackers?"

"Please." Ally's eyes were still damp.

When he left, she sobbed a little. "What did I do to deserve him?"

Sera gave Maddie an 'oh boy' look before they snuggled between Ally on the sofa. "My mom said she was a rollercoaster of emotions with us kids, so it's very normal."

"Oh, great." Ally sighed, blowing her nose.

"It's those baby hormones going bananas, Al. And Owen doesn't seem to mind one bit. Neither do we." Maddie rubbed her back.

"I feel like my life is a fairytale."

"You deserve it. Enjoy being doted on, little mother." Maddie smiled.

"Sorry, I feel like everything is about the baby. I'm like some black hole. I promise I used to be fun. Was I ever fun? Maybe I've always been this way." She hiccupped.

"We don't mind talking about the baby." Sera squeezed her arm.

"Are you sure?" Ally looked at Maddie.

"Why are you looking at me?"

"Because . . ." Ally's look was pointed.

"I'm *fine*. Honestly. I came to terms with my defunct ovaries a long time ago."

"Are you sure? Because I'd hate to make you feel—"

"I've known for a long time I can't have kids. I'm totally, a hundred percent fine with that fact. You don't need to feel guilty for being pregnant, Ally. Or talking about this little squoosh who I'm going to spoil rotten. I love hearing about bubs. I love watching you grow and talk about your family. I'm pumped to be an auntie. Again. Though Charlie has stopped letting me choose outfits for her."

Ally laughed. "If it's too much, just say so."

"Have I ever been the type to not speak my mind?" Maddie looked between them.

"Good point."

By the time Owen returned, they were hysterically laughing. He placed the plates down and backed out, shaking his head. She caught the look on his face as he did, and the tender joy made her heart turn over.

But Maddie couldn't help but feel a yearning for what was missing in her life. Trouble was, she hadn't a clue if she was ever going to find it.

CHAPTER THIRTEEN

Maddie spent the next week in a state of agony. Not because she had yet another late-night planning session with Gabriel, but because she had booked to see a psychic. Maddie had decided to pay a visit to Australia's most prominent fortune-teller, Madame Harrow. She'd seen an ad on social media and try as she might, she couldn't get the idea out of her head. Naturally, the thought of waiting months for the consultation made her want to tear her hair out.

She'd initially been offered a booking that was three months away, but as patience wasn't one of Maddie's strongest qualities, she'd requested to be put on a waiting list in the interim. When they called her a few days later offering a late afternoon appointment on Sunday, Maddie jumped at the opportunity. Hell, it could have been three in the morning and she would have agreed.

She hoped that this visit might shed some light on her father, especially as she now knew he was alive. Worse-case scenario, the woman was a fake, best case she'd help her find out the truth.

Given that she had barely turned six when her dad had left,

she didn't have very much other than his name and date of birth to help her. According to her mother, her father had never tried to contact them. Not once in nearly thirty years.

At the time, Maddie had found his disappearance alarming; her best friend in all the world had suddenly left, and she'd been afraid he'd had a terrible accident, which had been why she hadn't heard from him. But with every passing year, her mother's bitterness had grown, and Maddie had known he'd left on purpose. And that had devastated her.

For so long, it'd been easier to pretend he was dead. But that didn't cut it anymore.

She wasn't sure how she felt about seeing Madame Harrow. She was realistic about what she might hear, but a small part of her lived in hope that this stranger might tell her something that could help her find her dad.

Maddie expected a dimly lit room with woo woo music in the background, like she'd used to see in the fairgrounds when she'd been a child. But when she visited The Third Eye, she was greeted by a smart-looking, preppy-chic receptionist with short, trimmed black hair and a checkered shirt on his lean frame.

"Madame Harrow will be with you shortly." He spoke in hushed tones, as if speaking to a congregation at a funeral.

The space, while in a grungy part of the outer city suburbs, seemed newly furnished and sleek. The tarot symbols were framed across various parts of the reception room, with crystals and calming potted plants positioned in all corners of the room.

It gave off a warm, inviting atmosphere without being too psychedelic.

There was soft, rhythmic music floating in the background, accompanied by the faint smell of incense. It was, in every respect, everything that Maddie wasn't expecting.

Picking up a magazine from the side table, she tried to lose herself in a juicy scandal, but try as she might, her mind was out of focus, jumping from one scintillating headline to the next, always searching but never landing on an article to read.

Ten minutes later, right on time, the receptionist stood.

"Madam Harrow will see you now." He opened the door to the adjacent room, and Maddie felt goose bumps race across her forearms.

If the reception room was a surprise, the inner room was everything she imagined a visit to a psychic would be.

The space was dark, with enough light to make out the furniture and fixtures. A long therapist chair sat in the far corner next to a table with plants and crystals. Incense burned gently beside a few fat-wicked candles. On the whole, the atmosphere was relaxing and calm.

Madame Harrow sat at the far end of the room behind a small desk. She was in a long flowing dress, her midnight hair unbound along her shoulders, dark eyes bright with mischief.

Maddie was put at ease by the raspy warmth of her voice. Of a sense of the familiar.

"It's you." The woman's face was surprised, as if she'd broken through the veneer and revealed something she hadn't meant to.

Or maybe it was what she said to everyone who came to see her.

"Hi, I'm—"

"Yes, I know. You did register after all, Maddie."

She smiled, appreciating the woman's humor. Afraid her nerves would make her bolt out the door, she sat in front of Harrow, planting her feet firmly on the ground. Instinct told her that she'd made the right decision.

Harrow looked over Maddie's shoulder as if reading sentences from a huge storybook. She followed the psychic's line of sight but saw nothing out of the ordinary. She half-expected to see large cue cards or a teleprompter with Maddie's life story for her to follow.

"I'm reading your aura." Harrow smiled, explaining her behavior. "It's very strong. Bold colors, and yes, you're fire. You'll be a great match together."

"A match?"

"A love match. But he's also very stubborn. There's a lot of hurt there, but he tucks his heart away from everyone, so you shouldn't feel offended when he pushes you away. Don't mistake his reserve for lack of feeling or depth. He has pride, as do you."

"Who?"

"The answer to that will become clearer in time."

Maddie fidgeted with one of the silver bangles on her wrist. This woman was clearly on a different frequency. Love? A relationship? That was totally not on the cards.

Harrow peered at her. "That answer isn't sufficient for you. But I can only tell you what I see."

"I've no intention of being in a relationship, none whatsoever. I came here to ask about my father."

She looked over Maddie's shoulder again. "The two are linked."

Maddie's eyebrows shot through the roof. "*What?*"

"Past and present, old wounds and new, they're all entwined. But only if you're open, Maddie. That's the key."

"Open . . ."

"Let me read your cards and we'll see what they say. Shuffle this deck and stop any time you feel ready."

Maddie did, pondering over her words. She wanted to rush the process but told herself to slow down. When it was right, not when she thought it best to stop, she passed the deck back and split it.

Madame Harrow flipped the cards over, carefully revealing them.

"Yes . . . as I thought."

"What?"

"See this card here?" She tapped the one closest to Maddie. "There's a wound from your childhood."

"My father," Maddie explained. A part of her wondered if the woman was feeding her information she wanted to hear. Had she not brought up her father, would the psychic have 'seen' it in the cards?

"Your mother." Harrow pointed to the card adjacent. "Through her you'll find the answers."

"What?"

"I see correspondence. Parcels. Mail. Information. Something there."

"Okay."

She took her time to study the cards. "And the past is closer than you think." Closing her eyes now, she breathed in. "Oh . . . never been in love."

Maddie watched a range of expressions flutter across Harrow's face.

"Yes, I see the resistance there. But your time is coming. And the thing your mother told you when you were in high school isn't true."

Maddie's eyes rounded and she exhaled in one quick whoosh. How did she know about that? She couldn't have known. Was it just a good guess?

Harrow opened her eyes, her gaze direct. "Starting to believe now?"

Maddie bristled. "I've always had faith in the otherworldly, but I'm also pragmatic. I know that it's easy enough to spin stories based on generalities."

"Let's dig a little deeper, then. If you want to see?"

"Yes."

And she did, reading the cards and supplying information about Maddie that nobody could know. Information that she'd at one time repressed all those years ago. Wounds and words that had been aimed to hurt, scars she'd thought had faded, they all came to the surface. Therapy had helped her heal, but still, hearing it from a stranger's lips made it more embarrassing somehow. By the time Madame Harrow took her hand, she was literally on the edge of her seat.

"Ready for me to read your palm?"

Maddie nodded, watching as Harrow ran her fingers over the intersection of lines, reading what was seemingly illegible. "A good, strong heart line . . . Mmm."

"What?"

Madame Harrow's dark eyes speared directly into her own. "I believe you already know this, but it can be difficult news for a woman. You will not bear any children."

Maddie *did* know it. And she *had* made her peace with it. From a young age, she'd had problems with her ovaries and issues with her periods. After many visits to all sorts of specialists, it had boiled down to the one prognosis: she would never have biological children.

Her mother had shrugged it off, telling her she was better off without a burden to raise, but at the time, Maddie had felt nothing but anger. Then grief. She'd railed at her body for its inability to work properly, then at the doctors for their diagnosis, and finally and most especially at her mother for her callous manner.

Over time, Maddie had realized that she didn't want to have children. Whether biological or adopted, it simply wasn't something that appealed to her.

She liked kids well enough, she enjoyed teaching them, but she'd prefer to give them back at the end of the day rather than raising her own. In truth, Maddie had never felt that yearning that some women spoke of—a need or invisible longing that they couldn't describe.

Sure, she cooed over cute babies and loved playing with them, but that didn't mean she had a calling to raise one herself. If she'd been raised by a loving mother, Maddie wondered if she would've felt more of a loss at her barren state. As it was, she didn't feel anything.

Maddie blinked, coming back to the present. "I knew that already."

"And seem content with it."

"I am. Having kids isn't in my future, but it's comforting in an odd way to hear you confirm it."

"I only see what's there. You're a woman who knows her mind, and you need a man who also respects that."

"Easier said than done."

Harrow smiled as if she knew something but decided to keep the information to herself.

Maddie refused to settle for a guy who thought that she'd change her mind about being childless. The number of dates she'd been on with men who'd assumed that she'd want kids made her feel sick. It scared her to think she might meet a guy who simply told her what she wanted to hear or, worse, left her because they were incompatible.

"You need to open your eyes to what's around you. The answer to all of this is closer than you think. Sometimes right in front of you."

"Now that's super vague."

"If I told you who you'd date, that would be boring."

"So you know?"

"I see many things, but it's not for me to say."

Maddie swallowed her fear. "Can I ask about him?"

"You can."

"But you might not answer."

"I'll answer based on what I see. But I won't be giving a name, address, and social security number, if that's what you want. That's up to you to find out."

Maddie said what was on her heart, what secretly terrified her the most. "If this mystery man and I decide to date, will he leave me?"

"I can tell you with 100% certainty that this man will be faithful in this life and the next. He will cross countries and fight tigers. He will devote and worship you in a way that no man ever has or ever will again. But you must open your eyes. He's closer than you think."

Maddie was moved by the vehemence in Harrow's voice. The truth of what she'd said tiptoed over her skin. To be loved like that, to be with someone who loved her so completely, so faithfully . . . it was the stuff of dreams. Dreams that Maddie had long given up on.

She wanted to believe. She'd spent years hoping that she would find a great love. And now this woman, this stranger purported to know with utter assurance that it would happen. And soon.

It scared and thrilled her in equal measure.

"Wait a minute. I see a cupboard."

"The man's in the closet?"

Madame Harrow grinned. "No . . . this is about your father."

"Oh."

"I see letters in a cupboard." She was searching for more, her eyes vacant, waiting for whatever was downloading into her brain . . . or senses. Directly opposite her sat a woman who seemed to somehow know information about her father. Her future. It went beyond the realm of facts and reason. It *shouldn't* make any sense. And yet . . .

"There are babushka dolls. And a cupboard."

Maddie felt the presentiment steal over her. A vague recollection, a glimpse of a box with babushka dolls painted on the lid flitted across her memory from decades before. But it made no sense. The box she was thinking of belonged to her mother, not her father.

"And there are letters?" Maddie prompted.

"Yes. Letters. Notes. Correspondence of some sort. These will help you find the answers you seek."

"What's in them?"

"That's for you to find out."

"From whom?"

"Find those letters, find your father."

Maddie shivered.

Twenty minutes later, she sat in the driver's seat of her car, furiously typing all the things she remembered from the session into the Notes folder on her phone.

Madame Harrow's words echoed in her brain as she made her way home that evening. They sat beside her at dinner and kept her awake for most of the night.

Those words sparked something within her. And it felt a hell of a lot like hope.

CHAPTER FOURTEEN

*M*addie didn't wake up that Monday intending to storm through her mother's home, but as soon as she opened her bleary, sleep-deprived eyes, she knew she had to see for herself whether Madame Harrow had been right or just a really amazing actress.

It didn't matter that she would be cutting it close for work. It didn't matter that she had planned to begin the day with some yoga. Nothing would ease her mind but finding out whether Madame Harrow had been right about her dad.

She took what the woman had said about her future boyfriend with a grain of salt. Anyone could espouse crap about what someone's partner would be like. It was a lot harder to know things. Intimate things about a person's life.

But Harrow had known.

Like when her mother had told her in high school that she was too fat to be loved. That no man would ever want her looking the way she did. For so long, Maddie had internalized that, believed those lies. But not anymore.

Somehow, the information about her dad was connected to this jewelry box. A small part of her didn't want Harrow to be right. Because if she was, that meant that her mother had some way of knowing information about her father. She didn't want to believe that of her. Not when her mother knew how cut up she'd been about her father leaving. As monstrous as it had been growing up with that woman, Maddie didn't believe that her mother would rob her of her dad.

She wasn't *that* vindictive.

"Mom?" Maddie let herself in, tiptoeing through the darkened house. The lights were on in the kitchen, and she heard noises from the bathroom. "Mom?"

"What do you want?"

She heard the water sloshing through the closed door. Her mother was in the bath.

"I need a few documents I left in my old room for work," she said through the bathroom door.

"I've been asking you for years to clear out your junk. I'm sick of having it around the house."

"Sure thing."

Maddie crossed to her mother's room instead. It was still dark, with only part of the curtains drawn, but she knew her way.

Opening the cupboard, she began the search, half-expecting the box to be sitting there surrounded by a glowing light and dramatic music, but all she found was shoes. Maddie frowned but continued.

Giving up on the cupboard, she methodically searched every part of the room, from the dressing table to under the bed, but still she didn't spot the jewelry box. She was about to give up, certain that Harrow had been wrong, when she spotted a smaller set of drawers wedged in behind the single-seater sofa in the corner. She hadn't noticed it at first, as it was obscured by a stack of blankets and pillows.

Maddie shifted the sofa and knelt to open the top drawer. She rifled through the loose bits of ribbon and batteries before opening the one below. She shifted the pile of bills and pens aside, but there was nothing there to link her to her dad.

Sighing, Maddie stared at the flotsam and jetsam of the drawers, willing away the tears of bitter disappointment. As a desperate last attempt, Maddie snuck her hand in between the gap at the back of the drawer. When her fingers brushed against a solid rectangular box, she froze.

"Son of a bitch."

With a bit of jimmying, Maddie pulled out the drawers and then gently lifted the jewelry box, handling it as if it were a bomb. The edges were scuffed and worn, with a few nicks in the white finish. Painted over it were pictures of babushka dolls in all their varying sizes. Her mother had had this box since she'd been a little girl, and Maddie had never been allowed to play with it or even use it as a child.

With her heart pounding, she opened it, and after checking the drawers—now empty—she sighed. Nothing there. Maddie flicked the ballerina and was about to shut the lid when she noticed the material at the base seemed frayed, as if it had been cut away. Maddie settled the box in her lap then gave the ballerina a short, sharp tug.

She gasped as the base gave way. It had been cut around the edges, creating a secret compartment. And there, in a small pile bound together with string, were not only folded-up letters, but cards too. With shaking hands, Maddie picked up the first one and opened it. It was addressed to her. They all were.

Maddie reached into the back of the drawer and cursed as she found an envelope. And another. And another. Maddie retrieved a stack of envelopes that had been hidden beneath the jewelry box, all meant for her.

She stood abruptly, gripping the letters—so many damn letters—to her chest. The bile rushed up, scorching the back of her throat. Maddie steadied herself, head spinning, blood pumping through her body.

How could she? How *dare* she?

Before she could stop to think things through, Maddie stormed into the bathroom, and a sick part of her was glad when her mother started, jostling water over the lip of the tub.

"What the hell is this?" She waved the fistful of letters in the air, reveling in her mother's shock.

She wanted to shake her, to scream in her face, but then she would be no better than she was. Maddie had borne her mother's verbal abuse for so long, but in all the time she'd lived with her, she'd always felt pity for her life. Left by her husband. A single mother struggling, on her own. They might have argued a lot, but never in a million years would she have thought her capable of this level of deception.

"How dare you." Maddie kept her voice low, desperately trying to control the raging anger that burned through her.

"Get out!" Sharon hollered, covering herself with a washcloth.

"Answer me! All this time, you've been lying. Why the fucking deception?"

"Don't you speak to me like that."

Maddie stood her ground. "I'll speak to you the way you deserve. I want answers."

"This isn't the time."

"No. I want the truth."

Her mother's face was set in stone. Stubborn, not a hint of remorse.

"*The truth!*"

Maddie waited, chest heaving. With every breath, her anger bubbled and boiled, threatening to engulf them both. It took all her restraint not to jump into the tub and shake the answers out of her.

Finally, Sharon spoke. "He didn't deserve your love. He didn't deserve you."

"Who made you the judge of that?"

"He left us!" Sharon threw back.

"He left *you!*" Maddie's voice was shrill, slicing through the tiles and steam. It frightened her, this urge to close the distance and throttle her mother until she apologized. The red haze filled her from head to toe. "He left me with *you*, a broken, bitter woman who loved nothing more than to speak badly about my father. For years I had to listen to your hatred. For years . . . you made me think he didn't want me." Maddie's hands shook as she waved the stack of letters in the air again. "This proves that he did. That he fucking cared. Do you know what I would've given as a child to get just one of these? Do you know how that would have—" Maddie's throat closed over. Stealing short, sharp breaths, she continued. "This proves that you never really gave a shit about me. Never."

"I was protecting you."

"Bullshit! You were protecting yourself. If you cared about my feelings, you wouldn't have kept this from me. You wouldn't have lied. My whole fucking life—" Maddie's voice broke. The pain in her chest was so heavy, she wanted to sink to the floor.

It was only now that she understood why they'd moved so often, shifting from one apartment to another. Not because of Sharon's job, but out of spite. And still, the letters had come. Her dad had managed to find them. To find her.

It changed everything. Every thought, every feeling, every awful dream . . . none of it was true because her mother had fed her lies. For her whole damn life.

Maddie stood strong even as her legs trembled. She refused to crumble. "Every time I asked after him, every time I cried, saying I missed him, that I needed him, you lied. You were the one who kept him from me and—" Maddie's heart was broken at the betrayal. She couldn't stand looking at her anymore. "I will never, *ever* forgive you."

Her mother's tone was righteous. "I knew those letters

would turn you against me. I knew you would hate me. *This* is why I kept them from you. Because of him."

"No, Mother. You did that all on your own."

Ignoring her protests, unable to take it anymore, Maddie turned and fled.

Some people preferred to correspond via lengthy emails, others to leave voicemail messages, but Gabriel would much rather have a conversation with someone face-to-face.

Especially when the woman in question was Maddie Fitzgerald. He knew she ignored his emails out of sheer spite. And his Post-it Notes seemed to piss her off to no end.

Gabriel was petty enough to smirk. A perverse part of him did enjoy annoying her; watching the way her brown-blue eyes sparked with temper was a sure sign she was in a mood. Which was more often than not these days.

They'd been caught in this cold war for years now and neither showed any signs of surrender.

But Maddie had appeared on edge all last week. He wasn't sure if it was the workload or her role as acting head of arts, but there was something bothering her.

Not that it was any of his business.

Ever since she'd come over to apologize, he'd noticed that their interactions were fraught with tension. Something had shifted since that evening, but they were both wise enough not to act on it.

Which was a good thing. He didn't have time for distractions. Gabriel had spent the past week with his ailing father, coming to terms with the inevitability of his demise. He understood that Leo's heart was failing him, he knew logically that we all had to go at some point, but any time he thought about his dad, a wild panic seemed to seize him, robbing him of his peace.

Gabriel frowned at the document in his hands. Now was not the time to think about that.

Steeling himself for battle, Gabriel made his way across to Maddie's office, curriculum document in hand. He'd managed a few discipline issues that morning without incident, and if he could discuss these changes with Maddie and keep his temper in check, he'd take it as a win. Surely with the end of term approaching, they could be civil to one another. Gabriel cautioned himself. He was capable of self-restraint. Once upon a time, he'd been successfully able to keep his emotions in check, to practice control in all aspects of his life.

But no matter how many times he coached himself, he still couldn't seem to interact with her without wanting to take a bite. The need, that snapping, snarling, frenzied desire to claim her scared him. He wasn't that man anymore.

She was fire. He was ice. It was why they butted heads and didn't seem to be able to tolerate one another longer than an hour at a time. Leadership team meetings always left him walking away with itchy fingers.

The things he wanted to do . . .

Gabriel gripped the papers in his hands a little tighter. He recalled how she'd looked at him with his shirt off. He knew he had a good body; he wasn't ashamed of how he kept himself in shape. As an ex-model, your body was your currency. He was used to people ogling him, assessing him. But the way Maddie had stared . . . Gabriel swallowed. Best that they remained on either side of the battlefield.

"What are you two doing here?" He spoke quietly to two senior students loitering outside the toilets.

"Uh . . ."

"We . . ."

Gabriel stared. "Back to class. Now."

"But—"

Gabriel raised his eyebrows, and the students scuttled away. He checked the toilet stalls to be sure the boys weren't covering for a smoker, though they usually skulked on the back oval these days. He made a mental note to check on his way back.

He opened the sliding door of Maddie's office.

"Hey, Kara. Seen Maddie around?"

"Her seniors have a careers talk so she's free this period. Maybe try the old English block?"

"Thanks." Gabriel crossed the blue, patterned carpet and followed the steps outside to the 'old' English block. After the school's makeover, the old English office had been converted to a resource cupboard. Some senior classes were still held in that section, which made it handy when running exams during the year. Not so handy when he had to chase a sassy redhead about changes to the curriculum.

Gabriel swung through the corridor and leaned against the resource room door, which always seemed to be jammed. Because of it, he stumbled into the room and nearly floored said redhead, who was hovering at the entrance.

His arms instinctively reached out to steady them both, his phone and paperwork tumbling to the floor. Gabriel felt a sudden jolt at the contact. It singed his hands, the aftereffects pulsing through him in steady waves.

"Maddie, sorry, I—" Gabriel froze.

It was the anguish on her face that made his heart clench tighter than a fist. He wanted to draw her close to his chest, but instead he let go.

"Are you alright?"

"I-I—" She brushed at the steady stream of tears, her face red and splotchy.

"Okay, take a seat." Gabriel pulled out a stool for them both, thankful that the room was vacant. He found a box of tissues and handed it to her, watching helplessly as she gulped in air. It struck him that he'd never seen Maddie upset before. She was always bold, assured, a pain in the ass. It made him forget she was human too.

Gabriel picked up his phone off the floor. "Can I call anyone?"

She tried to speak then shook her head.

"I can see if Ally or Sera are free?"

The door flew open.

"Excuse me, can I get—"

"No." Gabriel stood, ushering the clueless student out of the room.

"We need paper," the boy whined.

"Try the arts supply room."

Gabriel closed the door behind him, crouching in front of Maddie, who had buried her head in her hands, sobbing into the tissue.

"Whatever it is, we'll figure it out."

Maddie's laugh was bitter, her voice thick. "Trust me." She hiccupped. "Years. Of. Therapy. Still. Doesn't. Help."

"So it's a personal matter."

She nodded, scrubbing away her tears.

"Do you need me to cover classes for you? What do you have for the rest of the day?"

"N-n-nothing n-n-now. Y-y-yard duty. M-middle sc-school—"

"I'll call."

Gabriel stood then placed a quick call to the daily organizer. He paced as he spoke, making sure she was taken off the extras list, and he offered to personally replace her on yard duty.

Teaching was a brutal gig. You couldn't lock yourself in a cubicle all day and give into your problems. To teach meant you were on show every day, at the beck and call of over a hundred different students with varying needs and attitudes. There was nowhere to hide. No grace, no soft place to land.

It looked like Maddie needed both right now.

When he turned back around, she'd stopped crying and simply stared at him, mouth agape.

"Why did you do that?"

"What? Cover your yard duty?"

"And everything else."

"You're upset."

She frowned at him, suspicion written across her face.

"What? Can't I be nice?"

"No. No, I don't think you can."

Gabriel's mouth twisted in amusement. "You still have to attend the curriculum planning session after school today. How's that for punishment?"

"That's more like the Gabriel I know."

"It was a joke."

Maddie sniffed, straightening. "I'll accept the cover for my yard duty, but I will be staying for my classes and the planning session."

Gabriel crossed his arms, wondering why she didn't take the offer. "Okay then."

A second later, her face crumpled. Gabriel stood stoic, feet glued to the floor, willing himself to stay put. Comforting her wasn't his job. Yes, his role as vice principal meant he was in charge of staff and student welfare, but that didn't mean he had to get involved.

Gabriel waited, looking around the room, focusing on the shelves filled with stationery and textbooks. There were copies of books he'd read as a teenager. *Animal Farm. Tomorrow, When the War Began.* Loads of Shakesp—

Fuck protocol. He couldn't bear to listen to her sobbing and not *do* something.

"What happened? Can I help?" He heard his tone and winced. It sounded harsher than he'd intended. But there was something about listening to her cry that made him feel like he had a swarm of wasps stinging his chest.

He crouched before her, uncertain of how to help but wanting to, *needing* to offer this woman comfort.

"This!" Maddie threw a slightly crumpled card on the floor between them.

Gabriel frowned, reaching for it. "May I?"

"Knock yourself out."

He picked it up, sitting back on the stool to read it. It was a birthday card dated close to thirty years ago, its edges slightly yellowed and worn. On the front of it was a glittery number six with a doll smiling in the corner. Gabriel swallowed, feeling suddenly ill.

Opening the card, he read the tight, neat handwriting.

Dear Big M,

Happy Birthday, pet. I'm sorry I couldn't see you on your special day. But I'll be going away for a while. Daddy and Mammy are taking a break for a time, and you'll be living with her until we can get a few things sorted. I'll be back soon. I left your gift by the TV. You be good and mind your mam. You're a big girl now.

Happy birthday again, dear Maddie.

Love and tickles,

Dad.

P.S. Say hi to Punky for me.

"I don't understand." Gabriel looked up.

"It's simple really. This is an example of all the cards and letters my dad sent for over a decade after my sixth birthday."

Gabriel handed her the card, trying his best to harden his heart, to not feel so much. But with every interaction, his armor was weakening.

"Okay."

"This—these . . . I just found out—" Maddie shook her head.

"If it helps, I'm sorry you're going through this, whatever *this* is. You don't have to tell me, but I'm here if you need someone to talk to. I know firsthand how much parents can suck."

Maddie looked up at him with startled eyes, and he wanted to take her in his arms, to speak words that he had no right saying.

The shrill school bell startled them both.

"Do you need anything before I go on duty?"

"You mean go on *my* yard duty."

"Mine for today."

"No, but thanks."

"If you need to cancel—"

"Thanks, but I'll see you at the planning meeting."

Gabriel nodded once then left the room before he said or did something they'd both regret.

CHAPTER FIFTEEN

It was moments when she hit rock bottom that Maddie felt blessed the most. Not because she was some masochist and derived joy from her pain, but because she had two of the bestest friends—sisters, really—in the whole wide world to help her through it.

When Sera and Ally had seen her face at work that day, they'd taken charge and talked her through it so she could survive the day without another major blip.

Knowing that she needed some space, they'd not come by Monday evening but had checked in on her on Tuesday to see how she was feeling.

By Wednesday, when she'd been steadier and less teary, they'd come over to her place after work with takeout food and a bottle of wine.

Their presence made her feel lighter, even though the pain was still fresh. It was only after dinner, with wine glasses in hand, that they began to chat in earnest.

"Have you heard from her since you found the letters?" Ally asked, sipping her soda. "Has she tried to contact you at all?"

Maddie shook her head. "No. And I honestly don't think I ever want to speak to her ever, ever, ever again."

"Fair call. I'd be raging as well," Sera replied. "I'm so sorry she kept this from you, Madds."

"I think I'm still in shock to be honest. I mean, even if she did call, I wouldn't answer her. Or if I did, I'd probably scream at her, to be honest."

"Have you read all the letters?"

Maddie picked up her glass of pinot grigio. "I haven't been able to read them all. It hurt too much after a handful, so I had to stop. I thought it best to save reading them for the weekend so I can at least wallow for a few days and not have to deal with teaching with puffy eyes."

"Has Gabriel spoken to you?"

Maddie smiled now, and the unexpected warmth that flooded her was actually pleasant. If she wasn't in such a despondent state, she'd be shocked by the feeling. As it was, she was grateful that he'd been there to support her.

"He's almost as bad as the two of you. But yes, he's been checking in on me every morning and afternoon. He does it with the pretense of bringing some work or clarifying some document, but I appreciate the gesture."

"I told you he was nice," Sera commented.

"Yeah, but you and Jack are friendly with him, so your judgment is colored."

"Well, I told you the exact same thing," Ally teased.

"Pregnant brain doesn't count—oof." Maddie nearly spilled her wine as the pillow sailed by her head. "Bless your terrible aim."

Ally laughed, placing her soda on the table.

"It's nice that you see the good in him. Gabriel is a great support. He was a rock when Owen and I got together—"

"Dating your student's dad. Naughty."

"Very. But he helped me through all the crap with parents and guiding me as I took on a leadership role."

"He's a regular knight in shining armor," Maddie drawled, but there was no heat in her sarcasm. Having his support had shifted something between them.

Or perhaps it was her lack of sleep that had taken the fight out of her. She'd been unable to switch off, unable to do much more than close her eyes while she'd remembered every moment when she'd ever felt abandoned growing up. All her milestone birthdays, the times when kids would tease her for being fatherless, her lonely graduation . . . she'd spent the past two nights thinking about how different her life might have been had her mother told her the truth. How different *she* might have been.

It was a betrayal that she would never be able to forgive. She wasn't the type to trust easily, but after learning of her mother's deception, Maddie wasn't certain she would ever be able to trust Sharon ever again.

If her own mother was capable of such a betrayal, who was to say a total stranger wouldn't be worse?

"Look, I'll admit that he's been attentive, but I was having a meltdown." At their twin looks of disapproval, Maddie rolled her eyes. "Just because he was nice to me doesn't automatically mean I think he's my best friend. We're civil to each other—kind of. And I'll keep being civil to him until the year is up."

"Uh-huh." Sera grinned. "So, had any more sex dreams about him?"

"I regret ever telling you two big mouths about that. And no, I haven't, thank you very much." Maddie sighed. Seeing him chopping wood had lived rent free in her head for the past few weeks. "Hey, thanks for coming over. I appreciate having you two to lean on. I honestly don't know what I'd do without you both."

"You're welcome, hun." Ally smiled then tried to stifle a yawn.

"Time to get this mama home, I think." Maddie winked at Sera.

"So, what now?" Sera asked, slipping on her boots.

After a few seconds of deliberation, she looked up at the two people she loved more than anyone else in the world. "Now, I suppose, I figure out what I want to say when I find my dad."

The prospect left her feeling both terrified and excited.

CHAPTER SIXTEEN

"Hey, you're early."

It was the first Saturday of the school holidays and instead of sipping cocktails on some far-off tropical island, Maddie stood on Gabriel's porch on a cold winter's day, ready for yet another planning session. This time, it would be in the comfort of his home. Or discomfort. The jury was still out on that one. Ever since she'd caught a glimpse of him half-naked in his backyard, Maddie had wondered what his home looked like on the inside. And it wasn't just curiosity about his bedroom either. "I can come back if that's a problem?"

She fought against the need to fidget, gripping the fruit platter in her hands as nerves danced up and down her spine.

"Not at all, come in. My best friend, Harper, is here. She was dropping off a few things, so I've not had the chance to set up yet. But she'll be leaving now."

"Friend?"

Gabriel shot her a dry look. "Yes, I have friends."

"Is this a *female* friend by any chance?"

Gabriel ushered her inside. "My oldest female friend, so dial it down, Miss Marple."

"The plot thickens."

"Uh-huh. How are you feeling?"

Maddie shrugged, still a little raw after the tumultuous two weeks. She hadn't spoken to her mom and had no intension to do so. "I've heard that question a lot lately." Maddie focused on the platter in her hands.

Even though she appreciated her friends' concern, she was looking forward to having a distraction. Anything to get her mind off the sick feeling that shifted her insides every time she thought about those letters. For years she'd thought herself strong and resilient, but these letters seemed to pour salt into what was still a gaping wound.

"I've no doubt Ally and Sera have had your back."

"They're the best."

Oddly enough, she wasn't dreading the planning session with Gabriel this afternoon. It had nothing to do with the fact that she wanted to be here or that Gabriel didn't pry. She appreciated his quiet 'need anything?' when he passed her office or 'all good?,' not forcing her to rehash any feelings but letting her know she could get support if she needed it.

It was very un-Gabriel-like. Or maybe it was exactly what he was like.

She wasn't really so sure these days.

Hanging out with Gabriel today would be like visiting an alien from another planet: weird and hopefully just unsettling enough to take her mind off everything. She looked at the quiet way he studied her and felt the need to add, "I'm coping and happy to have something to take my mind off it."

"Message received. I'm always one yard duty cover away next term if you need it."

"Roger, roger."

"I'll take that." Gabriel plucked the platter out of her arms and led her down the corridor. "I've put together an antipasti dish and thought pizza might be in order for dinner if that suits?"

"Sounds perfect."

"Let me set up first."

Maddie glanced at the rooms on either side of the high-ceilinged hall, noticing a study off the entrance. A sitting room followed sporting a huge fireplace and plush throws. She stopped to look at a series of photos of Gabriel on the slopes before she was distracted by a few of him with a bunch of equally hot friends at the beach. Lots of traveling around the world, which she totally appreciated.

She caught a glimpse of a dark-haired woman grinning behind oversized sunglasses, before Gabriel prompted her to catch up. There was something familiar about the woman's face. Surely they didn't have mutual friends. That would be . . . weird.

"Your home is gorgeous. I don't think I mentioned it the last time I was here."

Gabriel glanced over his shoulder, eyes warm. "I recall you might have been a bit distracted by the . . . view."

Maddie sputtered, surprised by his comment. Was he actually flirting? It made the man almost human. "We're in the kitchen," he continued, as if nothing had happened. She stared after him, suddenly overcome by the image of him half-naked and sweaty, axe slung over his shoulder . . . .

Ex-model, Madds. The guy has confidence up the—

"Wow. Gorgeous space." Maddie descended the few steps that led to the kitchen. "I thought the outside was beautiful, but it's so welcoming in here too." There were small bits of artwork and crafted wooden designs on cream walls that made the place comforting and homey.

"Thanks. You say it like it's a shock to you."

"I didn't know automatons had nice houses."

Gabriel smirked and placed the platter on the kitchen

counter. And suddenly she felt out of place. What the hell was she doing here?

An odd, unsettling feeling crept over her, and with that came a deep sadness. Everything about the past few weeks felt odd.

It was like when she'd been a kid and had first understood the moment that her father wasn't coming back. She'd been functioning normally on the outside, but inside, in her mind, it had been as if she were in a thick fog that had only seemed to increase in density with every step. She was looking at everything with new eyes, questioning everything she had once believed.

Why in the world was she standing in the middle of Gabriel's kitchen, acting like her world hadn't exploded?

It was too much to process all at once. And that feeling that seemed to press down on her now, the one that gripped the back of her neck, was grief. Crushing, debilitating grief. There was relief in knowing the truth, but also a depth of confusion she hadn't expected. She hadn't been abandoned by her father after all, but was very much loved. And from what she'd read, very much wanted.

It was more than she had ever felt growing up with her mom.

"I can take you on the grand tour if you like."

Maddie turned to find Gabriel leaning against the kitchen island, watching her in that quiet way of his.

"Sorry, my mind is all over the place." Maddie attempted a smile. "I'll take you up on that offer though. Your place is really inviting. I love all the light." She gestured to the large, rectangular windows that seemed to dominate the space.

"Did you think I lived in a cave?"

"I expected more . . . steel."

Gabriel laughed, and Maddie felt a rush of something beneath all her angst. It spread from her chest, traveling across every part of her body, making her feel something other than dread. She welcomed it despite herself. She had to hand it to him, the man had a great smile. Pity he was always scowling so much.

Maddie liked how the house played with different levels. She walked through the kitchen and down a few steps that led to a large dining table. To her right was yet another room. But it was the bright kitchen dining area that grabbed her attention. Maddie admired the floor-to-ceiling windows that showcased the late-afternoon light. She was so consumed by it that she almost missed the small, dark-haired woman who walked in.

A strange quiver of awareness stole through her. The woman from the picture.

Gabriel approached, gesturing to his friend. "Maddie, this is Harper. Harper, this is Maddie, my work colleague."

The woman looked up from her phone, and suddenly the large space around her began to shrink. All Maddie could see was the dark-haired, dark-eyed woman standing before her. It was as if someone had punched her in the gut.

"You're fucking kidding me."

Gabriel studied her face, his own blank. "What?"

She glanced at Gabriel and then the woman, head swinging back and forth, assessing them both for even the smallest sign of deception.

"Hello, Maddie."

"Is this some kind of a sick joke?" Her stomach rolled. Suddenly, all those fears resurfaced. What was she thinking, trusting Gabriel? He was just like everyone else. Deceiving her. Manipulating her.

Gabriel crossed his arms. "Excuse me?"

"Is she really a psychic, or are you having a laugh at my expense? I thought you were *nice*. One minute, you're covering my yard duty, and the next you're going behind my back, feeding her information?"

Maddie's body trembled. She wasn't sure if it was anger or something else. Her emotions had been tested to the extreme of late, and she couldn't trust herself to respond calmly.

"I'm not following."

Maddie hefted her bag on her shoulder. What the fuck was happening right now? She mustered every bit of patience to keep her voice measured. "This is a low blow, even for you, Gabriel."

"Explain this to me."

She marched out the front door, refusing to listen to his protests.

"Maddie!"

Stupid to have let down her guard. Stupid to have trusted him. She couldn't even trust her mother, for pity's sake. Lying to her for her whole damn life. Of course he would lie too. What was she thinking?

"Maddie, wait! What happened?" Gabriel stood between her and her car.

"You and your friend are having a great laugh. Swapping stories, pretending like you know me."

"I can explain." Harper stepped forward, her bag and keys in hand.

"It would be great if someone did." Gabriel stood, arms akimbo.

"Maddie is a new client of mine. She came to see me for a reading about a fortnight ago."

Gabriel scowled at his friend, then his eyes pinned Maddie in place. "How am I supposed to know that information?"

"Oh, come on, like you didn't tell your *oldest female friend* about my dad."

"What about your dad?"

Mercy, she couldn't think straight. Had she told Gabriel before the psychic visit about her dad? She shook her head, trying to clear it.

"Maddie?"

She'd told him her dad had left her, that she wasn't sure if he was even alive. Nothing more.

"What about the guy?" Maddie argued. "Closer than—" She crushed her lips together, horrified at her own line of thinking.

"What guy?" Gabriel's expression was hard, his mouth compressed in a thin line.

The only man in her life at the moment was Gabriel. Surely Harrow hadn't meant *him* when she'd made that prediction? Not that they were anything more than colleagues. Enemies at that.

Harper stepped closer. "Let me be clear, I maintain the privacy of my clients and I don't share anything I see with anyone. Not even my best friend."

Maddie's voice was firm. "I find that hard to believe."

"Believe me then," Gabriel interjected. "Harps never talks about her clients, and I had no idea you even went to see her. How would I know that? Yes, she's my friend and a close one, but I don't ask questions about her clients.

"What I know about your dad is vague at best and from your mouth only." Gabriel took her shoulders, and she couldn't help but look up at him. "I only found out about your dad from what *you* told me. All I know about the guy is that he's been absent for a long time, and that he sent you a card on your sixth birthday. That's it."

Maddie swallowed back the wave of pain. She recalled the moment in the storage room, the way Gabriel hadn't pried but had offered her comfort, all the same.

Was this a freak coincidence? Had she just happened to see the ad on social media that had recommended The Third Eye? Did Harper just happen to be Gabriel's best friend?

Maddie's shoulders slumped when she ran over the events of the past few weeks in her head. She rubbed at her stinging eyes, knowing she had jumped to conclusions. Damn her mother for lying to her. Hiding this from her. Damn her father for not trying harder to find her. Damn them all for screwing her over.

"You've had a lot going on lately, Maddie." Gabriel's gaze was direct, reassuring. "Maybe we can put this down as a misunderstanding? Or a really big coincidence."

All she wanted to do was sink into his chest and be held. Instead, Maddie stepped back, needing to keep her distance.

Harper shifted closer. "So you found the letters?"

"I did."

"I know it must hurt to find out the truth, but this will be good for you. Have a little faith that it will work out. There's a lot of mistrust in you which can cloud the process."

"Oh, is that what you see in your visions?" Maddie's voice was derisive, but she couldn't help it. She'd acted like a fool.

"No." Harper's mouth curved. "It's what you're showing me now."

Maddie glowered at them both.

Gabriel's expression, for once, was open. She realized that it was the first of a few rare moments that she could read him. It took her off guard. Sure, she could always tell when he was mad or annoyed, but seeing his concern, witnessing emotions that were real—that ran deeper than his usual polite detach-ment—was disconcerting.

"I've known Gabriel since I was five, and he accepts that I have a gift. He might not agree with what I see or know—"

"Far too reasoned for that."

"Exactly." Harper smiled now. "But he knows I have bound-aries and he's never one to press them."

"Right." Maddie squared her shoulders, shrugging off any lingering anger. "I apologize for getting it wrong. I—"

"Jumped to conclusions."

"I didn't—" Maddie paused. It was instinct to disagree with him. To fight. She stopped herself, recognizing when she was in the wrong. "Yep, I did. It's a hell of a coincidence, and I thought . . ."

". . . that we were playing some kind of prank."

"Yep." She hated being made a fool, being used in someone else's game. For decades, she'd been misled, told a story that hadn't been true. She didn't know how to accept that, how to move on. "I thought you might be getting back at me for the magazine thing."

Gabriel shook his head. "That's in the past, Maddie. Forget it ever happened."

"Sorry—to the both of you—for jumping to conclusions."

Harper nodded once. "Apology accepted."

Gabriel's mouth opened in mock surprise. "I didn't think Maddie even knew how to apologize."

"On that warm and fuzzy note, I'll be off. Let you two fight it out," Harper interjected.

"You know Gabriel all too well."

"I do." Harper turned to leave then stopped herself. "Hey, for whatever it's worth, I'm glad you found the answers you were looking for, even if it seems to have caused you pain."

Maddie swallowed back a fresh wave of emotions. "I should be thanking you for showing it to me. I didn't want it to be true, but you were right."

Harper nodded. "The pain will pass. And it'll all work out for you."

"Is that something you saw in the cards?"

Harper smiled, tapping her chest. "I know it in here. It'll work out for you, Maddie. Give it time."

She watched as Harper drove away, caught not by the woman's prophecy about her father, but what she'd seen about her personal life.

She glanced at Gabriel, taking a deep, fortifying breath. "Take two?"

Gabriel swung his arm out, leading the way. "Welcome to my home, Red. Would you like to come in?"

"Real smooth, Steele."

His deep chuckle as she stormed up to the front door seemed to do something very suspicious to her insides.

Perhaps she had better remain on her guard after all.

Maddie swirled the glass of wine, wondering if she was slightly tipsy or really, really tired. She'd only had half a glass, but she was feeling heavy and lethargic. She blamed it on the past few hours they'd spent rigorously designing the mid-year prac exam and internal assessment tasks for their senior literature students. She had to admit that Gabriel's ideas were damn good.

They'd eaten amazingly authentic pizza, indulged in the fruit platter and chocolate macarons, and were now settled on Gabriel's very large and very comfortable sofa.

Maddie felt like she could sink into a deep sleep. But she still had the drive home off the mountain, and if she didn't want to drive *off* the mountain, she needed to wake herself up a bit. Or grab a cab. Or crash at Sera and Jack's place, which was only six minutes away. Tempting.

Very tempting.

"I'd say that's a job well done, Red."

"It is."

"Then why do you look so sad?"

The heavy ache of her mother's deception and her father's letters wanted to smother any light or happiness inside her.

She'd lived for so long pretending like she didn't need a dad. All those years of recriminations and doubts . . . To know that she might have been a different person—it was all too much.

Bitterness, the acrid, burning taste of it scored her throat.

What must her dad think of her, never to once return a letter or get in contact?

She sat upright. "I can't stop thinking about those letters. I mean, all these years, he was writing to me. For over a decade. He sent me a birthday card every year up until my eighteenth birthday." Her voice wobbled.

She had read that card—the last one he seemed to have sent —over and over since finding it. She carried it with her in her bag, wanting to have it close.

She'd almost memorized it, too. He'd told her he wanted to see her, that he hoped she was well, that she was always on his mind. But he had never mentioned kids or a wife. Or hadn't up until her eighteenth birthday.

"To think *he* thinks that I want nothing to do with him. That I've ignored him for decades. I . . ." Maddie stood, restless now. "It makes me feel sick. If it wasn't for Harper, I'd still be in the dark."

"She helped you find the letters?"

Maddie nodded. "I kind of hoped that she wasn't right because that meant my mom was keeping them from me all these years. She—you probably don't want to hear this. Sorry, I'm tired, no filter."

"You've never had a filter, so why start now?"

Maddie laughed. "You're sharp, you know that?"

"Tell me." Gabriel sat beside her now.

"My mother has always been a bitter woman, and it seems like she was happy to keep me away from my dad for my whole life."

"I take it they're divorced?"

"He left on my sixth birthday."

"The birthday card you showed me." Gabriel nodded. "That's a long time to stay bitter."

"Trust me, my mother is the queen of bitter. If holding grudges were an Olympic sport, she'd be a gold medalist."

"Ouch."

"Mega ouch."

"Have you any way to contact him?"

Maddie opened her bag, retrieving the envelope from her father. "This." She handed it to him with a sigh. "There's a return address on this last letter. It was when he was moving and wanted me to know his details."

"And?"

"And what?"

"What are you going to do about it?"

Maddie pressed a hand on her stomach. "I've no idea. I mean, I want to see him, to find him, for sure, but there are so many questions. It's not simple after all this time. God, that's why this whole thing pisses me off so much."

"Often bitterness blinds."

"It poisons. My mother has some warped sense of justification for what she did. That somehow it was right of her to lie to me every single time I asked about my dad. I mean, I get how it would hurt at first, but surely after a while, any normal person would think, oh, it's a good thing for my child to know her father."

"There's no reason in emotion."

Maddie smirked. "That's such a Gabriel thing to say."

"It's the truth. It clouds judgment."

"Speaking from experience?"

"I am."

Maddie studied his face. "So you're aware that you act like a robot."

Gabriel bristled. "I do not."

"Oh, come on. You show no emotion at work at all. It wasn't until we started working together that I even caught a glimpse of anything remotely akin to human feeling."

"That's harsh. And perhaps says more about you than me."

"Okay, maybe a little harsh, but you can be distant, so what's a person meant to think?"

"Just because I'm not expressive with my emotions, doesn't mean I don't have any. Like I've said before, work is a chance for me to forget about everything else."

"But even now, in the comfort of your own home, you're distant."

"Technically, we're working."

"In the privacy of your home."

Gabriel stood. He took a few steps then turned to face her, his body taut. "I'm well aware of where we are, Maddie. Trust me on that."

A quiet but powerful sliver of awareness crept along her body. It heated her blood and left her wondering if what he was saying was, in fact, laden with dual meaning.

Or was she simply imagining it?

Maddie stood, uncertain.

Gabriel stepped closer and suddenly she felt like prey. Like the man before her was going to hunt her until she was his captive, until he could take one big bite. Mercy, in that very moment, she wanted to bend over and let him.

"But the thing is," he continued. "If I act on what I *feel*, I might find myself in big, *big* trouble."

Maddie sucked in air, very much aware of Gabriel, the man. Which was oh so different from Gabriel, the VP. His voice had deepened, becoming . . . intimate. That voice seemed to slide under her dress, sneak up her thighs, sending bolts of lust straight to her—

Fuck, no. Not him.

It galled her to think she had to take a few breaths to speak. *Rein in your hormones, girl. You're a little confused.*

Maddie cleared her throat. "You know that it's both normal and expected to act with emotion in your own damn home.

And—shock, horror—you can even act like a human at work too."

"Can I?"

Gabriel closed the gap between them, his face inches from her own. Too close to be considered anything but inappropriate. But her body didn't seem to mind one damn bit. She was tingling, *tingling* for heaven's sake. Her breasts were heavy. Her blood pulsed.

Maddie bit her lip, then she watched in fascination as Gabriel studied her reaction, his expression alert, intent.

"Because sometimes the things I want to do at work . . . could get me fired."

The noise she made at the back of her throat was incoherent.

She tried again. "Gabriel."

"Yes, Maddie?"

"I think that's enough emotion for now."

"What are you afraid of?" He was so close, so warm, so damn appealing. "Don't be a robot. You're so cold," he teased, throwing her words back at her.

"You're playing dirty."

"In case you haven't figured it out yet, I *like* playing dirty."

A beat. Another.

They both pounced.

Maddie jolted as his mouth claimed hers, a glorious consummation. As if in unspoken agreement, their bodies collided then fused together, both seeming to crave full contact.

It was everything she wanted and yet feared. Because now she knew, now she understood that being kissed by Gabriel was a million times better than her fantasies. He was wicked and bold, his mouth skilled and seductive.

And it was a lethal game that they were playing.

But she didn't care. All she wanted was more. They were connected at every angle, and Gabriel's touch left her burning.

He gripped her hips then shifted lower to grab her ass, pressing his body—hard and demanding—against her.

But his mouth—oh sweet sin—his mouth was punishing her in the most exquisite way possible. He was the perfect fit, and she never wanted him to stop.

Maddie opened to him, shivering as his tongue stroked hers, challenging her to match his pace. Never one to back down, Maddie kissed him back, reveling in the very low growl that it produced in response.

His hands fisted in her hair then roamed to explore her body in greedy strokes. She was burning, on fire, delirious and desperate for more.

She needed him. She would go out of her mind if she didn't have him. Now.

But this was Gabriel, not some random hot guy hook-up.

And as if by some new unspoken agreement, they both pulled away with a smacking 'pop' of their lips at the same time.

"If we don't stop . . ." His voice was gravelly, his eyes burning.

They both stared at the other, chests heaving.

Gabriel groaned, stroking her lips with his index finger. "The things I would do to that mouth."

She opened for him, biting at the tip of his finger.

"Maddie, if you were mine—"

"Gabriel." She sighed his name, uncertain of what to say. After a few moments, she found her answer even if it was the one that least appealed. "I think I should go home," she whispered, lips tingling.

"I think that's a good idea."

CHAPTER SEVENTEEN

Gabriel woke up that Saturday morning feeling like he'd been on a week-long bender. Which was ridiculous because those days of going until he didn't even know his own name were, well, behind him.

Sure, he was working most days to try and get on top of everything before the new school term began, but that morning he woke up restless and groggy.

It didn't help that every time he walked past his living room sofa, images of a certain redhead with a lush body and a killer mouth reappeared.

But that had been a week ago. And yet every evening since, he couldn't seem to stop thinking about her. About what had almost happened. Every time he thought about texting her, he talked himself out of it. And the few times they had messaged each other since, it had been strictly work related.

Perhaps it was for the best.

Not that it wasn't torturing him inside. He'd been fighting this urge for years, and he wasn't sure why his control was slipping now. Was it because he was working closely with her? Because he was getting to know her?

Gabriel told himself that she was still cut up about her dad, that she probably didn't have any headspace to be thinking about their kiss. He wished he could do something to help.

He debated whether he should call her when his phone rang. A stab of fear pierced through his sleep-fogged brain.

He answered with his heart in his throat. "Hello?"

"Gabriel, it's Eloise Templestowe, from Malton Mews. I'm calling to inform you that your father is asking for you, if you have some time to stop by?"

"I'll be over shortly."

Gabriel showered and changed, packing his car with the decorations he'd picked up for Ally's baby shower. Jack had enlisted everyone's help to make sure his sister-in-law's shower would be one she'd never forget. After a quick text to the group chat saying he would be late, Gabriel got in the car to visit his dad.

He prepared himself on the way, knowing that in the time it took to drive to Malton Mews, his father might have relapsed. Even still, the drive over didn't prepare him for the familiar flash of relief at seeing his father look at him like he used to, with recognition and a modicum of affection.

"Gabriel. Son."

Steeling himself, Gabriel walked into his father's room, sitting down on the chair next to him. There were fresh flowers by the windowsill, and his dad was dressed in a clean shirt and pants. An empty cup of tea and a saucer sat on the low table between them. Leo's room appeared cheery, even if a bit sparse. But his face—Gabriel shuddered—his father's face showed signs of decline, his body ravaged and thinner than it had been only weeks prior.

This whisper of a man was a reminder of all he'd lost. There had always seemed to be an invisible wall between them when he'd been a child. As the years had gone by, the wall had become a fortress, keeping them both on opposite sides. It was a cruel twist of fate that when Gabriel had wanted to have a relationship, his father's health had declined. It made the pain all the more acute.

"Dad. How are you feeling?"

"Lonely. Where are all my friends?"

"I don't know."

"What happened to that hot girlfriend of yours?"

"Which one?"

"The emaciated blondie."

Gabriel rubbed his face. "There were a few of those, Dad."

His old man chuckled. "An ol' chip off the block."

"Not quite."

"What, no girlfriend now? What's the matter with you? You're mixing with the New York set, son. You've got to have a flashy woman to go with the flashy lifestyle."

"We're not in New York, Dad." Trust the rare moment of lucidity to focus on his love life. "I'm happy enough being single."

"It's not healthy for a man to be on his own. I should know."

"You were hardly alone." Gabriel found it impossible to keep the derision out of his voice. He'd grown up in chaos, and it had all been his father's fault.

As a child, Gabriel had wondered if his mother had been a soft, sweet figment of his imagination. It seemed that his life had always been in the shadows, hiding from the overly familiar hands of strangers who thought Gabriel's presence only made his dad hotter. More desirable. A good-looking single dad needing a woman. And didn't they all want to save him.

But from a young age, Gabriel had learned how to make himself invisible, never understanding the funny feeling in his stomach for what it was. Grief.

But with the death of his mother came the death of anything he'd ever known and loved. Anything that was good and pure.

"I was alone. Nobody could replace your mother."

"You sure tried."

"What are you complaining about? I gave you food and shelter. I supported you when my heart was breaking. My heart is still broken."

Gabriel was torn between anger and resignation. He didn't want to fight with his dad in the rare moments that he had him back, but he also needed to know.

"What about mine?"

"Speak up, boy."

"What about my heart? I lost my mother. She was mine, my whole damn world. While you were off whoring around, I had to figure out how to deal with all that pain. All those strangers in our house while you weren't there. Or worse, when you were there, you were too drunk or high or hungover to even parent the next day."

"I did my best, didn't I?"

"You were lost, Dad."

"I don't need your blame."

"I'm not blaming you."

"Really?"

"You did that all by yourself."

His father never forgave himself for his mother's drowning. And instead of seeking help, he had sought self-destruction, taking Gabriel's chance of a happy childhood with him.

"If I hadn't insisted she learn how to swim . . ."

"It's done, Dad."

"She wasn't a strong swimmer."

"It's done!"

Leo's voice was raspy, wracked with despair. "It's my fault she died."

Gabriel rubbed his face. How many nights had he spent consoling his father, drunk and lost in his grief? How many days had he tried to get him to see a therapist? Tried to get him the help that he needed? But he'd been a teenager by that stage. And his dad had either been unwilling or unable to do it himself.

Leo's inability to get help had cost Gabriel his only remaining parent. Cost them their relationship.

"You can't keep blaming yourself, or even living life in the past. It happened. She drowned, and she's never coming back. But you were still living. You were there. And I— I needed you, Dad. I needed you to step up, to be there for me."

"Don't you see, Gabriel? She was the best of me. Without her, I was nothing. She saw . . . She saw the good in me. All I did was drag her down."

It was like talking to a brick wall. His father wasn't listening. He never listened. And every time it happened, it broke Gabriel's heart all over again.

As suddenly as it came, the moment was gone. Gabriel saw the shutters coming down. The far-off, distant expression. The blank incomprehension. The stranger.

He sighed, left once again with all the anger, the frustration and grief—all the heavy emotions—with no healthy place to go.

"Who the hell are you?"

Gabriel jolted, lifting his head.

"I—"

"Why are you so damn close? Get away from me!" Leo struck out, and Gabriel had only a split second to react, barely dodging the blow so that it landed not on his cheek, but on the side of his ear. Gabriel stared at his dad, the shock of what happened keeping him in place.

Stupid. He'd been lax, letting his guard down. He knew better than that.

Gabriel's head jerked back as a heavy object glanced off his cheek.

"What the fuck?" He shoved out of his chair and spotted the teacup on the ground.

It had been so long since his dad had remembered that Gabriel had forgotten about the rage, the disorientation that would come after.

A nurse rushed in, and Gabriel stepped out of the way.

"Get him out of here! I don't know him! He's trying to kill me!" His dad tried to launch at him again, but there was no strength left and he faltered.

Another nurse entered, and Gabriel slowly backed out of the room. He could never watch this bit. Couldn't bear the heartache of seeing his father shrink in on himself.

He walked back to his car in a daze, needing some space, the normalcy of everyday things. He sat behind the wheel for a few minutes, regulating his breathing until it was steady. Pulling down the rearview mirror, he winced at the mark on his cheek.

And like a ton of bricks, the rumbling emotion, the swell of it came crashing down on top of him.

For the first time in a long while, he let the emotion come, the heartache and anger and the bitter, bitter regret. He let it spew from his lips in frustrated curses until his voice was hoarse. And for the first time in a long while, Gabriel allowed all that pain to fall in silent tears for the dad he never had.

CHAPTER EIGHTEEN

Maddie had spent the first week of the school break recovering. She hadn't realized how much she'd been juggling until she was able to take a break. Being on school holidays meant she'd been able to cry when she felt sad, spend time exercising and seeing friends, and start marking the massive piles of essays at a leisurely pace. In short, she felt she had balance, even if she was still uncertain about what to do regarding her father's last known address.

Did she just rock up and see if he was home? Write him a letter? What would he say to her after all these years?

She had another appointment with her therapist this week, and she was hoping that getting a professional's perspective would help her out.

She was beginning to see that the letters were a blessing. Even though she would never get a chance to relive her youth, she would have this. She knew that she'd been loved and wanted. And for now, that knowledge would have to do.

She wanted to find him. She needed to know what had happened to him. But she was also terrified to find out the truth. And so she went back and forth, mulling it over until she kept herself up at night.

It was driving her crazy. Maddie knew a decision had to be made soon. But for now, decorating Ally and Owen's home for tomorrow's baby shower would be a welcome distraction.

Maddie bit her lip. She still hadn't told the girls about her kiss with Gabriel last weekend. Not that it meant anything. She opened another box of biodegradable cutlery, nearly nicking her finger with the box cutter. Okay, so maybe she was a little distracted by it. Which was fine. She was a grown woman and able to control her . . . urges.

Did she want him to kiss her again? Maddie put the box cutter down on the kitchen table. No. Uh-uh. It was Gabriel for heaven's sake. Why in the world would she want him anywhere near her lips?

Not those lips, you dirty whore.

The bell rang, startling her from the very wicked fantasy that had begun in her mind.

"Madds, can you get that?" Sera called to her from the stairs.

"On it!"

Maddie opened the front door, heart jolting at the sight of Gabriel in jeans and a dark blue sweater. It made his eyes stand out against—

Maddie gasped. "What happened to your face?"

"Biker gang." Gabriel stood on the step, sporting a bruise on his cheek and a relaxed attitude. It made him look dangerous and, she was loathe to admit it, a tiny bit appealing. "Okay, fine, I actually moonlight as a trapeze artist and I fell."

"With no broken bones? How lucky."

"I'm that kinda guy."

Maddie crossed her arms, waiting until she heard an answer that would satisfy her. "Those boxes look mighty heavy."

"Are you going to take pity on a frail man like me and let me in then?"

Not with those bulging biceps. "Not until you tell me."

"This isn't your home."

Maddie jutted her hip. "This is my friend's house."

"Did anyone ever tell you that you're nosey?"

"A modern-day Agatha Christie."

"Uh-huh."

Maddie caught a glimpse of something in his expression. It passed in a blink, but it was there alright. Her voice softened. "Are you alright?"

Gabriel nodded. "Looks worse than it is."

"You sound like you get shiners every day."

"In my old life."

"Oooh, hidden past. Do tell."

"You'll have to figure that one out on your own, Ms. Christie."

"I'm very adept at wheedling out information from recalcitrant people."

Gabriel stepped closer. "I'm sure you're a woman of many talents."

"Need any painkillers?"

"Yeah, I think so. And to set this box down somewhere."

Maddie pointed to the space in the hall and led him to the guest bathroom under the stairs. "Come with me." She opened the cupboard above the sink and filled a glass with water, handing him two paracetamols. "Need ice?"

"Not unless I'm drinking whiskey."

"I meant for your face."

Gabriel smirked then winced. "Ouch. No, afraid I'm stuck with my face the way it is."

"When did you get so funny?"

"What, you only just noticed?"

Something buzzed inside her. Yes, she was only just noticing a lot of things about Gabriel. One being a dry sense of humor.

"Be back in a sec."

When she returned with a bag of peas and a kitchen towel, Gabriel was leaning against the counter, his head hung low. When he made eye contact, something inside of her yearned to comfort him.

Something was wrong. She was well able to read it now that his usual filter had slipped, and the expression, the part of Gabriel she was certain not many people saw, was there. Raw, unfiltered. And in pain.

She shut the door behind her, approaching him tentatively with the bag of peas and the cloth.

"You don't need to tell me, but I can see that something is bothering you."

"It's nothing."

"It's something. But as it's private, I can respect that. I—"

She what? It wasn't her business. For all she knew, he could have been in a brawl at a bar, or been training at some karate studio, or—

"You what?" he echoed.

Why the hell did she care all of a sudden?

And then she remembered the way he'd covered for her at work when she'd been at her most vulnerable. The way he'd comforted her, distracted her, hell, had even made her laugh when they'd been busy planning the prac exam.

When had she started giving a shit?

"I suppose I wanted to say that whatever it is, I'm here to listen." Maddie chewed her lip, suddenly uncertain. She was never uncertain. She prided herself on being confident, on knowing her own mind, but when it came to Gabriel, she seemed to second-guess herself.

Why the hell was that?

Certain he wouldn't answer, she turned to leave when Gabriel's voice, low and troubled, held her in place.

"My dad hit me."

Maddie whirled around to face him, unable to contain her shock.

"He *what?*"

Gabriel pointed to the bruise on his face. His cheek had turned purple. There was also, she noted now, a little cut under his eye. Maddie shivered. He looked tortured and dangerous and not at all like the rule-bound vice principal.

"My dad's not well. He got angry and took a swing, threw a cup at me. I wasn't expecting it, got caught off guard. My own fault really."

Maddie stepped forward, absorbing the information. Without thinking, she reached out to touch the bruise on his cheek. Picking up the peas, she placed it over the angry mark, holding it in place.

"Does this happen often?"

Gabriel's mouth twisted in a bitter smile. "No. My dad's an old man, but he's still got deadly aim. It wasn't his fault. He was . . . startled."

"I'm sorry."

"So am I."

She didn't understand, wasn't sure what to say or if she would be crossing a line. It was in such moments that she was reminded how little they knew of each other. And was surprised to find that she wanted to know more.

"What?"

She studied him and shrugged. "I didn't say anything."

"I can see it on your face."

"I'm trying to understand, that's all. You'd mentioned your dad had a heart attack weeks ago . . . I'm trying to piece it all together."

"Better for both of us if we leave it at that."

Maddie's temper ignited.

"Now you're mad."

"Don't be so patronizing."

God, how could the man make her feel sorry for him and want to thump him in the same breath?

"I wasn't. Just commenting on your animated face."

Maddie stepped back, gripping the frozen packet in her hands. "Well, it's my damned face and I can animate it however which way I damn well like."

"I don't doubt that for a moment."

"This isn't tennis. I don't need a blow-by-blow commentary either." Maddie shoved the peas at his chest. "Here, you can sort yourself out."

And quick as lightning, his hand gripped hers, tugging her closer, keeping her in place.

All manner of protests died on her tongue.

"I like watching your face. The way your eyes flash with heat when you're angry. The way you toss your hair back when you're gearing up to make an argument. I like watching *you*, Maddie."

She felt the cold bag seep through her fingers, even as his warmth drew her in. His hand was firm on hers, his eyes bright with an expression she had never seen before.

What the hell was happening?

Her pulse skyrocketed. She was aware of every breath, every movement. And that intensity, the way he watched her with something like hunger left her breathless.

Flashes of her long-forgotten sex dream fluttered past, an enticing, teasing memory.

Why the hell did her mind go to the gutter? Like that would be happening, with him of all people, here.

But when he tugged her against him, the naughty dream and all the fantasies she'd had since they'd kissed flashed in her mind. She dropped the bag of peas, barely registering the thud on the bathroom floor between them.

Then Gabriel's mouth was on hers, and her whole body

came alive. He was firm and commanding, fucking her mouth with soft, hungry strokes of his tongue. He seemed to know exactly what he wanted—

Her.

And it was like Maddie had been waiting, hovering, balancing on the edge of her need ever since he had kissed her. Because when his mouth fit—oh so perfectly—against hers, she fell, tumbling headlong into her arousal. And while she was falling, she couldn't help but wonder how it was that someone with so much spirit could be so restrained?

Because the Gabriel who kissed her like this, with life and vibrancy and fucking skill, couldn't be the same man who was cold and reasoned and so bloody reserved. How could he be both?

And then, like the fierce whipping force of their kiss, understanding snapped through her. They couldn't.

One of those perceptions was wrong. Or both were right. Gabriel, the man who kissed with passion and power and *feeling* could not be the same as Gabriel, the vice principal, the colleague, who seemed not to react or respond to anything.

And as he tugged her flush against him, as his hands bunched into her dress, holding her close, it all made sense.

He was hiding.

His emotions. His feelings. His true self.

Gabriel Steele, vice principal, rigid colleague, and believer of reason over emotion, was a front.

No man who kissed like this, no man whose tongue teased like that could be so damn unfeeling. It wasn't possible.

He'd told her once that he had a wicked past, but she hadn't quite believed it. Until now.

Maddie wrenched back, needing to study his face, needing to see it. And the satisfaction and sheer relief at what she saw left her trembling.

There it was, proof that what she suspected was true. The raw, naked passion stamped across his face. His eyes were hot and intense, raking over her with a possession that left her stunned.

Gone was his reserve. Gone was his control.

Gone was the Gabriel Steele of old.

This man, who had kissed her with such fervor, looked annoyed and confused and hotter than hell.

But the thing that baffled her, what remained left to be answered . . . was why?

Why the duplicity?

Why the façade?

Why in God's good name did she even care?

At that moment, Maddie didn't. At that moment, she needed to feel something other than confusion.

She wanted this. She wanted this from *him*. She wasn't going to think about consequences right now. Not when his mouth was hot and demanding. Not when he was looking at her like the world's ripest peach.

No, she would happily screw it all to hell. And him.

"Did you kiss me to shut me up?"

"Like I said, I like watching you, but I like kissing you even more."

"That doesn't answer my question."

"I wanted to kiss you."

"You . . . wanted to?"

"I did. But I also know that now isn't the time or place to talk about all the things I want to do to you."

Beneath his passion, Maddie saw the pain. It frightened her how much she wanted to offer him comfort. He'd once told her that work was a place for him to forget about his life. What painful secrets was Gabriel trying to hide?

"So you're not going to tell me why your dad hit you?"

"Not right now, no."

"What is it?" Maddie saw that he was holding back.

"I've been thinking about this for a while now. And this morning has made me realize how much I want to help you find your dad."

Maddie saw the openness in his expression, the truth of his words. "Why?"

"Because I know how hard it is to have an absent one."

She wanted to ask, to know more, to understand, but she knew now wasn't the time. "And I think following up on the address you have will help you take control of the situation."

"Control. Reason. Logic. Do you ever do things spontaneously, Gabriel?"

He squeezed her hips. "I kissed you, didn't I?"

"You don't strike me as the impulsive type."

"I'm not."

And yet her gut told her that that wasn't the whole truth. She was starting to realize that the Gabriel she had hated for many years, the Gabriel she'd thought she knew, wasn't the real Gabriel at all.

"If I want to find my father, I'll find him when I'm ready."

"I'm in a situation where I can't reverse time, and regret is a heavy burden to bear, Maddie. I'm simply offering to help."

"Thanks all the same. But I can do this on my own."

"You don't have to. If you need support, you know where to find me."

The gentle knock on the bathroom door prompted them into action.

"I suppose that's our cue."

"Exit stage left." Maddie reluctantly stepped back and out of his arms. From the way he looked at her, it seemed he would've been happy to stay in the bathroom all day.

Tempting . . .

She stepped back again, rearranging her dress. She picked

up the bag of peas and discarded cloth, trying to act normal. Not that she knew what that meant these days.

"Ready when you are, Red."

Maddie sailed out of the bathroom, winking at a bug-eyed Sera when Gabriel followed close behind.

CHAPTER NINETEEN

"Well, well, well, look what the cat dragged in." Maddie took a sip of her Champagne and did her best to ignore the jolt in her belly. Gabriel was here.

She told herself she was responding as any woman would to an attractive guy. No big deal. It had nothing to do with his panty-melting kisses or the way he grabbed her ass.

There was this supercharged current between them, and any time he would look at her, Maddie was left with an odd, tingling sensation along her skin.

Jesus, woman, go get laid already.

He'd kissed her—twice now—because he'd wanted to. Which was surprising enough in itself. But it left her uncertain about where they stood. Did she ignore it, like the first kiss? Pretend like it didn't happen? That would be the smart choice. Especially given they worked together.

The last thing she needed to do was muddy the waters with some office fling. No matter how tempting he might be.

Not that it was something she should be thinking about at her best friend's baby shower. Today was a day of celebration.

Ally would be having a baby soon, and she would do well to focus on that and *not* the attractive blonde woman who'd walked in with Gabriel.

Was it some kind of statement? That he could pull a hot woman, that his kisses meant nothing more than letting off steam?

Typical.

Not that she cared.

But was it really appropriate to bring a date to a baby shower?

"Whose the chick?" Maddie nudged Sera, who was busy refilling the jar of marinated olives.

Sera looked up, following her line of sight. "Gabriel's date, I assume. Ally encouraged him to bring someone if he wanted to."

Maddie sipped her bubbly, noticing the way Gabriel's dark looks complemented the petite blonde. The bruise on his cheek looked angrier today, making him even hotter, if that was possible. "Did you know he was bringing someone?"

"Nope. No idea."

"I wonder if Al knew." Maddie tapped on her Champagne flute, studying the pair.

"Probably not. She's beautiful."

"Mmm, and slim." Maddie narrowed her eyes. "Totally his type."

Sera's eyes turned huge. "And how would you know Gabriel's type?"

Maddie shrugged. "Just do. She looks . . ."

"Hey now," Sera warned.

"What?"

"I know that tone."

"What tone?"

Sera turned to face her. "I get that whatever happened in the bathroom yesterday has brought out the green-eyed monster in you, but—"

"*Nothing* happened."

"I saw your face and I *know* it wasn't just a case of tending to his wounds." Sera's shot her a no-bullshit look. "Something happened. But if it was nothing, as you claim, then why care about who he's with?"

"I don't."

"Oh. My. God."

"What?" Maddie threw her a sideways glance.

"You *did* kiss."

Maddie toyed with the stem of her Champagne flute. "I don't—" Maddie rolled her eyes. "Oh, *alright*. We kissed."

Sera's eyes turned round. "I knew it!" she whispered fiercely. "Wait until I tell Ally."

"It wasn't the first time either."

Sera gasped. "Maddie Fitzgerald, you *are* holding out on me."

She shrugged, eyes glued to the petite blonde chatting to Gabriel and Ally. "Sorry."

"Wait a minute, *why* are you holding out on me? Do you have feelings for him? Is this serious? Are you and Gabe secretly dating?"

It was Maddie's turn to look horrified. "No! Nothing like that. It was—we were—" Maddie growled. "It just happened."

"Oh yes, your mouth *just happened* to gravitate towards his."

"It did."

"And?"

"And what?"

"And," Sera repeated, nodding as if she had figured out the solution to a problem. "It was amazing enough to make you insanely jealous that he brought a date."

"What? I do *not* do jealous."

That was ludicrous. Ridiculous.

And totally true.

It annoyed her that Gabriel had brought a date. No, it annoyed her that Gabriel had the gall to kiss her and *then* bring a date as if nothing had happened. And she hated feeling jealous of other women. So naturally, it was all Gabriel's fault for putting her in this position.

Didn't this prove her point? He was a closed book. Someone who she really didn't know anything about. What if this *was* his long-term girlfriend? Or even a woman he was dating. It was the first she'd heard about her. And if that were the case and the blonde in the figure-hugging white dress *was* his secret girl-friend, what the hell was he doing sticking that skilled tongue of his down *her* throat?

"Who wears a white dress to a baby shower anyway?"

Sera spluttered, choking on her wine. "Jesus, Madds."

Maddie thumped her on the back for good measure.

"Just saying."

But in saying it, she felt mean and petty and catty, which put her in a bad mood because she took pride in being a woman's woman. And suddenly this *thing* between her and Gabriel was jeopardizing all of that. So again, it was his fault.

A few minutes later, when Ally walked over with Gabriel and the svelte blonde in tow, Maddie cautioned herself. Preparing to be polite, she straightened her shoulders. She was calm. Cool. Totally unaffected.

"Hey, I saw the food platters. Maryam did a fantastic job." Gabriel gestured to one of the beautifully decorated plates.

"Be sure to tell her yourself. She was worried we wouldn't have enough." Sera grinned.

Her friend's affection for the man made Maddie want to scowl. She schooled her features, realizing that—too late—she was scowling already, which put her in a greater distemper.

Naturally, it was his f—

"I'd like you both to meet Natasha."

"Hello." Natasha beamed, offering a quick wave.

Ally gestured to the blonde with the very white teeth. "Girls, Tasha is my prenatal yoga instructor I was telling you about." Ally smiled, glowing from the pampering she'd received the day before. It had done wonders for the mother-to-be. She was utterly radiant. Seeing her best friend like that took a little edge off her anger.

"I bumped into her outside the florist on my way here," Gabriel supplied. "Tasha and I used to go to the same gym."

"I don't have a car. I got on the wrong bus, so I asked Gabriel how to get here by public transport," Tasha added.

"And Gabriel kindly offered her a lift." Ally's subtle eyebrow raise made Maddie's back go rigid. She drained her glass.

"That's so lovely." Maddie had aimed for sincere, but it came out with a little too much sarcasm. "Excuse me."

She didn't mean for it to come out that way, but she was starting to act like a jealous fool. And that made her self-conscious, which in turn made her angry. The last thing she wanted to be was pissed off at her bestie's baby shower. Or, worse, to cause a scene. She would *not* be the person responsible for spoiling her friend's day. No chance.

Why the hell was she letting him get to her? It was madness. *This* was madness.

For the next few hours, Maddie mingled with the guests, determined to enjoy herself and ignore Gabriel completely. And with the crowd gathered, it was an easy feat. She chatted with friends, helped with serving drinks and food, so by the time they had played a few baby shower games and cut the cake, she'd managed to work off her annoyance.

She had a lovely buzz going from the booze, which needed to be offset by some more food.

Maddie stood at one of the many dedicated food stations, deciding what delectable pastry she wanted to eat, when she felt *him* beside her. That damn prickling sensation along her spine was back again, a telltale sign that he was close.

Surely another glass of Champagne would solve that problem.

"Great baby shower."

"Mm-hmm." Maddie chewed on square of pastry with honeyed figs and feta cheese. She licked her thumb and finger, savoring the burst of flavor.

"That looks good."

Maddie swallowed, almost choking. That wasn't his polite voice, the one he used in company. *This* was his *other* voice. Lower, deeper . . . intimate. It was the tone he'd used after he'd kissed her.

"It is. You should try it."

"I prefer watching you eat it."

Maddie pressed her lips together, not sure of what to say. She felt the fig lodge in the back of her throat. And her body, her damned horn-bag of a body seemed to light up at his words.

"Great." She winced at her tone. Still carrying some of the mad, it seemed. "Why are you here?" Maddie blurted out, turning to face him. God, he looked good. And surprised.

"Is this a trick question? I was invited."

"No, no." Maddie waved her hand around. "Why are you over here. Talking to me?"

"Am I not allowed to talk to you?"

"You don't really like me."

"What makes you say that?"

"Because you spend most of your time either putting up boundaries or making me feel like I don't do anything right. All your Post-it Notes. All your comments for improvement. The way you didn't even tell me you were bringing a date."

"Natasha?" He looked shocked. "I told you, Natasha is a friend."

"Well, you looked a bit more than friendly today."

"How would you know that? You've been dodging me all afternoon."

"I know what I saw. Not that it's any of my business. Nothing seems to be when it comes to you. But I suppose we're not friends, so it doesn't really matter."

Gabriel stepped closer. "I don't hate you."

"Oh really? What do you feel then, if not hate?"

"You make me . . ." He looked out over her shoulder. She could see the emotions play over his face.

"What? Why don't you ever say what you mean?"

"You make me—"

"Spit it out, Gabriel."

"When I'm with you, when you're near me . . ." His eyes were cloudy now and intense, so intense, she had to keep still, afraid she would burn if she so much as budged an inch. "I feel on fire."

Maddie felt the heat of his words sear through her clothes. His voice was low and his admission, almost painful. The words coated the air, surrounding them with something that was dangerous, electric. And so very forbidden.

She wasn't expecting that. She also wasn't expecting her reaction. All that heat, all that awareness seemed to flood her senses. She wasn't supposed to feel anything but loathing for him. Right?

But even that old argument was beginning to sound fake.

"Oh."

Gabriel's eyes glinted. "Is that all you have to say? 'Oh'?"

Maddie swallowed. She was stunned. Speechless. What was a woman supposed to say to that? It made no sense. But sense she still had, it seemed, and the ol' familiar doubt wormed its way through. "Are you playing me?"

"Excuse me?"

"I mean . . . is it a good fire or a bad fire? Are you messing with me?"

"I think those glasses of Champagne have gone to your head."

"Don't speak to me that way." Maddie felt like an idiot, and because of it, she turned from him, away from the chatter and all the people, stalking out of the house and into the cold winter's day to the far side of the garden. She paced behind the small shed, sheltered from view.

She needed to get away because—God help her—the next thing she wanted to do was scream at him. Or kiss him. Or both.

She didn't know how to handle this. He wasn't supposed to flirt with her, or hell, even show any interest in her at all.

When she heard his footsteps approach, she tried her best to even out her breathing. She might as well have been sucking in air through a paper straw.

"You can't run away." He glared, blocking her escape.

"I don't have to listen to you."

"Yes, you damn well do."

"Stop being so bossy."

"Stop acting so stubborn."

"Oh *please*, I'm standing up for myself. You know, you've not been able to say a kind word to me from the moment we met."

"You were rude to *me*, if I recall."

Shut up, Madds. It doesn't matter anymore. Just walk away. Walk. Away.

But she stood tall and ground her feet firmly in place. "When you first came to Woodbury High, we had a staff briefing to introduce you to everyone. Do you recall? No? Well, I do. I tried for a solid ten minutes to talk to you, to make you feel welcome, but you barely said two words to me. Then, *then*, you excused yourself while I was mid-conversation, just up and left—"

"I'm sure I had a good reason."

"So you're justifying being rude to me?"

"I apologize if I was curt."

"Oh no, it's not just that day." Maddie tossed back her hair, bracelets dancing. "From then on, you were Mr. Freeze. You barely looked at me, let alone spoke to me. How about the times you deigned to show up at our English faculty meetings only to shut down my ideas."

"We had a budget that we had to stick to. I was only pointing out things cost money. That there are processes we have to go through to—"

"You only ever open your mouth to correct me."

"I thought you would appreciate constructive criticism."

"From textbook ideas to end of year activities, all you ever do is focus on the problems."

"Excuse me if I offer suggestions that are pragmatic!"

"Oh, *yes*, the ever-reasoned Gabriel strikes again!"

"I only ever make the suggestions to see if we can help bring *your* ideas to life. You seem intent on taking everything I do or say the wrong way. It's infuriating at the best of times." His eyes sparked with annoyance.

Maddie continued, needing to get it off her chest. "And what about the first staff Christmas party?"

"I'd been invited as a guest. I knew nobody there, as I had just been appointed in the role, and Jacinta thought it would be a good idea to attend to get to know everyone informally."

"And you stood there, silent and disdainful, judging everyone rather than participating. Hell, I even asked you to dance and you rejected me—"

"You didn't get it."

"Get it? Oh, I got it, alright. Message delivered loud and clear: back away, Fitzgerald!"

Gabriel leaned closer, his voice barely controlled. "I said, 'every savage can dance.' I was quoting a book!"

The words hung in the air, heavy and dense like a fog.

Maddie shivered, feeling the cool breeze bite through her blouse.

"Excuse me?"

The blood rushed to her head, her heart pounding.

"I was quoting a classic. *Pride and*—"

"*Prejudice*," she whispered, unable to contain the mewling sound of distress.

"I thought you'd appreciate the reference, but you stormed off. I assumed you were three sheets to the wind and didn't find my humor funny."

"I'm more of a Brontë fan," she offered weakly. "I thought you said I was a savage and couldn't dance. Plus I *was* really drunk that night and the music was way too loud. I'd assumed from our initial meeting that you didn't like me. I didn't know you—it didn't click—"

"You know what they say about those who assume."

"Funny."

"I thought given you were an English teacher, you'd appreciate the reference. But I realize it didn't land the way I'd intended."

Jesus, he'd been trying to make a joke and she'd taken it for an insult. She remembered that night, only because she'd had a massive row with her mother before the party and had been determined to have fun despite her sour mood. Perhaps she'd been spoiling for a fight.

"You know, I always found Darcy too stuffy for Lizzy. Lizzy needed a man that had Bingley's good humor combined with Wickham's charm. A Bingham."

"Or a Wickley."

Maddie's mouth curved. She'd spent so long hating Gabriel that it shocked her to find that he could be charming and funny when he wanted to be.

And opposites did attract. Right?

Like a montage, all the interactions she'd ever had with

Gabriel replayed in her mind on a loop. How the hell had she gotten it so wrong? Since that first staff meeting, she had kept him at a distance, typecasting him as cold and boring, not someone she wanted to befriend. But that was because he *had* been reserved and so very distant, right from the start. Perhaps now that she was getting to know him, she was seeing him in a different light.

Was she more understanding of him now, or had he simply let his guard down? It was hard to tell.

Gabriel's lips twitched. "In hindsight, I can see I was curt when we first met, and for that I apologize. I had intended to get to know you that night a bit better. Granted, the comment was a bit cutting, but I had meant it in a tongue-in-cheek way."

"I wouldn't know with you."

Gabriel shrugged. "I admit it takes me a while to warm to people."

"There's a reason kids fear you."

"Respect me. There's a difference. To be honest, you're the one who seemed intent on hating me."

"*You* seemed intent on ignoring me. All you did was point out my faults. It doesn't make me think very highly of you when you do."

"That isn't my intention. Not now. Not ever." He was close now, closer than her frayed nerves could handle.

"It's how it comes across." She should have spoken with greater conviction, but she couldn't quite muster the fire. Something in his expression seemed to melt away the bite of her anger, turning it into something else entirely . . . something sinful. She cleared her throat. "That doesn't excuse the fact that you've been distant and stand-offish for years. You would barely speak, let alone look at me that first year."

"And you've been antagonistic and dismissive ever since. We both have our faults . . . But tell me, for future quoting reference." He spoke softly, his expression curious. "What's your favorite Brontë book?"

She found herself caught in his thrall. The closer he stood to her—and now she was at an intimate proximity to him—the stronger her need.

"*Wuthering Heights*," she murmured, as if spilling some kind of dark secret.

"Why?"

"Because even across time, space, and death, Heathcliff loved her. In his own feral, fucked-up way, he loved her. And it killed them both, but it was eternal. For always."

"That means a lot to you."

"I've never known that kind of love."

"Some would say it was obsession."

"It was once pure and honest. They were children when he joined their family. From then, he loved her, and as they grew, he was smitten by the woman who was free but bound by societal expectations. But it turned into something unhealthy. I get that. It wasn't a love story, but a cautionary tale really. They were both a little fucked up. But when I read it as a teenager, I was struck by this concept of loving eternally."

"So Austen isn't fucked up enough for you then?"

"*Persuasion* is the only Austen I can't seem to stop rereading."

"Interesting." Gabriel picked up a stray curl that had clung to her cheek. He held it in between his thumb and forefinger, examining it before setting it behind her ear. "Why?"

Jesus, the way he was talking to her, looking at her, it felt like they were discussing anything other than books. His voice, normally tight and commanding, was gentle. It was how a man spoke to his lover . . . his woman.

"Why do you want to know?"

"Generally, when a man kisses a woman and tells that

woman that she makes him feel like fire, it's because he's interested to know more."

"Oh."

"I want to know why." Every word was punctuated softly with emphasis. It seemed to make her pulse climb to impossible heights.

"Hmm . . ."

Gabriel shifted them both so that her back brushed against the shed wall. He leaned into her, resting his hand above her head. He smelled like heaven and sin.

"Tell me."

"Because she loved him, even when loving was hopeless and pointless and beyond reason. She loved him for years. And he loved her in turn. There's something potent about a man who isn't quite whole without the woman he loves. Something appealing about the fact that it would destroy him if he didn't have her love."

And just like that, his expression altered. One minute his eyes were heavy with longing, and the next he looked pained.

"What? What is it?"

"Nothing." He shifted back.

And when she blinked, the hurt was gone. As if she'd never seen it there in the first place. It bothered her, the way he'd shut off, the way he'd suddenly locked his feelings inside so she couldn't get to them. She wanted to press him for an answer, but she knew from experience that he wouldn't budge.

"So you value constancy," he continued, as if nothing had happened.

"Yes. I've never known a love like that. One that would surpass time and reason. I can't say I've known an unconditional love at all. I've seen it happen to my friends, sure, but I've not experienced it."

"There's still time."

"I'm not holding my breath for a Captain Wentworth to sail

home to me. Knowing my luck, I'd get a broken and vengeful Heathcliff instead."

"I thought you liked the wild ones."

"I can like the idea of him but be realistic enough to know he would be toxic as fuck if he were real."

"And what if he were real?"

"Heathcliff?"

"Perhaps a mix of Captain Wentworth and Heathcliff rolled into one. A Wentcliff."

"Or a Heathworth."

"What then?"

Maddie smiled, enjoying the game, the playful tugging of her imagination. "Then I suppose I'd be head over heels in love with the guy. And be having the best sex of my adult life."

"Best sex?"

"Heathcliff—all that wild trying to be tamed. Wentworth—been at sea for all those years. I can only imagine what that pent up sexual frustration would be like once unleashed."

"What if I told you that you could have it?"

"Have what?"

"The best sex of your adult life. The kind that makes you wet just thinking about it. What if I said I could make you come over and over again until you begged me to stop. What would you do?"

She strained, yearning for more than his words, more than the hot gaze that seemed to rake over her, through her, inside of her.

"I . . ." She leaned towards him but was abruptly brought back to reality when her phone began to buzz in her back pocket. "Fuck," she muttered, seeing it was Sera on the line. It was probably her cue to start plating up take-home boxes of food for the guests.

Maddie closed her eyes briefly, letting the disappointment and frustration seep through her before stepping to the side.

"I'm afraid that's my cue."

"A shame, Red. I was just getting started."

Maddie studied him for a moment before heading back to the party. Her body yearned for his touch. While she was shocked by his candor, a very naughty part of her also welcomed it.

What would she do with an offer like that? The answer to his question scared her more than she cared to admit.

CHAPTER TWENTY

"You do know that winter is the time to let your garden go to shit."

"Hello to you too, Harps."

"I'd ask to move inside, but I see you're working through something. So I'll bitch about being out in the cold instead."

"Can you put a patch over that third eye of yours when you come over?"

Harper laughed, loud and brassy. "Nice one. But no. I've a flight to catch soon but wanted to stop by to see how you were before I left."

Gabriel was weeding out the overgrown garden, enjoying the way his muscles strained and pulled against the overgrowth. He needed to be here, in his own home, doing the simple, mundane things. The very act of burying his hands in the damp earth calmed him.

He had peace. And after the tumult of his childhood, it was such a relief to have lazy afternoons of doing whatever he damn well pleased. Yes, it wasn't glitzy and glamorous, but it was his life and it was stable.

Wasn't that what he'd always wanted?

He had a great job, one where he was actually making a difference. He had friends, his own home, and yet . . .

Something was missing. Gabriel wasn't sure if it was because he'd spent most of his youth searching for the next thrill, the next high, that now he was moving in the slow lane, it didn't seem so exciting.

He'd had plenty of short-term, mutually enjoyable 'things' over the years. They hadn't been quite what he would call relationships, but they had satisfied him enough.

Was he ready for more?

Images of a fiery redhead flashed in his mind. What would her answer have been had they not been interrupted? He knew he'd crossed a line with her, but for the life of him, he couldn't seem to stop.

What would happen next week when they were back in the office? How would they behave during the school term?

"How's your dad?" Harper sat beside him. "Any improvement since last week?"

Gabriel shook his head. "Worse. They called me on Monday to say he has fluid in his lungs, that he was struggling to breathe."

"Jesus, Gabe, why didn't you call me?"

Gabriel shrugged.

"You need to talk about this shit and not pretend like it's all okay."

"Old habits."

"I thought you'd moved past them."

He had. For the most part. But unlike his best friend, when the shit hit the fan, he needed a bit of time to figure out his feelings before talking it through with someone.

"I'm so sorry, Gabe."

"The nurses said it's days, not weeks left. He's in palliative care."

"Fuck."

"Yeah, like he wasn't dealing with enough shit."

"Have you had a heart-to-heart talk?"

"Kind of. I see him every day, just to be with him. I finally spoke to him about Mom yesterday. He had a few moments of clarity, which was both nice and also painful. But I'm never going to get him back. Not that I had him back anyway. That chapter is done. The father I wanted or needed isn't there anymore."

"That shit is tough."

Gabriel ran his hands along the earth, letting it ground him, soothe him. "I can't help but think every time I leave that it might be the last time I see him alive." He leaned against her, seeking the comfort she offered. He wanted to cry, but no tears would come. He was oddly hollow.

"How are you feeling about what they said?"

Gabriel sat up, rubbing off the excess dirt from his hands. "Sad. Annoyed. Accepting. I guess I figured he'd have more time in him, but he's led a hard life. I can only hope that when it's his time, it's painless. I'm going to spend some time with him this evening. In case . . ."

"Forgetting can also be a blessing for some."

"Mmm. The guilt he carried around for so long nearly killed him."

"It was his burden to bear, Gabe."

"I know it."

"You did the best you could by him."

"Did I?"

"Don't let your grief blind you to the truth. No kid should have gone through that crap. I was there, I saw it all, so you can't bullshit me. And I know, without a doubt, that they both would be proud of everything you've achieved. You're no longer the wild guy I used to know."

"Happier and healthier for it."

"But you're holding back."

"Holding back what?"

"It's like you've put up this perfectly friendly wall around yourself, but you don't really let anyone in."

Gabriel scratched his chin, trying not to take offense. "Not the first time I've heard it."

"Maddie?"

"How'd you guess?"

"She's a smart woman."

"A pain in the ass."

"You have to say that. But there's more there. I saw the way you looked at her that day."

"With utter contempt and loathing?"

"Like you couldn't bear to see her in pain."

"It's not up for discussion."

"Which means it's important."

"Why are you at this?"

"Because I give a damn, Gabriel. You're in your mid-thirties without a significant relationship under your belt, and don't start blabbing about being perfectly content."

"I am perfectly content."

"But not wildly, joyously happy. Don't you *want* to have a partner?"

He looked across the yard to his house. "I have everything that I want right here."

"That big ol' house ain't gonna keep your heart happy, Gabe. Just because you let loose a little and bend those rules, doesn't mean you'll go back to who you were. You're locking away a part of you that needs to come out."

But wasn't that what scared him the most? Giving his heart to someone? Risking losing them? Ending up exactly like his father . . .

"So, is she a good kisser?"

He dug at the dirt, shaking his head.

"I love how you're still surprised that I know things. You guard yourself when you talk about her, so I know she means something to you."

"Maddie and I are . . ."

"What?"

Gabriel shook his head. He felt uncomfortable talking about her, but also uncertain. The woman made him feel like he was going to erupt any minute. He couldn't control his emotions around her. Which put him on edge. He'd already lost his control—twice—by kissing her.

And yet, he hadn't had enough of her, not nearly enough.

That he wanted more, that she made him feel those wicked, out of control feelings of old should have scared him away. But lately, it only compelled him to act. To take. To consume.

As much as he would like to say he was unaffected and move the subject along, he couldn't.

"Something has changed between us."

"That's good, isn't it?"

"I don't know anymore. As reserved as I am, I get the feeling that she's holding back."

To be fair, he knew that he was too. But there were things about his dad that were shameful. Things about his childhood that made him feel embarrassed. Would she judge him? Would he ever feel comfortable sharing that with her?

"So you're both wary of dipping your toe in, so what? That's normal given that at the start of the year, you were bickering like an old married couple. Why are you pretending that it isn't affecting you? That *she* isn't getting under your skin. All I'm saying is, she's bulldozing through that wall that you keep up. And I'm wondering why you think you need it anymore. Maybe the two of you aren't so dissimilar as you think." Harper patted him on his back and gave him a kiss to soothe the sting. "I gotta go. But I'll chat to you when I land. Keep me posted."

"I always do."

Gabriel watched her walk away. If anyone knew him, it was Harper. She was like a sister to him, and it was in times like these that he missed having her around. She often traveled to give readings to celebrities or wealthy clients when she wasn't at The Third Eye, and he would sometimes go weeks without seeing her.

But she never let him hide from the truth. Even as a kid, when he'd wanted to push down those emotions, Harper had been there to drag them back up, helping him through it all, like she was now.

He might not like what she had to say, but she was right. He *had* built those walls because they'd served a purpose. But he was settled now. He had a solid career. Solid paychecks. A very comfortable life.

Why was he still denying a part of himself that was there, beneath the surface?

Gabriel realized that once he gave himself permission to pursue Maddie in a way that fed his hunger, then all bets would be off. He would awaken a part of himself—a ravenous part— that once released, would never be harnessed again.

He couldn't help but wonder, would that really be such a bad thing?

The very next day, Gabriel's father passed away.

It was the call he'd been dreading. One he'd known was coming. When the nurses told him it was time to say goodbye, he wasn't sure what to feel. His father's past was catching up with him, it seemed. But even still, Gabriel had thought they had more time.

All he could think about that Wednesday afternoon as he walked down the corridor of Malton Mews was what Maddie had said about loving someone beyond time, even past death.

He knew his father had been heartbroken about his mom's death. But it wasn't until recently, until listening to Maddie's thoughts about love, that Gabriel was able to put himself in his father's shoes, to really try and empathize with him.

He'd had tried many times over the years to do it, but something had always held him back. He was ashamed to admit that he'd been blinded by his own grief for so long that it had eclipsed any empathy he'd felt for his broken father. For all his life, the death of his mother had been felt as a son. He hadn't permitted himself to feel sorry for his father, who had lost his wife. His grief had been all-encompassing; it had been selfish. Just like his father's.

Maybe it was because Gabriel had never had anyone in his life—aside from his best friend—that he was afraid to lose. Maybe he'd never believed that he would find anyone he could love in such an all-encompassing way. Whatever it was, the guilt and trauma associated with becoming a widower hadn't been something he ever allowed himself to think about, but he was beginning to see it now.

What had changed?

Gabriel rubbed the back of his neck. Maybe Harps had been right. Maybe the wall he'd built was crumbling to the ground. Because he couldn't imagine anything worse than losing a life partner.

He shook the image of the fiery redhead out of his mind. Her words plagued him but also enabled him to view his father in a new light.

Gabriel slowed his steps, taking in the antiseptic smell, the murmured voices.

He'd called Harps on his way over, leaving a voicemail message on her phone, even though she was at a conference thousands of miles away. Not that she could have helped anyway. His father was beyond that now.

Gabriel was able to face this on his own. He knew he would

be fine because he had to be fine. When things had turned to shit as a kid and his father had needed support, it had been him waking Leo up for work with burnt coffee and bacon, all in the hope that he would somehow become the father that he had needed.

But Leo hadn't seen past his own grief.

If Harper and her mother hadn't moved in next door when he'd been five, he would've been lost.

But Gabriel didn't want to carry the bitterness anymore. It would kill him like it was killing his father.

Taking a deep breath, steeling himself against the pain, Gabriel gently nudged the door open. He watched his father, whose eyes were closed, his body still, in the middle of the bed. His nurses, Silas and Eloise, were there. Silas was talking to him, and Eloise held his hand.

Last night, Leo had had a burst of energy, one which Eloise had said was normal and a sign he was near the end. Gabriel had at first been startled by it, but he'd been cautioned about this, told not to give into false hope.

"Gabriel." Eloise smiled, spotting him. "Would you like us to stay?"

He looked between the two nurses, whose calm assurance helped settle his nerves. "No. But thanks for taking care of him."

Silas clapped him on the back. "It's what we do. And Leo was happy here, in case you need to hear it."

Eloise approached them. "He's slipping in and out. His body is doing what it needs to right now, so it's time we let that happen. Speak to him, do what makes you comfortable. We'll be outside and will keep the door open."

"Thanks."

Alone with his father, Gabriel sat at the edge of the bed and held his hand. At first, he simply watched his face, lined and drawn. It was a face that could light up a room—that was one thing he'd always wanted more of growing up: his father's smile. But Gabriel didn't need a trip down memory lane right now. He needed to be present.

"It's been a long time coming, Dad. But I know you'll be close to seeing Mom again. Tell her—" His throat closed over. "Tell her I miss her. I've always missed her."

His father didn't move. Didn't react. He wasn't even certain that he could hear him. But he spoke anyway, his heart aching.

"And I'll miss you, too. I spent so long wishing for things to be different. I know you were broken when Mom died. You can't blame yourself for something that happened so long ago. But I want you to know, I don't blame you. It was an accident."

"Gabriel." It was a garbled whisper. A final plea.

"I'm right here, Dad." He gripped his hand harder, the tears blurring his vision.

"I'm sorry. I'm sorry, son."

"It's okay." His throat closed over, choking his words. "I forgive you. For everything. You did the best you could. I get that now. I didn't before, and I'm sorry for it. But you don't need to worry anymore. You can let go now."

"I love you, son."

Gabriel started when his father inhaled, the noise loud and raspy. The harsh sound frightened him, a herald of death. And he sat there helplessly, holding his father's hand, knowing that there was nothing he could do to prevent it.

He leaned even closer, hoping that there was no pain, hoping to offer him comfort.

Gabriel kissed Leo on his forehead and whispered something he hadn't uttered in years.

"I love you, too, Dad. You can let go now. I've got you. I'm here. I'm right here."

"Annabelle."

And when his father took his final breath as the weak winter sun filtered through the windows, Gabriel held on. He clung to his dad as he once had as a child and allowed the tears to fall.

Gabriel held his father's lifeless body for a long time after he passed. And the very act of holding on allowed him, finally, to let go.

CHAPTER TWENTY-ONE

Maddie stood in Gabriel's living room that Saturday afternoon along with at least a hundred other mourners who had come to pay their respects to Leo Rossi. She wasn't sure what to expect, but a crowded house hadn't been one of them.

Attending the funeral, watching Gabriel's stoic face—hardened against any emotion—had been difficult. But Maddie hadn't expected fear to sit alongside her sympathy today. It had crept up on her at the cemetery, seizing her body with terrifying scenarios of her own father's mortality. How much time did she have left with him? He might be alive, but was he well?

Maddie bit her lip, understanding why Gabriel had offered to help her find her dad.

Even though a part of her was afraid of the answers she'd find, attending the funeral today was the reminder she'd needed. She wouldn't let fear stop her. She was going to go back to his last known address, the one she had on her letter, and find him.

"It was good of you to come along."

Maddie turned to see Harper beside her, brown eyes warm, her hair pulled back in a low bun.

What had Gabriel told her? Surely she knew what had happened between them.

"I thought he might need some extra support. A few of us from work are here." Maddie had lost Jack and Sera in the crowd, while Ally and Owen had left not long after the funeral. Ally was waddling now and in a hurry to have the baby born despite her due date. "I didn't realize there'd be so many people."

"How much has he told you about Leo?" Harper motioned for her to follow her down the hall to the kitchen. Finding a spare few chairs lined against the windows in the far corner, they sat down. The table on the opposite side of the room was positively overflowing with food. And crammed with people.

"Not much. You know Gabriel, a man of few words."

"Sometimes to his own detriment."

Maddie fiddled with her chignon, tucking in a stray curl before turning to Harper. "What was Gabriel's dad like?"

"Distant."

"Oh."

"Don't get me wrong, he was a captivating man. I mean, model good looks, a parade of women on his arm, the type of person who would charm a snake into submission, you know?"

"But?"

"But . . ." She lowered her voice to a whisper. "I know I'll be struck by lightning for speaking ill of the dead, but Leo was a dick. God forgive me, that's putting it mildly. He wasn't a great dad, or even a present one.

"I met Gabe when we were both five. It had only been six or seven months since his mom had died at that stage. My mom and I had moved into the apartment next door to him. And it took Gabe a long time before he even admitted that his dad left him to fend for himself in the evenings."

"What?"

"His dad was . . . absent, a lot. Look, Leo was a man grieving his wife's death and that grief consumed him. But it also ruined his relationship with his son." Harper studied the people milling about. "You know, Gabriel wasn't always so reserved. As a kid, he'd been sad, sure, but there was a warmth there, beneath the wariness. I was lucky enough to see it before he became so guarded. But with his dad the way he was, Gabriel had no choice but to harden up."

"But not with you." Maddie played with her rose-gold bracelet and wondered why it was Gabriel's best friend that was telling her all this. It also struck her that Gabriel might not want her to know. Which hurt. Because she wanted to know, not because of her innate curiosity, but out of a need to know *him*.

"No. Not with me. Leo didn't exactly lead a lifestyle suitable for little boys who'd lost their moms."

Maddie frowned. "How did he—"

"Why am I not surprised to see you two conspirators huddled together?"

Harper simply grinned.

"Trading secrets, Harps?"

"Wouldn't you like to know?"

"I dislike being gossiped about." Gabriel had lost his tie and the top button of his shirt was undone. The black suit accentuated his dark good looks. Maddie bit her lip. It was wrong to lust after someone when they had just buried a loved one.

And yet . . .

"I would have thought, given your job as VP, that you were used to it." Maddie smiled sweetly.

Gabriel was about to answer when he was called away by an older couple wanting to offer their condolences.

Harper giggled, showing Maddie an S.O.S text from her new boyfriend, Eric, who was still stuck talking to an overly affectionate octogenarian on the lookout for husband number four.

"I better go rescue him. But listen, I know you and Gabriel had your differences, but I think you'll find you've a lot more in common than you think."

"Hey—before you go . . ."

"What is it?"

"The guy you were talking about . . . at my reading. Was that —did you mean Gabriel?"

Harper grinned. "I think you know the answer to that." And before she could grill her any further, she left.

In need of some air, Maddie wandered out of the house to the far side of the yard. It was a question that had bothered her since the reading. But the answer didn't make any sense. The man Harper had spoken of was meant to be her soulmate. The thought that Gabriel was the man of her dreams freaked her out a little. Surely, Harper was wrong.

Pushing it out of her mind, Maddie focused on the throng of mourners milling about. There seemed to be a lot of fashionable people who had shown up to his dad's funeral. People who had known him from his old modeling days. It seemed Leo had spent most of Gabriel's youth hopping from one party to another, from one event to the next, never stopping or slowing down.

Not one story she'd overheard ever featured anecdotes about Leo's abilities as a dad. It was all about his fun-loving personality and the wild parties, but nobody seemed to mention his role as a father. She now knew why.

Maddie couldn't help but wonder about Gabriel's life growing up. She was trying to put the pieces together of who he was, but it was fragmented.

She found a swinging tire beneath the trees at the base of the garden. She sat on it, rocking back and forth, wondering about her own father. It was a loose thread that she couldn't seem to live with, not with any deep sense of satisfaction.

She was lost in her own thoughts when Gabriel walked

towards her with a blanket and glass in hand. His eyes, normally so calm and steady, seemed like swirling storm clouds on an overcast day.

She was noticing so much more than she had before. Feeling so much more.

"What's up, Red? You look troubled."

Gabriel arranged the blanket around her shoulders, and Maddie couldn't help but feel a fluttery sensation in her belly. "Nothing that's important."

Gabriel sat down on the bench beside the swing. He placed his glass of scotch on the grass then leaned back to look at the house.

"I bought this house when I moved to Woodbury High."

"Really?" She was surprised by his admission, but she waited patiently for more. She was beginning to understand how he operated. When Gabriel wanted to share, he took his time about it.

"The agent had just put it on the market, and I was one of the first to see it. I was barely halfway through the inspection when I knew I wanted it. Made some upgrades and moved in as soon as I could."

"It's a beautiful home."

"It's my sanctuary." He watched her. "I'm sure Harps told you my sob story."

Maddie shook her head. "She only told me what I already knew . . . or suspected."

"That my dad was a dick?"

"Something like that."

"Did she tell you about Mom?"

"No . . . only that you lost her as a little boy."

Gabriel nodded then sighed. "My mom—Annabelle—" He cleared his throat. "She drowned."

Maddie's stomach churned. "Oh. I'm so sorry." She slipped out of the tire swing, crossing to sit beside him on the bench.

She placed the blanket on her lap, offering the other end to him. "Gabriel, how awful."

"My dad was there."

"Shit."

"He blamed himself for her death. She was caught in a rip and exhausted herself trying to get out." Gabriel cleared his throat. "He'd been teaching her how to swim. His idea to do it in exchange for her teaching him how to read."

"Oh . . ."

"Dad was dyslexic and had neglectful parents of his own who thought he was thick. He made his living with his body and his good looks. Until he met Mom."

"She saw something in him."

"She did." Gabriel's smile was sad as he remembered. "He always said she made him better. She calmed him, made him slow down a little. But after she died, he never forgave himself and went off the rails. I lost my mom *and* dad on that day."

Maddie's heart twisted. She ached for the small boy, for all the pain Gabriel had to deal with even today. She knew that kind of hurting didn't go away.

Perhaps they did have more in common than she initially thought.

Her eyes stung. "I'm so sorry, Gabriel."

"So am I. And I couldn't even hate him. Well, not lately. The dementia, as hard as it was for me, was a blessing for him. It took away those memories, took away his pain."

"Your bruise." She was beginning to understand everything now. To understand him.

"He would get aggressive when he slipped back. He would remember and then forget, and in forgetting he would get scared or startled. And I would bear the brunt of it."

"That's awful."

"I was angry at him for not being the dad I needed. He used to—"

"What?"

Gabriel shook his head, as if deciding the memory was too painful. "When I grew up, I did everything I could to rebel."

"You wanted him to notice you."

Gabriel nodded. "I wanted a father, a role model, but he was in so much pain that he couldn't cope with a kid, a reminder of what he'd lost. I never spoke to him, not in a way that counts. I was so bitter about all the shit in my childhood, I saw the world through angry eyes.

"I eventually got my shit together and realized—thanks to therapy—that I needed to have an honest conversation with him. We were slowly building a relationship again, but then he got sick and all that residual anger had nowhere to go. No outlet."

"Why did you choose teaching?"

"My parents." Gabriel shrugged. "Mom would always read to me whenever she was home from shifts. She was a nurse and was really big on education. Apparently, she took an interest in my learning, or at least that's what I can remember.

"I still have those camcorder recordings of her reading to me. Growing up with an illiterate dad, I was doing most of the heavy lifting. If there were forms to fill out or paperwork to read, I was the one having to do it. By the time I was six, I was reading chapter books. But the pain was too much, and by the time I hit my teens, I'd lost focus. Got out of control."

"How out of control?"

"Everything but drugs. Couldn't stand to touch the stuff. I saw what it did to people at my father's parties, and from a young age, I knew it wasn't for me. But unfortunately, I did everything else to feel alive and took everything else to numb the pain. Prescription pills are as bad as illegal drugs. Then I got clean and decided I needed every thrill-seeking activity except without proper harnesses, all because I wanted to push the limit."

"I'm surprised you're still alive."

"Broken a few bones skydiving, BASE jumping, racing cars. Lived in the jungles of South America for a while. For a time, I thought I'd get into stunt work. I was all over the place. But I wanted to feel something other than rage. The modeling paid the bills, but all I wanted to do was forget everything, so I'd go on week-long sex benders, booze-fueled parties that just made me tune out. I look back on that time and I wonder who the hell I was. I don't even recognize that person anymore. But I was young and stupid."

"How did you go from wild and free to stoic VP?"

"Nice rhyming."

"I try."

"I was in a small beachside town somewhere in Europe, can't recall where. I was hungover, waiting for the coffee to kick in, and I went into a bookstore. First book I saw was this little story about a kid and an owl my mother used to read to me as a child, and everything clicked into place. Not that I wanted to be a teacher at that stage, but I knew that I needed to change my life."

"A sign."

"I took it as such. The night before, I'd gone to the beach and asked my mother for guidance. I was desperate and so broken, I didn't care if it was stupid."

"Did you buy the book?"

"I did. That book reminded me of my roots. I was lost, not sure what in the world I was going to do next, and I knew I didn't want to keep drifting. The next day, I got my tattoo. *Per sempre*. I made a promise to myself to make the right decisions, and this tattoo is a reminder of that. I vowed that the woman I would marry would be someone I'd be with forever. I caught a plane back home the day after that, stayed with Harps until I found a rental, and six months later, I enrolled at the university."

"Do you ever regret it?"

"No. I wanted to do something good, something worthwhile with my life. And when I saw education on the list, it made sense. I saw how not being able to read screwed my dad over, and I wanted to do something to give back to society."

"That's decent, Gabriel."

"I didn't do it for brownie points."

"I'm not saying you did. But all the same, it's a good thing. You chose to do something that was difficult, and that takes guts."

Silence settled upon them; they both watched as mourners gathered in small groups to laugh and jest even in remembrance of death.

This was what she had wanted from him. This connection. It made her feel something she couldn't quite put her finger on.

"So have you made a decision?" Gabriel finished his drink before placing it on the ground again.

"About what?"

"Your dad."

"I have actually. And I can't believe I'm saying this, but you're right."

Gabriel frowned. "I think that's the second time I've ever heard you say that. Do you have a fever?"

"Funny."

"What am I right about specifically?"

"I get what you meant about not having the luxury of time with your father. I've lost so many years already, and I want to know if there's a relationship to salvage before it's too late."

"I think you're brave for doing this."

"Or stupid . . ."

"Has your mom called you?"

Maddie scoffed. "No chance of that happening."

"Will you call her?"

"Doubt it. I'm still angry with her, and I don't know if I'll ever forgive her for lying to me like that." Maddie fidgeted with the hem of her black dress. "You know, you're like the last person in the world I thought would understand my predicament."

"Is that meant to be a compliment?"

Maddie huffed. "For once, yes. It's coming out like a back-handed one. What I mean is, it's nice to be able to have someone in my life who understands. I appreciate the offer to help and your concern."

"You're welcome."

Maddie's head jerked back. "What? No counterargument?"

Gabriel shifted closer. "Not this time."

"Gabriel." She had meant it as a warning but found herself melting as he tucked an errant curl behind her ear. His fingers caressed her cheek, his warmth making her shiver.

He slipped off his jacket, draping it over her shoulders.

"I can't seem to stop myself from touching you."

"I find that hard to believe."

He cupped her cheeks then kissed her softly, the blanket between them falling to the ground.

"The things I would do to that mouth." He groaned. His thumb rubbed against her bottom lip, arousing her beyond measure.

"Gabriel, you can't say that."

"Can't I? Why not?"

"Because . . ."

He raised one dark eyebrow, his mouth curving wickedly. "Because it scares you? I never took you for a coward, Fitzgerald." Her temper flared. "There she is, my hellcat."

"I'm not your—"

"But you will be. Soon."

"You think very highly of yourself."

"No, I think highly of you. I want you, Maddie. I thought I made myself clear on that."

"You—I don't—"

"I don't kiss every woman I work with, you know."

"Aside from the fact that it's frowned upon and against workplace regulations."

"I've read the rules. And there's nothing to say two consenting adults can't fuck like bunnies if they want to."

"Since when do you break the rules?"

"When it comes to you, Maddie, I'd break every one of them a thousand times over." His eyes locked her in place, his expression heated. "Do you know how many times I've watched you in class, in those hot outfits you wear with those impossibly high heels? All I've wanted to do is bend you over your desk, slide down your panties, and fuck you until you begged me to make you come."

She drew back, breaking contact. The X-rated image frightened her because deep down inside, she knew she wanted it too.

"I—"

"There are plenty more of those fantasies. But I keep them locked away because I'm a grown man who knows better."

"So why now? Why break those rules?"

"Because I'm a grown man who knows better. And better is you, Red."

Maddie stared at him in shock. She heard the words that were coming out of his mouth, but her brain was processing everything as if on a delay.

"But you hate me," she whispered.

"Hate you?" Gabriel shook his head. "Sure, you're the most infuriating woman I've ever met, but I don't hate you."

"I'm so confused."

"*I want you*, Maddie. And from the way you've kissed me back, I think you want me too."

I do. She wanted to say it, but for the first time couldn't find the courage. *I do want you. More than I should. More than you'll know.*

Gabriel continued. "I think this is the part where we raise the white flag."

"Surrender? Never."

He smirked. "Coward. Look, we got off on the wrong foot, and we've both had our moments, but something has shifted between us. I've made my intentions clear, but I want to know how you feel. You never answered my question the other week. At Ally's baby shower."

"Gabriel . . ."

He studied her for a moment, his eyes heated. Whatever it was he saw made him stand.

"I won't push. That's not my style. But I want to take this thing between us to the next level. I want you, Maddie. But only if you say you want me too. Think about it."

As she watched him walk away, shoulders hunched against the biting breeze, Maddie wasn't sure what to think, but she damn well knew how she felt.

And it scared the hell out of her.

CHAPTER TWENTY-TWO

"Hey, what gives?" Maddie poked her head in Gabriel's office then stepped inside. "You're supposed to be on leave this week, not in the office. What the hell are you doing here? At half-past seven at night?"

He'd been ordered by the principal to take the first two weeks of term three off as personal leave. He'd lasted four days. What the fuck was he doing here anyway? He hadn't been thinking straight and needed to do something normal. He'd gone for a drive and the next thing he knew, he'd parked in front of the school. With nothing better to do, Gabriel had let himself in.

"My dad's dead."

Maddie frowned, walking over to where he sat. "I know. I was there at the funeral last weekend. But what are you doing *here*? I thought you're still on leave for another week."

Christ, it was only Thursday. What the fuck was he doing?

Gabriel blinked, taking in her concerned expression. She perched on the edge of his desk, bangles dancing at her wrists, her floral scent curling around him.

"I can't stay at home."

"You can't stay here either."

"I'm cutting my leave short. I don't need it."

"Like hell you don't. You look like you haven't slept since the funeral. Maybe you're in shock?"

"Not shock . . . I don't think. I know he's dead." Gabriel rubbed at his face. Maybe he was still in shock, but he didn't *feel* numb. If anything, he felt too much; he had no outlet for all that emotion. He craved contact in the same breath as he did isolation. It was driving him crazy.

"C'mon, you need to go home or get some fresh air before the cleaners kick us out. You could go—"

"Could you stop talking for a goddamn minute?"

Maddie flinched. "Your dad died, but that doesn't mean it gives you the right to act like an asshole."

"I can't think. I . . . stop for a minute."

It was building. He felt it, but he couldn't stop it, didn't think he wanted to, even though a part of him was screaming in protest.

"Why the hell should I?"

Gabriel stood, kicking back his chair in the process, and, in one fluid move, yanked her against him.

"So I can do this."

Gabriel's control snapped. He could almost hear it cracking in the air, a whiplash of lust. And while a part of him—the good, honest, *controlled* part of him—was hollering in protest, there was another side, an edgier, persistent one that was hot and hungry and desperate to feel something other than this smothering grief.

To touch.

To taste.

To let go of those fucking restraints he'd kept harnessed on his desire for so long. He didn't want to hold back anymore. He didn't think he could.

Slowly, deliberately, he walked her backwards towards the

small interview room sandwiched between the VP offices. It was private, out of sight from view, and perfect for what he wanted to do.

Gabriel broke them apart long enough to relish the shock and surprise that crossed her face. Beneath all of that was an awareness. A very elemental understanding of the electric spark that had ignited between them.

"Make no mistake, Maddie." He shut the door with his foot, not stopping until he had backed her into a wall.

She shouldn't smell this good.

She shouldn't look this good.

She had no right to tempt him.

"Gabriel? What are we doing?" she muttered between kisses.

"Do you want a fucking essay on it, or can I start pleasuring you?"

Her wicked laugh thrilled him.

"Have you thought about it?"

"About it?" she echoed.

He pulled back and then rejoiced in the passion that clouded her vision. "Sex. With me. Do you want me to keep going, Maddie? Or should I stop now?"

She blinked a few times. "Don't stop. I want you, Gabriel. Now."

A feral, elemental victory pounded in his blood. The pulsing beat of awareness throbbed between them, heavy and close. He was drawn to her eyes, bewitched by that mouth. How long had he hoped to see a lick of desire across her face rather than her usual disdain?

His ego was goading him to keep going, to take that flash of lust and stretch it until it reached the point of yearning. Of longing.

For him.

Gabriel ground his teeth together. Every inch of his body was hard.

"You feel so damn good, Maddie." She was lush and curvy, ripe for the taking. He simply couldn't help himself, and leaning in so that her heavy breasts pressed against his chest, he whispered, "Can you feel what you do to me?"

"I—"

Gabriel grinned, enjoying her stunned silence. He couldn't quite believe it himself, but he'd started something and by God he was going to finish it.

The need to claim her was a basic driving force, and because he wanted to, because he could, he breathed in her scent at the hollow of her throat, and it was like breathing in fire and ice at the same time. His blood burned, his body strained, but still he held back. He wanted her satisfaction, to feel her wet and sweet on his tongue. He needed it as much as he needed to breathe.

"Do you know what I want to do to you?" he whispered close, blowing against the dangling green stones that hung from her ears.

He watched her, the lovely way her mouth worked to speak, the way she swallowed then whispered, "What?"

"I want to start by tasting every inch of that sweet body of yours."

She trembled now. Trembled because of him. Trembled *for* him.

Fuck. Gabriel fisted his hands, hands that wanted to cup and caress and explore.

"Do you want it?" he pressed.

"Want . . ."

"No games, Red. Not now, not when you're pliant as a lamb and trembling against me."

A flash of fire burned in her eyes. Yes. *This* was what he craved. *This* was what he yearned to see when he touched her. Her spirit, her arousal.

He wanted to step into all that fire until he burned.

"I'm not trembling."

Gabriel grinned then waited a beat. "Yet."

He couldn't say who reacted first. But it was like a bolt of lightning, sudden and striking. She gripped his T-shirt, he pulled her close, and then that mouth, that glorious, soft, pink mouth was fused to his, and Gabriel couldn't see anything but her.

She overloaded his senses so that his tongue feasted and explored, his hands roamed and ravished, and still he wasn't satisfied. She tasted like peppermint and honey, and she kissed him back with equal force, equal strength, so that he was sure *he* was the one now trembling.

She nipped at his bottom lip, and he jerked against her. Fuck yes. He wanted the pain and the pleasure. He wanted her so damn bad, he would die if he didn't have her.

"Witch."

Her eyes flashed in satisfaction and the kiss turned feral. It was hard and urgent, and his hands sought more than just the lush outline of her hips or the curve of her ass. He wanted flesh.

Dragging her dress up to her waist, he groaned feeling smooth skin.

Maddie jerked. "I haven't shaved . . . down there."

He felt the soft thatch of curls on the edge of whatever dainty thing she was wearing, and he had to see.

Gabriel crouched down, drawn to the triangle of lace where auburn curls decorated the edge of her underwear, peeking out. And the contrast of the soft white skin of her thighs and the unbound curls sent him into overdrive.

"That's hot."

He heard her disbelieving huff.

"I want you unbound, natural, real. I want all of you."

He buried his face there, and she yelped. He wanted to

remember her smell. To imprint her to his soul until he could taste her on his mouth every fucking day for all time.

"I want to taste you, Maddie."

He looked up, struck by her beauty. When she murmured her agreement, he wasted no time in drawing down the scrap of lace.

Gabriel feasted.

The first long lick had her hips jerking. Straining. And the second left *him* seeing stars.

She moaned, soft and low, and he knew right at that moment that he would never be the same again. He would have her, and in having her, he would always want more.

She was his addiction. His salvation. His sin.

Maddie Fitzgerald belonged to him now.

God help him, but the old Gabriel—the one who had lived for heady thrills, the one who had longed to feel this way for a woman—resurfaced.

He took his time, parting the soft folds until he found her warm and wet. He stroked, reveling in the murmured words that spilled from her mouth.

Maddie gripped his hair, and he couldn't help himself. He wanted to tease and torture her for a little longer, to draw out her arousal until she begged him to fuck her. But more, he wanted to heighten her pleasure until she all but exploded around him.

Gabriel took a deep breath, calming himself, easing back on the ferocious hunger that made him want to devour her whole. Instead, he toyed with her pussy, circling her clit until she was rocking against his fingers, straining for her release.

He stopped and looked up at the way her mouth was parted, her cheeks flushed. His gut twisted. She was glorious. Breathtaking. He'd never seen anything so mesmerizing before in his life.

Maddie opened her eyes. "Why are you stopping?"

"You're stunning." He stared for long enough to see the shock on her face before giving her what she wanted.

His mouth worshipped her. His tongue punished. And Gabriel coaxed and cajoled, teased and touched until she panted his name. He smiled against her swollen clit, keeping her on the edge of her orgasm.

But when her thighs began to tremble, he continued in steady, measured strokes, maintaining the same persistent rhythm until she lost control. Panting and writhing against him, Maddie shattered around his mouth, coming with such abandon that he felt every bit of her pleasure course through him.

Gabriel stood then kissed her reverently. "Now you know how sweet you taste."

Twin marks of embarrassment stained her cheeks, and at that moment, Gabriel wished he were good at painting so he could capture the expression on her face.

He realized with sudden panic that there was more here than he'd thought.

Before he could succumb to the fear, Maddie gripped his hips, taking his zipper down slowly. He wasn't strong enough —not nearly selfless enough—to deny it. He'd dreamed about those lips around his cock, the way he would disappear deep inside of her mouth, fucking her until she gagged.

He tugged down her dress and bra, exposing her breasts, heavy and round. Her dark pink nipples strained for attention. He palmed them now, wanting to bury his face between her breasts, to fuck them until he came on her chest.

Maddie pushed him back against the wall, taking her time to tug down his jeans, freeing his cock. Her small gasp made him feel—stupidly—proud of what she saw.

He was harder than iron. Thick and long with wanting.

She teased him, just as he'd suspected she would. First with the tip of her finger, tracing his cock as if outlining it, and then eventually making her way down to where his balls sat heavy and full. So fucking full with the need to come, the need to hoist her up in his arms and slide his cock in all that wet heat.

This was his pain. This was what drove him to distraction—he was walking a tightrope—on one end there was control, the other abandon. He was equal parts both, pulled in either direction.

Right now, with those witchy eyes watching him, with that mouth soft and red from his kisses, he didn't fucking care. He wanted wild, craved reckless. He needed to let go. With her.

When Maddie took him in hand, stroking softly, building a steady rhythm, he gnashed his teeth together, taking deep breaths. She tugged at the length of him, palming his balls, squeezing and pulling until he thought he would die from the sensation. Happily fucking so.

But Gabriel waited. And watched.

"You're so hard, I think you might come on my face."

"I'd rather come in your dirty mouth and then on those glorious fucking tits."

"A marathon man, are we?"

"You have no idea what I can do, Red. Now blow me before I lose my fucking mind."

Maddie's eyes narrowed in mock annoyance. She stopped pleasuring him and he groaned. This woman was going to kill him. At this point, death by sex didn't seem a bad way to go.

"Say please."

"Hellion."

"*Please.*" She drew out the word, enjoying the power.

Fuck, she was glorious.

"Blow. Me."

She did, breathing air on his cock then smiling a smug, satisfied grin when he groaned.

"Very clever." He bunched his hands in her hair, tugging her head back.

"You need to say please, Gabriel."

"Or what?"

"Or I'll leave you hard for hours. You know I will."

"I don't doubt it. Do you get off on being in charge? Is your pussy wetter when you make me beg?"

"If you must know, I get off on sucking cock. Makes me think about the ways that I'll be getting fucked."

"Then I'll be a gentleman, for tonight. For you. *Please* will you suck my cock, queen?"

Maddie's laugh sent a quick thrill up his spine.

Glorious.

She didn't waste any time, taking him in her mouth, using her tongue at his tip.

"Maddie." He groaned, lost in her soft mouth. It was better than his fantasies. He was mesmerized by the sight of her, by the way she made him feel. The sensation left him lightheaded.

Gabriel watched her tits bounce as she sucked his cock, and he wanted those breasts in his mouth. He wanted to make her come over and over again until she could barely stand.

Watching her on her knees, her red hair trailing down her back, her shoulders and breasts bare to him, made him lose control. As his body clenched, he gripped her hair, groaning as he came inside of her warm mouth. Maddie drank every drop like a woman starved until there was nothing left.

And fuck if it didn't turn him on to see it. `

Gabriel was lost, wonderfully lost in her, and he wasn't sure what it all meant. With unsteady legs, he slumped down to the ground, propping himself against the wall beside her.

"I don't know what to say," Maddie whispered, wiping her lips.

"I'll take that as a win."

When she giggled in response, Gabriel felt like a king. He wanted to hear that sound over and over just as much as he needed to hear her pleasure.

He looked over at Maddie and something inside of him clicked into place. He didn't know what the hell it meant, but right there, sitting on the floor beside her, half-naked and a little sweaty, he was right where he wanted to be.

As crazy as it seemed, Gabriel was at that very moment blissfully happy.

What startled him the most was that he'd never felt this way before. What scared him even more was the thought that he might lose it.

CHAPTER TWENTY-THREE

"Hey," Gabriel whispered, crouching down beside her at the end of the row.

Maddie's heart galloped. It had been a week since their naughty romp at school. And every night since then, she'd spent alone and thinking of Gabriel. She wanted to have sex with him—full-on, go all the way sex—so bad she thought she'd scream from the sexual frustration. Every minute of waiting had proved to be torturous.

The dirty texts he'd sent her since then had only increased the pain.

And of course, seeing him at school had turned into some sexy, prolonged foreplay, to the point where she'd had to go home and get herself off every night this week.

Not that she would ever tell him that. The man had been walking around with a swagger since he'd returned to work, a week earlier than he'd planned. Not that she'd minded one bit. It seemed she couldn't quite get enough of seeing him. Maddie was certain that if she didn't get his cock in her vagina soon, she would break her vibrator from overuse.

The only reason she didn't turn up at his house in a trench

coat and six-inch heels was because it had only been two weeks since his dad's death. And even though *he* had been the one to come on to *her*, she knew that grief could make people go a little crazy sometimes. So she wouldn't push it.

Not yet anyway.

"You're late," she whispered back.

"Jacinta needed me to talk to Kaden's parents."

"Kaden Wood, the expelled kid?"

Gabriel nodded. "Don't ask."

When the principal required you to fight fires, then you best get your hose.

Her eyebrows shot up at his open collar. "Undressing for the occasion, are we?"

"If I don't have to wear a tie, I won't."

"Huh. And here I thought you were a sucker for punishment."

"In time you'll find out just how wild I can be."

Maddie stared. She wasn't expecting that. "Well, well, well. You think you know a VP."

"Buckle up, Red. You're in for a ride."

Great. Now she had images of Gabriel tongue-fucking her on a loop in her brain. She recalled her sex dream last term and knew, without a doubt, that reality was far more satisfying than any fantasy.

Who knew he had all this passion? For her. It beggared belief.

But Maddie was torn between joy and fear. Whatever it was that was happening between them was sending her body into overdrive. She wasn't sure about where they stood now. The lines were blurred and the clear-cut boundaries that were once in place had vanished.

"The great Maddie Fitzgerald speechless?" He raised an eyebrow, but Maddie refused to smile.

"Not choosing to dignify that with a response."

"Sucker."

"Shh, I'm listening."

But she wasn't, or couldn't, not fully. She was too aware of the warmth of the man beside her. The way he would whisper a comment every now and then or shift as he wrote down notes. When a chair became available a few rows ahead, she breathed a sigh of relief. The farther away from her, the better.

But now she was noticing something different. The way the women around him sat up straighter, fluffing their hair or adjusting their clothes. Preening themselves. For Gabriel.

Maddie gripped the edges of her electronic notebook a little tighter. She put the stylus back in its holder, afraid that it might snap in her hand.

Was she meant to endure this now?

But Gabriel seemed oblivious to the ripple around him, not once taking his eyes off the presenters at the front of the room. Not only was Gabriel one of the very few men present tonight— a common plight in English departments—but he was the only startlingly good-looking one.

And he was hers.

She squirmed at the possessive thought.

The idea that women were lusting after him shouldn't bother her. But it did. How many women had he slept with? Had he ever been in love? Did he want a proper relationship, or were they just fuck buddies?

Give the guy the benefit of the doubt, Madds.

But her knee-jerk response was to see Gabriel in a negative light: cold, robotic, inhuman. It had served her well . . . but now? Now she was beginning to realize she didn't know him— the real him—at all. Sure, they were getting to know each other, but that was a slow process. And it wasn't like she was going to rush into anything deep and meaningful. This was just fooling around. Right?

As the examiners fiddled with the PowerPoint, Maddie

watched the 'Gabriel effect' take hold. The woman next to him whispered to her colleague, who whispered to another colleague, who had the attention of another woman in front of them, who had turned around and then nudged her friend. All of a sudden, there were covert glances and murmurs, and by the time the examiners asked people to break up into smaller groups to take part in moderation and networking, there was a positive wave of female pheromones on alert for the unicorn in the room.

The hot English teacher unicorn.

No doubt the fact that he wasn't wearing a ring as well had put the women on hyper-alert.

Maddie was about to approach him when he seemed to be swallowed whole by the sea of women chatting and batting their eyelashes at him, vying for his attention. Biting back a disgusted sigh, Maddie walked in the opposite direction, only to hear the rising cacophony of what was no doubt more women swarming around him.

It was distracting.

Maddie introduced herself to a group of men and women whom she didn't know. Some were from private schools and other public, but they were all focused on figuring out what they needed to do to understand the exam assessment criteria.

Unlike some people.

Maddie looked over at Gabriel and tutted. What was meant to be two tables had turned into one large one, with Gabriel at the head. She watched now with a mixture of annoyance and fascination as he led the group in their discussion. He was comfortable, clearly in control of the situation, and holding every single female's gaze in the process.

Maddie dragged her eyes away, intent on focusing on the essay on her electronic notebook. She was already spending way too much time with the man, so much so that she understood his mannerisms and gestures.

Like now, when he pressed his lips together, his eyes narrowing. Clearly whatever the brunette was saying wasn't something he agreed with and he was wondering how best to cut her in two. She'd seen that expression countless times, usually aimed in her direction.

Or now, when he leaned back, crossing his arms on his chest, a sure sign that he was gathering his thoughts to lash out with some whopper of a reply.

Maddie jumped when one of the examiners came by to check they had the right sample on their devices, placing one or two paper copies for those who came without.

What the hell was she doing? *Focus, Madds.*

Once they began reading the sample essay, Maddie's attention shifted to the task at hand. The examiners had shown them a sample paper rich in ideas. It only had a smattering of evidence here and there, but the student clearly knew the text, and the way in which they were incorporating the evidence that was there was seamless. It was an essay she would have expected from some of their students. How heavily would they be penalized though?

"Thoughts?" Maddie prompted after their ten minutes were up.

Some people were convinced it should score highly because of the sophistication of the ideas, but Maddie wasn't so sure with the lack of detailed evidence. Eventually, when all samples and groups were completed, the examiners revealed the ranges.

It prompted some debate, but on the whole, most people were on target with their range, but what was arguable was the specific mark allocated to the paper. How much to reward? What were the examiners looking for when they read an exemplary piece?

By the time the evening ended, Maddie felt a lot more comfortable about what to look for in developing their students' skills for the end of year exam.

She was also confident that their focus for the past few years on developing interpretations and ideas was going to reward them, but their students were still struggling to get their detailed analyses up to par.

After networking with a few schools and picking their brains, Maddie was ready to call it a night.

She was halfway out of the door before a hand on her arm halted her progress.

"Hey, wait up."

Maddie jolted as Gabriel's hand brushed the side of her breast. It had been accidental, but Maddie hadn't expected the little pitter patter of awareness that danced across her chest because of it. Didn't expect or care for it one bit.

"You were preoccupied, so I thought I'd see you tomorrow."

"You're angry."

"No, I'm not." Maddie walked away, trying her best to school her features.

"You are," he said, catching up with her. "And I'm intrigued to know why. One of the examiners piss you off?"

"No, actually." Maddie stomped down the stairs. "You did."

"Me?" Gabriel held open the door for her as they left the building. "I thought you'd be used to that by now."

"Me too."

"How could I have possibly pissed you off? I barely spoke to you all night."

"No, you didn't." Maddie whirled to face him, standing in front of her car. "But you did flirt with every other woman in the room instead."

Gabriel's smug smile had her baring her teeth.

"Easy, Red."

"You're insufferable! You know that? The whole point of this evening was to network with other schools, to take in information for the end of year exam, not to hit on every attractive woman you could find!"

"I *was* networking."

"Oh, come on, I could see their pheromones from across the room."

"You're mixing metaphors."

"Screw you, Steele."

Maddie jabbed the button of her car remote then growled when Gabriel's hand shot out, keeping the door closed.

She whirled around to face him, startled by his proximity.

"So what if I did flirt with every woman. What's it to you?"

"It means nothing to me."

"Clearly." His sarcastic drawl made her see red.

"Except that it's grossly unprofessional in this setting and so typical."

"Uh-huh."

"Surely you can go to a club for that?"

"Why would I when I have women throwing themselves at me?"

"Uh!"

Gabriel studied her and then grinned. "You're jealous."

Maddie scoffed, unable to answer for a good minute. "I am not."

She recalled the way he'd touched her, as if he'd known the parts that would make her sigh or scream. Like he'd known and touched her before.

A man didn't get to that expert level of skill without practice.

So who were the women before?

A tiny sliver of jealousy left her feeling annoyed. She didn't *do* jealous. It was a wasted emotion, and she'd never really liked anyone that much to let it get to her. Not that she liked Gabriel. Not like that. They weren't even exclusive with one another. The very idea only added fuel to the fire.

Gabriel leaned forward, the open collar of his shirt seeming to draw her gaze. Anything better than looking at his eyes. Not so pale gray anymore. They were almost a light blue.

"I know you're jealous." Gabriel leaned closer still. "Why else would you care who I'm flirting with? Why should it even matter to you?"

"I said it doesn't." Maddie's voice was shakier than she cared to admit. "I was just saying . . ."

"I'm listening."

"It was unprofessional." Maddie pressed her backside against the car door. "Why are you so damn close?"

"Because, Maddie, if I wanted to flirt, I would flirt. And the woman, or women . . ." He paused a hair's breadth from her lips. "Would be under no doubt that I wanted them. That I craved them. Make no mistake, Red. If I want a woman, I'm going after her, and she's going to feel every inch of my desire when I do."

Maddie swallowed. Waited with bated breath.

Everything inside of her was screaming to push him away, but all she could do was grip her car keys until they marked her hand.

"I wasn't flirting. Because contrary to your opinion of me, I don't have the hottest oral sex with one woman one week, just to go hit on another the next. But let's be clear so there's no doubt in that fiery mind of yours. When I'm eating you out, when my cock is buried deep inside of you, there *is* no one else. Understood?"

Maddie tilted her chin up, embarrassment filtering through her anger. "Who says your cock will go anywhere near m—"

Gabriel's laughter cut off her remaining reply. "C'mon, Maddie. We both know where this is going. So when it happens, and I say *when,* it'll be because we're both ready for it."

"What if I'm never ready?"

Bitch, please!

Gabriel pressed his hips against hers and she felt his rigid length bulging against his trousers.

"Then I'll be walking around with blue balls for a very long time."

Despite her foul mood, Maddie laughed. "Good."

"Thought you'd like that, you vixen. Ultimately, whether we go beyond amazing oral sex is up to you, Fitzgerald." Gabriel pulled away, and it was as if all the oxygen in the world rushed back into her lungs.

"Me?"

"I made the first move. And in answer to your earlier accusation, I did get a whole heap of contact details from *platonic* women. That way we can liaise with a few of their schools to do some close analysis work. A couple are studying the same texts, with full units mapped out. I thought that would be of use."

Maddie nodded, feeling on uncertain ground, unsure of how to proceed or what to say.

In short, she felt like an idiot.

"But we can talk about all that tomorrow. At work."

"Tomorrow."

Gabriel stepped back, motioning for her to proceed.

She glanced at him and gritted her teeth at his smug expression.

Bastard.

Maddie yanked open her door and without so much as a glance in the rearview mirror, she drove home.

CHAPTER TWENTY-FOUR

"*I*f someone told me six months ago that you'd be the person sitting beside me on the day I'd be reunited with my dad, I would've laughed in their face."

"Ouch."

Maddie sat in Gabriel's car, questioning her impulsive decision to go find her father when they should have been moderating student essays.

"Sorry, that was mean. I'm bitchy when I'm nervous."

"No comment."

Maddie nudged him. "Maybe we should go back to my place."

"I stand by my earlier idea of cross-marking essays naked, but it's your call."

"Naughty, but no. After last week's seminar, we definitely need to be on the same page with these essay gradings. Which I promise we'll get started on as soon as I satisfy my curiosity and see whether my dad is living in that apartment." She jerked her head towards the block of flats behind her. "Sorry I dragged you into this. I don't know what got into me."

"You don't need to explain."

As soon as Gabriel had walked into her apartment that Saturday morning, she'd felt an overwhelming urge to take him to find her dad. She couldn't explain it, but all she knew was that she wanted to see if Dermot was still at the address he'd given her. And she wanted Gabriel with her when she did.

"The last thing you need is getting involved in my twisted family dynamics."

Gabriel frowned at her. "I'm the president of the twisted family group. You know my childhood was far from picture perfect, so I think I'll be fine."

Maddie toyed with the letter in her hands. She had written it after deciding she was going to find her dad. In it contained all the things she wanted to tell him but couldn't say.

She looked up at Gabriel. Perhaps that was why she'd wanted him to come with her and not Ally or Sera. Perhaps it was because she'd known that he would understand and wouldn't judge her for it.

Or maybe she felt oddly comforted by his presence.

"I feel like there should be some magical arrow pointing to the apartment or momentous music playing in the background."

"I'd offer a beat, but I'm a terrible rapper."

Maddie gripped her phone.

Gabriel reached out to hold her hand. "Are you sure about this? Normally you don't miss an opportunity to roast me alive."

"Yes?"

"That should've been a reply, not a question."

"Mmm."

"You don't have to do this, you know."

"I want to." She pressed her hand on her stomach, willing the queasy feeling to disappear. "This situation is so weird. I kind of pictured it differently."

"As in, you were a kid when you found him again?"

"Well . . . yeah, but more like he was coming to find *me*."

Gabriel shifted back. "You can do this another time."

Maddie chewed on her lip. She hated being indecisive. It gave her a stomachache to stew over things. She either did something or she didn't; prevaricating was not good for her digestion.

"I can. But I don't want to."

"Okay."

Gabriel was calm, sitting behind the wheel as if he went to random people's apartments to find absent fathers every day. A bubble of hysterical laughter threatened to derail her focus. She would not fall apart. She was simply nervous as hell.

"What if he tells me to fuck off?"

"Then you come and get me."

Maddie clutched his arm. "What, you're not coming in?"

Gabriel frowned. "I thought you'd want to do this alone."

"Right. Yes. I do." Maddie breathed out. "And I don't."

"Say the word."

Maddie swallowed, studying the unassuming cream building. It looked like any other in the neighborhood outside of Melbourne's CBD. Nothing flashy, but not dilapidated and rundown. Her dad must be doing an okay job at life to be living here. Which was a good sign. She couldn't bear to think he'd been living in poverty. That would only make her feel ill.

She swallowed the fear. "What am I going to say?"

"Hi."

"Well done, Einstein. Then what?"

"I thought you'd have that figured out."

"I'm flying by the seat of my pants here, Steele."

"Give him your letter to start. Talk about what this means to you. I'm sure you'll think of something after that. You're not the type to be speechless."

"Smart ass. Okay, I'm going in."

She was about to turn when he caught her chin. The kiss was firm and with just enough heat to distract her.

"Good luck."

Maddie walked up the sidewalk, trying desperately to keep calm. Nerves were normal. She was going to meet her father for the first time in decades. She was bound to be jittery.

Maddie lifted her chin, squared her shoulders, and approached apartment number six. With shaking hands, she knocked on the door then waited.

She could hear the television in the background and the sound of plates and dishes. She smoothed down the fabric of her woolen dress, trying to keep calm. Finally, the door opened.

A little blond-haired boy, around seven or eight, answered.

"Hello?"

Maddie felt breathless. Children. She hadn't thought her father would have children or a new family. Surely he was too old for that? Maybe they were adopted? Why would she assume that she wouldn't have other siblings? Half-siblings.

She crouched down.

"Hi. Is your daddy here?"

"He's at work."

"Oh. Is your—"

"Martin! What did I say about opening the door to strangers?" A woman in sweatpants and a sports top came to the door. She wasn't much older than Maddie. On her arm was a fussy baby, its face covered in some kind of orange food.

"Sorry. Busy feeding this little bear some pumpkin. Can I help you?"

"Umm. I wanted to know if Dermot was home? Dermot Fitzgerald?"

The woman bounced the baby on her hip. "There's nobody here by that name."

Maddie felt relief and disappointment flood through her simultaneously. It left her a little lightheaded. "Are you sure?"

"Yes. My husband, Rick, is down at the aquarium."

"Umm, can I ask how old your husband is?"

The woman frowned. "Forty."

"Sorry, I think I have the wrong house. I . . . I'm looking for my father and I had this old address and . . ." Maddie sighed, feeling dejected.

"How long have you lived here?" Maddie jerked as Gabriel placed a hand on her back.

She breathed out, relieved that he was there.

"Oh, we've been here at least four years."

Maddie pressed her lips together as she noticed the woman fluffing back her blonde hair.

"And you wouldn't happen to know who the previous tenants were, would you?"

"Uh, no. But, oh wait, we do get mail that isn't ours on occasion. Wait here."

The woman disappeared and came back a few minutes later. "Sometimes people forget to cancel memberships and things."

Maddie took the mail, but the only name that was there was that of a Millicent Kenny.

"No, this isn't what we're after, but thanks anyway."

"Best of luck finding him."

Maddie nodded, walking back to the car with Gabriel. She sat in the passenger seat, letting it all sink in.

"Sorry," Gabriel offered, squeezing her shoulder.

"It's okay. I'm kind of relieved. Or disappointed. I don't know anymore."

"Give it some time to settle in. There are plenty of other ways to find him."

Maddie shrugged. She'd hyped herself up so much. She hadn't quite expected to walk away without answers.

"I don't know. Chasing dead ends for months at a time sounds pretty shitty. I feel a bit stupid now. He sent this letter to me when I was eighteen. It was a long shot to think he would still be living here."

"You know, you don't have to do it yourself. You can hire professional services."

"What, like a private investigator? Aren't they pricey?"

"Some can be. Others are pretty reasonable."

"Maybe I'll never find him."

"Let the disappointment settle. Then you can come back to the search with a plan."

"That ol' reason and logic."

"Hasn't failed me yet."

She wasn't so sure about that. "You haven't been using any of that logic when it comes to pursuing me."

Gabriel shifted, placing his arm on the back of her headrest. She felt a shiver of awareness, that familiar spark.

"I suppose I haven't . . . . I have a weakness for kissing beautiful women."

The guy was smooth when he wasn't being a pain in the ass.

"So you do this often, do you?"

"Not at all. Perhaps I should rephrase that. I seem to have a weakness for you."

She gasped, caught by the lovely sentiment, and then she was burning.

The kiss, initially gentle and soft, fast turned into something that spoke to every need inside of her. It was like she was caught in a storm, whipped around in a frenzy of fervor. His mouth drove her to distraction, his tongue teasing her until she strained forward, craving more contact.

As if she had spoken aloud, he speared his hand beneath her thighs, plucking her off her seat and onto his lap.

"I can't get enough of you," he whispered against her lips, squeezing her hips as he took his fill. Every part of her yearned for more. She wanted his hands on her, inside her. She needed to feel the weight of his body crushing her into her mattress.

Maddie gripped his hair, tugging at the dark strands, moaning when his tongue taunted her. She shivered as those hands ran up her back and then leisurely down again.

When they parted, chests heaving, she knew that he was just as aroused.

"I've wanted to do that for hours now," he murmured.

"I'm glad you did."

"If you sit on my lap for much longer, I'm going to coax you into the back seat of my car, and I don't think you'd appreciate that."

"Perhaps not . . . but I have a very comfortable bed in my apartment."

Gabriel studied her for a few moments. It was long enough to make her second-guess herself.

"What?" She huffed. "You're not going to make me beg, are you?"

Gabriel's mouth curved. "Tempting. Maybe later."

Her body vibrated gently, as she was thrilled by his words. Maddie shifted back to the passenger seat, heart pounding.

She couldn't analyze what was happening too closely. She didn't dare take a deeper look for fear of what she would find.

There would be time for thinking later. Right now, she was going to enjoy the anticipation of having a very skilled lover fuck her brains out.

She wouldn't have thought in a million years that said lover would be Gabriel. But now that it was going to happen, she didn't mind it one bit.

CHAPTER TWENTY-FIVE

It was totally normal to feel nervous. She was about to have proper, go all the way, fully naked and sweaty sex with Gabriel . . . . Maddie pressed a hand to her chest. Jesus, there was nothing in the world that was going to settle her nerves. Her heart bounced like a rabbit in her chest the whole car ride home.

If what they'd done in the office was anything to go by, then going the whole way was going to be epic.

Normally, she would be waxed and landing stripped, but after Gabriel's reaction to her *au naturale*, she found that it would be a waste to deprive the man of something that turned him on so much. It made her feel sexy to know he wanted her as she was.

Maddie placed her handbag and the letter for her dad on the kitchen counter, wondering how this would all play out, when Gabriel came up behind her, gripping her waist.

"I want you."

When he drew her back against his hard chest, she knew she'd been deluding herself with all her calming self-talk. She was unbelievably aroused and thrilled to have sex with him.

"I've been watching you all morning, wanting you."

Maddie breathed out slowly as his hands roamed across her belly and cupped her breasts. He squeezed, making a low rumble of satisfaction that vibrated through her. When he tweaked her nipples, she shivered, clit throbbing.

"Your breasts, enough of a glimpse in this dress to leave a man salivating for more. I want to devour you."

"Then what are you waiting for?"

He whipped her around now, watching her every reaction. His eyes were like the stormy sea, his expression hot, hungry. Suddenly, the knee-length, woolen dress she'd worn that day was stifling.

"You."

And his kisses, Jesus in heaven, his kisses were enough to drug her into submission. But she was eager and willing in her own right. She'd yearned for this kind of intensity. To have a man make her feel desirable and sexy. The way he looked at her, the way he touched her made her feel whole.

Gabriel gripped her ass, kneading it, teasing her until every other intrusive thought in her head melted away. She felt him jutting and hard against her and couldn't help but reach down to squeeze his thick length.

"Did I tell you that I find you sexy as fuck? The way you took my cock in your mouth was—" Gabriel groaned, gripping her tighter.

Maddie's pulse, already peaking, spiked again. "The way you talk to me . . ." She cleared her throat. "It's hot. It's like there are two Gabriels—and the bad one, the *wicked* one comes out every time you touch me."

"I mean every word. You gotta stop teasing me like that, *witch*, or I'm going to explode." He gripped her hand, drawing it up so he could bite at the tip of her finger.

"I don't mind watching you explode. We have all afternoon."

Gabriel grunted. "Then I better get started."

He whipped her back around so that she leaned over the kitchen counter. She yelped when he smacked her ass, then moaned as his hands trailed up over her tights.

"How much do you like these tights?"

Maddie frowned for a moment. "Not that much."

"Good."

She gasped as he ripped them, rending it in two so that there was nothing left to cover her crotch or ass. A thrill shot through her, adrenaline pumping.

He muttered an approval at her underwear. "Black lace."

"I love how it feels on my body. How it looks."

"That makes two. I can't decide whether I want to fuck you naked or half-dressed." He leaned against her, chest pressing against her back. "It makes me hard to see you like this."

He slipped his finger inside her panties, rubbing at her swollen clit.

"Oh."

"Come on my fingers."

"Is that an order, *boss*?"

"You'll be punished for that. Later."

Gabriel tugged her dress higher, bunching it at her waist. Her ass jiggled at the next smack.

"That ass. Jesus, you're perfection."

She blushed. Heaven help her, she blushed as if she were a schoolgirl speaking to her crush. She was a confident woman, and that confidence came from years of self-affirming love. But when Gabriel spoke to her like that, she felt something bloom inside.

Maddie rocked back and forth, desperate to come on his hand.

"You're so fucking ready, I could slide my cock inside that heat and fill you up."

"Not without protection." She moaned.

"I've come prepared this time."

Maddie squirmed as he continued to tease her, keeping up the steady beat, driving her a little wilder, a little wetter with each stroke.

"So why don't you fuck me, then? Right here." She gasped. "Right now."

"You love to run that mouth of yours, don't you, Maddie?"

He pressed harder, firmer, setting her pulse to a frenzy. Her body was so hot. She wanted him to rip off her dress and take her.

"I love to get what I want."

Gabriel stroked slowly. "And what is it that you want?"

"You."

He eased back, slowly taking off her ruined tights and lace panties. Maddie bit her tongue, stepping out of them. She would not beg. But oh, how she wanted to.

Before she could speak, he turned her around then gripped her waist and lifted her onto the counter.

"I want to tease you first."

"That's not nearly as fun."

"You'll change your mind about that soon enough."

She huffed. "You're so arrogant."

"Honest . . . and I have a confession to make." She didn't dare take her eyes off his handsome face.

"What is it?"

"I don't want to fuck you like that. Not the first time."

"Oh . . ." Maddie shivered.

"I have a fantasy of you riding me, your tits bouncing while I watch you work your hand on that pussy."

"Fuck."

"But first, I want to watch those juices drip on your kitchen counter. I want to smell you when I walk back into this room. You're wondering why, I can see the question in your eyes, and it's plain and simple really." He spread her legs wide, his voice seductive.

Gabriel rubbed at her clit again then inserted one long finger inside. He started slowly, keeping the motion steady until she was panting for more. For him.

"The answer," she whispered. "What is it?"

"Because I know how sweet you taste. And I want to be reminded of that again and again."

"That's . . . kinky."

Gabriel grinned, and it was like a transformation. His smile was charming, arresting, and she found herself wanting to see it again.

"I've a lot of kinks, Red. And you can bet we'll be christening every room in my house so I can surround myself with your scent. Fuck, I'm hard just thinking about it."

And he continued, torturing her with his hands then crouching lower to suck and lick until she was slick and wet. He moaned against her and the vibration had her scratching at the counter, desperate for purchase.

She was so overwhelmed by the need to come that she didn't care that she was spread-eagle, in an unflattering position. Gabriel was eating her up, literally.

"I can't help it. I want to torture you, but I'm afraid you're going to have to come," he muttered against her pussy, wicked and teasing.

The exquisite building began, the spirals of pleasure coiling tighter and tighter until she couldn't keep her eyes open any longer. He was relentless, plundering and pleasuring her with his tongue until she gripped his hair, shattering against his mouth. She shuddered, gasping for air as her orgasm crashed through her, sharp and sudden.

When her body grew limp, Gabriel stood, licking at his fingers, wiping his mouth. Maddie felt her cheeks redden.

"Think you can walk to your bedroom?"

"Not a chance."

His rumbling laugh warmed her. And with a contented grunt, he plucked her up off the counter. When he set her down, Maddie wasted no time in removing the rest of her clothes. As did he.

She liked her men big, and Gabriel lived up to those expectations. She ran her hands down his arms, stroking at his hard length.

"I want to fuck your mouth, Maddie. I need those lips wrapped around my cock. I've been dreaming about it since that evening in my office."

"I'm always up for an appetizer."

"Tell me if I'm being too rough."

A small lick of fear and excitement heightened her arousal. How rough was rough?

"I take no pleasure in hurting a woman. But every woman has her limit, and if this is going to be pleasurable for me, it means it needs to be pleasurable for you."

"I told you, I like sucking cock."

"We'll see about that. On the bed."

"Bossy in and out of the bedroom," she muttered, lying down.

"You love it." Gabriel climbed on top of her, shifting up to straddle her face, his cock hovering over her mouth. "Tap out, remember?"

"Just so you know, I'm going to imagine you fucking my pussy next."

"That mouth." Gabriel swore. "That dirty fucking mouth."

Maddie moaned as he thrust into her. He extended back out and made sure she was okay before entering her again, this time a little firmer, a little deeper.

She had a good gag reflex but knew he hadn't gone the full length, so she relaxed the back of her throat, moaning now.

He was muttering to her, dirty words, sweet words, words that left her wet and wanting.

Maddie grabbed his ass, encouraging him to keep going. It didn't take him long to pull out, his body taut, cock twitching. He looked at her in a way that made her heart pound erratically.

"Move to the end of the bed." He stood now, waiting proud and hard for her to respond.

Maddie blinked at the sudden change in position but scooted across.

"Let your head hang over the side a little. I want to watch your tits bounce. And while I'm face-fucking you, I want to see your hand disappear beneath those tight curls. But do you know what I really want, Maddie?"

She swallowed, watching him upside down. He bent to whisper in her ear, dragging her hair out from under her so it hung off the side of the bed in messy curls.

"What?"

"I want to hear the sound your pussy makes when you finger yourself."

"Like this?" Maddie teased, spreading her legs, fingers buried beneath her curls. Fuck, she was wet and desperate to have him inside her.

"Perfect."

When he entered her mouth this time, she writhed on the bed, inserting one finger inside of her. But it wasn't enough. She bunched her knees to her chest, inserting another few. She imagined his eyes raking over her body, and it made her feel sexy and desired.

"Your breasts . . . Jesus in heaven, they're perfection."

Gabriel continued thrusting and palmed her tits, tweaking and pinching her nipples until she was whimpering with need.

"Fuck." Gabriel pulled back, panting.

"What? No pearl necklace?"

"Not this time."

Gabriel reached in his jeans pocket for a condom, dragging it down over his glistening cock then lying down on the duvet. Maddie took out the lube from her bedside drawer, smearing it over him.

She swallowed, caught by his dark beauty, the very picture of masculinity as he lounged on her bed, arms behind his head, waiting for her with a hard-on. God, he was one sexy fucker.

"Giddy up, cowgirl." He smirked.

Maddie crawled her way towards him, loving the way his eyes slid over her swinging tits.

"You're so fucking sexy." Gabriel ran his hands up her thighs, pinching her hips before squeezing her tits. "You've got the sweetest, most sinful body I've seen. And I want to watch you fuck me, Red."

She hovered over him, shaking a little with anticipation. Slowly, exquisitely, she eased herself down onto his cock.

"Oh." She had no words for the stretching sensation. The heavy fullness inside of her. "Fuck, that feels amazing."

Maddie tipped her head back, rising and falling over him, taking her fill, torturing them both.

"Do you know how long I've wanted to do this?" Gabriel muttered, brushing the back of his knuckles on her nipples. The sensation was like bolts of lightning down her chest, powering through her body.

"How long?" She gasped, looking down at him now.

"Years."

The admission made her stiffen, and Gabriel took the opportunity to thrust beneath her, bouncing her tits, fucking her hard.

Maddie pinched his nipples in turn, still reeling from his confession.

"Hellcat."

"I thought you wanted *me* to fuck *you*, Steele."

She pressed down on his chest, riding his cock. Maddie

arched back, building the waves of arousal bit by bit until she thought she would die from the pleasure. But that need to come was overwhelming. When she tried to toy with her clit, Gabriel shoved her hand away.

"The pleasure's all mine," he ordered, his thumb working over her, matching her rhythm.

His desire for her was what brought her to the edge. The way he looked at her as if she were like no other woman in the world. The way he touched her like she was precious and price-less and . . . *his*.

Maddie's throat tightened. She wanted to be claimed. She wanted to be his. To be taken and touched and whole.

Maddie yearned to belong to someone. And the very thought of it overwhelmed her.

So when her orgasm built, dancing at the edges, teasing and goading her, she took that leap. She was so full of him, hard and slick and pumping in time to her unspoken rhythm, she couldn't seem to breathe. Greedily, eagerly, Maddie came over his cock with such force, she cried out. Shaking and shuddering, she let go, rejoicing in his firmness and her pliancy, allowing wave after wave to carry her to completion.

And when she was still coasting down, he took her higher again. Dragging her towards him, Gabriel buried his face in her breasts, biting and sucking at her nipples, pounding into her now with such speed, she had to grip his shoulders to hold on.

Rearing up, Gabriel held her, sitting upright, pounding her close. His arm was like a band of steel around her waist. He nuzzled at her breasts, groaning her name in between bites.

"Shit, Gabriel, don't make me come again."

"You're gonna fucking lose control on my cock, Red. You're gonna come because I tell you to fucking come."

And unbelievably so, Maddie did. The orgasm was different. It pulsed deep inside her, not as strong but there, heating her body, shocking her.

It was a pressure like no other, a pleasure that seemed to echo through her in a way that wasn't sharp and edgy, but a soft release. And with it came a trickling wetness.

"Oh my god." She gasped. She had never come without touching herself before. She'd also never squirted. She nearly passed out at the feeling.

"That's it. Come all over my cock."

Maddie shuddered, riding out her orgasm.

"Fuck yes." Gabriel groaned moments later, and she could feel him pulsing inside of her as he came. He buried his face in her neck, his body hard and slick with sweat.

All Maddie had the strength to do was hold on.

It had taken a considerable amount of time for her heartbeat to return to normal. More before she could string together a coherent sentence.

"You seemed surprised by that." Gabriel lazily ran his hand up and down her arm as she sprawled out on top of him. Apparently, he was a snuggler after sex. Who knew?

Maddie shifted back to watch his reaction. How much to reveal? How much did he already suspect?

"I've never . . ."

"What?"

She cleared her throat. "I've never come twice like that before . . . or even from just penetration."

Gabriel brushed back her hair, his eyes serious. "Was that your first time squirting?"

Maddie nodded. "You're going to get a big head about this, aren't you?"

"Too late for that, sweetheart."

Maddie swatted his chest. "Figures."

A part of her wanted to stop time, to bask in this moment for as long as she could. How was it that this man aroused her and offered her . . . What? What was it she was feeling? Maddie frowned.

"What is it?"

"Nothing."

"Liar."

"How did we get here?"

"In your bed?" Gabriel's lips curved, and Maddie was momentarily distracted by the sight of him. Had he always been this sexy? Gabriel continued. "Let's see, I came over to your—"

"I meant in the position that you're in my bed in the first place."

"I don't know."

"Doesn't it bother you?"

"No . . . Do we have to have an answer for it? Can't things just be enjoyed?"

She frowned. "Who are you and what have you done with Gabriel?"

His smile was rueful. "I've been known to go with the flow."

"Once upon a time. But that's not the Gabriel Steele I've known. Hey . . . Steele."

"Yeah?"

"No, *Steele*. Why are you called Steele and not Rossi?"

"Rossi was a name I associated with my old life. With my father."

"So you changed it?"

"Legally, yeah. It also gives me something to remember my mother." He was playing with the strands of her hair, twirling them around his finger. When he looked back at her, she saw the pain etched into his face—an old hurt that hadn't dulled with time.

"That's lovely."

"Not to my father. At the time, he was incensed that I was changing it. He thought I blamed him for her death."

"And did you?"

"At first, no. I was so small, I only saw it for what it was: a horrible accident. But then I grew up and I couldn't see for all the rage I had aimed against him."

"And now?"

"It's always going to be painful. But I think I've made my peace with it. Something broke loose when my dad died. It was as if any lingering anger I had deflated. I don't know how long that will last, but I hope it's for good."

"Mmm."

"What?"

"That's probably a really healthy position to be in."

"You'll get there too, Maddie." His hand trailed down her arm.

"I don't know about that. I don't even speak to my mom and have no idea where my dad could be."

"You're making a choice there." Gabriel held up his hand in defense. "And before you go turning me into a toad, hear me out."

Maddie sat up fully now, pulling away from him. Gabriel merely rested his hands behind his head, grinning indulgently.

"Go on." She tossed her hair over her shoulder.

"This isn't going to be a fight, Fitzgerald."

"Uh-huh."

"All I wanted to say is, you have all the clues you need to solve the mystery of where your father is. And I think you should see a private investigator sooner rather than later. Today was a disappointment and a long shot to think he'd still be at that address."

She knew it had been, but she'd wanted to do something, however small, to prove that she was making progress. But in reality? She'd been hiding. Licking her wounds. Distracting herself with every other thing she could, from work to volunteering to Ally's baby shower, so she wouldn't have to make the next big decision.

"I know this."

"What are you afraid of?"

Finding out he didn't want her. Learning that he had a new family.

"Being disappointed." Maddie shivered at the admission.

"Seems to me you'll be feeling that either way. Disappointed in yourself if you never find out, disappointed in him if he proves to be a man you don't remember."

"Great."

"I know this is going to be one of the biggest decisions you'll make in your adult life, but at least with a private investigator, you'll be able to see for yourself."

"Lecturing people in bed is a mood killer, you know that?"

"I only say it because I care."

Maddie felt a current of something akin to surprise zap through her annoyance.

"You care?"

"Isn't that obvious?" Gabriel gestured to their naked bodies.

"News flash, Steele, lots of people have great sex without caring."

"Who said this was only great?"

Maddie huffed, feeling the color creeping up her chest.

"If I recall." Gabriel sat up now then flipped her so she was beneath him. "And I know I'm right, you thought this was pretty damn fantastic."

Gabriel nuzzled her neck, licking and biting until she squirmed. He pulled back. "But you can feel free to deny it. To call it whatever you like."

"Mmm."

Could it be she cared for him? Was that why their sex had been—

"Out of this world, brilliant . . . but it's true, Maddie."

She pouted.

"Maybe I need to convince you one more time." Gabriel kissed her now, sending all her thoughts and feelings into one chaotic jumble. "To be thorough."

"Hmm." She wrapped her arms around him. "Maybe you're right, just this once."

Laughing, Maddie let him prove her wrong.

CHAPTER TWENTY-SIX

Maddie had always flirted with getting a tattoo. She had wanted to do it when she'd been younger but never quite knew what kind to get. She wasn't into having random images or symbols on her body if they didn't actually mean something to her. But her gut instinct told her that now was the right time. And that she wanted her best friends there with her for moral support.

Somehow, having sex with Gabriel last weekend had unlocked clarity in her that hadn't been there before.

What Gabriel had said had affected her. She'd put off finding her father up until now and it was starting to mess with her head. She'd known going back to the last known address had been a long shot, but she had pursued that line of inquiry anyway.

She was afraid to find him. Afraid of what she would find out. But he'd been right. She needed to hire someone. But who?

Naturally, she had spent the car ride telling Ally and Sera about her failed attempt at finding her dad and the amazing sex she'd had with Gabriel after it. Not that they'd been surprised.

Which had irked as much as it had shocked her. Had she been so blind all this time?

Funny how she had begun to look forward to the days when they could spend it together. They were careful to keep their distance at school so nobody would suspect anything, but Maddie couldn't help but feel a little pitter patter in her chest any time she caught a glimpse of Gabriel across the room. She had on one or two occasions sauntered past his office to tease him. It was the sexiest form of foreplay and had led to Gabriel knocking on her apartment door last night and showing her how much her antics had affected him during the day.

"So what is your tattoo going to look like?" Sera flipped through the booklet of images, drawing her out of her reverie.

Ally peered over her shoulder. "Where are you going to get it?"

"And how big is it going to be?"

"Oooh, butterfly, pretty." Ally rubbed at her bump.

"Definitely not a butterfly." Maddie half-looked up from her own booklet of tattoos. "But you're more than welcome to get one yourself, Al."

"I'm getting kicked around enough from the inside of my body. I don't need to add to any more of that pain."

"I won't argue with you on that. Some of these are so intricate," Maddie murmured. What would Gabriel think of her tattoo? Oddly enough, she wished that he were here with her now to help her choose something. Knowing him, he'd just piss her off and she'd end up getting something out of spite.

"We have loads more of these folders out back." Chase, the tattoo artist whose whole left arm was covered in a sleeve of tattoos, gestured. "I can get more, but a lot of time people come in asking me to sketch something for them that isn't something we've done before."

"Like custom-made." Sera looked up.

"Exactly." Chase sat back in his chair, totally at ease. He was a wiry guy, with a mop of long dark-blond hair tied back at the nape of his neck and a selection of nose, lip, and face piercings that seemed to make him appear even friendlier, if that was at all possible. Maddie briefly wondered what he would look like without all the lead and ink and didn't think he'd be nearly so vibrant.

Clearly, she wasn't going to pull a Chase and get the whole shebang, but she wanted something true, something that was meaningful and her own—

She gasped. "I think I've got it." Maddie took a pen and notepad and sketched a symbol. Beneath it she wrote one word. "Can you do something like this, but with the scroll intertwined through it?"

Chase took it from her and started his own sketch. Maddie made a few adjustments and stepped back from it, admiring his work. "It's exactly what I want."

When she looked back at her best friends, there were tears in her eyes. She was overcome by so many feelings, but most of all she was overwhelmed by her friends' support.

She knew then that she might never have a proper relationship with her dad, that she might never have the closure that she craved, and that was okay. She refused to stop herself from living because she was afraid or, worse, waiting for something to happen. That wound she'd had since she was a child would always be there.

Reality was, the people who had always been beside her, supporting and giving her strength were here. She was lucky to have friends that were family.

Maddie knew right now, that was everything she needed. And then Gabriel's face swam into view, wreaking havoc with her system.

Well, maybe not *quite* everything . . .

"Alright, take a seat, Maddie." Chase grinned. "Let's get you inked."

"I found your father."

Maddie stopped short in Gabriel's kitchen. It had been a week since she'd seen him last. A week since she'd gotten her tattoo, which she'd been about to show him before he'd dropped that bombshell. She'd barely placed her bag on the counter when he'd said it, those three little words that seemed to tilt everything on its axis.

"Excuse me?"

Her head had been floating in the clouds, her body tingling with anticipation at the thought of sex with him. But all of that arousal seemed to fly out the window the moment he'd opened his mouth.

Gabriel took a step closer, and it was only then that she noticed the envelope in his hands.

"I found your dad."

Maddie was unable to do more than stare.

"Maddie?"

She'd heard the words. She understood them. But it was as if there were a long, thin, threadbare string that connected his words to her brain, so that the sound was tinny and small.

"I'm not sure I'm following really. *You* found my father? What, you bumped into him at the education conference in Sydney or something?" Her heart was beating erratically, fearfully. She didn't know why she was feeling like thousands of tiny spiders were rushing over her skin.

"Sit down."

"I don't want to."

"I think you should."

"Don't coddle me, Gabe. Spit it out."

Gabriel sat on the stool by the kitchen island. He tapped the envelope against the table, marking a beat, infuriating her with every passing second. She knew him well enough to wait it out.

"I saw how disappointed you were when we couldn't find your dad. I know it means a lot to you, so I decided to hire a private investigator before I left to try and find him."

"And?" She was trembling, a mixture of shock, anticipation, and anger.

"And to cut to the chase, she found him."

"She found him."

"I have her details and the report she wrote up, which for the record, I didn't read. I simply gathered the information for you. But Kate confirmed that he's still alive and well and currently living in the city. We have his contact details so you can call him. Problem solved."

"Problem solved? *Problem solved*?" Maddie tried to speak through gritted teeth. "Could you be any more unfeeling?"

"I didn't mean it like that—"

"Really? Going around and searching for *my* father is none of your business."

"You wanted him found, didn't you?"

"That isn't the point!"

"Then what is?"

"It's not *your problem* to solve. It's my life, and it's personal."

"I'm failing to grasp why you're so upset." Gabriel's voice, normally calm and reasoned, was raised.

"You don't have to understand it. I don't need you to interfere."

"So all those conversations about actually finding him meant nothing? Do you want to know the truth, or do you enjoy playing this game?"

"How dare you! This isn't a game."

"Then what? You want him found, then you don't. I was there with you at the apartment. I saw how disappointed you were. So instead of prolonging it, I thought I would help. Maddie, I've taken out all the hard work, the worry, the guessing for *you*. I thought you'd be pleased."

"I didn't want you doing that."

"Well then, what the hell did you want?"

Maddie wanted to pull her hair out. He was frustrating beyond belief. How could it be that someone who was so educated could be so obtuse? It made no sense at all.

"It's complicated."

"I've uncomplicated it."

Maddie stepped closer. "Then complicate it again!"

"This makes no sense."

"I didn't ask for any of this."

"Neither did I."

"What's that supposed to mean?"

"You had a problem; I solved it."

"There we go again with the logic. Well, you know what, Gabe? I don't want to be anyone's problem."

He stood, looking frustrated. "You pulled me into this drama, Maddie. So what did you expect me to do? Stand to the side and watch you torture yourself over it? I see how it hurts you, how it affects you."

She absorbed the burn, letting it fuel her anger. "I actually thought that we were—"

Maddie sucked in air, trying her best to keep all those emotions he seemed to throw in her face in check. She had no problem with her feelings. Hell, she'd never been ashamed of them, but right now she refused to show any vulnerability.

God, how could she have been so wrong? How had she possibly begun to think he was different? He had no clue how she felt at all.

Maddie crossed her arms, righteous in her initial judgment. He was as she'd thought. Rude, arrogant, and cold.

"I'm angry that you felt you could do as you pleased without consulting with me."

"Consulting? I was trying to do you a favor. To help you."

"This isn't like finding my lost phone or covering for me when I'm late to work. It's personal."

"I thought I could help," he repeated, raking his hand through his hair.

"In order to help, you'd have to understand how I'm feeling. And in order to understand *that*, you'd have to have emotions."

"I have enough to last me a lifetime, a thousand lifetimes when I'm around you." He gripped her arms, yanking her close.

Maddie was angry enough to revel at the pressure and feral enough in her frustration to crave more.

She wanted to kick and hit and spit her rage, to take all the fear and anger and let it bubble and spill over like molten lava, burning them both.

Maddie didn't think she could keep it in even if she tried.

"Everything is extreme. Larger than life, unbound, and reckless with you. Damn it, woman, I'm trying to help you because I—"

Something cracked in the air around them. She could feel his heat, his own anger as he drew her closer. Through the mist and fog of her temper, there was an awareness, a sliver of it, that what she was doing was dangerous. Destructive. But she didn't care.

At that moment, she didn't care about a damn thing.

"Because you *what*, Gabriel?"

"Damn it, Maddie."

A flash of confusion crossed her face before she was lost in his kiss.

It was powerful and hungry and every bit as raw and elemental as their argument. It was utterly perfect. She craved the snapping energy, the rough, harsh power. In it, he spoke volumes.

Ever since their first kiss, she'd been thinking about him in ways that confused her. She'd told herself she was unaffected by him, that this was all surface level, but she'd been fooling herself.

She wanted to provoke him, to see every part of him. Unbound, unreserved, like this. She wanted him to unravel. More so, she wanted to be the woman to do it. To figure out all the parts to him, to understand why it was he acted like a pompous ass. No, that wasn't right . . . . She knew enough about him to know that.

He pulled back, watching her with glittering eyes.

"I wanted to find him for *you*, Maddie. Nobody else but you."

Tears, angry and hot, blurred her vision. "Then for my sake, you'll stay out of my business."

Snatching the envelope, Maddie turned and fled.

The next day, as Maddie sat in the office of Kate Riccardo, ex-cop turned private investigator, she couldn't help but stew over the latest turn of events. She'd made the appointment mostly out of spite. And anger. But deep inside, she'd made it because she was hurt.

How dare Gabriel think he could interfere with her life like that? He had no right. Couldn't he see through that thick skull of his that this wasn't his business? This was something she wanted to do on her own. In her own time.

She replayed the argument over in her head. He'd been so arrogant to assume that she would fall to her knees in thanks.

Taking the next step was a big deal, but it was one she wanted to make of her own volition, not because some guy did it for her.

Maddie bit her lip. But Gabriel wasn't some guy, was he?

He cared for her. Wasn't that what he'd said when they had first slept together?

Was this his way of showing it? What a joke. He saw her as a problem. He'd said as much, hadn't he? And problems needed fixing.

Well, she refused to be anyone's burden. She'd grown up believing that her very presence had ruined her mother's life. She wouldn't be with a man who didn't consider her feelings. Or worse, who thought her life needed fixing in some way.

Had her initial view of him been right all along? Was he too cold for her hot-blooded liking?

"Sorry for the delay." Kate walked in, pausing to shake Maddie's hand before sitting behind her desk. "We've been slammed this afternoon."

"Thanks for fitting me in at the last minute." Maddie toyed with the strap of her bag. "You know, this isn't what I thought a private investigator's office would look like." Maddie noticed the flowery wallpaper and potted plants. Pictures of sunny horizons and towering waves decorated the large space.

"I'm no wise-talkin', cigar-smoking man from the 1930s, but I do get the job done."

Maddie laughed. "That's exactly the stereotype I had in my head."

"So, your friend enlisted my help."

"Yes . . . Gabriel."

"And did you read through the report?"

"I did briefly." It had detailed all the practicalities, from her dad's current address to his work history. There had been more, but Maddie had been too angry to take it all in.

The one thing that had stood out to her was that he'd become a music teacher. No more working on oil rigs. It made her shiver to think that perhaps they might be more alike than she ever thought.

"I'm glad you came in because there's more on file that I didn't give your friend Gabriel."

"Oh?"

"He assured me that he only wanted the basics, but I have pictures. I was able to trace Dermot's phone number, all off public records, which is in the report. Your friend said you'd probably want to come in and speak to me eventually, to obtain the pictures yourself."

Something tickled at Maddie's spine. How was it that he could be thoughtful about that but still went ahead and found the information without her permission? The man was infuriating. "I do."

"Let me get them for you then."

After chatting to Kate for a half hour about a few of the details of her father's life—he lived in the city, had never remarried, and had no criminal convictions—she picked up the envelope and left.

It was only when she sat behind the wheel of her car that she looked through the photos. And what she saw shocked her beyond measure.

Not only was it a dagger to the heart to see her dad with wrinkles, his once-long red hair cropped and coppery, but it was whom he was photographed with that left her heart broken.

Because the person sitting in a wheelchair, the woman inviting him into their family home was none other than Sharon Calway Fitzgerald. Her mother.

Maddie closed her eyes at the images, tears streaming down her face.

At that moment, when her pain seemed to suffocate her entirely, the only person in all the world that she wanted to call was Gabriel.

CHAPTER TWENTY-SEVEN

"Not cool, my friend."

Gabriel shoved his hands in his pockets and wandered farther down the path. He could always rely on Harper to call a spade a spade, but in this instance, he'd thought she might be a bit sympathetic.

He'd only tried to help, but instead of gratitude, Maddie had thrown his kindness back in his face. He didn't understand why she couldn't accept he was doing her a favor. Perhaps he'd gotten a little heated, but he'd been frustrated by her response.

Christ.

When it came to that woman, he had no control. Everything he'd worked so hard to keep in check for so long disintegrated the moment he held her. Arguing with her was confusing and . . . God help him, unbelievably arousing.

What the hell did that say about him? He prided himself on becoming the man he was today, on changing his bad habits, but . . .

All those lush curves. That sweet, soft mouth.

She was temptation. She was sin.

She was everything he craved but had never really believed in.

Gabriel scowled, now remembering her anger.

"I did it to help her. I saw how disappointed she was when we couldn't find her dad initially. I thought I was helping her out by taking the hard part off her hands. Now that she has his contact details, she can make the choice if she wants to see him or not. Why is this such a problem?"

"Have you ever thought that perhaps she might want to do the hard part herself? That the process of it would help her heal?"

Gabriel studied his friend's face, letting her words sink in.

"You know, for a man as educated as you, you can be a little thick sometimes."

Gabriel scratched his jaw. "You know, I came to you for advice, not insults."

"No need to get pissy with me. I'm simply telling you the truth. And as a woman who likes making my own decisions, having someone make that decision for me, especially one that's so important to me, would make me furious."

"Why?"

"It's personal."

"She made it my business. Look, she had a problem, and I helped her solve it."

"You know it's not black and white like that."

He also knew what it was like to be estranged from a parent and to not have the opportunity to do or say the things that were important while there was still time.

"Not everything is going to be solved with logic, Gabe."

He felt the sting of it, the burn, an echo of what Maddie had thrown in his face.

"What I feel for her isn't logical!" His frustration exploded from him. Gabriel paced, talking to himself as much as confessing to his friend. "She gets under my skin and seems to infect every reasonable part of my brain so all I think about is her. When she laughs, it's like the sun is shining, and when she cries, it's like a thousand daggers piercing my chest. It kills me to see her in pain."

His chest heaved with the force of his emotions, so many damn emotions he couldn't get a hold on just one. But he also knew the danger of living life this way; it had been logic that had saved him all those years ago. When he'd been living a life that was fast and loose and based on whims, he'd actually only been destroying himself. As soon as he'd made that change, that choice to be better, to do things differently, his life had improved.

"Does she know that you love her?"

Gabriel sighed, feeling the frustration gently ebb away. Harper always could see through the unspoken layers. "No. She knows I care about her, but . . . no. It's too soon to say anything."

"You're afraid she'll bolt."

"For all of her talk about me being emotionless, I think sometimes the big emotions scare her too."

"So, are you going to admit you crossed a line, kiss, and have hot makeup sex?"

Gabriel grinned. "So what you're saying is, I was in the wrong."

"I think you crossed a line. I agree your intentions were pure—"

"I honestly wanted to help her out."

"I think there was another way of doing things, like telling her about the private investigator you found and suggesting maybe she could go down that route."

Gabriel's conscience pinged.

"Oh boy." Harper's tone was dry. "You already had."

Gabriel cursed, remembering the conversation they'd had the day they'd been prepping Ally's baby shower. Hadn't she said she'd wanted to find him on her own? Hadn't she already rejected his help?

But that had been before he'd felt his heart rip out of his chest and fall at her feet. Before he'd fallen in love.

Gabriel groaned, accepting that perhaps he'd crossed a boundary.

"Surely if she'd wanted you to help her, she'd have asked."

"Have you met Maddie?"

Harper chuckled. "Regardless, that would be her choice to make. And if she wanted your help, she'd have asked," she repeated. "Like she did when she took you to the apartment to meet her dad. What you've done is eliminate her agency in this whole situation, which has taken her power."

Which was something Maddie's mother had done. Hiding the letters, making the decision for her.

"Fuck." Gabriel rubbed at his face. "That wasn't my intention. I really did fuck up."

"Yup. And I think it's time to start groveling on your knees, Steele."

"My favorite position."

"There are so many things I'm mad about, I don't even know where to begin." Maddie huffed.

After her meeting with Kate, she'd driven straight to Sera's house and demanded that she go for a hike up the mountain. With Ally already past her due date, Maddie didn't want to disturb her or, God forbid, have her go into labor while on a climb.

And given her foul mood, she needed to walk at a pace that was slightly faster than a tortoise.

"Start with what has you itching to slap someone. I can see it on your face."

"My mother has been secretly seeing my father at the house."

Sera tripped, catching herself just in time.

"What? Your—he—oh my god, Maddie. How do you know?"

"Which brings me to the second thing that has me pissed off. Gabriel hired a PI to find my father even though I told him I didn't need the help."

"You need to explain this to me like I'm a child."

Maddie did. She poured out all her anger and disappointment while Sera nodded and sympathized and listened. In some ways, she expected such betrayal from her mother—Sharon had never seemed to take into account Maddie's feelings growing up—but it hurt even more that Gabriel had acted without her consent.

"Have you spoken to Sharon about it?"

"I haven't called or seen my mother since the day I found Dad's letters."

"Fair enough."

"I mean, she's got some sick justification as to why she kept the letters a secret, but to know now they're in contact, that she's *been* in contact all this time? That's another level of fucked up. I—" Maddie's voice cracked. "Where's any thought for me in all this?"

She dashed away the tears and felt Sera's arms wrap around her. She cried for all the things that had been taken from her. For their deception, even now.

Maddie pulled back, scrubbing at her face. "Why hasn't my dad come to see me? How long have they been in contact? Months? Years?"

"What did the PI say?"

"She only had a snapshot, taken from a few days of snooping on him. I mean, does he not want to see me?"

"Oh, honey, I don't know if it's as black and white as that. He might have just seen her that week."

Maddie threw her ever-optimistic friend a disbelieving look. "Doubtful."

"So what will you do?"

"I still want to meet my dad, but I'm angry at him and my mom. I need to work through all that before I actually make the call."

"Does Gabriel know?"

"I'm not speaking to him at the moment."

"Why does it bother you that he found that PI? It sounds like he was trying to help you out."

Maddie groaned. "Not you too."

"Hear me out."

"Mercy."

"He knew you wanted to see your dad, to find him, right?"

"Yes, but—"

"And he crossed a major line doing it. But he did it for you."

"He—"

"Saw that you needed help and he helped you. It wasn't done maliciously or to one-up you. Granted, it's your personal business and your decision and you've every right to be angry that he took that away from you—"

"Yes! Exactly. He took that away from me, and I want to tear him limb from limb."

"Want me to help hide the body?" Sera winked.

"Yes, please. I don't insert myself into his business, do I?"

"No."

"That's right. You know why?" She didn't wait for a response. "Because he doesn't fucking let me in!"

But even as she made the argument, a part of her realized that it wasn't entirely true. That Gabriel *had* revealed things to her—personal things about his childhood, his life, that perhaps he hadn't shared with others. But there were still times where she felt he was holding back. She couldn't put her finger on it, but it felt like there was something he wasn't telling her.

And if she wanted a relationship with a guy, one beyond the physical, then she needed to know he could communicate with her.

"I can't speak for your relationship, but I thought you two were building a friendship this year, and now that you're sleeping together, it seems like it's turning into something more."

"Well, friends share things with one another."

"Exactly."

"Friends make decisions together."

"Definitely."

"Friends—"

"Also help each other out when they need it."

"Yes! Wait, what?"

"He's trying to be a friend in that take charge way of his. And you're probably feeling like everything in your life is exposed and that makes you vulnerable."

"All my life, I've been lied to. He totally stepped over that line by making that decision for me. He assumes he knows best. How arrogant is that?"

"People show they care in different ways, Madds."

"He knew I wanted to do this on my own."

"So time to reinforce some boundaries. He made a mistake; there's no denying it. You need to decide how big of a deal this is to you and what you'll do if he does something like this again. Is this really a dealbreaker, Madds, or are you hurt because this has touched a nerve?"

They walked in silence for a while, slowing down their pace as they reached the lookout point.

"He said it was a problem and he wanted to fix it."

"Oh, honey." Sera turned to her.

"It made me feel like a burden, you know?"

"Like how your mother treated you." Sera nodded. "I get it. The hurt runs deep."

"It always does."

"So, do you think you'll talk to him?"

"To Gabriel? Not a chance."

"What happened to the old Madds? Quick to burn but never held a grudge."

"This is different."

"Really?"

Maddie nodded. "This time, it's personal."

CHAPTER TWENTY-EIGHT

addie was true to form.

She held a grudge through the Monday morning briefing, all the way to Tuesday's afternoon planning session. But by Wednesday night, her jaw was starting to ache from all the tension.

They were on baby watch given that Ally was fit to burst and in immense discomfort, which seemed to only add to the stress.

So when Gabriel rang the buzzer of her apartment that Wednesday evening, she was of two minds. It was tempting to let him stand in the cool evening air until he left, but she'd learned that Gabriel was a bit like a bulldog; he wouldn't give up.

With a resigned sigh, she waited for him to reach the landing.

He'd changed.

Gone was his suit and tie, and in their place were black jeans and a black T-shirt that sat very nicely over his broad shoulders.

She told herself not to, but as she wordlessly ushered him

inside, shutting the apartment door behind them, she couldn't help but notice how well he looked.

Or how much she missed him.

The gale-force wind warnings were in full effect and the storm that raged outside seemed to do outrageously sexy things to his thick, dark hair.

"Take a seat." She motioned to the sofa, but Gabriel remained standing. "Or not, that's good too."

"I know you're angry with me."

Maddie nodded. "I am."

"And I want to talk about it because we're both adults and this needs to be resolved. We also can't keep avoiding each other at school."

"You could always find another place to work."

"Very funny."

"Does it look like I'm joking?" Maddie folded her arms. She was nervous all of a sudden. A bundle of frayed wires, exposed and charged. She once again couldn't read him, and that made her want to kick and claw.

"I wanted to find your father for you because I saw how disappointed you were when he wasn't at that address."

"But that's my business."

"It is. I thought, as a friend, that I would be doing you a favor, protecting you so you wouldn't have to go through the disappointment each time you failed."

"Failed? You don't think much of my abilities then, but I suppose that's always been the case."

His temper ignited. She could tell by the way his eyes turned cloudy, not dissimilar to the storm outside. "You know that's not true. I meant it when I said I did this with good intentions. I can see now that I overstepped the mark."

"How?"

"Excuse me?"

"How did you see that?"

Gabriel scratched his chin, a rueful smile on his face. "Harper tore me a new one."

"Wise woman."

"That she is. And it made me see things in a different light. Look, I'm not saying this to manipulate you, but I just lost my father. A father who was absent for most of my life. Yeah, he may have been physically present, but . . ." Gabriel took a deep breath in. "He was absent in every way that counted. I've spent years wishing I had it different, and then even more years being estranged from him. I didn't have a relationship with him that was functional in any way, and I don't want that for you.

"Your father's alive. I want you to say your piece or build a relationship or do whatever it is you want to do because you have the chance. Now. While he's around. I've lost out with my dad, and I have so many fucking regrets."

"And I'm supposed to accept that you'll steamroll over my wishes because you have a valid justification, is that it?"

Gabriel took a step closer. "No. I know that I crossed a boundary. I should have listened when you said you wanted to do this by yourself. I thought you were being stubborn and afraid, and I stupidly thought I could eliminate the hard part for you."

Maddie crossed her arms. "Is this supposed to be an apology? 'Coz you kind of suck at it."

Gabriel's voice lowered. "Do you want me to beg?"

Maddie felt a thrill race up her spine. Not at his supplication, not entirely, but at the dangerously wicked tone coupled with the heated look in his eyes. It made her want him even more.

"The offer is tempting."

To her utter shock, Gabriel fell to his knees, his arms outstretched.

"Maddie, I only realized how hurtful this might have been to you after talking to Harper. I could only see it from my perspective, and I realize now this isn't about me at all. Harps knocked some sense into my thick skull, and it made me realize that I was doing something that took away your agency, something your mother has been doing to you your whole life. She took away your right to choose whether you wanted a relationship with your dad, and I went and did the same."

Maddie swallowed past the knot in her throat.

Gabriel continued, "I didn't get that it would have only turned the knife deeper, and for that, I'm truly sorry. I know you said you wanted to do this on your own, and I went and did it anyway, and I can see now that was the wrong call. But I had tunnel vision. I did it with the best of intentions, but I still hurt you, and I apologize. Forgive me?"

Maddie waited a beat, watching him. Then everything inside of her seemed to crumble. Because he understood. He'd finally taken the time to understand why what he'd done was hurtful. And she could see the remorse on his face. He took responsibility for his actions when nobody in her family ever had before.

She knelt in front of Gabriel, giving him a quick, hard hug.

"I've had my mom make these decisions for me for so long that I was so angry when you decided you knew what was best. When you said it was a problem, I felt like *I* was the problem, and I grew up feeling like a burden."

"She took away your power, and I did the same. She made you feel small and less than, and I'm so damn sorry that I did too."

Gabriel rose, drawing her up in his arms. "But you're more than that, Madds. You're not a burden to me. You're not a problem. You're a woman who makes me feel things I've been shutting down for a long time. You make me vulnerable, and that scares me. But I want you. I want this thing between us to work, so that means I'll apologize a thousand times in a thousand different ways if that means I get to have you."

Maddie cleared the emotion that had stuck in the back of her throat. "Maybe you're not so bad at apologizing after all."

"Something tells me I'm gonna have practice at it for a long time yet. So am I forgiven?"

"I accept your apology. But don't ever cross those boundaries again."

He wrapped his arms around her waist. "I promise. You have my word."

"Good . . . and maybe I was quick to judge your intentions because . . . well, you mean something to me too. Not just the sex."

Gabriel's grin was full and fleeting. "So, what now?"

"There's something else. I went to visit Kate Riccardo after our fight, and she found out something big."

Gabriel tilted his chin. "What happened?"

She told him everything, from her dad's job history through to his secret rendezvous with her mother.

"Fuck, Madds."

"I know."

"What are you—"

Maddie shook her head. "I don't know what I'm going to do. I still feel so damn angry at them, mostly my mom, but my dad too. I mean, he must have known that I wanted to see him, so why wait? Why not come and find me?"

"I wish I could give you those answers."

"I know. And I know there's only one way I'm going to find out, but it scares me." Maddie shook her head. "I don't think I can talk about this right now. It makes me feel sick to think of it."

"Then take some time. Take however long you need. There's no point rushing it when you don't feel steady and strong in taking the next step."

"You're singing a different tune."

"I'm realizing I was blinded by my own relationship with

my dad, that I was forcing those views onto you. Whenever you're ready, know that I'm here."

"That's all I need to know." Maddie smiled, drawing him in for a kiss. "Make me forget, Gabriel. Even if only for tonight, make me forget about everything in the world except us."

"Yes, *boss*."

She squealed when he did exactly that.

Gabriel was weak. When it came to Maddie Fitzgerald, he was the weakest man in the world. Because when she looked up at him with her mismatched eyes, begging him to make her forget, he couldn't say no. Wouldn't. He seemed to yearn for her every minute of the day.

He yanked her close, kissing her with an intensity he'd held in check since their argument. Her mouth was soft, her tongue teasing. She moaned against him, her body vibrating, driving him crazy.

He'd missed her. Missed this.

It felt like a lifetime since he'd touched her, tasted her. And he never wanted to stop.

"Gabriel?" Her startled gasp sent his desire through the roof.

Maddie's expression was heated. She looked at him in a way that made his blood pump frantically. His body was burning for her, and he didn't think he could restrain himself. Not when this fiery need seemed to rip through him.

"I need you, Gabriel."

"Fuck, Maddie, I've missed you."

She trembled. That delicate shiver ran through her, and it seemed he would never get enough. He ached for this woman, for her warmth, for that mewling sound she made at the back of her throat when he touched her.

Perfection.

He nuzzled her neck, hearing that sound, biting her shoulder to make her gasp. She arched against him, and with trembling hands, he whipped up her hoodie, taking her T-shirt with it. He sent a silent prayer of thanks that she wore no bra.

She was glorious. Stunning.

All his.

He muttered it, a chant, a prayer, a hymn of sorts that would make him whole.

"Gabriel?" she asked again, cupping his face.

"You're all mine, Maddie. Fuck what is right and PC and proper. When I'm with you, you're mine. There is no other man for you. Do you hear me?"

"You're so—"

"Tell me, Maddie, there's no one else."

"There's—" She gasped as he toyed with her nipples. "Nobody but you, Gabriel."

He kissed her hard. "I'm never going to stop wanting you. Ever. You're like a fire in my blood, and I'll burn for you always, Red."

"Say it again."

"I burn for you."

She sobbed in her next breath as he bit her breasts, swirling his tongue around her puckered nipples until he thought his cock would rip through his jeans.

He was achingly hard. So ready to fuck, to claim, to bury himself inside of her until he couldn't breathe.

A part of him cautioned against the wild, whipping need, the feral possessiveness that clawed at his control. But the intensity was everything. He chased it. Craved it. Knew that it was different from anything he'd ever felt before.

Because this woman before him was everything. And it nearly knocked him on his ass to admit it.

Gabriel stripped out of his clothes, covering himself with a condom, then watched hungrily as she shimmied out of her sweatpants.

"I'm sorry," he muttered, yanking her by the cotton waistband of her panties.

"For what?"

"This."

And he gathered the seam of her underwear and ripped it in two.

Maddie's gasp, her widened eyes made him feel feral, territorial. And, fuck it, every inch the possessive caveman. But the lust that leaped into her eyes, the yearning that replaced it made him want to do it again and again.

"You seem to do that a lot."

"I'll buy you a new pair," he muttered by way of an apology.

"I think I'll need lots of new ones then 'coz that was hot."

His grin, he was sure, was wolfish. He backed them both up against the living room wall, reveling in the lush woman against him.

Gabriel pinned her arms above her head then froze. Slowly, he removed his hands then fingered the fresh tattoo on the inside of her wrist.

"When did you get this?"

"The other week."

He grinned a little, running his finger along the Celtic knot; wrapped through it on a small scroll was one word. "What does this mean? *Misneach*."

"Courage." She spoke softly.

"The knot?"

"The triquetra. Some say it represents the three stages of womanhood."

"Very befitting."

"I thought so too—oh!" Maddie gasped when he lifted her leg up and stroked her soft, swollen clit. He toyed with her, watching the way her eyes fluttered closed, only to open in desperation. She clawed at his shoulders, and he hoped she left a mark.

Gabriel swirled his fingers at her entrance then slid them inside. She was molten. Sweet heaven, she was hot and wet and smelled divine.

"I think your tatt is sexy, Maddie. Just. Like. You."

He kissed her again then reared back. He was heavy and straining and so damn ready, he thought he'd explode. Finding the right angle, he thrust into her. And when they both groaned, taking their pleasure, it was like nothing he had ever experienced before.

She wrapped her legs around his waist, moaning with each thrust.

That need, that yearning for her was unmatched by anything else he'd ever felt. It was a joining like no other. And he knew he would be lost without her.

Gabriel stilled, taking in the moment, the perfect simplicity of their joined bodies. And when he looked at her, his vision swam. He didn't fight it, didn't analyze or shove it away. He accepted it, this breaking open inside himself. The beauty of it. The beauty of her.

Maddie's face was flushed, her pale skin marked by his earlier attentions. He was alarmed and yet satisfied in equal measure that his passion branded her. But it wasn't the same as it was before. He wasn't the same. Where once it was lust without any substance, now it was both. There was need and desire. Substance and sex.

It was with this woman, only this woman, that he found it.

Gabriel gripped her ass, pumping into her without restraint. He felt the soft spot deep inside of her, felt the walls of her pussy bearing down on him, clenching and releasing with every thrust. Her breasts bounced against his chest, and the smell of her left him salivating for a taste.

"I want you like this always." He rutted her now; there was no other word for it. And she matched his every thrust with her own fervor.

When she muttered filthy words, she might as well have cast a spell. She bound him to her with her body, and he could have roared from the primitive force of it.

His desire was a snarling, snapping beast and it would be sated. His arousal knew no bounds when it came to her, so he took and took. And she gave and gave until she was muttering incomprehensible words.

He wanted to make her come, to feel her soaking his cock while he filled her. And one day, he would fill her without protection, without restraint, and the image of it was so damn sexy that when he heard the telltale sound of her arousal, he didn't stop. The trickle became a gushing sound, and Gabriel sucked and bit her nipples until she shook, finding her own orgasm on a long, drawn-out cry of pleasure.

He felt the warmth on his cock, felt the effects of her orgasm trickling down his thighs.

That delicious sound coupled by the sensation of her coming sent him spiraling into his own pleasure. Gabriel buried his head in her fiery hair as he came, her name a sacred oath on his lips . . .

And forever inside his heart.

CHAPTER TWENTY-NINE

fter checking in at reception and being given the all clear, Maddie walked through the maze of rooms at St. Augustus Hospital, where Ally was recovering after pushing an eight pounder out of her wazoo.

She'd heard from Owen the moment her best friend had gone into labor and had been impatient to find out that everything was okay ever since.

When the news had come through that Ally had given birth to a healthy baby girl, she had shed tears of relief. After a grueling twenty-two hours of labor, Ellie Mae Davies had been born.

Maddie had been able to see her via video chat, and the plump little pudding had blue eyes like her daddy and a shock of her mom's dark hair. Charlotte, Owen's daughter, had been given the honor of naming her from a short list, and according to Ally, her stepdaughter wasn't ready to leave her little sister's side.

Maddie had waited a few days before visiting, torn between an eager need to meet this little human and the desire to give her bestie and Owen some space.

She found 16B and gently knocked then entered. Maddie blinked, overwhelmed with the shock of teddies and flowers that covered every free surface.

Sitting on the bed amidst the plush toys was her friend, looking utterly worn but somehow glowing. In her arms was a podgy little babe, dressed in frilly green boots and mittens, burrowing into her mama's neck.

And whatever residual anger she was feeling about her own screwed-up family life dissipated in an instant.

"Oh, Ally, congratulations!" She hugged her friend, overcome by a swell of love and emotion. This was how they'd all begun. This was how *she'd* begun, with her own mother and father so many years ago. Had they been happy at one point? Had she been wanted? Growing up with her mother, being made to feel like a burden had worn down her self-worth for such a long time. She could only hope that at some point in the past, when her parents had been together, that her presence had made them happy.

But knowing that her mother had lied to her all her life, that her father had been visiting Sharon for God knew how long, never once reaching out to her, was a kick in the teeth.

Seeing just how much love Ally had for this newborn made her proud to be her friend. She knew that Ellie Mae was going to be the most loved-up baby on the planet.

"She's absolutely beautiful." Maddie sat at the end of the bed, overcome with so much happiness that tears stung her eyes.

"We think so, but I keep telling Owen we're totally biased."

"And how are you, Marathon Mama?"

"Tired. Like, bone-achingly so, and my vagina is unrecognizable."

"Nice."

"Be grateful you don't have to see it."

"Immensely. But apparently you're not supposed to recognize your va-jay-jay after labor."

"You're only saying that to make me feel better."

"Hey, I read up on all that stuff in the lead-up to this momentous day and it's true. But yes, I'm also saying it because you need to hear it. Once the swelling goes down, you won't be able to tell the difference."

"The midwives said the same thing, but it's hard to not feel panicked about all that stuff."

"First time you've given birth, so take it easy on yourself, Al."

"You're the best." Ally squeezed her hand. "Want a cuddle?"

"I'll just wash my hands."

"You *have* been reading."

"See? Totally supportive auntie here. Though, I mentioned to Sera that I might bring in some snacks for you and Maryam nearly bit off my hand. She was over at their place enlisting Sera's help, the two of them cooking up a storm for when you come home."

"She's been amazing."

"You mean coming in to feed you even though you get hospital food? I'm shocked." Maddie spoke over her shoulder, scrubbing her hands in the basin.

"Sera told you." Ally laughed, patting Ellie Mae's bottom. "She wouldn't take no for an answer, and after sampling what they offered, I'm kinda glad I was talked into it. It's nice to be doted on as well."

"I'd take Sera's mom's food over anything, any day."

"I'm not complaining."

Maddie dried her hands on the paper towel. "And your folks?"

"They were here. Polite and happy to have a grandchild. Of blood relation."

"Yikes." Maddie shook her head. "But it's not the same, is it?"

Ally sighed, fiddling with the lace cuff of Ellie's sock. "No, not even close."

"Sera's parents are like unicorns. And they're love bombers, so it puts our parents to shame."

"My parents will never be like them, and I accepted that long ago, but it still hurts a bit, you know? I was smothered by Maryam and Tony when they came in and couldn't even get my child off them if I tried. Total opposite of my folks, who were so, so . . ."

"Distant?"

"Yeah."

"I'm sorry."

Ally shrugged. "It is what it is."

"Still sucks."

"Yep. I've accepted that's who they are, but in moments like this, I think I forget. I want them to be different people."

Maddie sat on the bed with a sigh. "Don't I know it."

"Are you okay?"

"I'm fine."

"How did it go with your mom?"

"I haven't spoken to her yet. Or Dad. I still can't believe they've been seeing each other behind my back. It really hurts."

Ally held her hand, squeezing it. "I'm so sorry this has been so difficult."

"It is what it is. But hey, not going to bring bad energy in here. Not with this gorgeous, little person in the room."

"So how about a cuddle then?"

"Sounds wonderful."

Maddie gently cupped her honorary niece in her arms and gazed down at her in awe. Her friend had housed this person inside of her, growing her for nine long months. There was no better person to be a mother. Ally would care for Ellie Mae and love her with the same warmth and generosity that she did her stepdaughter.

"You did it, Al. And she's gorgeous."

A twinge of something like envy sprang up like a jack-in-the-box to then disappear just as fast. She didn't want a baby. She knew she didn't have it in her to be that selfless, and she refused to be turned into a bitter woman like her mother, resentful and regretful because of a child.

Maddie had the life she wanted, the life she deserved, and knowing that a child had no place in it felt right to her. But her life wasn't settled. And that was why she'd felt jealous.

She didn't know where she stood with Gabriel. She was for all intents and purposes in a relationship, but did that mean he was her boyfriend? He wanted an exclusive relationship, as did she, but she had no idea if he even wanted children. What if he did?

She couldn't, wouldn't deprive someone of their dreams if they desired a child. It would be just as bad as forcing someone to have one when they weren't ready. It wasn't right.

She'd spent so much time getting to know Gabriel on a deeper level, but there was still so much to figure out. She got the feeling he was holding something back, and it left her a little more than panicked.

Where was it going? What happened after their sex frenzy died out? Did he want marriage? Kids? Travel? To live in a remote cabin chopping wood?

"You seem sad."

Maddie blinked, jolting out of her reverie. "I'm not. Or at least, not for the reason you think. I'm totally fine with not having a little one of my own, but it's made me realize I need to talk to Gabriel."

"Uh-oh."

"No, not bad. We need to figure out if we're on the same page."

"That doesn't sound convincing."

"I don't know if he wants kids."

"Oh . . .."

"Yeah."

"That one will need some gentle handling."

"Kid gloves. I'll wear them."

"Uh-huh, suuuure."

"Is your mommy being mean to me, Ellie Mae? Oh, I think that's a yes."

Ally grinned. "Thick as thieves already."

"You bet. What you're doing is the hardest job in the world, Al. If you need me at any time, I'm here."

"I know it."

"Good."

When Ellie Mae began to fuss fifteen minutes later, Maddie changed her nappy then gave her to Ally for a feed.

"I'll come by tomorrow to give you and Owen a chance to sleep."

"Auntie duties already?"

"Pulling the night shift for you after work will be my pleasure. How else will this kiddo know I'm the best auntie in the world?"

"Ha ha."

"Love you."

"Love you too. And good luck with Gabriel."

"Mmm."

Something told her she was going to need it.

CHAPTER THIRTY

"*Fitzgerald.*"

Maddie smirked. "*Boss.*"

"I thought you'd left hours ago."

"I had every intention of leaving after the staff meeting but a few of my seniors wanted some help with their solos." Maddie dumped her bags on the chair then stretched out her back. It had been a long day. "What's your excuse?"

"Prepping for school council meeting tomorrow night."

"Fun. There's something I wanted to discuss with you."

Gabriel stood. "Actually, I've got something I want to get off my chest too."

"You first."

He took his time to approach her, as if gathering his thoughts. "This has been on my mind for a long time, and after our argument at Ally's baby shower, I've realized how my actions when we first met may have given you the wrong impression. It served me well at the time to have you think that I disliked you, but that wasn't the truth. Not entirely."

There was an intensity in his expression that she hadn't seen before. "You accused me of being cold to you when we were introduced, and you were right. I was curt. Looking at you stirred something in me. And I was afraid of letting my control slip. There was something about you that drew me in. It made me feel like the old Gabriel, the one who would've had no issues with coaxing you into a spare classroom and fucking you until you screamed. And that scared the hell out of me. So I panicked. Shut down. I told myself that it was for the best. That staying away from you was the answer. But the truth is, I was afraid that you'd be a temptation I couldn't resist."

"And how did that work out for you?" Maddie replied, a little breathless.

"Turns out I was right. You're still a temptation I can't resist."

Maddie was thrilled by his words. Shocked and stunned and totally turned on by his confession. It changed everything.

"Why are you telling me this now?"

"Because you need to know. You need to understand that this passion I feel for you consumes me. I can't get enough of you, Red. I'll never get enough."

"For the record, I feel the same way."

Gabriel grinned. "Good." He crossed the room, drawing down the blinds of his office. When he locked the door, Maddie gasped, anticipation tingling across her skin. "You know, I once had a fantasy where you were wearing a skirt and blouse not dissimilar to what you have on now."

Maddie's mouth turned to ash. "Oh?"

"Except, you know what the difference was?"

She shook her head, unable to offer more than a strangled reply. "What?"

"The difference was"—Gabriel held her waist, drawing her closer—"I had my cock buried inside your pretty pussy."

Maddie heard the mewling sound she made at the back of her throat and knew they wouldn't be making it back to her apartment. At least not for round one.

She also knew that all hopes of having a serious conversation disintegrated the moment he'd locked his office door.

"Bend over."

Maddie tilted her chin. "What if I don't want to?"

Gabriel rubbed his thumb between her lips. "Then you'll be punished."

Slowly, he unbuttoned her red blouse until it hung open.

"I can't decide if I want to eat you out now or fuck you." He bit at her earlobe, sending one dangly earring dancing.

"Please."

"Please, what?"

"Fuck me."

Maddie trembled. She felt the pooling between her thighs at all the dirty things he was saying to her. He squeezed her breasts then tugged down her bra to finger her nipples, teasing them until she squirmed.

But he was a master of distraction, of drawing out her desire. This was his fantasy, and for once, Maddie appreciated his bossy personality.

Gabriel pulled up her skirt slowly, bunching it at her waist. His low whistle made her giggle.

"Thigh-high tights and black lace, straight out of my dreams. I approve."

"I know you do."

"Very naughty, Miss Fitzgerald." Gabriel slipped his finger inside her panties, stroking her clit with slow, gentle movements.

"Yes." She gasped, never wanting him to stop. He had a wicked way of knowing exactly what she liked and kept her begging for more. The smug bastard.

"Show me that pretty pussy, Maddie. I want you bent over my desk."

With unsteady legs, Maddie turned. She reached out to clear

some space, when Gabriel gripped her waist. His mouth hovered at her ear, his erection pressed against her ass.

"I want you to leave everything where it is. I want to see evidence of you on this desk after I'm through fucking you. Your red lipstick on those reports, your nails digging into the table . . ." Gabriel bent her over the desk, his chest flush against her back. "I want evidence of what we did here every time I walk into this room. Is that clear?"

"Yes, *boss*."

"You know what drives me wild, Red?"

Maddie trembled. "What?"

"This." He shifted back then grabbed at the round curve of her hips, squeezing and releasing with such gentle pressure, she thought her legs might give way. "This part of your body drives me wild. Not gonna lie, I watch the way your hips sway in those sexy dresses and tight skirts, and I want to take a bite."

"What are you waiting for then?"

Gabriel swore and sunk his teeth into her. Maddie yelped, covering her mouth in case the cleaning staff came to investigate.

"God, you smell fucking incredible." He slowly pulled down her underwear until it pooled on the floor.

When she felt his tongue at her snatch, she cried out, nails scratching against the desk. He rocked back and forth, dipping his tongue inside her pussy, spreading her ass so she was exposed.

"Gabriel," she moaned.

"That's it. Beg for it."

"I hate you."

"How much do you hate me?"

He inserted a finger, making her gasp. "So much."

The low rumble of laughter drove her wild with longing. But a wave of something else overwhelmed her now, intensifying her desire for him. Maddie swallowed, overcome by her feelings for this man.

Her heart hammered in her chest.

"I want to feel your thick cock stretching me."

"Tell me," he rasped.

"I want to feel you hitting that spot inside of me to make me come."

She heard his belt buckle, then his zipper. There was a whisper of material before his cock jutted against her ass. He ground himself between the line of her ass cheeks, making her tremble.

"Stop teasing me."

"You love it."

"I—" Maddie swallowed the confession. It rocked through her, this realization of what she felt for this man.

Love.

She shook now with the force of it. But even through her shock, she knew it to be true.

She loved the enemy. She was in love with Gabriel.

She knew without a doubt that it felt so right. To want him like this made her ache in ways she had never thought possible.

"Gabriel . . ."

"Maddie."

"I want my punishment."

She could feel him grinning. "I suppose you've been a very bad girl."

"The worst."

He bent over her a few seconds later, his red tie in his hands. Taking her wrists, he bound them together. "Is this too tight?"

"It's perfect. What's my punishment?"

"A bit of spanking on that ass might teach you a lesson, Miss Fitzgerald."

"With what?"

"You have a choice." He stroked her back as he spoke, his hands tangling in her hair. "My belt or a ruler."

"Ruler."

"Good choice."

Gabriel reached across to retrieve the long wooden ruler on his desk. It looked old with nicks and scratches along its length, but it seemed sturdy enough for their purpose. He stroked her ass now as if preparing her. "Do I need to gag you, or will you be a good girl and stay quiet?"

"If by gagging you mean stuffing your cock in my mouth, then yes please."

She felt the light sting as he brought the ruler down on her ass. She was thrilled at the power dynamics, his display of control, and the pooling wetness between her thighs.

"I didn't say you could talk back."

"Yes, *boss*."

"You need a safeword."

Maddie muttered the first thing that came to mind. "Apple."

"If you want me to stop at any time, say the word. I'll go slow and build from there."

Maddie nodded, anticipation racing along her spine. He spread her legs apart even farther, then taking the ruler, he gently rubbed it along her clit. The firm, cool pressure made her jump.

Gabriel used the edge to trace up the line of her ass, then without warning, he brought the flat end down on her cheek. Her heart jolted in her chest at the sudden sting.

"Harder."

Gabriel trailed the edge of the ruler down her spine. She could feel it through her blouse. When it sailed down on her ass again, she squirmed, the pleasure-pain racing through her.

"That better?"

"Yes."

She felt the quick sting as he smacked her again.

"Yes, what?"

"Boss." She shuddered, chest heaving.

Gabriel ran his hand over her cheek. "So fucking sexy." He brought down the ruler again, speaking filthy words that turned her on. Words that made her dig her nails into his desk.

By the time he was done, she felt wonderfully sore and painfully aroused.

"You're positively dripping on the carpet, Red," Gabriel murmured, kissing the spots on her ass that were tender. "I think that's punishment enough. Protection?"

"In my handbag."

A few seconds later, she heard the condom packet tear open. Maddie gasped as Gabriel tilted her hips, and without more than spitting on his palm to coat his cock, he thrust into her.

They both groaned.

Gabriel was harder, rougher, wilder than ever before. He tugged at her hair, pounding into her pussy, saying filthy things in that way of his that made her want to come on the spot. His voice was seductive, his touch commanding, and Maddie would surrender to him a million times over to have him love her like this.

Unbound. Wild. Fucking free.

She leaned up on her elbows, her tits bouncing, the tips of her nipples grazing against his chronicle. Maddie gripped the papers beneath her, fisting them in her hands. She could only feel the building pressure inside of her, the need, persistent and pressing, to come.

"I can hear you getting wetter. That's fucking sexy."

"I don't think I can last, Gabe."

"Then come." Gabriel tugged her back farther, pinching her nipples as he pumped into her. The pressure became so intense, Maddie thought she would pass out from it. But his smooth, hard cock hit the place inside of her that set her whole body alight.

Trembling now, Maddie called out, begging him for more.

"I want to see you drench my cock. Come for me, witch."

It was dazzling power that coursed through her now, and the trickling down her leg turned into a gushing release. "Gabriel!" She screamed his name, shaking and shuddering as she came on his cock.

Still, he pounded into her, relentless in his pleasuring.

It was only when she slumped against his desk that he stopped, placing a kiss on her shoulder.

"Maybe this wasn't only my fantasy."

Maddie laughed, gasping for air.

"But I'm not finished yet."

And with one sweeping motion, Gabriel shoved aside the items on his desk, uncaring where they landed. He picked her up, turning her around so that she sat on his desk now, sweaty and disheveled.

He unbound her hands then kissed her. Hard. His tongue worked her mouth, his hands fisting in her hair, until the beginnings of desire stirred anew.

Maddie unbuttoned his shirt. His chest was hard, warm, and begging for her mouth.

But Gabriel's need seemed impatient, and he gripped her face in his hands and kissed her until she clawed at his waist, wanting more.

"I want to watch your face when I come. I want to see you take my cock in that sexy snatch until I fill you whole."

He rubbed at her clit and sparks of pleasure shot through her. Oh god, he was going to make her come again, and she wasn't sure if she could stand it.

Gabriel shifted her knees back so that her heels rested against the desk, her pussy exposed and glistening. "Such a pretty, pretty pussy."

He thrust into her again, impatient with his need.

"Work your clit, Maddie. I want to see you lose control."

His eyes raked over her pussy, and the way he watched his cock disappear beneath the thatch of curls at her thighs spiked her arousal. She touched herself and the yearning grew, different again; it left her on edge. A grasping, searching desire built until she was flushed and whimpering.

He fisted her hair, kissing her with a ferocious need that set her body alight.

"Fuck, you're so sexy. I want you to come for me, Red. I'm close."

His labored breathing as he fucked her was the biggest turn-on.

When he pushed her to lie flat against the table, the forbidden nature of what they were doing hit home. It was hot as hell.

Her tits bounced with every thrust and she arched her back, desperate for release. When she caught a glimpse of his hooded, hungry expression, her body shattered and she sobbed his name as she orgasmed.

And then he pulled out, ripping off the condom to come over her tits in hot, silky waves. His jaw was clenched, his eyes closed, and Maddie had never seen anything sexier in her life.

She loved this man. It was a persistent thought that chanted through her brain. She loved this man and wanted to be with him in a way she'd never felt before. She loved the wild way he fucked her. The way he made her feel sexy and beautiful. She loved everything about him.

It filled her mind as he cleaned her gently with tissues. It invaded her body as he whispered sweet words of praise. It blurred her vision as she dressed back into her clothes.

And when Gabriel grinned at her—boyish and sweet—her heart simply fell at his feet.

She hugged this sensation to her chest, even though it terri-fied her. She couldn't help but tremble from the force of it.

Because Maddie knew that once they had the talk, that she might lose him. And she knew that she would never recover from it if she did.

CHAPTER THIRTY-ONE

*I*t was the final week of term three when it happened. Finally. After being estranged for so long, Maddie was going to meet her dad. The anticipation had been building steadily, so much so that she wasn't certain of her feelings. It was surreal to think that her dad was waiting on the other side of her door, wanting to see her. Even though her movements were slow, her mind raced with a thousand different scenarios of how this might play out. She was disconnected from her body and felt like she was drifting through some kind of fog.

Maddie had plucked up the courage to call the number she'd been given from Kate, the private investigator. But she hadn't expected the onslaught of emotions at hearing his voice again. It filled her with nostalgia that was comforting as much as it was painful. She'd left a breathless voice message asking him to make contact, and a part of her had been surprised when he'd texted her back late that evening, asking for details of where to meet. The fact that he had replied, that he'd wanted to see her was a good sign.

For the first meeting, Maddie had wanted to be on the front foot, and having him visit her at home had seemed the best option. But now that he was waiting behind the door, she wasn't so sure.

Taking a steadying, fortifying breath, she opened the door, and like a burst dam, nearly thirty years of angst and sadness engulfed them both.

"Big M."

"Dad."

She wrapped her arms around him, uncaring that he might feel uncomfortable, uncaring that he might not be a man who showed affection. It was what she needed. And when his arms came to hold her, she felt something inside her break.

Dermot held her tight against him, and she was assailed by his scent: licorice. That aniseed smell that always used to bring her comfort as a little girl wrapped itself around her now. She buried her face into his neck, pouring all the complex emotions into that hug.

It felt like an age when they let go. She wasn't surprised to see the tears swimming in his blue eyes. She was barely able to control her emotions either.

Dermot cupped her shoulders. "Let me have a look at you, my girl."

And that accent, the promise of Kildare and the green, grassy stud farms galloped around it.

She would have to go to Ireland. The thought popped into her head. The sudden need to understand, completely, the man who'd left, who'd abandoned her, filtered through any of her bitterness and anger at him leaving.

"Pretty as a picture."

Maddie laughed, tears streaming down her face.

He still sported a beard, robust and full even if a little faded in color. She remembered the way he would tickle her face and belly with the soft tufts of hair. How she would howl with laughter and the desperate need to wee if he didn't stop.

Yes, his fiery red hair had lost its vibrant hue, but he was still her burly, barrel-chested father, with arms so strong and comforting that she thought she would never feel fear again.

She had all these memories inside of her seeping out now, unable or unwilling to be contained any longer. She didn't know how to reconcile those feelings with the man before her. The one who broke her heart.

But she would try. She needed to try to understand.

Swallowing her emotions, Maddie stepped back, ushering him in.

He had aged. Not only in face, but in those blue eyes. They were shadowed with sadness where before she only recalled the humor. But she'd been a child and had viewed the world differently then.

"Cup of tea?"

"Sure, go on."

She nodded, motioning for him to follow her through to the kitchen.

"You've a lovely place here, Madeleine."

"Maddie." Only her dad had ever called her by her full name. She'd always thought she preferred Maddie, but now she knew why. It was too painful any other way.

"Daughter. I hardly know what to call ye."

Emotions squeaked and bubbled inside of her, making her feel unstable.

"Maddie is fine."

"I'm glad you found me."

"Are you?"

She turned around, the stove at her back. She still kept up the tradition of a pot of tea on the boil. It soothed her knowing it was something her dad used to do. Some things she just didn't forget. But she could tell he was nervous, perhaps more so than she. And for some reason, that put her at ease.

"Cookie?"

"Some things don't change." He patted his belly.

"Chocolate orange okay?"

"Some things *certainly* don't change."

"I don't know what I remember or what I have as my personal preferences."

"We have a lot of catching up to do."

When the tea had brewed and they both sat on the sofa, Maddie felt stable. The out of body feeling was beginning to fade at the edges. Holding the steamy, hot mug in her hands was grounding. Normal.

She was just having a cuppa with her estranged father of thirty-odd years in her home. *Totally* normal.

"I still can't believe I'm sitting in my apartment with my dad, drinking tea."

"You've no idea how long I've wanted this for, Maddie."

"Really? So how long have you been seeing Mom for then?"

"Straight to the point."

"Oh, I'm sorry if I'm not quite happy with the fact that you've been visiting my mother for God knows how long and neither of you bothered to tell me. You never once contacted me. I'm in my thirties for heaven's sake, not some clueless six-year-old. I deserve to know the truth. For so many years, I was afraid you were dead." She felt anger rush through her. "Do you know Mom never gave me your letters? I only found them three months ago. I never even knew you wrote to me, and now I find out you're seeing her?"

Her dad frowned. "I didn't know that. I—she said you didn't want to see me."

"Well, she's a damned good liar."

"I didn't contact you because she said you were happy. That you'd moved on. That you had no interest in me."

"They're all lies. I've wanted you back since the day you left us." Maddie shook her head. Why did her mother hate her so much? What had she done to deserve such ire? "How long have you been seeing her?"

"Six months maybe. And only every other month. I'd hoped to get some information from her about where you were, a number, anything to know you were okay."

"Why now?"

"I'm sorting out my will—"

Maddie's heart leaped. "Are you ill?"

"No, no, I'm grand, but I'm getting old. And I want to make sure you're provided for when I do end up kicking the bucket. It hurts that I wasn't there for you. I wanted to reconnect, to see you."

"All these years . . ." She sipped her tea, swallowing her bitter regret. "Sometimes I wished you'd tried harder."

"I know it. I kept telling myself that you probably hated me, that you didn't want to see me. So when I didn't hear from you, I assumed that was the truth."

"I hate her for keeping you away from me."

With a labored sigh, Maddie began explaining her mother's deceit. She started with her meeting with Madame Harrow, the PI, in short, everything.

"Mmm."

"Is that all you have to say? The woman you married has been hoodwinking us both and you say 'mmm'?"

"Simmer down."

Maddie leaned forward. "Don't you have an opinion on it?"

"Not anymore."

She stared at her father for a moment before putting down her tea. "I don't understand."

"I left your mother a long time ago because of her deceit."

Maddie frowned, heart racing. "What are you talking about?"

Dermot sighed. "Why do you think I keep visiting her? For the past six months, I've been going to that house, seeing the pictures of you as a child, trying to figure out a way to get through to her, to get to you. Why do you think I wrote to you all those years? Because I know what kind of woman she is."

"You should have tried harder."

Dermot nodded. "But I was afraid she would take you and run away. It was bad enough that she moved so often. She didn't want me contacting ye, so I sent the letters. I was afraid if I did more, I'd never see ye again."

"I want answers."

"It isn't my story to tell."

"Bullshit, it isn't. She's the reason you left, the reason I grew up without a father, and I want to know why."

Dermot placed his mug on the table, shifting back. "Do you remember your uncle?"

Maddie searched her memory but found it lacking. "What has this got to do with it?"

"Your uncle, Colm, has everything to do with it."

Maddie's mouth felt suddenly dry. She heard the weary anger in his tone, but she needed to know the truth. "I want to know what happened." She waited even though she wanted to poke and prod. She waited until he seemed to gather his thoughts—or enough strength—to tell her.

"My brother was trying to emigrate. He'd been talking of it since I left Ireland. He kept saying he wanted to come on a working visa and we could go into business together. Always some grand idea with Colm. But I told him I wanted none of it. If he were to come, it was on him."

"Okay."

"All my life, Colm wanted what I had. If I said I was joining the army, he was enlisting the next week. If I said I was retraining as a firefighter, you could be sure he'd be holding a feckin' hose and practising drills. That was the type of man he was."

"Were you close?"

"For a time. He was my kid brother, so it was endearing

when he was a lad, but as we grew, his inability to live his own life suffocated me. Eventually, like every man in Ireland at the time, I grew sick of the rain and the lack of jobs and I left.

"I traveled for a bit around Australia before I met your ma at a pub, fell in love, got married. Suddenly, Colm was yapping on the phone about wanting to come down.

"He visited for the wedding, then again when you were a wee thing, each time begging for us to take him in. God knows how he paid for them flights, but he was a feckin' swindler, he was. Charm the pants off the pope if he got a chance."

"Sounds swell."

Dermott chuckled. "I don't know how he managed to get across again, but he did with a working visa. I was reluctant to have him, but your mother, not so."

The dread swirled in her belly.

"I was away on an oil rig. I wanted to make good money for us to save up a bit more for a bigger house. With Colm over and yer ma complaining about the space, I thought I'd try to get money together, get us settled, and hopefully get Colm off our case. Then I'd be able to go back to college and get a teaching job and the like."

"But?"

"But I came home a few days early, wanting to surprise ye, and of course there's Colm and yer ma . . ." Dermot gestured.

Maddie's mouth fell open. "Oh god."

"There ain't no delicate way to put it, I'm afraid."

"Eww."

"That weren't the words I was hollerin' that day, you can be sure o' that." Dermot shook his head. "I used my fists. Not on her, mind, but on him before kicking him out."

"Where was I?"

"School."

"Oh."

"I know it doesn't excuse my actions."

"It doesn't. It explains why you were hurt, but it doesn't explain why the hell you left."

Dermot's mouth disappeared in a thin line. Whatever it was ate at him until he eventually spoke, his voice barely above a whisper. "She . . . Your ma said you weren't mine."

"What? And you believed her?"

"I did at first. She convinced me that the affair started when we were married. That Colm kept coming over to be with her."

Maddie felt sick. "Wait. Hold on. A-are you actually saying you're not my dad?"

"That's what I was told."

"And what's the truth?"

"Looking at you, I couldn't believe you weren't mine. We did the tests and confirmed what I'd always known, that you're my daughter both in looks and temperament. When yer ma cottoned onto the fact that I'd be up for child support payments, she was only too happy to facilitate those tests. And, sweet child, believe me when I say I wanted to take you with me."

"But you didn't."

"She was saying Colm was wanting to marry her and she wanted a divorce and she would fight for you. I knew her to be bitter and vengeful enough to do it. No matter how much it hurt me, most of all, I didn't want that for you. I didn't want you caught between us and in courts, and I—" He sighed, his heavy shoulders lowering. "I foolishly thought it was a phase. That maybe one day, we could be a family again."

"You were hoping she would take you back?" Maddie stared at him, struck by the realization that her father loved her mother. Against his better judgment. Beyond all reason. He loved her so much that he would have tried to win her back again so that they could be a family. Cheating didn't switch off that love. Even though he knew better, he still had feelings for her.

Her mother didn't deserve his loyalty.

"And did you try? To get back together again?"

"Aye. I did many times. I called, I visited at the beginning, but she wouldn't let me see you. She said you were happy at school and they were a family now and it was best I didn't upset you further."

"And that didn't strike you as odd? Didn't you question it? Try to see me?"

"I was a mess. I was broken and angry and gone for so long, I was starting to believe it. I asked if I could write to you and she agreed."

"I still can't believe you left."

"She was threatening with courts. I didn't want to lose any more rights. Feck'n hell, Maddie, I was working on rigs. That was no place for a chil' of your age. I wouldn'ta had a chance o' keeping you."

"Well, it didn't feel like you fought very hard."

"I did the best I could. I see now that it wasn't good enough. But I thought Colm had replaced me as her husband, that he was your stepdad."

"So what, she asked you to write and then out of spite didn't give me your letters? That's sick."

"I'd hoped that she'd keep to her word and gave you them. But she always liked to fight dirty. I managed to find you with each move, certain if you at least had my letters, you'd know me."

Maddie shook her head. The deception was so deep, so entrenched in every aspect of her childhood, she couldn't believe it. "You should have stayed."

"I'm sorry, pet. I was angry and scared and confused. I took the coward's way out."

"You were scared of her."

She saw the truth of it flash behind his eyes. Even though her father was a big man, much bigger and stronger than her mother, she knew without a doubt that the hate and vitriol that had been spewed her way since she'd been a kid was merely a fraction of what her father would have copped when they were together.

Her mother was an abuser.

But she could imagine that her father coming forward, saying anything about her mother's verbal assault and threats would have been dismissed back then. But she knew it to be the case because alongside the loving memories of her father reading to her or building Lego towers were the twisted memories of her mother hurling abuse and—oftentimes—objects at her father in her fits of rage.

How much had she blocked out of her memory? How much had she internalized?

"So why did you keep writing? All those years when I never replied, why did you keep sending me letters?"

"Because I had hope."

Again the tears blurred her vision, and again her heart twisted painfully in her chest.

"I had hope that one day you would forgive me and seek me out. I had hope that you would know that I loved you dearly. That I never meant to leave you. It killed me every day knowing you were there. I didn't even know she wasn't with my brother until he came back to find me ten years later as if nothing had happened."

"Jesus."

"Jesus, Mary, Joseph, and all the saints and sinners, he did."

"And?"

"He said he'd left your ma not long after your sixth birthday, not long after I'd left. The novelty of living my life had gone once I was no longer around. But she'd been telling me that ye were happy families."

It was odd. Even though she had just reconnected with her dad, she believed him. There was an honesty in his recount of the past. A haunting truth to his words that brought up all of her pain again.

"But why would she keep up the farce? What's the point? Especially if you were still in contact?"

Dermot shrugged. "Pride? Your mother's a complicated woman."

"I doubt that."

"To be honest with ye, Sharon didn't have the greatest of starts in life."

"That doesn't excuse her behavior."

"No, it doesn't. But it gives you a thread to follow, to lead you back to where it all began."

"Sounds like excuses to me."

"Haven't you ever met someone whose past makes you understand them that little bit better? It's not that you excuse their behavior, but everything makes sense. And yes, in some cases you allow for them being overdramatic or anal retentive or hypervigilant because you understand where they come from, and so you bend a little or make room a bit more."

Maddie swallowed the truth. She did, in fact, know a person, and because it startled her to think of her mother and Dermot as anything like her relationship with Gabriel, she paused, refusing to answer.

Not that her relationship with Gabriel was anything like her parents', but she knew he'd had a rough childhood. One that— by his own admission—had made him wild and a little destructive. And didn't he overcompensate with rules and order and the shield of a cold exterior to never get hurt again?

Knowing him now, the possessive, passionate, stubborn man behind the mask, didn't she like him best of all? Better than anyone else she had known?

Maddie shook a little, a fine tremor beginning, breaking through her reasoning. It wove a path from her head all the way

to her heart, rattling her resolve, breaking apart her justifi-
cations.

But now wasn't the time to think about Gabriel and his
heartache, or even her feelings for him, ones that scared the hell
out of her.

Her father was right. She got it, as her father seemed to
know that she would. She understood now why he would give
her twisted mother the benefit of the doubt at times, why he
didn't give up hope.

Love.

And maybe for her father, there were some deep-seated
boundary issues.

But it was love that filtered through his sadness even now,
shimmering in the late-afternoon light. Because at one point in
time, he must have felt that way for her and she him.

But love is behavior, as her therapist had once said. And
treating someone badly and justifying it as love wasn't healthy.
It dawned on her that what she felt for Gabriel was a far cry
from what her parents had shown one another. She was
breaking the cycle, refusing to accept abuse in her life.

But what of her parents? From what her dad had shared
with her, their relationship had been complicated, made harder
by their inability to seek help.

She imagined that at the beginning, Dermott would have
fallen for her mother's direct manner, for her big laugh and love
of all animals, especially birds.

Maddie had thought the magpies and crows had come to
visit their home because her mother was a witch, but she'd not
allowed for the fact that her mother loved those birds with a
tenderness that didn't seem to make sense. Loved them sometimes above her own child. Beneath all the layers of bitterness,
there was a woman who once had the capacity to show and
receive love from this man sitting before her.

But her mother's issues warped their love until it was a

broken destructive force, until it poisoned everything they'd once shared.

"I'm not saying her past excuses her behavior, but she wasn't well, Maddie. She had demons that haunted her—"

"Which you thought you could love away."

"I'm ashamed enough to admit that I did. It was a different time back then."

Maddie tried to process it all. She wanted to fight against this new understanding, but she couldn't. She wasn't the type to rail against reason for the sheer, stubborn need to be right. She smiled, knowing that Gabriel would be shocked to hear it.

"I get why you wanted to believe in your marriage and in Sharon, but there comes a point where you have to accept that some people won't change. She's hurt me so much, and I don't know how to forgive her for that. Or you."

"You don't have to."

That wasn't the response she expected. But given that the man sitting opposite her was a stranger, she wasn't sure what to expect. "No, I suppose I don't."

"Not everyone is capable of forgiveness, and that's okay so long as you don't become resentful."

So long as she didn't become her mother.

A part of her didn't want to think of her mother as someone who was anything other than a bitter woman who hurt everyone she'd ever claimed to love.

Hateful. Resentful. Manipulative. Bitter.

She clung to that image, clung to that persona because she couldn't quite believe there was someone who had been worthy of love beneath all of that. It also hurt to think that had her mother managed her issues, Maddie would have had a very different upbringing. But then, they were both at fault. Her father for allowing himself to believe that his only daughter was better off without him and her mother for throwing away the only person who had probably seen the good in her. The only person who had loved her, knowing her past.

Maddie frowned. Her mother had never been forthcoming about her parents or even her youth. Any time Maddie had asked, Sharon had told her that her grandparents were dead and she was without a family.

"Is what Mom said about her family true? That she's an only child?"

"It is and isn't. Her dad was unfaithful to her ma. Her stepfather wasn't a good man. She . . . uh, well . . ." He cleared his throat. "She lived in terror of his footsteps at night. He abused her for many years."

Maddie gasped.

"She had stepsiblings who were only happy enough to look the other way at their father's abuse, most likely relieved that it wasn't them anymore, that he had found a new child to be his favorite."

"That's sick."

"Aye, it is. And I was the only person in all the world that knew it. She never uttered it to a soul, and when her stepfather died, she went to his funeral so she could spit on his grave."

"Good."

"She's a hurt woman. One who desperately wants to love, to be loved, but doesn't know how. Like a baby bird with a broken wing. The urge is there to fly, to be free of all the pain, but she's trapped by her body, by her mind."

"She won't ever be free."

"Human beings can change."

Maddie scoffed. "You'd need a miracle for that to happen."

"You forget you're half Irish. We come from a land of saints."

"And sinners."

He nodded. "Aye, that too."

"So what now? Does this mean you want to be in my life? Are we going to go our separate ways?"

"Ye kiddin' me, lass? I'd have crossed the wild Atlantic in a rubber dinghy to see you again. To apologize. I took the coward's way out, and you've paid for my sins long enough. But Maddie, let me say this." He reached out to hold her hands. "There wasn't a day that went by where I didn't think about you and love you. Not a day. To have you here, to speak with you and hear your voice is beyond any words."

Maddie closed her eyes briefly, feeling something shift into place. Or was it a letting go? Either way, that constant dissatisfaction that she carried with her, that ringing echo inside of her became muted. Even if a fraction.

Here was the first man she had ever loved, the one who had promised to look after her and care for her, apologizing for what he'd done, loving her always in his own way. And it was everything that she needed to hear. It was the balm on a childhood wound, and even though she'd learned to be cynical, she was incapable of it now in the face of such honesty. Because it hadn't been about her. She'd been caught in their dysfunctional relationship, but it wasn't her fault he'd left or that her mother hated the sight of her.

She witnessed his pain, his need for reconciliation, as much as she accepted her own. Taking in a cleansing breath, Maddie rotated her hands so that she could grip his in return.

She clung to her father, accepting his olive branch nearly thirty years too late and yet, in some ways, perfectly on time.

CHAPTER THIRTY-TWO

"Where is this going?" Maddie watched the confusion play out over Gabriel's face. Once upon a time, she wouldn't have been able to read him, but now that she was in love with him, she understood.

Every subtle twitch, every heated look, they all made sense to her because she knew him. And because she knew him, she had to ask, had to figure it all out.

"You obviously don't mean the state examiner's advice." Gabriel looked up over his laptop.

The truth was, she knew her own heart and she had to protect it. Love sometimes wasn't enough. Her parents were proof of that . . . and she wouldn't let what she had with Gabriel disintegrate into something nasty.

Her father coming back into her life had changed everything. He wanted a relationship with her. He wanted to be connected in a way that she'd only ever dreamed of. Some days she was torn between love and anger, but she was still processing it. Her dad was back in her life, and she was grateful for it.

And through it all, Gabriel had been by her side. Solid,

dependable, secure. So instead of watching what they had waste away, she would make the first move. There was no point being in a relationship for months or years until they both would be hurt by the bitter realization that they were on separate paths, wanting separate things.

"No. I don't. There's something I have to tell you."

"Okay." She watched as Gabriel shut his laptop and looked at her across his kitchen table. His movements were careful, but she could tell he was annoyed by the interruption.

They were flat out spending their two-week break working in the lead-up to the end of year literature exam. Maddie knew he was as focused as she was on marking papers, creating practice exams, and finalizing the internal assessment. Now was probably not the best time to talk about their relationship status.

But if not now, when?

Maddie knew it was easy to just enjoy their very healthy sex life, the romantic dinner dates, and weekends away, but it would be much harder to face reality.

She was old and wise enough to know that it wouldn't be roses all the time. She felt a desperate need to lay her cards out on the table and tell him the truth, and if that meant having kids was a dealbreaker for him, then so be it.

"I can't have children," she blurted out.

"Okay."

Maddie traced one of the keys on her laptop with her finger, circling around it in quick, repetitive movements. "I'm not sure you understand. I've lived with the knowledge of my infertility for most of my life, so it isn't something new. It's pretty much impossible for me to conceive. Even if I could, the truth is that I don't want to. I don't want kids. Not now, not ever. I know a lot of guys want a family, and if it's something you do want in the future, then that's totally fine. What I'm saying is, I'll understand if you don't want to continue this."

"I want to continue this." His response was instantaneous. His tone, even.

"It doesn't bother you?"

"No."

"Do you want kids?"

"No."

"No?" Maddie blinked. "Are you sure?"

"Why ask me a question only to doubt my answer? If this is going to work, then you need to learn to trust me."

"I'm sleeping with the enemy . . . or ex-enemy. Surely that shows you how much I trust you."

"Okay."

"What, that's it?"

"I'm not going to ask for a doctor's note detailing your medical history if that's what you're getting at, but I can if it'll make you feel better."

"Why are you being so . . ."

"Reasoned? Logical?"

"Annoyingly calm. Most guys would be running for the hills."

"How about I walk towards you instead?" Gabriel approached, drawing her up and into his arms.

Maddie wanted to feel relieved, and a part of her did, but something was off. And she didn't know how to fix it. Dear Lord, was she simply incapable of being happy?

Gabriel's embrace was firm, and even though she wrapped her arms around him, she couldn't seem to relax. For some reason, the sinking sensation in the pit of her stomach wouldn't abate. She didn't know what the answer would be, but she was certain that this wasn't it.

As if sensing her distance, Gabriel pulled away, planting a kiss on her temple.

"Tell me. What's troubling you still?"

"What are your plans for the future?"

"I didn't have any until I met you."

She felt a sick fear creep up her spine. She didn't want to hear what he was going to say, she couldn't bear to hear her own heart breaking, but she continued to ask the question. She *had* to know for her own selfish preservation.

"That's all well and good, but what does that mean specifically? We need to be on the same page. Do you even believe in marriage? What party do you vote for? Do you donate to charity?"

"Why does any of this matter?"

"It matters to me."

"Why?"

Maddie sighed and stepped back, trying to make sense of what she was feeling. She wouldn't let her temper cloud the clarity that was needed for this conversation, but she couldn't seem to help it. The more she thought about it, the greater her anger.

"Because it does."

"That's a thirteen-year-old's answer."

"Are you calling me juvenile?"

"I said what I said." She knew he was goading her, but she was beyond caring. "You need to give me a better answer than that, Maddie."

"Because I'm not so green as to assume that we can make it work because we want it to."

"Why can't we make it work?"

"There are fundamental differences between us."

"What about them?"

"Fundamental differences in a relationship means friction, friction means arguments, and arguments equal dissatisfaction."

"Are you trying to use logic on me?"

"I'm not joking." She was afraid that their propensity to

disagree would mean they'd always be arguing, just like her parents.

Gabriel reached out only for her to step back again. He sighed, shoving his hands in his pockets. "Who cares if we disagree? I would've thought we're pretty used to that."

"So what, you want to argue all the time?"

"I think healthy disagreements are normal."

"I don't."

"You'd give up the chance to have a fulfilling and happy relationship because we could argue?"

"It's not only that."

"Then what? Relationships take work, Maddie, and that means making a choice every day to be with that person even through arguments and differing values. It's not like I'm going to change who I am overnight."

"It goes deeper and you know it."

"Break it down for me then."

"Relationships are hard enough. Marriage is a forever thing for me. I saw my dad walk out as if it were the easiest thing in the world to do. One day we were a family, and the next we were broken. *I* was broken. If I'm going to even entertain the idea of marriage, I want to know that I'm doing it with someone I'm compatible with."

"Are you proposing?"

"What?" She reared back, startled.

"You're talking of marriage."

"I-I'm not proposing."

"Well, I hope not 'coz as far as proposals go, that one kind of sucked."

She laughed in spite of herself. "You're twisting this, Gabriel, making it harder than what it needs to be." Why the hell had she brought up marriage? What the hell was wrong with her? She had no idea how this man felt about her. Hell, she was still processing how *she* felt about *him*. "We already piss each other off as it is."

"I'm finding it hard to understand the problem. We're allowed to fight, Maddie. We're allowed to be in a happy relationship and disagree. We're passionate people. And I don't hear you complaining about the makeup sex."

"Funny. But I need to know your values."

"I agree. Values are important."

"Good. And if they differ, then we might need to think about whether this is the right relationship for us both."

"It is."

"I want to be on the same page. Now. Before we get in too deep."

"Speak for yourself. This is deep whether you like it or not."

"Gabriel." She huffed. "Honestly, we can't presume we'll have some fairytale happily ever after because we're in love!"

The air crackled between them, and Maddie froze, realizing what had come out of her mouth.

Fuck.

"We're in love?"

"Oh god."

Gabriel held her, his eyes bright, a smile playing at the corners of his mouth. "In love."

"Forget I said it."

"Why?"

"It never happened."

"Why?"

"It just slipped out."

"*Why?*"

"For God's sake, Gabriel, why *what*?" She was beyond reason, unable to think clearly but running on the pumping adrenaline that burst through her. She wanted to throw a book at his head. She settled for throwing her hair back in anger. Why had she ever entertained the idea that she loved him? It was ludicrous.

"Why would you want to deny it, Maddie?"

"I—"

"Why is it a problem?" Gabriel's eyes were bright but somehow also serious. "Do you love me?"

Maddie shook. "That's beside the point."

"Is it?"

"I was saying it as an example." Her cheeks flushed. "It's beside the point."

"You keep saying that. So what *is* the point?"

"I—we hate each other."

"Do we? Maybe at the start, but not now. You seem so certain that this won't work out. If I'm in a relationship, I'm all in. But I want a partner who's the same."

Maddie's mouth opened then closed again.

"You know what? You don't have to answer anything right now. I think you need to think about whether you want to be with me or not. This isn't an ultimatum, but you're throwing this stuff back in my face and I'm wondering why. What do you need from me to feel secure in this? Whatever it is, we can talk about it, and I'll try my damn best to give it to you. But Maddie, I want this. I want you. Surely that should be enough?"

She turned to leave, but he held her close.

"Don't. Stay with me tonight, Madeleine."

His voice was low, a deep rumble that vibrated through her, reaching every part of her body. Every part of her soul. If she had had any reservations, his vulnerable request would have dashed them aside.

She wanted to run and hide, to lick her wounds. She also wanted to stay.

"Nobody calls me by that name anymore."

"I know. Just like I know a lot things about you. Important things. If it makes you feel better, we can finish up early tonight, get a pizza, and start talking about the serious stuff all night if you want."

"And then what?"

"Then you can wake up with me in the morning. No slinking out in the dead of night."

Something was shifting. Breaking or settling into place, she wasn't sure. It scared and excited her. Not wanting to hide, not wanting to run from it, she leaned forward. His kiss was gentle, a balm to soothe the fear and hurt.

She didn't understand what it was about him that was drawing her in, but she was going to follow it to wherever it would lead.

"I've never slunk away before."

"I'm covering all bases here. I want to wake up beside you, Maddie." He stroked her cheek gently with his knuckles, his touch tender.

"I didn't bring any of my things."

Gabriel sighed. "I'm afraid you'll have to be naked for the rest of the weekend then."

Maddie swallowed, suddenly nervous. She hadn't felt that way about a guy in a really, really long time.

"I think I can handle that."

"I bet you could, you naughty witch." Sweeping her up off her feet, he led her upstairs.

CHAPTER THIRTY-THREE

Gabriel held Maddie close, enjoying the way she fit against his naked body. He had taken the time to explore every part of her, to savor and devour and love her in the way she deserved. After the events of the evening, he'd needed to reconnect because her words made him more than fearful. She had her doubts about their relationship, and he wanted to banish them all away. But he realized he couldn't do that unless he let her in. Really let her in.

She was right. Values were important. But he was also right. Love was everything. And he knew that telling her how he felt would freak her the fuck out. She needed to work through all her concerns before opening her heart. He could see that now.

As fiery as their relationship was, she grounded him. Lying together, feeling her close filled in the gaps that he'd started to notice were missing.

He felt it was time to share what bothered him the most. What shamed him about his childhood. So she knew and could make a decision about whether this was something she wanted. Yes, values were important, but so was complete honesty.

"You know that my childhood wasn't ideal."

"I do." Maddie turned to face him now as they lay on their sides.

"To be honest, if I didn't have Harper, I don't know how I would have navigated life being on my own with my dad. So I'll always be grateful to her for being there."

"You know, she told me that the man I'd be with was closer than I thought. I didn't realize at the time just how right she was."

"She's pretty amazing. She helped me a lot growing up, but even with all her support, it didn't take away the pain completely. Even if I crashed next door on her mother's sofa, I would still have to go home eventually. I'd have to face the shit-show that was my father's way of bringing up his only son."

"I want to know. I want to understand." Her expression was open, inviting.

Gabriel knew she did. He could see the concern on her face. He understood that she wanted to connect with him. He yearned for that, craved it with this woman. He'd convinced himself that he'd gotten over the shit with his father. And he *had* dealt with it, sought help, cleaned up his act. But ever since Leo's death, all the pain had resurfaced.

Since getting to know Maddie, he realized that the way he'd been living had been pleasant enough, but somehow lacking. It wasn't what he wanted anymore, not what he needed for his future.

The woman beside him was his future.

If only he offered it. If only she accepted.

In order to do that, they needed to be open and honest with each other.

"So, you know that my father was a model. He was obviously very good-looking, and even though he was wild, when he met my mother—who actually treated him in triage after a motorbike accident—he fell head over heels for her. Totally smitten, couldn't stop seeing her, and according to my dad, she felt the same for him. It was instant. A strong connection that sparked something more. A few months later, that was it. He swore to marry her and he did."

"That's so sweet."

"Those first five years of my life were magic." Gabriel grinned. "You can tell in all the pictures they were madly in love. After they got married, they had me, and it seemed like we were a happy family. At least for a time."

"Not many people get that ever in their lives. They were lucky to have it. To have each other."

"I know it. Which is what makes what happened next harder to deal with."

"Your mother's drowning."

"That and . . . after. They would go to the beach, and he would teach her how to swim, and it was simply bad luck that she got caught in a rip. He naturally jumped in to try save her but got in trouble himself. He was a stronger swimmer, but I nearly lost both my parents that day."

"Where were you?"

"At a friend's house for a playdate."

Maddie squeezed his shoulder, and he drew her close, resting his arm around her waist, needing to be connected.

"But then my dad became depressed. It was like he forgot I existed. And that's when I began taking care of him, bringing him water and painkillers after he'd drowned his sorrow in booze. Until eventually, he seemed to snap out of it, and I thought finally, finally, I'd get my dad back."

"I get it. I know what it feels like to wait and want."

"I think my dad decided he'd had his once in a lifetime love. So somewhere in his mind, he figured if he couldn't have that again, then he would do the opposite. Chase every thrill, every high, to forget."

"What does that mean?"

"He lost out on a lot of modeling gigs. The booze wrecked

his ability to hold down jobs or make call backs on time. So . . ." Gabriel took a deep breath. "My dad became an escort."

Maddie's shock flashed behind her eyes, her mouth opening in disbelief.

He hadn't told anyone about it other than Harper. All the women he knew or had dated didn't know. And he'd preferred it that way.

Until Maddie.

She needed to know the truth. He needed to tell her, to share it with her.

For so long, his father's job had made him feel dirty. As if the seedy side of being paid for sex had somehow rubbed off on Gabriel. He couldn't describe it, but that was how he'd always felt: tainted by association.

"Like a . . ."

"Prostitute. First to anyone, then eventually he realized socialites with money to burn didn't mind a handsome face. They'd all heard about my mom's death and were only too happy to pounce on that opportunity. It gave my dad something . . . I don't know, a connection, a sense of being for a brief time. So then he'd get sober, make good money, then months later he'd be back on the alcohol, lost for weeks on end. Sometimes he brought the women home and I was told to hide away. If he remembered that I existed, that is.

"But when he started to bring the parties home on the regular, that was when everything exploded. The booze, then the drugs and more loose women, I couldn't escape it. As I grew up, I saw the truth of it, and I hated his weaknesses. Hated him. So then I got wild in my teen years, searching for love and sex and fulfillment in every empty relationship and experience."

"I'm so sorry."

"Don't get me wrong, modeling gave me the money to change careers and get myself an education and a house and everything I wanted. But it didn't cure the hate and anger. One day, I woke up and loathed myself so much, I didn't recognize who I'd become. I looked in the mirror and all I saw was my father staring back at me.

"You asked me a while back why I got into education, and my mother is a huge part of that. But I think it was the moment my drunk, drug-addled whore of an absent father said he was proud of me that made me snap. I didn't want his pride. I thought I was rebelling, but I was turning into him. Someone I hated. And for so long, I've felt ashamed of him, ashamed of myself, but not anymore."

"That's awful, Gabriel." She cupped his cheeks, her expression soft, accepting. "I get it now. I get why you do what you do, the reasons behind it. But you don't have to be ashamed anymore. It doesn't make you tainted to come from a father who made the wrong choices any more than it taints me to come from a mother who did the same. But here we are, carrying their shame and their burdens as if they were our own."

Relief washed over him. To be accepted by her was more important than he'd realized. And that niggling discontent, that sense that something wasn't right, that he was missing something vital, had dissipated.

It was peace.

Her words healed him in a way that nobody ever had before.

He wanted her. On a deeper level. He craved from her what he feared he would never want, what he feared he was better off *not* wanting.

But this vibrant, vexing woman made him believe that love was worth the pain; for her, he would risk his heart a thousand times over.

"Gabriel, you don't have to live your life with hard rules and restrictions. You can be a little wild and emotional. Because those experiences are a massive part of who you are. And that's okay."

He studied the soft curve of her cheek, the warmth in her expression. His heart twisted.

"My mother would've loved you."

Her sweet gasp hovered between them, and he watched as the tears pooled in her eyes. His mother *would* have loved her. He knew that without a doubt. Just as he loved her.

It spread through him. The acceptance of it. The wonderful joy in it. He wasn't bound anymore by self-imposed rules. He was with someone who accepted him. The parts of himself that were ugly, the parts that scared him. And just then, he realized what his father must have felt. That lightning bolt, that feeling of being whole and loved; it gave him life.

He finally understood what it must have been like for his father to have lost it. Now that he'd found the woman who was his world, it was tortuous to think he would have to endure life without her.

He hadn't understood his father's pain. How could he? He'd been a kid, mourning his mother, the life that was wrenched brutally away from him. He'd hated his father, blamed him for not being what he'd needed for so long.

But Gabriel wondered what he'd be like if he ever lost Maddie. It didn't bear thinking about.

"Hey, can I ask you something?"

"I'm an open book, remember?"

"Who's Punky?"

Maddie stiffened in his arms. "How did you—"

"The birthday card Dermot sent you. I didn't want to ask at the time as you were upset, but I've wondered since then if Punky was a pet?"

Maddie closed her eyes, and when she opened them, he saw the pain.

"She was the doll my dad gave me on my third birthday. It was one of the only things I had left of him."

"Tell me." Gabriel held her, hoping his presence would comfort her.

"I did something my mother didn't like. I can't remember what heinous crime I committed. But she had a quick temper and a mean spirit, even more so after dad had left. I told her I'd learned my lesson, but she didn't seem to think that was enough, and she knew that I loved Punky, that I used to talk to her about dad, that it was a comfort to me. And . . . she took her, made me sit down in front of the chair by the fire, and watch as she burned her."

"Christ."

"I couldn't do anything about it. I tried. But I was only six years old, and back then she was a strong woman, not bound by a wheelchair. I screamed and cried and told her I hated her and that I would never forgive her. That she wasn't my best friend anymore."

"I'm sorry."

"She—fuck, Gabe—she *laughed* when I said that. Said she didn't want to be my friend. That I was naughty and that was the reason Dad had left."

"Jesus, Maddie."

He gently wiped away the tears that fell.

"She blamed me for so long for him leaving. I thought it was something I had done, and it wasn't until I got myself into therapy that I realized that I wasn't to blame. That it was ridiculous to even think that I was somehow responsible, but as a kid, I didn't know better."

"And as your mother, she should have."

"Yes. She should have. I loved her. I wanted to make her happy, and for so long she would cry and I would try comfort her, but I hadn't a clue what had happened until my dad told me everything, about her cheating with his brother, about her own awful childhood. I was ignorant of the truth as a kid and took the blame as my own.

"And when I grew older and she kept blaming me, I thought well, it must be me. If my mother, the woman I loved so much, said I was bad, then I was bad. If she said I was responsible, I was responsible."

"And you carried that your whole life."

"I did. And I told myself when I was older and wiser that the bitterness she felt wasn't against me, not really. It was against my dad to a degree, but really, deep down inside, it was against herself. She's never once apologized or taken responsibility for her actions. She never admitted she was wrong. Never admitted that she made mistakes or drove him away. It was always someone else's fault."

"A true mark of emotional immaturity."

Maddie looked at him. "Yes. Yes, you're right. But she'll never change. And after years of living with her commenting about my looks, how I was too heavy to be loved or whatever it was that she wanted to pick on, I made a plan to leave. And I still can't seem to forgive her."

"Maddie, know this. You're stunning, inside and out. And I think you're perfect as you are. I don't want you ever feeling otherwise."

"I know this. Well, most of the time I do. Sometimes I still get caught up in those negative thoughts, but I'm a lot stronger than I used to be. And I don't know if living with my dad would have been the ideal life I once imagined, but I'd hoped that it would've been a lot less abusive. More peaceful. He's a chilled-out guy, a coward by his own admission, but he never once made me feel small and weak. And he still doesn't. He hurt me and abandoned me and that was bad enough, but he was always gentle with me."

He squeezed her close. Cupping her face, he kissed her, pouring every part of his heart into it, giving her what his words seemed to lack. But he would find them. Those words were important, not just to her, but for him too. He wanted to say them, to put it out there into the world. To claim her as his.

"I'm sorry she hurt you."

"I know. But it feels good to share this with you. To understand."

"It's like a weight off your chest."

"It is."

"Look at us, getting along." Gabriel pulled her on top of him. "I know of another thing we do really well together."

"Again?" She laughed.

"Always."

Wild need whipped through him. To claim. To possess. He had to have her or he would die from the wanting.

This fiery, bold, intelligent woman would forever make him want. She brought out a part of him he'd feared had no place in the world. Through her eyes, he saw how ridiculous he'd been.

He'd wasted too much time already, and he would be damned if he made that same mistake twice.

CHAPTER THIRTY-FOUR

"So you guys had a fight?" Ally asked, walking slowly as she pushed the stroller with a sleeping Ellie Mae in the bassinet attachment.

"I think so?"

"But you're not angry with him?"

"No . . ."

Maddie glanced at Ally as they made another loop around the block. She was still tender and sleep-deprived but had texted saying she needed some air and grown-up company. Maddie had happily come straight over, detailing what had happened on the weekend.

"Explain this to me again?" Ally puffed her cheeks, stopping to rub at her back before walking again.

"Do you want to go back inside?"

"No . . . but milky boobs weigh a ton and it sometimes feels like my vagina is going to fall out."

Maddie laughed, grabbing her own breasts. "Don't I know it. The boobs thing. These puppies are torture on the back and shoulders. And I don't even have milk in them."

"I think I need to sit." Ally squirmed.

Maddie steered her to the bus stop bench, helping her sit down before perching beside her.

"You okay? Vagina falling out sounds painful."

"It is. It doesn't last thankfully, but that's my cue that I need to lie down."

"Want me to call Owen?"

"No, I need to sit for a bit." Ally sighed. "Distract me with your love life drama. What's bothering you?"

"He wasn't affected by my confession."

"That you can't have kids?"

"That I can't and don't want to have kids. I wasn't going to blame it on my infertility. I genuinely can think of nothing worse in the world than raising a child—no offense."

"None taken. What did he say?"

"He said okay."

"Okay?"

"Yes, okay. He doesn't want kids either."

"And this is a problem because?"

"Why would he be okay with it?"

"Now you're questioning why he doesn't want kids? Madds, that's mental."

"It is."

"Maybe you should trust him, perhaps? You've trusted him so far with all your family issues, with your body . . ."

Maddie frowned. "I never thought of it like that."

"Whether you like it or not, you need to work through those trust issues that will rear their ugly head when you least expect it."

"I don't think I have trust issues."

Ally looked at her for a moment then held her belly, laughing. When she had a chance to draw breath, Maddie was pouting.

"Not funny."

"Oh . . . too funny." Ally wiped at her eyes. "Look, you were just harping on about not trusting the fact that he said he doesn't want kids. If that isn't major trust issues, then I don't know what to tell you."

"That I'm right?"

Ally pulled a face. "Can't lie. Won't lie."

"Yeah, yeah." But she knew that she *did* have issues with trust. She'd all but admitted it to herself in the past, but hearing it from someone else wounded her pride a little.

"Your dad left you as a child, and your mom has major issues with men, so I'm not surprised that it has filtered down to you, especially now that you're in a relationship. The whole guys say one thing but act in another way spiel, is bound to leave you a bit guarded."

"Mmm. He said I needed to figure out what I wanted from the relationship, what I needed to feel secure. That he didn't think I wanted to be in a relationship with him."

"And do you?"

"Yes, I do."

Ally shifted. "You and Gabriel had a very grown-up, measured discussion about a big relationship thing. One where you both agreed. What about this is bothering you?"

"I'm not sure."

"Does he treat you well?"

"Yes."

"And do you enjoy spending time together?"

"Well, yeah. It's surprisingly easy being with him. But we disagree about things."

"And you think that's a bad thing."

Maddie sighed. "It makes me scared. My parents fought a lot."

"Your parents had a toxic relationship, Madds. Your mom

was abusive in every way. This is different. Gabriel's telling you he's committed to making it work despite your differences, but all you've known relationships to be is tumultuous. Which makes you freak out. Trust the fact that this is going well. You're looking for problems and because you haven't found any, you're getting antsy and convincing yourself something is wrong."

"I don't trust myself to know what's right."

"You will. Because you'll figure this out together. Gabriel won't leave you like your father did."

She knew that what Ally was saying was right, that Gabriel would be faithful. And knowing it made her scared that she would lose the one person she loved more than anything.

"Did I tell you about the time I thought Owen was super angry at me?"

"Tell me so I don't feel so pathetic."

"It was when we were dating and it was over Charlotte's welfare, and I was so sure that he was going to storm off in a huff after our disagreement."

"But he didn't?"

"He asked me out for a steak dinner."

"Ha."

"Because he said he'd rather be angry at me and talking through it than to give me the silent treatment like some child. That communication with me was what he valued and put above all else." Ally sighed, a dreamy expression transporting her to that moment in the past.

"Shit, that's so sweet." And wasn't that essentially what Gabriel had done? Asking her to stay the night? Sharing things from his childhood that made him feel vulnerable? He'd made sure that she'd known he wanted to be in a relationship with her. They had spoken of their values and beliefs, what they needed from a relationship. So what was her damn problem?

"It showed me that Owen was the type of guy that was

unlike any other man I'd known. That he wouldn't freeze me out like my parents did and that communication was important to him. But Madds, I didn't know how to deal with that. At the time, I was certain he would behave the way my father did, how anyone I ever dated did. And it left me feeling uncertain."

"So you're saying that this jittery feeling that makes me want to puke like I'm on a roller coaster is normal?"

"Very normal. You'll learn how to have a healthy relationship by living it, not running from it."

"Al . . ."

"Hmm?"

"I think . . . In fact, I know, well, the thing is . . ." Maddie threw her hands up in the air. Why was this so fucking hard to admit? "I'm in love with him."

"Oh!" Ally beamed at her. "Oh, Maddie, this is wonderful! I could see it, but I didn't want to scare you by suggesting it. Oh Madds, Gabriel is making you feel things you didn't think possible. You're finding all these excuses or reasons as to why you can't trust him. Why you aren't compatible together."

"So I'm looking for reasons to push him away."

"Exactly. You forget he's been there this whole year, helping you out with your family, showing you the type of man he is. It isn't just sex anymore. Which if I know you, you probably convinced yourself it was."

"He said he cared for me."

"That's so lovely, Madds."

"Is it?"

Ally nodded. "It is . . . but you're afraid it's not enough."

"I don't want to be like my father, loving my mother beyond what was healthy. And I don't want to be like my mother, pushing away a good thing because I have issues."

"You're nothing like your parents. What you have is special, but you need to let him know how you feel. Gabriel is not your dad or your mom. They abandoned you in different ways, but he's been nothing but loyal."

Maddie leaned forward, groaning. "I thought I'd worked through all my shit in therapy." And then it hit her with utter clarity, why she carried this uneasiness. Beneath her inability to trust and her fear of losing Gabriel was her unresolved past. She knew, without a doubt, that she would never find peace unless she confronted her mother. She needed to tell her how she felt, even if it was one last time. She needed it to finally move on.

"That shit is lifelong, girl. And I hate to preach, but you've never met a man like Gabriel before. All the guys you've dated haven't stood a chance. But Gabe has gotten past those defenses and is now telling you that you need to trust him a bit more."

"Like it's so easy."

"It's the hardest and also the easiest thing in the world."

Maddie placed a hand on Ally's forehead. "God, you must be sleep-deprived, talking gibberish like that."

Ally rolled her eyes, swatting her away. "The first bit of surrendering is petrifying, but the more you do it, the easier it becomes, until you can't remember a time when you didn't trust that person."

"What if I fuck things up?"

"Then you fuck 'em up." Ally shrugged. "You've clearly forgotten how I nearly lost my job when Owen and I started hooking up. I made a shit ton of mistakes, which you're allowed to do. It doesn't mean it's the end of your relationship."

Maddie shivered. "Ally," she whispered, afraid to say it. "I can't believe that this is happening, that he's real. I mean, the Gabriel I know now is . . ."

"What?"

"Everything," she whispered softly, as if still stunned. "I'm still shocked at how he's become such a huge part of my life. It's like one day I looked up and there he was."

It shook her, knowing that at every turn, for every important life event, she wanted him there.

She understood what he'd meant now. It didn't matter that they were polar opposites. It didn't matter if they disagreed or argued, so long as they came together at the end of the day as one.

And there was nobody she wanted to come home to at that moment other than him.

CHAPTER THIRTY-FIVE

$\mathcal{M}$ addie knew that she had to face the past in order to have a future. She wanted to tie up loose ends so that she could focus her time and energy on her relationship with Gabriel.

And the biggest loose end in her life right now was her mother.

She had always felt a modicum of guilt whenever she'd resented her mother as a child. She'd convinced herself that she was bad for thinking such ungrateful thoughts for the woman who'd sheltered and fed her. Now she only felt anger.

Maddie stood on her mother's doorstep, her father at her side. It was surreal to be in this position, but then again, her life over the past six months had hardly been predictable.

When the door swung open, Maddie was petty enough to enjoy seeing her mother's shock. "Surprise!"

She pushed her way inside of the house, standing beside her mother, who was holding onto her walker. Maddie knew she was able to walk but chose the walker and wheelchair for maximum manipulative sympathy.

"You know, I contemplated doing this on my own, but given

that you've been lying to me for my whole life, I thought it best to bring proof."

"May I come in, Sharon?"

Her dad was still standing on the step, waiting and watchful. Respectful still after all these years. It would have made Maddie spit-fire mad, but now she was beginning to understand that it showed Dermot's integrity, his character.

It took Sharon a good minute before she sighed. "You're here now."

Maddie bristled, biting back a scathing remark. It bothered her that she was still so affected by her mom, even after years of therapy. And after the recent betrayal, she knew she would need more.

So while it was petty to taunt her mother with her father's presence, she was okay with that. Yes, vindictive, but also healing. Maddie was happy enough to admit that she had that inside of her. She didn't care for continuing a relationship with her mother, and knowing it now, accepting it without any guilt —totally and completely—was freeing.

"Tea?" her mother offered, settling on the sofa as if this were a social call.

Before her father could reply, Maddie cut in. "Let's not pretend, you've never been good at that. I won't be staying long at any rate."

"You've a bee in your bonnet, lass."

"That's putting it mildly, Dad. I'm here to tell Mom how I feel, and after I've said my piece, I'm leaving."

"You've never been one to hold your tongue." Her mother's reply was disapproving. As usual.

"And you've never been one to listen."

"I've heard it before."

"No, not really you haven't. And I hope what I say will help you to get some help. You've lived your life a bitter woman. And you've somehow tried to blame me for all the problems that you've created. You cheated on Dad then somehow had the gall to make me feel responsible for him leaving, and I will never ever forgive you for that."

"Always with the drama. Didn't I feed you? Provide a roof over your head?"

"Those are the basic necessities." Dermot cut in. "That's not something you should be disgruntled about, Sharon. Not to a child."

"And you have no right to judge me, walking out like some coward."

"Walking out? You all but kicked me to the curb. In your little love club with my brother, telling me I wasn't wanted. I tried to contact you, to keep in touch with Maddie."

"Bullshit. You ran away like some coward. It was only later on that you thought it best to come back for your child, and by then we'd done well enough without you."

"I sent her letters, which I'd hoped you'd look past your hatred to give to her."

"You weren't here."

"I worked remote. And you kept moving."

"I couldn't afford that place on my own."

"Not when my brother abandoned you."

"Stop!" Maddie interjected. "That's between the two of you and not my concern. I want to say my piece and then you can have at it." She faced her mom. "I lived my whole life wondering about my dad, asking you if you heard any news, and every time you lied to me as if it were nothing. As if I meant nothing. And I will never forgive you for that."

"I did the best I could."

"No. You deceived and lied, not for my benefit, but because you selfishly didn't want me to have a relationship with Dad. You punished me because he didn't want to put up with your abuse."

"Always the victim."

"No, I'm a survivor, actually." Maddie stared at the woman who was supposed to have cared for her and found herself feeling nothing. "You didn't do right by me. I needed more from you. For you to be honest, to not spew your abusive hate, to not make me feel like I was the worst person in the world for needing the basic things in life.

"You've only ever opened your mouth to criticize and I'm sick of it. You need to get therapy and move on because all that bitterness will kill you. I hope one day you realize that and seek help. But for now? I'm done. I had a miserable childhood because of you, one which I'm still healing from. I don't know if I can forgive you, but I'm trying hard to forget and move forward. I'd say don't call me, but you never really do unless to criticize. So from here on in, I don't have a mother. And you no longer have a daughter. Consider yourself absolved of all duty."

"You finished?"

Maddie crossed her arms. "I am."

"You can never know then what it was like to have to raise you on my own. Yes, I cheated on your father, but Colm was around. Not absent all the damn time for work. I wanted a husband, not a roommate. And Colm was here. He showered me with attention. We didn't mean for it to happen at first, but it did and I don't regret it. Not a bit." Her mother's mouth twisted in bitter remembrance. "But then Colm proved as flaky as your father and that was it. I was once again left scrambling to make things work."

"I told ye I was working towards getting my degree so I could teach. There was more to it than that, Sharon, but ye fail to acknowledge anything but your view."

"I don't regret a damn thing. You weren't around. Wouldn't have been around, and I didn't want a damn child on my own. I had dreams, Dermot, ones which I put off because you wanted a career change, you wanted a kid, and you wanted a family."

"Jesus, Mary, and—"

"I think I've heard enough." Maddie stood.

"Oh, that's it, twist my words. Maddie the dramatic." Her mother rolled her eyes.

"You've all but said I wasn't wanted. And you know what, you've done a great job in making me feel that way."

"You think whatever you want to think."

"You can't seem to admit when you're wrong, can you? Would it kill you to say sorry? To understand that you hurt me? At least Dad is able to apologize."

"Oh, and now that he's back, he's the savior and can do no wrong. I knew you'd think of him that way. I knew if he came back, he would twist it and I would be the bad guy. We were better off without him."

"He was better off without you!" Maddie's heart hurt. "But I wasn't. I needed him, and you drove him away."

"You can go ahead and think whatever you like, child. But don't think you can come back into this house after the way you've spoken to me."

Maddie snarled. "You don't need to tell me twice. I'll happily never set foot in this house, especially when you can't even do the decent thing and apologize."

"I'll never accept anything."

"Then I feel sorry for you. But it's not my problem anymore. Good luck to you, Mother. I hope you learn to find whatever it is that will make you happy. Because I'm at a loss as to what that is."

With one last look at her parents, Maddie left, knowing that everything had changed in her life. Because *she* had changed. She had become a strong, resilient woman in spite of her mother and father, not because of them. Finally, she was moving on. And she vowed in that moment that she would never look back again.

CHAPTER THIRTY-SIX

The sealed envelope was sitting on her desk when she returned to her office that evening. The after-school session with her senior drama kids had been successful. The kids were ready for their solo exams, and while she was utterly exhausted, she was also proud. She wanted to get into her jammies and maybe read something light and swoon-worthy when she got home—anything except literature practice exams.

Gabriel was out this evening, and she found she craved a bit of alone time. She was still dealing with fatigue from her confrontation with her mother. It felt right, but as usual, going head-to-head with that woman always left her drained. That and the fact that she didn't know how to talk to Gabriel about how she felt.

Why was it so damn hard?

Why did she feel like she was going to drop off the face of a cliff if she did?

Maddie picked up the envelope. There was a Post-it Note on it saying: Read Me. She recognized the handwriting instantly.

With the spring rain knocking against the window, Maddie

sat down, stifling a yawn. She opened the envelope and gasped at the heading.

If You Were Mine - A Love Letter

She tried to breathe, but it was as if there were a tight fist squeezing her chest. She continued:

Maddie,

I know you have your reservations about us, so I thought I would tell you all the things I've been feeling for you, in the hopes you will believe me. Keep in mind, to me, you're already mine in all the ways that are important. In all the ways that matter. Unlike a certain fictional character—rhymes with Mr. Arsey—I won't tell you how I feel in spite of all of your faults, but because of them (and let's be real, Darcy didn't help our relationship in the beginning, so I'll refrain from quoting him now). To me, your struggles make you who you are —strong and brave and kind—in short, the woman of my dreams.

I love your temper, your fiery, fighting spirit. The way you call me out on my behavior, and the way you pout when you know I'm right. I love your stubbornness, your openness, the way I know how you feel by looking at you. To me, these are qualities that are what make you, you. And I wouldn't want to change them.

For years, I had a persistent thought that would keep me up some-times at night. If I could call you mine, what would I say or do? Now that you are mine, here's the (by no means extensive) list.

If you were mine, I would:

1. Tell you I love you. I wanted to say this to you in person for my own selfish reasons, but in getting to know you, I've come to understand that you'd feel safer knowing how I feel, and I believe in this relationship enough (and suspect you might feel the same after that slip-up of yours) to tell you first. That way, if you don't feel the same or need more time, you have it without the pressure. I love you. I have for some time now, and I only want to continue loving you, if you'll let me. I want to tell you in person. I want to see the expression in your eyes when I do because there's no one else for me. You're it. You're mine. I feel like you always have been.

2. Argue with you. One of the things I love the most about you is your mind. You're sharp, witty, intelligent, and damn funny—even when you're stubborn. That little flick you do with your hair drives me insane. But I don't care if we disagree. It's what I love best about you. About us. Don't fear it, Red.

3. Have sex with you on my desk. I know we've done this, but I want to do it again and again. Forgive me for the juvenile fantasy, but you do something to me that no other woman has ever done before. Sex with you is even better than all my fantasies—and yes, I have plenty of those—so I want to touch you in a way that makes you realize that you are mine. So yeah, lots of sex.

4. Build a home with you. I told you I don't want kids and I meant it, but I want a home with you. Whether it's mine in the mountains or perhaps something by the sea. Something that's ours. I find myself dreaming of lazy mornings of lovemaking. Marking essays in bed together. Cooking in the kitchen. Living life and creating a home side by side. If that means traveling, I'm up for any adventure—home is where you are. If you want a pet, we can negotiate that too.

5. Marriage. I want you as my wife. To wake up beside you every morning and know you're mine. You asked what I wanted for our future, and it's marriage, with you. I know that for certain.

• • •

I know this is a lot to take in. So I understand if you need time to process everything. Just so you know, I'm in agony waiting for your response. I want to know how you feel, even if it's to say you need more time. Or to shove this letter where the sun don't shine.

But know this, I'll wait forever for you, Maddie.

Love Always,
   Gabriel
   xx

Maddie stifled a sob, tears falling in a steady stream. Her heart, the last tiny piece she had reserved in self-preservation, was now completely his.

She wanted to tell him how she felt, wanted to make him understand what was in her heart. Because above all her fears and trust issues was the blinding truth that she loved him. She wanted to keep on loving him through it all.

She might not have had the greatest role models growing up, but she had built a family around her that loved and supported her.

It was with Gabriel that she could begin this next chapter. He'd seen her at her worst and still believed she was the best. And she wanted more than anything to prove to him that she could love him completely, in the way that he deserved. It was as if the heaviest weight had been lifted off her chest.

All the way home, Maddie hugged the feeling close. She couldn't wait to tell him.

It was pitch black by the time she drove up the mountain. Now that Gabriel had confessed his feelings, Maddie felt silly for wanting to wait until after exams were over. She knew that she'd been afraid of his response, which was why she'd stopped herself from saying anything. Because if he didn't return her love, she would have been devastated.

But now that she knew his heart, she could take that leap. It had been cowardly of her to hold back, but Gabriel meant so much to her that she couldn't bear the thought of losing him.

It wasn't until she rapped on his front door that it occurred to her that he might not be home. He'd said he was going out this evening, hadn't he? Or was it a red herring?

She thought back to when she had come to apologize for the magazine incident all those months ago. So much had changed since then. She'd gone from love to hate within a year, yet it felt like the most natural thing in the world.

Maddie knocked on the door again. Of course he would be home. Nobody left a love letter on someone's desk to just flit off into the night. Did they?

Disappointment washed over her. She stomped down the stairs then froze. She heard the faint but rhythmic clapping sound coming from the backyard. Following it, Maddie walked through the open side gate and down the garden path. At the far end of the yard was Gabriel, back turned to her as he chopped wood in nothing but a T-shirt and shorts. The evening spring air was cool, the earlier rain soaking the grass and his shirt. He was illuminated by the garden lights, and the muscles of his arms and legs rippled in the glow.

Maddie couldn't help but grin at the sight. Here was the man whom she loved and adored. The man who made her believe that happily ever afters did exist.

Gabriel was about to lift the axe to swing but paused, dropping it to his side instead. Slowly, he turned to face her, and it took every bit of self-control not to burst into tears. She wanted to tell him how she felt before she turned into a puddle of emotions.

Gabriel took the earbuds out of his ears, shoving them into his pocket. He met her halfway, his face illuminated by the porch light.

"Well?" He watched her with a wary expression on his face.

"I read your letter."

"And?"

"Are you going to talk in monosyllables all evening?"

"Depends."

"On what?"

"You."

Maddie smiled even though she wanted to shake him. "What are you doing out here in the cold?"

Gabriel shrugged. "I was sick of waiting by the phone for you to text or call. I wanted to let off a bit of steam."

"Gabriel . . ." Her eyes clouded over.

Gabriel brushed away her tears. "Tell me."

Maddie felt the swell of emotion in her chest. "I've never felt this way for anyone else. Your letter meant everything to me. To hear you say those things, to know that I needed to hear it made me feel so secure, so loved." Maddie looked him in the eye; despite her nerves, she needed to tell him how she felt. "I love you."

Gabriel's smile could have lit up the night sky. "I've been waiting hours to hear you say that."

"I went overtime with my drama students."

"Typical."

"Dedicated."

"Workaholic."

"Diligent."

"Love of my life." He stepped closer, winding his arms around her waist.

"Love of *my* life."

He raised an eyebrow. "This isn't meant to be a competition, Red."

"I thought you loved arguing with me."

"Always."

She felt like she was floating. "You had the courage to say it first, and that's something I didn't even know I needed. We didn't exactly get off to a great start, and I made assumptions about you that aren't true. You're someone I didn't understand at first, but I do now, Gabriel. I see you. And I want you. Always."

"Nothing else matters to me but you. Damn it, Maddie, I want forever. You challenge me and drive me insane, and I wouldn't want it any other way. I'm always going to fight for you and have your back. Always."

"I'm so afraid."

"Good."

"Good?"

"It means you care. It means that what we have matters. I'm afraid too. Of living this life without you in it. I'm so petrified of potentially losing you that some nights I wake in a cold sweat. But those are fears. They're not true. And I refuse to waste a life-time holding onto my fears when all I want and need is to hold you."

Maddie trembled. Nothing she had experienced before even compared to this feeling. Cupping his face, she kissed him. And in his arms she felt loved and safe and whole.

"I love you, Madds. Get ready to hear it every day because I'm gonna be saying it *a lot*."

"I don't know why I found it so difficult to tell you—well, I do, and you were right. I have trust issues, but I'm working on that. I'm not perfect, but you need to know that I do trust you. I've been so afraid to love you. So certain that I hadn't fallen in love with you."

"And now?"

"I know I love you in a way I've never loved before. It's real and true, and sometimes it hurts because of the fear of losing you too. But you're right."

"Wait, let me record that."

She swatted him, smiling. "Yes, you're right. I'm not so stubborn that I can't admit it. When it's true, that is."

"What am I right about?"

"That this, what we have is worth the fight. You're worth all the times I'll be annoyed at you, all the times I'll fuck shit up because of my fears. I want only you, Gabriel. I didn't think I'd find this kind of love ever, but I love you, am in love with you."

"I'm in love with you too, Maddie. Just in case you needed to hear me say it. Again."

"So what now?"

"Now," Gabriel murmured, picking her up in his arms. "I get to show you how much I love you. With your permission of course."

Maddie grinned. "Sounds perfect."

CHAPTER THIRTY-SEVEN

It had been a whirlwind few months, and Maddie couldn't quite believe that life could be this amazing. Their students had finished their exams, they were nearing the end of the school year, and she had just found out she'd been appointed as the new official head of arts. Gabriel had absented himself from the panel for merit and equity reasons, and when Maddie had been phoned by the principal with the good news, she couldn't help but feel like life was finally working out in ways she'd only dreamed.

All of the worries that she'd had at the beginning of the year about her life seemed to have dulled. Especially now that she was in a committed relationship with a man whom she loved.

Finally, the niggling feeling of doubt that had plagued her for years had gone. She was working on building a relationship with her dad and not feeling any guilt for severing all communication with her mom. Gone was the queasy panic in her gut. Her life was by no means perfect, but she was enjoying every minute of it. And that felt good.

Glancing at the clock in the kitchen, Maddie took the chicken from the oven to baste. The roast potatoes were crisping up nicely, and the veg was caramelizing too. The whole gang was coming over for an early dinner and she wanted to have everything prepped and ready to go. Cooking in Gabriel's kitchen was magic. Everything about Gabriel's house was.

"Did you find the napkins?" she called out down the hall. She'd begun moving all of her boxes from her apartment over; they'd decided it made sense that she move in with him, given she was spending so much time at his place anyway.

Though Maddie had yet to finish moving some of the furniture, by Christmas time, she hoped to have her apartment renovated and leased out. In the meantime, she had moved in with Gabriel, and life was very much proving to be something straight out of a fairytale. *Her* fairytale.

"You kept them?" Gabriel walked over to her.

"Kept what?" She turned with the oven mittens in hand and froze.

"These?" He waved the Post-it Notes in the air, an incredulous look on his face.

"Where did you get them from?"

"They fell out of your old chronicle while I was looking for the party stuff."

She'd forgotten she'd shoved them in there. "Oops."

"You kept them." Gabriel grinned, walking slowly towards her. "Why?"

Maddie slapped the mittens on the counter behind her. "I don't know. I just did. And I feel a little silly for doing it right about now."

"Even a few scrunched-up ones I see." He looked delighted with himself. And so very smug.

Maddie cringed. "Your ego doesn't need any more boosting after this morning, Steele."

"Uh-huh." Gabriel pulled her against him, cradling her in his arms. "I have a theory."

"Here we go."

"Hear me out because I think you'll like it."

"So you say."

He spoke slowly, his eyes dancing with mischief. "I think that you've secretly liked me . . ." He leaned closer to whisper in her ear. ". . . for years." He bit at her earlobe, and Maddie felt an electric current pulse through her.

"There's that healthy ego talking again," she murmured. But she wound her arms around him, enjoying his teasing.

"Why else would you keep these notes then?" He nibbled at the curve of her neck and her legs turned to jelly.

Maddie raked her nails down his back, squeezing his ass. "That's easy. Because you hmm . . . Because you annoyed me."

"Annoyed you?"

"Mm-hmm."

His hand trailed up her shorts, cupping her sex.

"I think the word you're searching for, Miss Fitzgerald, is 'aroused.' Just like you are now."

He bit her lip then kissed her in a way that made her ache for more.

Maddie muttered a curse when the bell rang. "Saved in the nick of time."

"Lucky for you, we have all night to settle this argument." Gabriel winked and turned away.

She was going to enjoy every minute of it.

Late that evening, once everyone had gone home, and the kitchen was tidy, Gabriel watched Maddie sleep. He'd known from the first time she'd slept in his bed that he wanted to wake beside her every morning for the rest of his life.

The moonlight pierced through the half-open blinds, illuminating her soft skin. She looked peaceful, ethereal, and all his. Ever since they'd declared their love, a possessive desire to claim her would often seize him, compelling him to hold her close or kiss her passionately. Gabriel accepted that this was what she brought out in him, this wild and wicked need that he'd once been so sure would signal his ruin.

But he was a changed man, or perhaps a wiser one.

Being with Maddie, declaring how he felt for her was by far the best thing he'd done in his life. He wanted to be better— for her.

Gabriel stroked her arm. She slept naked, her skin warm and soft, and he was torn between wanting to wake her and letting her sleep.

He placed a gentle kiss on her nose and turned over, trying to settle.

A few minutes later, he felt her stirring. Maddie's hand curved around his chest, followed by her soft body.

"You're still awake," she muttered sleepily.

"It's late, Red. Get some sleep."

She all but purred and her hand danced down his abdomen, stroking his hard cock.

"Fuck," Gabriel muttered.

"Sounds like a great idea." Maddie switched positions, straddling him. Her mouth was firm, arousing a snapping, snarling passion that called to his own. He stroked her clit until she moaned and rocked over his fingers.

Gabriel enjoyed her startled squeak of surprise when he flipped her on her back. He wanted to love her thoroughly, to show her how much he cared.

He caressed her breasts, feasting on the pebbled peaks until she arched against him. He loved the way her fingers fisted his hair, the way she urged him on with soft sighs or muttered pleas. He trailed kisses down her stomach, then shifted lower, until he reached the triangle of hair between her thighs. There was something about her earthy smell that evoked a wicked need in him, one that wanted to feast until he was sated. With her, he knew he never would be.

"Beautiful, you're so beautiful."

He parted her now, exposing her sex to him before taking one long, luxurious lick. She cried out, and the sound traveled straight to his cock. He did it again, wanting to hear her scream. Gabriel repeated the movement until she was begging and writhing against his mouth, but he held back, wanting to be inside of her when she came.

Satisfying this woman was the only thing that mattered to him.

"Maddie . . . I need you."

"I'm yours," she whispered.

He reached for the condoms then froze.

Maddie gripped his hand, stopping him. "We don't need it."

Gabriel's body shook with restraint. "Maddie," he warned. "We—"

"I'm sure. We've both been tested, I'm on the pill and you know I can't have kids. We've done all the sensible things to protect each other. Let's be wild and reckless. I want to feel you inside of me without any barriers between us."

"If you're sure?"

"A hundred percent."

Hadn't he dreamed of this . . . taking her without protection, feeling her soft and warm and wet, wrapped around his cock? The thought of it made him groan.

Shaking now, Gabriel parted her thighs, positioning his cock at her entrance. And slowly, unbelievably slowly, he entered her. She stretched around him, fisting his cock with such exquisite pressure, he thought he might come on the spot.

Gabriel cursed, losing himself in her wet heat. He'd die from the pleasure of it.

"That's it, milk my fucking cock." Gabriel kissed her, rocking inside of her with slow, controlled movements.

She wrapped her legs around him, and the hot, possessive, hungry need snapped and snarled, wanting to take over. Still, he took his time to kiss and caress until his arms strained and his body shook.

He feasted on her neck, loving the way her breasts pressed against his chest, soft and so damn full. She was sexy and fiery and all his. He thrust deeper now, a little faster as their desire built. Her mewling cries urged him to keep going.

"Gabe . . . faster."

"No chance."

"I want to ride your cock."

"Not happening."

"I hate you." She gasped.

"I love you too." He grinned.

The change happened suddenly, swiftly; like a bolt of lightning, terrifying and bold, his control snapped and the frenzy began. He could deny this woman—*his woman*—nothing.

He fucked her harder and faster then reared back, wanting so desperately to come he thought he would explode.

"I want rough, Gabriel." Maddie grabbed the silk tie from the bedside drawer and draped it around her neck.

"Safeword?" he muttered, loving how she was comfortable enough lately to explore new kinks.

"Apple," she replied, kneeling on all fours, lush and curvy and ripe for the fucking.

He knelt over her, his mouth at her ear. "I love you."

She shivered. "I love you, Gabriel."

"I want to watch you."

Knowing his meaning, Maddie crawled over to the far side of the bed, facing the floor-length mirror on the opposite side of the room. From here he could see everything, but still it wasn't enough. He reached over and turned on the beside light.

"Much better."

He kissed her shoulder then reared back, thrusting into her

again, reveling in the sensation. He took both ends of the tie in his fist and tugged.

Her throaty moan vibrated through him. Her neck was arched back, her breasts dangling, aching for his mouth.

"Is this what you want?"

"Mm-hmm."

"Tell me you love it."

"I love it."

"Tell me you love me."

"I love you." She gasped against the tie.

"Fucking right." He slapped her ass, loving the way it jiggled.

Gabriel let go of the tie and fisted his hands in her hair, drawing her back up against his body. They both knelt upright, so he could see her in the mirror, her ivory skin flushed and red, her tits gloriously heavy. He fucked her harder, wanting more.

"Play with that sweet pussy."

Her fingers danced through the thatch of curls, and she rubbed and pressed until she panted his name.

Gabriel ground his teeth together at the sounds she was making. Her ass pressed against him; her tits bounced wildly. He let go of her hair and they both dropped to all fours.

"You're so fucking sexy, Maddie. I'm gonna explode in that sweet pussy."

"I want you to come inside me."

"Tell me."

"I want to see your cum dripping down my thighs. I want you to rub it on my tits, marking me with it."

Christ, she was glorious. And knew exactly what turned him on.

"That dirty mouth is gonna get you into trouble one day, Fitzgerald."

"Good." She moaned, watching him in the mirror.

The sounds of sex filled the room, her scent, his sweat, the earthy desire circling them both, until he couldn't hold back any longer.

But he waited until she bucked and writhed against him, shattering around his cock before he lost control. Crying out, chasing her release, he came, squeezing her hips as he filled her, lost in her soft, generous body. The sensation was mind-numbingly good. To be inside her, to feel every soft spot, every ridge was sexy as fuck.

He withdrew from her with a groan, wanting to do it all again.

Maddie shifted, lying on her back. He watched as she dipped her fingers in her sex, smearing his cum on her tits.

Reaching down, he toyed with her nipples then sucked them.

"Dirty witch."

"You love it."

"I do."

"Totally worth the sleep deprivation."

Gabriel placed a gentle kiss on her lips. "I had every intention of taking this slow."

"I'm glad you didn't."

He covered them both with the duvet, enjoying the feeling of her sticky, sweaty body cocooned against his. He loved caring for her, loving her, the after sex as much as the anticipation of the before.

Maddie curled up against him, her breathing slow and steady, and everything inside him relaxed. His heart was full.

Tomorrow, it would be complete.

Maddie woke up the next morning feeling rested. She tried to open her eyes then frowned. There was a Post-it Note stuck on her forehead. Peeling it off, she giggled then turned it over.

Follow me, it said.

Maddie looked around for another note, finding it on the glass of juice waiting for her on the bedside table. *Drink me.*

She smiled, enjoying the freshly squeezed juice.

Maddie found her robe lying at the foot of the bed. *Wear me.*

She slipped it on and opened the bedroom door. Maddie stepped out onto the landing and gasped. Strewn across the floor were rose petals of all colors, and they seemingly led downstairs.

She followed the path to the front door. There, by the hall table, was one long-stemmed rose. *Smell me.* Maddie picked it up, inhaling deeply. Her heart danced at the romantic gestures.

She walked down the corridor, following the petal path until she reached the kitchen. There on the island was a chocolate heart. *Eat me.*

She did, enjoying the burst of milk chocolate and caramel.

Savoring the taste and the romance, she walked through the kitchen and around to the living room.

There on the coffee table beside the fireplace was a small black box. Maddie gasped, crossing to it.

On top of the ring box was a note that read: *Open me.*

Maddie crouched before the table, hands trembling. Slowly, as if in a trance, she opened the lid then huffed. It was empty.

She stood swiftly, turning to find Gabriel on bended knee, a Post-it Note attached to his forehead, a ring between his fingers.

Her heart all but bounded out of her chest. She peeled off the note and gasped, looking at the ring again. Sitting on top of a thin gold band was a line of different colored gems. Diamonds, rubies, and sapphires, all of different shapes, glittered in the morning light.

Marry me, the Post-it Note read.

"I wanted to give you a ring that matched your personality. Stunning, eye-catchingly beautiful, and strong. I don't have my mother's ring, as that was lost long ago, but I chose this after getting some advice from a few of your friends." Gabriel grinned. "And I knew it was perfect for you. I also know that you'll tell me to my face if you hate it."

"I love it. I love you."

She heard the fear in his voice, this man who was on bended knee, this man who loved her enough to love her the way she needed. The way she had only ever dreamed.

"I promise I'll love you until my last breath. I want to wake up knowing you're my wife, my lover, my friend, every day. I want to make this commitment to you. So . . . Madeleine Fitzgerald, will you marry me?"

Maddie nodded, letting the tears fall. "Yes, I'll marry you, Gabriel."

He stood, placing the ring on her finger. He kissed her hand, then the tips of her fingers, and finally her lips. Her heart danced in her chest knowing she was the luckiest woman in the world to have him.

"I want to marry you, Gabriel, for all that you are. You're kind and passionate, protective and thoughtful. And I want a future with you as your wife."

"My wife." Gabriel grinned. "I like the sound of that."

Maddie laughed, drawing him in for another kiss. With this man, she'd found love and acceptance. With this man, she'd found her home.

She knew without a doubt that it would be forever.

THE END

SUBSCRIBE FOR ALL THE NEWS!
If you want exclusive access to giveaways, ARCs, sales, and

new release alerts first, then subscribe to my monthly
newsletter, With You in Romance.

WANT TO GO BACK TO WHERE IT ALL BEGAN?
Read Before You Were Mine

OR TELL ME WHAT YOU THINK, BY LEAVING A REVIEW!
Amazon or Goodreads

ALSO BY IDA BRADY

To Tango with Love

Teacher Chronicles Series

Before You Were Mine

When You Were Mine

If You Were Mine

A Sweet, Sexy, Scandalous Series

Sweet Spot

Sex and the Stage

Secrets and Scandals

The Gamer's Girlfriend Series

Virtue

Voyeur

Vixen

SUBSCRIBE FOR ALL THE NEWS!

If you want exclusive access to giveaways, sales, and new release alerts first, then subscribe to my monthly newsletter, With You in Romance.

LEAVE A REVIEW HERE:

Amazon or Goodreads

ABOUT THE AUTHOR

Ida Brady writes contemporary romance novels that promise humour, heartbreak and a happily ever after. With all the sexy bits! A lover of chocolate (milk or dark) and thunderstorms (the bigger the better), she's usually dreaming about her next cast of characters or what she's going to eat for her next meal. When she isn't trying to tame her intractable curls, she's running after her kids, usually with a book in hand.

Ida used to live in Melbourne, but has shifted to the other side of the world to live in the Emerald Isle with her Irish husband, two daughters, one very big cat and their out-of-control collection of books. She sometimes daydreams about having a huge library in her apartment but will settle for stacking novels in the kitchen drawers instead. In her past life, she taught VCE Literature and English to a gaggle of teenagers. While she misses their enthusiasm, she sure as hell doesn't miss marking papers. You might find her dancing the sexy Argentine tango in her spare time, which isn't very often these days. She loves travelling with her family, observing strangers at café's, and getting lost in a good story.

Want to hear more?

Sign up to my Newsletter, With You in Romance for giveaways and prizes! http://www.idabrady.com

Follow me on Instagram, Tiktok, Facebook! and or leave a review on Goodreads.

ACKNOWLEDGMENTS

I've been waiting patiently for YEARS to write Gabriel and Maddie's story, and you have no idea how much of a relief it is to end this series with a bang! If you've read *Before You Were Mine* and *When You Were Mine* you'd know that Gabriel and Maddie have been at each other's throats for a long time. Which makes their relationship and HEA so utterly delicious!

They're strong characters, with strong ideas, but I've enjoyed showing their vulnerabilities and their strengths. Even though they are polar opposites, I wanted them to acknowledge that they actually have a little more in common than they thought. And that it's these opposing traits that lead them to have an amazing relationship! While it's sad to see the end of this series, I'm leaving on a high. I really wanted to do this story justice, so I hope you enjoy it!

To Team Brida: Brian, Adria, Niamh and Hugo. I can say I'm the luckiest woman in the world to have you all in my corner. All that love and support, not to mention sweet little hugs, have kept this sleep-deprived mama going when some days it was just bloody tough. Love you all to the moon and back!
To Norma Gambini, girl, you are a treasure! Honestly, your support and utter faith in my work over the years makes me want to cry happy tears. Your eagle-eye edits are the best, and I'm eternally grateful for all that you do. Thank you, soooo much!
To Ebony McKenna, thanks so much! You've no idea how much

I appreciate all the advice and time you put in. You're a lifesaver.

To my family, as always for the love and support both near and far. I miss you loads, and absolutely love all of our family chats more than you know.

To my wonderful writer friends, my Meetup girls, your advice, feedback and general support really makes me feel like I can do this. I wouldn't be where I am without your friendship and support, so thank you! Missing you a lot, but I know we're just a virtual chat away.

To my With You in Romance team, (Alpha, Beta and ARC readers) thank you for all the feedback, encouragement and support. I'm so very lucky to have your help along the way. Y'all ROCK!

Finally, to my readers. Whoever you are, wherever you may be, I hope that this novel gives you a chance to escape from reality, even if for a chapter or two.

With you in romance,

Ida Brady